The Legions
of the Mist

ROMAN BRITAIN 115 A.D.

INCHTUTHIL●

CALEDONES
(PICTI)

SELGOVAE

TRIMONTIUM●

CASTRA EXPLORATORUM

VINDOLANDA●   SEGEDUNUM●

LUGUVALLIUM● CORSTOPITUM●
ALAUNA●

VINOVIA●

BRIGANTES   CATARACTONIUM●

●ISURIUM BRIGANTUM

EBURACUM●

DANUM●

MAMUCIUM●

LINDUM●

DEVA●

CORITANI

ICENI

CAMULODUNUM●

VERULAMIUM●

ISCA SILURUM●

LONDINIUM●

AQUAE SULIS●   CALLEVA ATREBATUM●   RUTUPIAE●

VENTA BELGARUM●

GESORIACUM●

HIBERNIA

CHANNEL

0   50   100
ROMAN MILES

The Legions of the Mist

A NOVEL OF ROMAN BRITAIN

Amanda Cockrell

ATHENEUM

NEW YORK

1979

Library of Congress Cataloging in Publication Data

Cockrell, Amanda.
  The legions of the mist.

    I. Great Britain—History—Roman period, 55 B.C.
—449 A.D.—Fiction. I. Title.
PZ4.C665Le [PS3553.028]   813'.5'4 79-51353
ISBN 0-689-10989-X

Composition by American–Stratford Graphic Services, Inc.
  Brattleboro, Vermont
Printed and bound by R. R. Donnelley & Sons,
  Crawfordsville, Indiana

Designed by Kathleen Carey
First Edition

For John

*Wherever the Roman conquers,
there he dwells.*

SENECA

Contents

Contents

The Legions
of the Mist

Historical Note

Sometime during the beginning of the second century A.D., the Ninth Legion Hispana marched into the mists of Roman-occupied Britain and disappeared forever.

Rome erased their name and number from the legionary rolls, and so far no British farmer has turned up a buried graveyard with his plow, to show where they lie.

Perhaps they turned their backs on everything that was of their own world and melted into the native tribes. Perhaps they were ambushed and cut down. All we know for certain is that they vanished as surely as if the ground had opened to swallow them, taking with them their Eagle, the life and honor of the Legion, and leaving behind only the few men who happened to be detached from the Hispana when it marched out that last day.

I have reconstructed these last years of the Ninth Hispana from the opinions and research of many distinguished historians, with admitted leaps of imagination in between. None of the people in this story, with the exception of the Emperors Trajan and Hadrian and certain other historical figures, exists outside these pages, although someone very like them may well have walked the paths which I have set Justin and Vortrix in, and followed the road the lost Hispana took.

Amanda Cockrell

3

Glossary of Place Names

Roman	Modern
Alauna	Maryport
Antium	Anzio
Aquae Sulis	Bath
Calleva Atrebatum	Silchester
Camulodunum	Colchester
Castra Exploratorum	Netherby
Cataractonium	Catterick
Corstopitum	Corbridge
Dacia	Transylvania and Rumania
Danum	Doncaster
Deva	Chester
Eburacum	York
Grannona	Bayeux
Gesoriacum	Boulogne
Hibernia	Ireland
Hippo Regius	Annaba, Algeria
Isca Silurum	Caerleon
Isurium Brigantum	Aldborough
Lambaesis	Lambèse, Algeria

4

Lindum	Lincoln
Londinium	London
Luguvallium	Carlisle
Mamucium	Manchester
Moesia	Upper: Serbia
	Lower: Bulgaria
Nicomedia	Izmit, Turkey
Pannonia	Hungary and Yugoslavia west of the Danube
Parthia	Northeast Iran
Rutupiae	Richborough
Segedunum	Wallsend
Selinous	Selente, Turkey
Tarraco	Tarragona, Spain
Trimontium	Newstead
Valentia	Lowland Scotland
Venta Belgarum	Winchester
Verulamium	St. Albans
Vindobona	Vienna
Vindolanda	Chesterholm
Vinovia	Binchester

I

Eburacum Fortress

"THERE YOU ARE." The decurion of the supply train escort gestured with his riding crop where the grey dominance of Eburacum Fortress rose above the blue-green of the surrounding plain. Outside its stone and timber bulwark there was nothing for miles but the empty land and the wild, sorrowful cry of the curlews. "It may not look like much, but it's all that keeps the north under wraps, I can tell you."

The cohort centurion beside him nodded and turned a grim gaze on the fort. He was young, and a few locks of wavy brown hair which not even a military haircut could disguise rippled under the rim of his helmet in the light breeze. His brows were sharp-angled and expressive above an almost unnecessarily Roman nose, and the irises of his eyes were a startling amber color. He regarded his destination with every evidence of distaste.

"Not what you're used to, I expect." The decurion of cavalry grinned at him with the friendly malice of the horseman for the foot soldier.

"No," Justin said shortly.

"Now *my* lads," the decurion went on, "they're used to sleeping just about anywhere there's fodder for the horses. Haven't had time to get too fine in their ways. But you won't find it too bad, I expect."

"I haven't seen such a piss poor example of the Emperor's service in my life," Justin said frankly. "And I've been around." They halted outside the fortress gate and he dismounted, handing his reins over to the cavalryman. "Thank you for the escort and the mount," he said. "I firmly hope I shan't be here when next you pass this way, or I'd invite you to stop in."

The decurion of cavalry raised his crop in a friendly salute and wheeled his troop round onto the main road again. Twitching the folds of his cloak into place (it smelled vaguely of horse, he noted), Justin gave his name and business to the sentries at the gate, and they passed him through into the Via Praetoria.

Eburacum Fortress, planted like a rock in the bend of a river, would have made ten of the quarters which Justin's cohort had shared during his last posting at the African seaport of Hippo Regius. But compared to that Legion's home base, the shining modern military city of Lambaesis, British Eburacum wore the gone-to-seed air of a passed-over general.

The town, which huddled under its ramparts as close as the intervening river would allow, had been equally unimpressive, a hodgepodge of wine stalls, shops, houses, and dog kennels, cheerfully intermingled with temples to an amazing variety of gods—British, Roman, Greek, Egyptian, native gods, and those adopted by soldiers in every province in the Empire. And it was cold, as cold as his old commander had predicted, with a chill that seemed to bite into the bone.

A detachment passed him in full marching gear, and swung south out of the main gate, Auxiliaries and native drafts mostly, with a few legionary troops thrown in, bound, he supposed, for the Emperor's Parthian wars. He had passed several more on the road north. It was a wonder there were enough troops left to garrison this fort, he thought, as he halted outside the command quarters in the Principia and gave his name to the Optio on duty. Above him loomed the great, golden Eagle of the Legion, perched on crossed thunderbolts with its silver wings swept back, above a staff impressive with gilded wreaths of honor. Justin paused to read its number and titles: *Legio IX Hispana, Triumphalis, Macedonica.*

Legions might be named for the Emperor who raised them, like the Third Augusta, or for their prowess, like the Sixth Victrix, or for their country of recruitment. The Ninth Legion Hispana had been born in Spain, a proud Legion which had seen distinguished service in Pannonia before it had come to Britain with Claudius Caesar's invasion force.

The cold sunlight glinted on the Eagle's beak and talons, and it seemed to soar above its disreputable surroundings. Justin saluted it quietly, the incarnation of an ancient service, and felt the gentle tug of the safe, the familiar. The last Eagle he had saluted had cast its winged shadow on the hot sands of Africa, but the feeling had been much the same . . . .

"Centurion Corvus?" The Optio regarded him impatiently. "If you are quite ready now, the Legate will see you."

"Oh, of course. I'm sorry." Justin turned and followed him across the courtyard to the Legate's office.

"Centurion Julius Justinius Corvus reporting, sir." Reluctantly he handed the Legate his orders.

Metius Lupus glanced at the tablet. "From Africa, I see."

"Yes, sir."

"I trust you had a satisfactory crossing. What was your transport?"

"The *Nausicaä*. She wallowed like a pig, sir," he added frankly. "I came north from Londinium with a supply train."

"I can't say that I blame you," the Legate said. "That channel crossing always turns one's stomach inside out. Well, well, you'll find it very different here, I imagine." He nodded his dismissal. "You can report to duty in the morning, Centurion. The Optio will show you where to find your quarters."

"Yes, sir." Justin gave a crashing salute and followed the Optio to the door.

"Straight down there, sir. You'll see the officers' block on the right."

Justin thanked him politely. The Optios, attached to headquarters staff and other departments, saw to the myriad inner workings of a Roman camp, and could assure an officer's comfort or outright misery in a new post.

Justin went where the Optio had pointed, past blocks of barracks, storerooms, and workshops. Eburacum was immense, a fully self-contained fortress sprawled over some fifty acres, with great stone walls at either end and ramparts of timber and earth. At the river dock, supply ships put in to unload sacks of meal from the corn country to the south, and everywhere legionaries and auxiliary troops bustled back and forth, their cloaks whipping about them in the stiff breeze. A troop of cavalry clattered by on their way to drill, and a group of "on report" miscreants with mops in hand turned reluctantly into the latrine under the eagle eye of a centurion. The armorer's hammer rang against the shouting from the parade ground, and the bugler shrilled "Change of Sentries." To anyone not used to the din that 5,000 soldiers could make, it would have been unbearable, but to Justin that much, at least, was the sound of home.

Another centurion, a slim young man with curling dark hair like a faun's and the uniform of a cohort commander, met him at the door of the officers' quarters.

"You'll be the one come to take over the Eighth," he said. "I'm Favonius, Third Cohort. You're in 15, I think. You've just time for a splash before dinner." He eyed Justin's grimy uniform. "Expect you'd like to soak off the march. Hai, Martius, wait!" he called after another centurion just disappearing around the corner. "Bathhouse is that way," he added, sprinting to catch up to his friend.

Justin wandered down the row of small limewashed, identical rooms until he found number 15. He dropped his kit thankfully on the bed, followed by the vine staff of his rank, a dagger and short sword in leather scabbards banded with bronze, an iron helmet crested fanwise with red, and a rectangular shield overlaid with wings and jagged bolts of iron barbed like arrows at the ends. On a lower corner, it bore his name and rank, and now the number of the Ninth Hispana. He struggled out of his breastplate and harness tunic and added them to the pile of gear on the bed. Then, catching up his cloak, scarlet for a cohort centurion, he went in search of a bath.

The bathhouse was crowded with laughing, naked figures who greeted him amiably and returned to their pursuits, soaking out the day's work in the steam chamber, splashing happily in the main pool, or braving the invigorating rigors of the cold bath. Justin was filthy from the long march and his muscles ached. He rinsed and scraped himself clean, and then slipped gratefully into the hot pool.

He lay aloof, soaking and searching vainly for the golden words that might have swayed the commander and kept him in Hippo Regius, until he realized that the bathhouse had grown empty, and he was going to miss dinner. Pulling himself up on the side of the pool, he applied a hasty towel and slipped damply into the folds of his uniform tunic.

"Wait, friend!" he called to the last occupant of the baths, a man fastening his sandals on the far side of the pool.

The man slipped the buckle home and stood up. He was older than Justin by a few years, with a tanned complexion and a very slight limp in his stride. "In a hurry?" he inquired mildly.

"Just lost," Justin said. "And I want my dinner." He came round to the other man's side. "I'm Justin—Justinius Corvus. I'm to command the Eighth Cohort."

The dark-haired man held out a hand. "I'm Gaius Licinius. Senior surgeon. Come along then, and I'll put you on the right road. I was heading that way myself."

"My thanks. I met one of the other cohort officers, Favonius I think he said his name was, and he showed me the baths, but I forgot to ask about the mess hall." Justin fell into step beside Licinius.

"Young idiot!" the surgeon said irritably, apparently referring to Favonius. "I had one of his men on sick parade this morning, said he'd slipped down the stairs from the North Rampart. Not a mark on him, but he 'felt awful peculiar, sir.' If I was his centurion, I'd have made him feel more peculiar yet."

They reached the mess hall, and Licinius took Justin off to sit with him, introducing him to some of the other officers, and to the Legion's junior surgeon, Flavius, a brown-haired boy with a cheerful face. It was a mixed bag of men, many of them young, as junior officers were apt to be, career men, following the Eagles as their fathers and grandfathers had. Most were Roman by citizenship only, offspring of Army families born in the four corners of the Empire.

For the most part they seemed eager enough, but there was also an air of carelessness and an underlying tinge of depression that Justin had not encountered before. Listening to Favonius and Centurion Martius chatting happily about a wager on a cockfight, he wondered just what was behind the surgeon's animosity toward Favonius. Then he shrugged and applied himself to a plate of bread, eggs, and fish, washed down with routine-issue wine. He was hungry, and although Army food was never more than serviceable, there was at least plenty of it.

Lying on his back on the cot bed in his quarters that night and staring wakefully out the one high window, Justin turned the day over in his mind. The Legate, a heavy pink and grey man with a harassed expression, had stopped him after dinner and asked him how he liked Eburacum so far, and Justin had lied in his teeth and said that he liked it very much, sir, privately deciding to put in for transfer the minute he could decently do so.

Exploring the great fort, he had discovered that it was indeed as unkempt as it had appeared on first impression, and a number of the men were sloppily dressed as well. Even the walls were in bad shape, although he noticed signs of recent repair in some places. It was none of it bad enough to be outstanding, but compared to Lambaesis, Eburacum was a mess. To make matters worse, most of the officers, although *they* looked fine, seemed indifferent to any problems. Except perhaps for Licinius. The surgeon had a military acumen more usually found in the Centuriate than the Army Medical Corps, and Justin suspected that there was a good deal Licinius could tell him about Eburacum, most probably none of it good . . . .

So here he was, proud commander of 480 bad examples . . . . There was a thin line of moonlight coming through the window, and Justin wiggled one foot idly, watching the patterns it made on the heavy blanket. He remembered the commander saying that the Ninth would provide him with enough work to keep him out of trouble. So he had known, Typhon take him. Suddenly he laughed and rolled over, drawing the blanket up around his ears and thinking regretfully of the soft African nights. Before he slept, he said several short prayers that the commander found his next post in Britain.

The next morning Justin encountered more evidence of the general state of affairs in Eburacum when he received his orders and found his cohort assigned to repair duty on the northwest wall, which most certainly needed it.

The five young centurions under him were good men, if a trifle carefree, but that couldn't be said of the men. They were lazy and bad tempered and sloppy, the greater part of them. And what was worse, it appeared that his predecessor had been letting them get away with it. They were clearly surprised when he set them to redoing yesterday's work, most of which looked as if it would have come down again at the slightest pressure.

Justin spent a frustrating day trying to impress a sense of discipline on men who, apparently judging him by their previous commander, showed a regrettable tendency to think that the centurion was only being funny. After having sent one man to the guardhouse for the rest of the day to reflect on his sins, applied the vine staff to the shoulders of another, and told a third that if he did not take the time to mix the mortar properly, he, Justin, would personally cement him into it, the work went better, but Justin knew that any time he turned his back it still stopped, and it was still being done sloppily for all his orders. Nor, he thought, doing a quick count, did the cohort seem to be up to its paper strength.

By the time he came off duty, covered with a fine white dust, he was tired and thoroughly irritable, a mood which remained with him as he stalked into the mess hall, his hair still damp from the bath. He met Licinius at the door. The surgeon took one look at his expression and took Justin off to sit with him.

"You look mad enough to chew a sword in half," Licinius said placidly, drawing out a bench at the far table. "What's the matter?"

"Incompetent . . . lazy . . . underdisciplined. . . ." Justin ticked his grievances off on one hand.

"I see," Licinius said, cracking open an egg.

"And falling apart. Even Hippo Regius was better kept up."

"Is that where you were before?"

"I had the Sixth Cohort of the Third Augusta out of Lambaesis. We drew garrison duty there for a while. If I had any brains, I'd be there now."

"The Sixth." Licinius studied his plate.

"It wasn't anything to do with my command," Justin said hastily. "I took on a rather silly sort of bet and got booted down two cohorts for it."

"What was it?"

"Well, Posides, who had the cavalry command there, was going on about what strict training the gladiators go through," Justin said, feeling, in retrospect, a little foolish, "and I said that that might be true in Rome, but that in a place like Hippo Regius a man with ordinary military training could easily hold his own. Of course the end of it was that he bet me I couldn't, so I took the net-and-trident's place in the Volcanalia games to prove my point. Made Posides put up the bribe for the arena master, though," he added, and Licinius choked on his egg.

"If the Legate hadn't come out from Lambaesis that week, I mightn't have got anything but a few days confined to quarters, but as it was, the commander was having heart failure for fear he'd see me."

"So I should think," Licinius said when he had recovered.

"That and the fact that he'd put a week's pay on the sword-and-buckler man before he found out the other one was me."

Licinius gave an undignified whoop of laughter that made several men near them turn and stare. "Did you win?"

"Yes. They say the net-and-trident man has the advantage, and the arena master assured me that his men rarely got killed, but along about halfway through it dawned on me that arena masters have been known to lie. I didn't kill the other fellow, of course."

"And the commander packed you off to Britain for your sins."

"He'd have sent me farther, I think, if the Empire had *gone* any farther."

"We *are* rather at the end of the world. Britain grows on you after a while, though."

Justin looked about him with distaste. "It hasn't so far."

He never liked Eburacum any better, or the Hispana either, for that matter, but his transfer applications were routinely turned down with the comment that he was needed at present—the centurion could feel free to reapply next month. Meanwhile he tackled the appalling project of working the Eighth Cohort into shape, and did his bit to mend the walls of Eburacum. And slowly he grew grudgingly used to the place, as he grew to be friends with Licinius. They hunted together when they were off duty, in the woods to the west or the purple heather hills that rolled like an ocean to the northward; or wandered into the cluster of buildings that made up Eburacum town, to drink in one of the wine stalls or poke about in the shops selling perfume and rubbing oil, hunting spears, jewelry, hides, and bright native weaving. Licinius found endless fascination in the shops of the potion peddlers although, as he told Justin, he suspected that most of their panaceas were compounded mainly of hope and goose grease.

And the surgeon served as balm to Justin's mood. "Keep your

temper," Licinius advised him once when Justin had complained that the wall repairs—they were replacing the old and rotten wood with stone—ought to have been made long ago. "Some was done six or eight years back, I think. I wasn't here myself then. But after that it was let slide again. Mithras, don't you think I know how it is? I've complained til I'm hoarse and all it's got me is young fools like Favonius being so gay and amusing about the whole thing that I want to knock their heads in. They think they're playing some kind of game. They're all such little Roman gentlemen. A pity they haven't more brains."

It was a late afternoon in the first days of winter, and they were sprawled in a clearing westward of the fort, their hunting spears on the ground beside them with a bundled wolf skin, the product of the day's hunting. They were finishing the last of a meal of mutton and barley bannock, tossing a piece now and then to Whitepaw, Licinius's hunting dog, who was flopped contentedly at their feet. They were almost within sight of Eburacum, and their guide, one of the local tribesmen who supplemented his income in this fashion, had parted from them a short distance back.

"Licinius, the Ninth wasn't always like this," Justin said, cleaning his dagger, with which he had been slicing mutton. "Hades, it has enough wreaths of honor to satisfy an Emperor. What happened to it?"

"I don't know. Maybe it's been too long from Rome. The Ninth came over here with Claudius, you know. Or maybe it never recovered from Boudicca's rebellion. Rebuilt legions tend to think themselves unlucky. It almost happened again in Domitian's reign— the Picts had the whole damn Legion surrounded, and Agricola's reinforcements only just pulled their asses out of the fire in time. Or maybe it was the few years of peace after Agricola's campaign that did it. Nobody really thought of Britain as a threat, and they recalled Agricola, and the Legion was allowed to get soft. I don't know. The Second Adiutrix was withdrawn then too, and *that* was a mistake. For years now we've been marching out to put down one small tribal rising after another, piecemeal. And the minute we turn our backs, it flares up again, or another one does. There was a bad one ten years ago, the last time we pulled back in the north. The younger officers, and some old enough to know better, regard it as a sort of game, but this ineffectual dodging about and striking here and there wears the men's nerves down." Licinius shifted one leg to a more comfortable angle and regarded it with disgust. "Now you've got me doing it, curse you, and I'm in even less of a position than you are to change anything. I suppose I'm lucky. If it hadn't been for a bad knee, I'd have gone into the Centuriate, and then I'd be more frustrated than ever. Well, I'm like to have plenty on my hands with my own craft soon enough."

Justin sat up straight, putting his dagger away. "Trouble?"

"I don't know. I'm only the surgeon here. My job is to put men back together, not take them apart. But the tribes are stirring all along the frontier, especially the Brigantes, and we're sitting right smack in the middle of their territory. From what Cunory the Hunter said to me yesterday, we shall have them down about our ears soon if we aren't careful."

Oh, splendid. A tribal rising, and a wonderful cohort like his to meet it with. "It's a good thing we mend our walls, then," Justin said disgustedly.

Licinius picked up the wolf skin and whistled the dog to heel, and taking their spears, they set off homeward. As they came in through the Dexter Gate, they saw a tall, fair-haired man with the luxuriant mustache cultivated by the Britons, settling the last of a pile of baled skins on the packsaddle of a small pony which braced its shaggy legs against the weight, swelling up its belly when the man came to tighten the cinches.

"Ah, would you now, oh lazy one?" the man said in the soft-voiced speech of the Britons, kneeing the beast sharply in the ribs. The pony let out its breath, and he pulled the cinches tight before it could draw it in again.

"Going, Cunory?" Licinius asked, coming up to him, while White-paw and the Briton's pack of hounds eyed each other suspiciously.

"Aye, this is my last trip this winter. I've sold all I can here, and there will be snow soon, and lambing season. My tribe will need every man to keep the wolf guard. I will sell the rest there." He was dressed in plaid woolen breeches and cloak and carried a light throw spear. A heavier boar spear was fastened to the side of the packsaddle.

"Was it a good hunting?"

"It was very good," Cunory said. "And I have brought back something alive as well, that will bring me as much as the skins." He pulled back a flap of hide toward the front of the bundle to disclose three very young puppies in a nest of skins, curled round

16

each other for warmth. Cunory lifted one out and held him up. His coat was a fine dark steel color and he had feet apparently designed with a much larger animal in mind.

"I bought them from one of the Painted People to the north. The mother died at the birth, and they said they would likely not live. But see, they have lived well enough. They will be good dogs, and one is a female."

Justin, who by this time had a fair knowledge of the local language, listened with interest.

"Gods," Licinius said, looking at the puppy's feet, "I think it's going to be a horse."

"No, they're wolfhounds," Justin said. "I had one when I was a boy that my father bought from a trader out of Hibernia. They make the best hunting dogs there are."

The little female was still snoring peacefully among the deerskins, but the third puppy had sat up and was looking curiously about him, his tail fanning happily back and forth.

Justin reached out and picked him up. "Will you sell this one?"

"Aye, I will sell either of the males. They are grown so that there is barely enough room for two on the pony."

Licinius regarded the puppy dubiously. "He'll eat you out of half your pay."

"What else am I going to spend it on in this delightful place? Where do you kennel Whitepaw?"

"With Aeresius at the Head of Neptune. He might have room for another."

An hour later, having haggled with Cunory over the price, and bathed—Justin barely preventing the puppy from leaping in as well —they were walking down the Street of Neptune, which took its name from the wineshop at the corner, with the dog clutched firmly under Justin's cloak. He had already stopped in the odds-and-ends shop kept by Barates the Syrian and bought him a puppy collar of soft leather studded with brass.

They halted before a doorway crudely carved with a head of Neptune, badge of the Ninth Legion. Aeresius was an ex-legionary himself and had served his term with the Eagles in the Hispana. Inside was the warm glow of lamplight and the sound of someone singing, horribly off-key, one of the songs the Legions marched to.

They pushed through the crowd about the door, Whitepaw padding at Licinius's heel, and took one of the farther tables, where the surgeon sat rubbing the stiffness from his knee. A blue-eyed girl with long brown braids and a bright tunic of blue and saffron checkered wool brought them wine.

"Good evening to you, Licinius the Surgeon. And you, Centurion," she added, looking curiously at Justin.

"Hello, Gwytha," Licinius said. "I have brought Whitepaw back, as you can see, and we would like something to eat and to speak with Aeresius."

"I'll fetch him. He's shaking dice with one of the Optios from the fort. Perhaps I can catch him before he shakes this shop away."

Justin looked after her. "Aeresius's daughter?"

"No, he never married. A trader left her for a debt a year or so back. Aeresius wasn't very pleased, but since the trader had sold all his goods and *claimed* he'd been robbed of his money, Aeresius had to take what he could get." Licinius laughed. "He says he got her cheaply because she talks so much."

"I am very useful," the girl said indignantly, coming back. "And what is more, I am the only one who can keep the books straight."

Justin raised his eyebrows. A British slave girl with a turn for mathematics was unusual, to say the least.

She set two bowls of stew down before them. "And you needn't goggle like that, Centurion," she added tartly. "A Greek clerk taught me, in Calleva, and I'm very good at it." She turned away as someone called for more wine, and Justin sat looking after her.

"A most unusual slave," he murmured, when she was out of earshot.

"She is from the Iceni to the south, and wellborn in her tribe, I think. She was quite young when a slave trader found her wandering alone, and—well, it happens often enough. Here's Aeresius."

A square, greying man in his fifties, his sword arm crossed with the scars of twenty years' service in the Legion, pulled up a chair beside them. "Gwytha says you wanted to talk to me."

"This is Centurion Corvus, new commander of the Eighth Cohort," Licinius said. "He wants you to kennel this monstrosity he has bought from Cunory the Hunter."

Justin took the puppy, who had been squirming madly the past ten minutes, from under his cloak and put him on the table; only a firm hand on his collar prevented him from jumping immediately to the floor where Whitepaw, for whom he had apparently devel-

18

oped an attachment, was lying at his master's feet. Thwarted in this attempt, he stuck his nose in Justin's bowl.

"Finn!" Justin snapped. The puppy withdrew and sat back on his haunches, looking up at him.

"So, he obeys you already," Aeresius said, watching him. "He will make a good dog when he's grown."

The matter was settled quickly. Justin set the puppy next to Whitepaw and sat idly listening to the hum of conversation around him. In one corner a group of soldiers were arguing the relative merits of two fighting cocks, while another two disputed the outcome of an arm-wrestling match with loud invitations to come outside and be convinced. The discussion was quieted somewhat as the mailed footsteps of the Watch clattered by in the road, their swinging lanterns setting the shadows to leaping on the building across the street, but it was taken up again as soon as they had passed. On the far side of the room, the Optio had apparently found another dicing partner and was speedily winning his opponent's accumulated pay.

Licinius had been drawn into a discussion with two other young officers, and Justin turned, for want of anything else to do, to watch Gwytha as she wove her way between the tables, a flask of wine in her hand. She was a tall girl, nearly as tall as he was himself, and her thick red-brown hair must have hung below her waist when it was unbraided. She was pretty enough, even by Roman standards, but he couldn't imagine any Roman woman in that brilliant saffron and blue tunic. His mother, for instance, would have rolled up her eyes and turned pale at the mere thought of putting on such a garment.

It seemed a shame the girl belonged to a wineshop keeper. She was quite obviously fit for better work, and the customers at the Head of Neptune could make it uncomfortable for a girl as young as she was.

There was a loud crash and Justin was startled to see Gwytha box a drunken legionary's ears with a force that sent him spinning off the bench and onto the floor.

"If you try that again, I'll knock your teeth out the back of your head," she said calmly, picking up the wine flask again. "I'm here to serve you wine, not to keep you amused."

The legionary looked up at her, startled. "Then give me some more wine," he said sullenly after a moment.

Gwytha regarded him with distaste. "Nay, then, you've had enough. Go and cool your head somewhere, and when you come back, remember your manners." She turned her back on him to serve the men at the next table.

The chastened legionary looked as if he were going to argue, and then thought better of it. He picked himself up and strode self-consciously to the door, followed by a brief wave of laughter from the room behind him.

"Eugé, Gwytha, that was well done, hellcat!"

"Hai, Manlius, didn't I tell you Icenian women have minds of their own?"

"Remember what Boudicca did to us!"

Justin grinned. Apparently Gwytha was well able to take care of herself.

Licinius saw him and grinned back. "Inspires you to protect the helpless little thing, doesn't it?"

"It inspires me to protect Manlius." He called Aeresius over and the three of them went together to make the puppy a bed in the storeroom, Whitepaw following at Licinius's heels.

Aeresius piled some old meal sacks in one corner of the dirt floor and Justin put the puppy down on them, telling him firmly that he was to stay. Finn yawned and seemed content with the arrangement, but Whitepaw nosed his way in between the men and, picking Finn up by the scruff of the neck, took him off to his own corner and curled himself up beside him.

"So, they're going to be friends," Licinius said. "A year from now we'll have a fine hunting team, if we aren't off hunting Brigantes or the Pict instead."

"What are they like?" Justin asked. "The Picts?"

"Like smoke. The Brigantes are fine fighters, but we can fence them in, given enough men. The Pict can hide behind a pilum shaft and come and go under our noses. We found that out in the last war in the north."

"Aye, we go looking for him and can't find him," Aeresius said, "and when we turn around we find his little barbed arrow in our back instead."

II

The Hunt

AS THE TWO MEN came out into the street again, Licinius looked up at the sky where a few stars shone through a ragged hole in the enveloping clouds. The air was still and not quite as cold as it had been. He took a deep breath.

"It's going to snow soon," he said, and as he spoke, a few white flakes came drifting down around them, spiralling to the ground where they vanished as they landed. Somewhere, far off in the hills, a wolf howled, a long, drawn-out note, quavering and eerie, the voice of winter hunger.

Justin shivered. He hadn't known a wolf could be so intimidating.

Licinius nodded. "Cunory's going to have trouble with the wolf guard this winter," he said. "I think it's going to be a rough one. They'll be howling all round the lambing pens."

"Half-witted animals, sheep, at best," Justin remarked. "I've always considered a midwinter lambing season just one more proof of it."

"They're not bright," Licinius agreed. "I once saw a whole flock jump off a cliff because something had frightened *one* of them."

"There's something so wasteful about stupidity. Speaking of which, here's young Favonius."

"And a couple of his brothers-in-arms, out for a night on the town."

"The gods help the town. Greet him politely, smile nicely. That's it. We can be little gentlemen if we try. Maybe it isn't snowing after all. I don't see any more coming down, and there's another break in the clouds, over there."

"Little enough you know about it, my boy."

It did snow, starting heavily the next night, and the wind came up again as well, howling round the roof and piling great drifts against the walls of the fort. It was still coming down the following morning, the wind dying and rising by turns, blowing the snow into little feathered ridges along the ground, and clawing at doors and windows. Even where hot air from the hypocausts flowed through the wall flues, the buildings were icy and iron braziers were set up, their glowing flames jumping in the wind that somehow found its way inside and whistled across the floor. The grey cloaks of the sentries were almost lost in the blur of the driving snow, and Justin, slogging his way disgustedly across the fort to put in his monthly request for transfer, saw that someone had wrapped the single rosebush outside the Principia with a sack to keep it from the frost.

The Legate's staff greeted him as an old acquaintance, handed him the proper request forms, and waited, grinning, while he copied them out. This usually served to infuriate Justin, but today he grinned reluctantly back at them. He wasn't going anywhere in this weather, anyway.

It was impossible to work in the blinding storm, and the men were set to marching in the drill shed or sent to the armory to check and mend equipment. The sentries, who kept only half watches each now, returned, cold and stamping the snow from their feet, to strip their sodden leggings off and stand shivering at the braziers.

Justin, drilling his men that afternoon, abandoned the usual practice of keeping a supervisory eye out from a distance and marched with them instead. It was warmer that way.

"What did I tell you?" Licinius asked, encountering him in the mess hall that night. "Hippo Regius. Oh, my innocent!"

"Oh, stow it. What have you got for frostbite?"

"Another layer of wool in your leggings and don't thaw out so quickly when you come in," Licinius said unsympathetically.

Justin sat up late that night, having experimented and found that it was colder when you were lying down, dutifully writing a letter to his mother at Antium by the flame of the little bronze lamp. He had meant to do it sooner, and should have, he thought guiltily, closing the two leaves of the tablet and sealing them. It would take longer than ever to reach her now, with winter making the roads bad.

By the next morning the sky had cleared and the temperature dropped, freezing the top layer of snow. In the early half-light of dawn Justin set out from the fort with his hunting spear at the head of one of several foraging parties sent to bring in extra meat for what looked like an unusually bad winter.

He led them into the wood that he and Licinius had hunted before, the hounds—many of the soldiers kept hunting dogs—lolloping on ahead of them. Almost immediately they came onto the fresh trail of a big dog wolf but passed it by, whistling the hounds away. It was meat that they were after. You could eat a wolf, of course, but there was no point in it if you didn't have to. They pushed further into the wood, the rising winter sun coming through the bare trees to splotch the snow with pink and saffron. The air smelled clean and clear after the stuffiness of the barracks and somewhere a sparrow was chattering to itself about the weather. Soon after, they ran onto deer tracks and turned to follow them, angling to the westward until early afternoon, when they brought him to bay, backed up against a fall of rock, and made their kill. When they had skinned the buck and wrapped the meat in the hide, Justin set up a small altar of packed snow and frozen turf dug out with his dagger blade, and, whipping the hounds off the rest of the carcase, they laid it across the altar for the gods of the place, and turned back east again. They killed a second time on the way back, a boar, and arrived at the fort, converging with several other hunting parties and feeling very pleased with themselves.

But Licinius, when Justin came by the hospital on his way in, was in no mood to hear hunting stories. He was engaged in binding up the shoulder of Centurion Sylvanus, Favonius's second in command, who had been foolish enough to disregard the orders about bringing in meat, and had gone off after the same dog wolf whose tracks Justin's party had passed that morning, getting badly bitten for his pains. Favonius, leaning over Licinius's shoulder and getting in his light, was chattily recounting his own day's hunting.

"—a thundering great boar, as big as I am, with tusks like sword blades, so we—"

"Ow!" Sylvanus winced as Licinius tightened the bandages around his shoulder and pinned them into place. "We nearly had him too, biggest wolf you ever saw," he continued with his own saga.

Justin decided not to tell him about the buck.

"So I said to him, 'You work your way around the far side—'" The salve jars rattled as Favonius leaned comfortably against the table. " '—and we'll have him rolled up.' "

"A thundering great bore indeed," Licinius said when they had departed. "This *is* a hospital, you know, and not the Forum at Rome."

"They do run on, don't they?" Justin said. "*We* killed a buck, but I shan't mention it except in passing. Here, let the orderly clean up, and come away. You've had enough."

"No, I always clean my own instruments," Licinius said. "It's something my uncle taught me."

"He was a surgeon too?"

"Yes, and a very good one. He lived with us in Judaea. I grew up there—my father was stationed with the Fretensis. I never thought of being a surgeon myself, though, until I realized this knee wouldn't hold up on the march. My father's family have always been soldiers."

"And mine. Odd, isn't it, how it always seems to be a matter of family. My father died when I was quite small, but I never really thought of doing anything else when I was grown."

"I suppose it comes of growing up with it," Licinius said, stacking the salve jars away. "When I joined, I hoped I'd be sent to the Fretensis too, and I did serve my training year there, but after that I was posted to Vindobona in Pannonia, and then here when I got senior rank."

Justin laughed. "And I grew up at Antium and went from there to Africa, by way of the Rhine. Gods, what a lot of ground the Empire covers. I can still remember when I was about eight, lying on my back beside the pool in the atrium, looking up at the sky, thinking what an awful lot of it there was, and wondering what particular bit of it I was going to wind up under. I don't suppose I need add I did *not* have Britain in mind."

"I always wondered too, except that I didn't much want to go anywhere except Judaea. I can't think why, now."

"And now we're both at the end of the world."

"That's what I thought when I got my orders to Britain. Strange, though, how much I like it now. Because it's so green, I think. Judaea's sort of mud color."

"Will you go back there, when your service is over?"

"How do I know what I'll do in ten years? But I don't think so. My parents are both dead, and my uncle as well. The only family I really have left is an aunt, and she's one of those women who are always doing things to you for your own good. The farther away from Aunt Vipsania the better, I imagine. No, I'll probably settle here."

"Licinius, the snow's got into your brain."

"No, I'd like it. Get a grant of land somewhere in the south and raise horses. There's always a demand for good cavalry mounts. What will you do?"

"I don't know. Stay with the Legions maybe."

"And rise to be Emperor?"

"Oh, shut up."

"Licinius! Licinius!" There was the sound of running feet in the corridor, and a breathless legionary burst through the door. "The Dexter Gate!" he panted. "Quick!"

"What happened?" Licinius was already gathering up his instrument case and a roll of bandages. "Bring this, will you, Justin?"

"Forage party—attacked. Brigantes, curse them. We've got two wounded. The rest are bringing them down, and I was sent to fetch you. I think Manlius is hurt bad. He's got a spear in his back and we're afraid to pull it!"

Licinius caught up the rest of his gear and ran for the door, the others behind him.

When they reached the gate, the sentries were already helping in seven bloodstained and weary men who, among them, carried two others. From the back of one of these protruded the broken-off haft of a spear. It was Manlius, whose ears Gwytha had boxed at the Head of Neptune.

Licinius took a quick look and said, "Get him to hospital, quick! Put him on the big table and tell the orderly to get my kit ready. You!" He grabbed one of the hunting party. "Go and find Flavius and send him to me. Justin, help me with this."

He slit open the other man's tunic and wrapped a strip of linen tightly around the gaping wound in his chest to stop the bleeding which had been only partly arrested by a piece torn from someone's cloak. It was Centurion Geta, the grizzled, middle-aged commander of the Seventh Cohort.

"That should hold. Bring him along." He left the blood-soaked scrap of wool sinking crimson streaks into the snow and ran for the hospital.

Justin slipped his shoulder under Geta's arm, nodding to a man with a bad gash in his sword arm to follow, and they picked their way over the ground, which by now had been frozen into icy ruts wherever the cart wheels had passed. They reached the hospital as young Flavius, Licinius's junior surgeon, came flying round the corner, his instrument case in his hand.

Licinius was carefully cutting away Manlius's tunic from around the spear shaft as they laid the centurion down on the other operating table.

"Flavius, see to Centurion Geta," he said, looking up briefly. An orderly came in with a stack of lint and bandages, and a tray of instruments. "Put it down there and get me a packet of ephedron. Then stick around. I'm going to need you. Justin, tie something around that man's arm to stop the bleeding. Everybody else clear out."

Flavius had unwrapped Licinius's temporary bandaging and was cleaning Geta's wound while the centurion gritted his teeth and gripped the edge of the table until his knuckles were white.

Justin bound a strip of linen round the other soldier's forearm and secured it in place. "That'll do well enough until someone can see to you. I'm afraid I'd only make it worse."

"It's all right." The man shook his head wearily. "I'm only tired. We had a long way to come, carrying the two of them."

"What happened?"

"We were miles to the north of here, on the track of a boar, when we heard the commotion. They had jumped Manlius's patrol and pretty well torn them up by the time we got there. We beat them off, but we weren't in any position to chase them, with Manlius and the centurion wounded, and who knew how many more waiting behind the next tree for us. We lost two of our men, and all but Manlius of his patrol. We'll lose him too, by the look of it."

"How many of them?"

"Ten or twelve, I think. I hadn't time to count."

Flavius finished cleaning and stitching Geta's wound and Justin helped the orderly carry him to one of the four-man wards lining the corridor, while Flavius attended to Antonius, the man with the gashed arm. Licinius had cleaned away the blood from around the spear shaft in Manlius's back and was examining it gingerly. Mercifully, the man had fainted. Getting enough opium down him to do any good would not have been easy.

"How is Geta?" Licinius asked, not looking up.

"He'll live," Flavius said. "It's bad, but not as deep as it looked."

"When you have finished, come and help me here." There was a fine-drawn edge to Licinius's voice that brought Justin, coming back into the operating room, up short in the doorway.

Flavius salved Antonius's cut and rebandaged it while Licinius worked steadily, trying to discover how deep the spear had gone, and whether it was barbed at the point or not. He thought so, but it was difficult to tell for certain.

"What about it?" Flavius asked, when he had finished and sent Antonius off to be taken care of by the orderly.

"I don't know. If I pull this, he may live, but most likely not. It's deep, and I think it's gone through the lung. If I leave it, he'll die in a day or two, of course." Licinius's face was taut and pallid under his tan.

Flavius was silent. He was very young, and this was his first posting since his training year. He looked at Licinius.

"Right. Let's get on with it," Licinius said. "The ephedron may slow the bleeding enough. Justin, get me some more light. It's getting dark in here."

Without stopping to wonder how he had ended up playing orderly, Justin fetched three lamps and set two of them in stands on either side of the table. The third he held in his hand, shifting it as Licinius and Flavius worked, so that the light fell always on the wound. Licinius moved slowly, working a long spoonlike instrument down past the spear shaft. He nodded in satisfaction as he felt the bowl of it slide under the point. The smooth sides of the spoon would keep the spearhead from tearing the flesh further as it came out. Manlius stirred and murmured something.

"There now, be.still. It will be all right," Licinius said gently. He glanced at Flavius and pulled the shaft.

Manlius cried out as the blood rushed up out of the wound like

27

a fountain. Justin fought down a sick feeling in his throat and held the lamp closer as the two men struggled to stop the crimson flow. They worked feverishly with the tiny, snub-nosed forceps to catch and tie off each vein while the orderly clamped lint against the un-staunched side of the wound, retracting it out of their way and trying to seal off the red and deadly river until they could stop it.

Manlius whimpered, as if he had no strength to yell, and Licin-ius's face went a shade whiter, but he kept on working, Justin hold-ing a lamp in each hand now, for the sun had gone completely, and it was black night outside, broken only by scurrying shadows as someone carried a torch or lantern by.

In the end, though, it was no use. Manlius quivered and his fingers, which had been gripping the sides of the table, slackened and fell limp. There was one soft, sad little whisper, "Mama . . ." and he was still. Licinius worked on for a while, but then he straightened and laid the forceps down. He picked up Manlius's body and turned it over gently. He brushed a soft hand over the soldier's face, closing the staring eyes before he drew a sheet up over him. He looked at Flavius and said wearily, "You may as well go back. I'll see to the rest," and turned and began to gather up his instruments.

Flavius, ashen faced, looked as if he were about to say something, then changed his mind and slipped quickly from the operating room.

Justin, realizing that he was still holding the lamps, set them down and silently began to help Licinius. He had seen men die before, in battle, but he also remembered a man of his own cohort who had died in his arms in the African sun because there was no surgeon to be found, and he remembered how sick and helpless he had felt.

Afterward, Licinius sat at the desk in his office where the records were kept and requisitions made, and put his head in his hands.

"Do you know," he said finally, "I was praying to every god I knew that that man would live. Dear gods, we know so little."

There was no reply to make, and Justin sat silent for several minutes. Then he said softly, "There was something wrong about that attack, Licinius. There were ten or twelve of them, Antonius said, to our patrol of ten. They shouldn't have cut them up like that. Did you notice Manlius was out of armor?"

Licinius looked up. "What?"

"He wasn't wearing his armor on patrol. They couldn't possibly have got his breastplate off with that spear sticking out of his back."

"I don't like that," Licinius said slowly.

"No more do I. I'm willing to bet the rest of his patrol was un-armored as well. Poor Manlius—he hadn't a chance."

"Who's the fool who let them out like that?"

"Their centurion, most like, and he's a dead fool now."

"Something's got to be done, or we'll *all* be dead fools if Cunory the Hunter was right."

"Is he of the Brigantes? That seems strange."

"No, he's from the Coritani to the south, but mostly he hunts to the north. And news of any sort goes through the tribes in ways which I still haven't figured out. I expect he takes them news of us too, but in any case the Brigantes could tell this Legion's rotting just by looking at it. And with the Emperor fighting his damn war halfway across the world, they know we can't get reinforcements."

"And when spring comes, we'll have the Brigantes on our hands," Justin said. "I think this had better go to the Legate."

"Take it to the Legate by all means," Licinius said bitterly. "Some-one's got to persuade him to clamp down before it's too late. But with the Emperor treating us like a recruiting station for his wars in Dacia, and then saying he thinks maybe he'll keep our detach-ments a little longer for his Parthian campaign, I wonder how long from now 'too late' is going to be."

They buried Manlius and the rest of his patrol the next day, in deep graves hacked out of the frozen ground in the cemetery out-side the fortress. Later a row of stones were set above them:

MANLIUS VERUS, OF THE V COHORT
OF THE IX LEGION HISPANA,
LIVED THIRTY-THREE YEARS.

Justin, seeing Licinius stop before the row and murmur a few words over Manlius's stone, thought that he was praying for the dead man's soul. He was wrong. Licinius was praying to Aesculapius.

Since Centurion Geta was badly hurt and still in hospital the next day, Justin went to see him, and then took the story of his suspicions to the Legate.

"You are certain they were out of armor?" Metius Lupus re-garded him sceptically, his dark eyes very bored, in a face which maintained a perpetual shade of pink.

"Yes, sir. I have checked it with the other men of Geta's patrol to be sure that he and Antonius weren't mistaken."

"I will see that their centurion is disciplined for this."

"Their centurion was disciplined by the Brigantes, sir. He's dead."

"Well, I shouldn't think that particular century will make that mistake again," the Legate said drily.

"No, but others may if discipline isn't improved. And the Brigantes will be waiting for it."

"Centurion, the Roman Legion is the best fighting force in the world, and the Brigantes know it."

"And the Brigantes are the best warriors in Britain, or so I hear, saving the Picts maybe, and we're sitting right in their laps. They'll know an advantage when they see one."

"Centurion Corvus, what precisely are you driving at?"

"That if we slip up, they'll walk all over us. All they need is a chance. Sir, I think, and Licinius too, that there's a tribal rising brewing—especially if they get any more examples of our weak spots."

"Licinius is upset because he didn't save that man. And a surgeon is not a military expert."

"Not only that, sir—" Justin was getting exasperated. "It was the way it happened, sir."

"Centurion Corvus, considering that you weren't there yourself, I think that you are making a war out of a chance skirmish, and the stupidity of ten men who have already paid for it." The Legate flipped the bronze lid of his inkstand open and began making notes on a supply list.

"I have spoken to Centurion Geta, sir," Justin said. "He agrees with me."

The Legate put his pen down. "I begin to understand why the commander at Hippo Regius thought he would be better off without you," he said.

"No, sir. That was a silly prank. I had no business doing it, but it had nothing to do with my duties."

"Nor, I may say, does this. I suggest you worry about your own cohort. As far as I can tell, you've spent all your time since you got here trying to get transferred, which you aren't going to be for a while, I can tell you. Now, it doesn't pay to be overly dramatic," he went on in a more kindly tone. "The Brigantes were fighting *themselves* last fall."

"What if they all join together, sir?"

"There is too much rivalry among the clans for that. Dubric tried it and found he couldn't hold them together."

"Dubric died last fall, sir. And from what I have heard, the outcome of that fighting was a new High King."

"His nephew Vortrix, who is very young."

"He managed to take the kingship, sir."

"A tribal skirmish is not the same thing as a full-scale war. I wouldn't worry greatly over this, Centurion. Rome is more than a match for a few tribes of barbarians. And the Brigantes have been peaceful for years."

Justin forebore to point out that that was what Quintilius Varus had thought too, before he lost three Eagles to the Germans, and contented himself with saying that Rome and most of her forces seemed to be occupied elsewhere at the moment.

"Very well, Centurion, I will look into it, if it will make you any happier," Metius Lupus sighed. "But undermanned as we are, I don't propose to stir up trouble unnecessarily. We have managed to maintain peace thus far, you know."

"A rather precarious peace, it seems."

"It's peace nonetheless," the Legate said with a certain amount of irritation. "Which, after all, is what we're here for. We aren't Claudius Caesar's invasion force, you know."

"No, sir."

"Very well, Centurion, you may go. I am pleased that you should be so concerned, but now I have work to do. I must check these supply lists if they are to go out today, and Jupiter knows we're going to need the extra grain this winter."

Justin saluted and left. He vented his feelings somewhat by bumping into the clerk in the outer office and swearing at him. He then remarked that Vortrix the High King of the Brigantes had need of a record keeper and he had best get his application in before the rush, and stalked out.

The clerk, a mild young man with a squint, goggled after him for a moment, then shrugged and went back to work. The Legate discouraged any pauses in his activities.

Justin turned down the Via Praetoria and, with a word to the sentry on duty, started over the stone bridge into the town. He stopped midway out of sheer irritation to pitch a snowball against the icy surface of the river, but seeing two of his own men watching him with evident curiosity from the rampart, abandoned this undignified idea.

By the time he reached the Head of Neptune he had cooled down. He knew the Legate wasn't going to pay the least attention to what he had told him, but they'd wear their armor out of fright for a while. And since improving the Legion's attitude was probably next to impossible as long as it remained undermanned, as Licinius had said, he supposed it didn't really matter. He remembered the detachments he had met on the road north last fall, going the other way. One of them had been from the Hispana. Probably from his own cohort. The gods knew it had been robbed of men at some point. Oh, what in Hades did he care anyway? He wasn't going to be here any longer than he could help.

He called an order for a cup of wine to Gwytha and went into the storeroom, wondering what on earth the Emperor wanted with Parthia anyway.

Finn, who had sat up at the sound of his step, yelped joyfully and bounded over, leaping about Justin's knees. Whitepaw wagged his tail in a friendly manner but stayed in his corner. Whitepaw was very much Licinius's dog although, as Justin discovered, he made an exception for Gwytha.

"Down!" Justin said as the puppy bounced up in excitement and fell over his own feet into an empty bowl. Finn subsided and sat waving his plumed tail back and forth on the dirt floor. Justin knelt down and scratched his ears, pulling some strips of deer meat from a sack in his tunic. He put the greater part down for the puppy, but tossed a piece to Whitepaw, who regarded it suspiciously for a moment and then, apparently deciding that if Justin hunted with his master he was all right, ate hungrily.

Someone ducked under the leather curtain from the shop, and Justin looked up to see Gwytha standing in the doorway with a bowl in her hand.

"I thought you would be in here," she said. "I put your wine on the corner table."

She came and knelt down beside him, holding one hand out for the puppy to sniff. Finn, who had gulped down the last of the deer meat, put his black nose forward tentatively. Gwytha held her hand still and he sniffed it for a minute and then licked her fingers. Only then did she move to scratch his ears. Finn wagged his tail and butted against her knee.

"You have a way with dogs," Justin said.

"I grew up with the hounds in my father's house," the girl said. "It is only knowing how to go slowly with them. Puppies are readier to make friends than grown dogs. It took me longer with Whitepaw. This will be a nice one—no, that is not for you." Finn had pushed an inquiring nose into the bowl she carried. "That is for Whitepaw. You have eaten, little pig. You can have some more later. Aeresius usually feeds them, but he's out hunting. We thought we wouldn't be crowded today, with it being so cold and everyone busy at the fort getting ready for the winter, and with what happened two days ago."

"You know about that?"

"If you keep a wineshop you know everything that happens, from the business at the fort to the smith's wife's new baby." She paused a moment. "I'm sorry about Manlius. It's in my mind that I wish I hadn't boxed his ears."

"I expect he had it coming," Justin said.

"All the same, I wish I hadn't done it."

She set the bowl down in front of Whitepaw and Justin followed her back into the shop, snapping his fingers for Finn to follow. He sat for a while over his wine, idly tapping the table with his ring, a twisted band of red gold, flat across the top and cut with a stag's head. Finn turned round two or three times in the rushes on the floor and went to sleep with his head on Justin's foot. It was still afternoon, and there was no one else in the shop. He watched Gwytha dusting the tables, her rounded figure jiggling attractively under her tunic. No luck there, probably, but he called out to her anyway.

"Come and talk to me. I want company."

She stared back at him, obviously deciding whether it had been a request or a command.

"Please. I'll start to talk to myself in a moment."

Gwytha came and sat across the table, looking at him carefully. "You look like a mind with something bad on it," she commented finally.

"I was cursing me for a fool, and the rest of the world to Hades," Justin said, with an honesty that surprised him. "Vortrix of the Brigantes along with it."

"He would rule it very well. He's going to make a good king, is young Vortrix."

33

"Good for whom?"

"For the Brigantes, of course," Gwytha said. "I only hope it doesn't bring them something worse in the end. When Rome makes up her mind, she may come and leave the Brigantes with nothing but children and old women, as they did with my people."

"In the meantime, of course, the Brigantes may leave us with nothing but corpses," Justin pointed out, "as your people did to us." Boudicca of the Iceni had slaughtered a Legion and three cities before Rome brought her rebellion to a halt.

Gwytha looked at him sideways. "You forget I'm not a Roman."

"I'm sorry. I suppose you have little enough reason to love us. Was it a Roman who—?"

"No, it was a Gaul," she said shortly, "who are kin to us."

He looked at her dubiously, unsure how to react. "Was it very bad?"

"I thought it bad at first, of course. I was only ten and I nearly died of fright and loneliness, but my first mistress was kind to me, and she had other slaves, and somehow the company made it more bearable. That was where I learned mathematics, and to write. She was a good woman, but old and extravagant, and when she died she was very much in debt, and we were sold to pay it. A magistrate from Venta Belgarum bought me then."

"What was *he* like?"

"He was one of those Britons who become very Roman because it's fashionable. It's like that in the south, and all the Romans who settle in Britain find it fashionable to be very British. I hated him," she added, and Justin was startled at the venom in her tone. "Not because I was his slave—there is slavery among my own people. Because he was so busy with himself and what face he put to the world that he had no caring for anyone else. It was a pleasant enough house, but it is no enjoyment, I assure you, Centurion, to be a piece of machinery, kept running smoothly so it can work a loom and sing for the guests, and maybe sleep with them if the host feels generous." Justin caught a knife-edge of bitterness in her voice that chilled him to the bone.

"I wasn't alone," she added. "His wife hated him too. He died soon after, and she put up a stone for him. It said, 'Here lies the body of Mutius Servianus. The gods be praised,' which you could take any way you chose. I rather liked her."

34

"What happened then?" It was a window on a world he had not encountered from that perspective before.

"I was sold again. His wife moved to Aquae Sulis with only a few of her oldest slaves. She was careful to sell the rest of us to good masters, but mine got drunk one night and fell to dicing with Morgan the Trader." She laughed. "I learned later that no one should dice with Morgan the Trader. His fingers are too quick. He didn't really want me, but I was the only stake my master could put up. And I was strong and a good worker, so he took me with him. I rather liked it, tramping all the length of Britain. But I didn't like sleeping in the rain, and I have managing ways and too quick a tongue, so Morgan said. Poor Morgan. So he left me with Aeresius to pay a debt. I have been lucky, I think, all in all. Aeresius treats me more as his assistant than his slave. He would sell me my freedom, I think, if I asked him for it."

"And you haven't? What of your own people?"

"It's been twelve years since I've been with my own people. They might take me back, I suppose, but it wouldn't be as if I had never left. They have no love for the Roman, or anything the Roman has touched. If I had stayed with my clan I would have been married long ago, and have babes now." A soft, wistful note crept into her voice. "I've been too long with the Roman kind. What man of the Iceni would ask for me now?"

Justin was touched; although seeing the softness of her skin and the gloss of her hair, he wondered briefly how many other men there had been and whether Aeresius was one of them. It seemed likely enough, but he didn't ask. "Have you never sent a message to tell your family it is well with you?" he said instead.

"No. My mother will have stopped grieving for me now and begun to forget that once she had another daughter at her hearth." The girl's eyes were focused on a point somewhere beyond the far wall. "If I can never go back, it's better they forget."

Justin was silent, at a loss for anything to say which wouldn't sound foolish and thoughtless.

Then Gwytha seemed to shake off her own mood and smiled at him. "If you are feeling sorry for me, Centurion, stop. It makes me uncomfortable. As long as we are exchanging stories, Aeresius said you were new to the Legion, and I haven't seen you before. Where do you come from?"

"Damn near everywhere," Justin said, relieved. "Hispania, originally, like the Legion. We lived at Tarraco while my father was stationed there. When he died—I was three, I think—my mother went to live at Antium where she could be comfortable and fashionable again. Antium's rather like going to live at Aquae Sulis. Very civilized. Hispania might have been more fun to grow up in, but I liked Antium."

"I've always wondered what Rome was like," Gwytha said. "Where this new world has come from."

"Well, Antium isn't Rome, though it's near enough to it. My most vivid memory of it is shying a mud ball at a sparrow and getting a senator instead."

Gwytha chuckled, a gurgling sound that seemed to roll back the years. "I set a snare once to trip a boy I didn't like, and the priest set it off instead. I hid for days."

"Italy's nice," Justin said, casting a baleful glance at the doorway, where a brisk wind was whipping flakes of snow in over the sill. "It's the countryside I like. It's all green and golden, with the warmth of the sun in it. People who've never been there go and goggle at the buildings in Rome and sit in the Circus Maximus and watch men and wild beasts slaughter each other, which you can see in any arena in the Empire, if you've a taste for it. I don't."

"Aeresius told me that in Africa you—"

"Never you mind what Aeresius told you. I'd like to know who told it to him. If it was Licinius, I'll—"

"Good stories have a way of getting around. And in any case, I asked Aeresius about you, so blame me. It wasn't Licinius, I shouldn't think. He doesn't gossip."

"But you do. Still, it was my own fault, and I'd probably do it again," he added with the ghost of a grin.

"Why? It was stupid the first time. If the centurion permits me to say so," she added hastily, seeing his expression.

Justin laughed. "You'd say so anyway. Morgan the Trader was right. Roma Dea, woman, I don't know why. Because it seems to me better to get rid of irresponsibility in that way than in your duties with your Legion."

"You're very serious about your Eagles, aren't you?" She looked at him curiously.

"It's the only life I know," Justin said.

"Or want?" she asked.

"That too, I suppose." He tried to explain it. "I'm a Roman, and the Legions *are* Rome. More than anything else is, even the Senate, or the Emperor. The Senate is losing power, but you can go from one end of the Empire to the other on the roads the Legions built, and speak the same language all the way, the language the Legions brought with them. And lately the Emperors too come from the Legions."

"And what when there are no more Legions and no Rome?"

"Oh, I know it will happen. There's never been an empire yet that's lasted forever. But the world is young for us yet. And then— then, someone will do it all again, I suppose."

They sat for a moment, the old world and the new one, looking at each other in the lamplight. And then a group of cavalrymen burst laughing through the door, and the mood was broken. Gwytha rose and began to see to the business of the night, and Justin pulled his cloak around his ears and made his solitary way back over the bridge to the fort.

III

The Watcher

ALL THAT LONG WINTER, hunting parties went out again and
again after meat, whenever the weather allowed. Justin saw to it
that his men at least were armored and carried more than their hunting spears, a rule he enforced with a ruthlessness that seemed to be
new to them. A spate of howling storms had almost completely
blocked supply lines from the south, both by river and by the roads
from Lindum and Mamucium. In every northern garrison the men
were finding that they had to shift for themselves, and the sense of
isolation did nothing for an already sagging morale. At least the
attack on Manlius's patrol seemed to have taught some of them
caution.

The attack was not repeated. The Brigantes were busy finding
meat for their own people and keeping the wolf guard round the
lambing pens. The wolves were growing gaunt and unusually hungry, even for wolves.

A punitive expedition had been sent out from Eburacum to the
villages of the closest clan, the most likely culprits in the attack,
but they had simply evaporated into the hills, taking their families
and livestock with them, and in this weather it had been impossible
to do anything more than set the roof thatch in flames, hoping that

38

the rebuilding would give them something to think about. The Brigantes were used to rebuilding. They had a long history of rebellion, broken only by occasional periods of peace under rulers of Rome's choosing.

After that brief excitement, the Legion returned to winter drill, or mock engagements fought amid loud complaints in the stone arena outside the fortress walls. Justin was grimly determined that *his* men at least would not go soft over the winter, and by his constant presence he made it harder for them to indulge what appeared to be a universal aversion to hard labor. The wall repairs went on as well, and when the weather was impossible they checked and rationed supplies in the storerooms, took inventory, and made repairs in the armory, or saw to their own gear, which in wet weather required constant oiling and burnishing to keep it in shape. And one by one the great catapults were tested, taken down for overhauling, reset, and tested again. When this had been done, there was catapult practice, a nightmare way to spend the day when the wind had blown the covers off the great machines and the skeins were wet.

Over the whole fort there was a feeling of restlessness and boredom, of being hemmed in, despite the constant duties of the day. At night the wineshops and beer stalls did a lively business. When Licinius had had a particularly trying day at the hospital, or Justin had found yet another foundation put in wrong and his last transfer application had come back marked "try again," they would take the dogs out for an hour or so, near to the fort, and make up the dinner they had missed with a bowl of stew and a cup of hot wine at the Head of Neptune.

At night Gwytha would sometimes produce a harp and sing, mostly tunes of the Legion. She had a soft, pure alto voice that seemed to get at the heart of a song, and Justin remained curious about her. Aeresius, he had discovered through other channels, was *not* bedding her, preferring the lighter-hearted if more expensive company of Venus Julia's "girls." (The standing joke held that Aeresius said Gwytha was bossy enough already.) But after that first talk of her early days, she had returned to her usual self-contained state. She was friendly enough, but it was as if she threw up her own defenses against the world. Justin had made a half-hearted pass at her once, mostly because she looked good in the lamplight and there wasn't much else to do, and she clipped him across the ear and then resumed the conversation as if nothing had happened.

Justin had a philosophical attitude toward women, derived from being more attractive than he knew. When the mood struck him, he had discovered that he could generally find what he was looking for without much trouble, although it never occurred to him to wonder why. So he had simply shrugged his shoulders, rubbed his stinging ear, and proceeded to treat Gwytha with brotherly indifference.

He liked her, though; she was pleasant company. And the few times that she had let her defenses slip, he had got a glimpse of a world as harsh as any that he had ever known.

Sometimes when he and Licinius took the dogs out, if the record books were put away and the wineshop ready for that evening, Gwytha would tie on the same heavy leggings that the men wore, fling her mantle over her head, and come with them. Justin and Licinius, in their scarlet cloaks, stood out against the snow like bonfires beside her rough brown mantle and the brown and grey coats of the dogs.

Once she caught Justin on the back of the neck with a well-placed snowball, and he pitched her in a snowbank to teach her better manners while Licinius laughed loudly and impartially at them both. They went on, brushing the snow from each other, but when Licinius turned his back, they jumped him. Then, laughing, the three stopped on a little ridge above the river and stood looking out over the winter-bare landscape.

"It's as frozen as ever," Gwytha said. "I was watching the sentries on the wall today. They're almost pretty against the snow."

"You wouldn't think so if you were up there," Licinius said.

"When was it you told me that this thaw of yours was going to thaw, Licinius?" Justin inquired acidly. "Wait until spring, you said, and Britain will be beautiful."

"It's beautiful now," Gwytha said. "Only you have to be looking at it on a full stomach from beside a fire to appreciate it."

"That does make it harder."

"This winter is different," Licinius said. "It's one of those events that the country people date things from. 'Aye, two years after the Great Winter, that'd be'."

"And every man in the Legion who went through it will be perfectly insufferable," Gwytha said. "Somebody will only have to breathe the word 'cold' and you'll pipe up with 'You should have been out in Eburacum in the winter of Trajan's nineteenth year. Talk about cold! Well, it was so cold that we were sleeping with a brazier under the bed and burned our—' "

She was silenced by a handful of snow in the face and they walked companionably on, their mood sobering as the wind came up again.

"I hope it thaws soon," Gwytha said. "I'm cold to the bone, and this is my country."

"So are we, and it isn't. The camp is about ready to start walking about on the ceiling," Justin said.

Gwytha pulled the folds of her mantle closer around her face. "Aeresius saw a wolf while he was hunting. It was dead. He thinks it *starved* to death. It's *got* to thaw."

By the end of another week, Justin was beginning to feel the same way. The suffocating white world seemed to be closing in around him. He was unnaturally relieved to wake to the sound of water dripping from the roof some two weeks later.

The man lay flat out along the ground, one elbow braced against the rocky outcrop at the hill's crest, and peered down into the valley below. His golden hair was tied back with a thong, and he was bundled against the cold in a grey wolfskin cloak which blended with the surrounding rock. There was a fine, misting rain coming down, to which he appeared oblivious.

Not so the two other men huddled out of sight behind an overhanging clump of thorn and rock, sullen and wet in the late thaw. They had been on the hunting trail all day and this detour was not to their liking.

"What's the good of staring at a few Romans from up here, like vultures. There aren't enough of us to take them," grumbled one.

The watcher in the rocks was silent, his golden head bent intently toward the men moving along the valley floor. Two of them carried a buck deer between them, but there was an awareness in their movement that showed they had more than the hunt on their minds. The centurion with them kept a wary eye both on his men and on the skyline, and changed their formation somewhat as they approached a clump of windblown trees. He turned a hawk-nosed profile to the watcher above him, and the golden-haired man nodded to himself.

"Armored and in formation. That one's no fool. The new centurion, think you?"

"Aye, lord," the second of his companions volunteered. "I saw him with Licinius the Surgeon in the Roman town."

The patrol passed out of sight, and Vortrix slid back from the hill crest. "A good day's hunting."

His companions grimaced at each other and slogged along behind him to rejoin the rest of the party which had been left safely out of sight, with orders to stay there and let well enough alone with the Romans. A new cohort commander at the fort was bound to stir Vortrix's curiosity.

Curiosity and a watchful eye were what had kept him alive in the years that his uncle Dubric had turned a regency into a takeover, and in the months when Vortrix had fought Dubric's brother Rhiada for his father's throne. And it was his watchfulness, coupled with an iron will, which now held the clans as one people after the bloody fighting which had left Rhiada dead and Vortrix in the High King's place.

There was much bustling in and about the little hill steading where the High King's household was keeping quarters as the hunting party straggled in. Three still-laden pack ponies were standing dejectedly under a tree. Several small boys dashed up to take the hunters' gear and bear their kill off to the kitchen, and Vortrix headed at a trot for the hall.

A dark-haired man in grimy traveling clothes was warming his hands at the hearth. "The sun and the moon on your path, Vortrix the King."

Vortrix shook the rain from his hair and mustache like a dog. "And on yours, Eri. You are always welcome at my hearth."

"I have brought you more than copper cook pots and eardrops to please the women this time, Lord Vortrix."

"New spear blades, I hope," Vortrix smiled. "We can't make anything to touch what you can bring us."

The rest of the hunters, having spotted Eri's shaggy little ponies, were gathering round the hearth to warm their hands and listen, while the women, whose ears had pricked up at the first sign of the

42

trader, fluttered about the bolts of cloth and gleaming kettles which lay already unpacked in the far corner.

"Send a few of your hounds to bring the rest of my packs and I will show you."

Vortrix whistled to a couple of small boys standing goggle-eyed at the edge of the throng and they scurried to the door. As Eri supervised the unloading, the men ambled over to inspect the cook pots and jewelry while their wives offered vivid descriptions of the size of the hole in the current kettle, or a hitherto unfulfilled longing for amber eardrops. Cathuil, the old chieftain whose lands marched closest to the Roman fort at Eburacum, and who was hence a not inconsiderable power, strolled over to inquire about the success of the hunt.

He eyed the array of gold and copper, amber and onyx and soft folds of cloth. "Eri always manages to turn the women upside down," he muttered. "There will be no peace at the hearth tonight for any man who doesn't buy."

"It has been a long winter with little softness in it," Vortrix said in the carefree tone of a man whose house contained no wife to demand new cook pots. "You can hardly blame them."

"Aye, perhaps he comes at a good time. It is in my mind it is time to buy Branwen her bride goods."

"See, here is Eri with something even more important," Vortrix murmured, turning away with a smile. Cathuil had a daughter of marriageable age, and Vortrix suspected there was something more on his mind than cook pots.

The men gathered round again as the little trader unrolled the first of his packs, and Vortrix nodded to a few of the new arrivals, including his kinsman Cawdor, a reluctant vassal since the death of his father Rhiada.

"So Eri brings us new teeth to bite the Romans," Cawdor said, looking ferretwise at his kinsman. His red hair reflected the firelight like the copper pots, and he twitched a fold of his kilt in nervous fingers.

"Aye, and something better, I hope." Vortrix's eyes were alert under the twin blue spirals tattooed across his temples. He watched in silence as Eri unrolled pack after pack, spreading out spear blades and arrowheads and new sword blades glinting in the firelight.

As the men squatted down to look and bargain, Vortrix nodded to Eri, and the little trader brought out one last bundle. He pulled out the thongs that bound it and spilled out five more blades, shining blue in the firelight.

"Look well, brothers!" Vortrix's voice brought silence in the room as he picked up a sword blade and bent it against his knee.

"Ah, they are fine." Niall the old armorer knelt down to examine them. "They will not break against the Roman blades as ours do."

"Can you get us more, Eri?" Vortrix asked.

"Aye, but the price comes high."

"It will be paid."

"And with *what* will it be paid, oh kinsman, when the better part of our corn goes in tribute to the Romans?" Cawdor leaned against an upright beam at the edge of the circle, still pleating his kilt edge between his fingers.

"It will be paid with whatever we can raise," Vortrix said, "so that there will be no more corn given to Rome, ever."

Cawdor looked as if he were about to speak again, and for a moment the tension was drawn so fine between them that there was no sound in the hall but the faraway call of a plover and the little wind that whipped in spurts around the door. Then Galt the Harper, who led Vortrix's household warriors, turned with exaggerated reluctance from the little pile of golden jewelry he had been fingering, and picked up one of the new blades.

"I will buy, Eri. I've a longing for a new arm ring, but this seems like to be the better bargain." There was a murmur of laughter, and a joke or two at the expense of Galt's vanity, and the moment passed.

Vortrix knelt beside Galt to make his choice of the new blades, and took also a wicked little dagger with a silver hilt which Eri pressed upon him as a hearth gift. It was small enough to fit in a sleeve, and he wondered if, after observing Cawdor, Eri thought he needed it. Cathuil bought also. He owed the Romans a debt over the matter of burned thatch.

The warriors having completed their purchases, Eri rolled the remaining weapons back into his pack—he had many such stops to make among the tribes—and turned to the women clustered about the goods which were nearer to their hearts than new war gear.

Cathuil inquired ostentatiously when Eri expected to reach *his* hall, and, setting aside certain objects from the pile, informed him that he would be there. Vortrix smiled. He had certain ideas of his own on the subject but had no intention of discussing them at a time not of his choosing. He waited while Galt lovingly sheathed his new blade and then drew him away from the rest to his private lodging.

Galt had ridden in from the north but a moment or two before the High King's hunting party, and his harp still hung in its leather case on his back. He loosened the straps and let it slide to the floor. "She has kept me company on a lot of long rides," he murmured, running a hand softly across the case. "But she grows old, and I have given Eri some gold in trade for a new one from the harpers of Eire when he passes that way. Perhaps I will give this one to young Dawid. He shows signs of having the music in him."

He opened the case and ran his fingers along the strings in a half tune. "The new colts show promise," he said, and the tune changed to a frolicking, undisciplined thing that sang of open country and new grass and a foal tumbling along at his mother's heels.

Galt was the finest horseman among the warriors, and if he saw promise in a new herd, it was there. Vortrix had sent him north to the Tribe's main horse runs as soon as the weather had made the journey possible, with instructions to report on their status.

"The yearling crop is the largest we've had yet," Galt said. "I'm afraid this year's batch won't be as good—it's been a black winter, and we've lost some mares as well. But the two-year-olds are shaping well, and there are many of the three-year-olds chariot-broken to draw on."

"That is good. It is in my mind we may be needing them."

"We had best keep a close watch on them, then," Galt said. "There are stirrings in the heather that the Painted People will be raiding south again this spring. A hard winter always drives them this way."

"The Painted One never moves unless he has the advantage," Vortrix said. "If the war band holds its strength, they'll stay clear."

Galt ran a questioning string of notes across the harp and looked up at him sideways. "Then keep an eye on Cawdor," he murmured. "His ambitions reach as far as the war band, if not the High King's throne."

"The one makes a good stepping-stone to the other," Vortrix said drily. "No one commands the war band but me."

"Nor ever will," Galt said. "But there are one or two to watch, all the same. I wonder occasionally why you have not seen fit to rid the tribe of that ferret."

"There has been enough blood shed in this Tribe," Vortrix said. "I will kill no more kinsmen if I can help it."

"I can think of some who might be improved by it," Galt answered lightly, but Vortrix just shook his head. "Then I will make you a wrist sheath for that dagger Eri seems to think you need."

As it had been a long winter, it was a long thaw. The snow about Eburacum melted only to freeze again into icy ruts and glasslike pathways that sent many a careless soldier sliding on his way on his backside. Justin, seeing the Legate skating helplessly across the courtyard of the Principia, retired around a corner to have a private fit of hysterics. The supply lines were got open after the first few days, but they were slow and unreliable, and it was the first day of May before the last ice had melted.

Looking down from the west wall, where he had gone to see to his sentry posts, Justin felt oddly isolated. Behind him in the fort, light shone warm in the barracks and the windows of the Praetorium, and torches glowed along the ramparts, but below the town lay dark. Except for the pale light of a lantern where the Watch made its rounds, there was nothing to be seen beyond the rim of the sentry walk. The thin horns of the moon, too new to shed any light, hung along the horizon.

It was the Feast of Beltane when all fires were quenched and the people gathered for the yearly miracle that would wake the new spark to light the world once more. Soon the friction of the fire drill would set the flames to leaping in the great piles of bracken on the low crest of the hill, but for now the world lay ink-black and desolate, with only the chanting of the priests on the hill to mark the presence of any living thing outside the walls of Eburacum.

Then, from far off, there was a sudden flash of light that glowed in triumph and leapt higher. Justin turned to find Licinius standing beside him.

The surgeon looked out over the rampart at the distant glow that spread now into several smaller glimmerings as torches were lit from it. "Come along. You mustn't miss your first Beltane. It's the Night of New Fire, the ritual death and rebirth of the tribe that has its counterpart in every religion in the world. And for all that Lugh Shining Spear is not my god, I find it awe-inspiring."

They crossed the bridge into the town and, whistling the dogs from the dark shop, set off toward the great twin fires on the hill.

By the time they reached them, the first leaping flames had died down, and the people were beginning to drive the sheep and cattle and shaggy little native ponies through them, to make them fruitful in the coming year. The animals, lowing and neighing with fright, streamed through the fire and down the far side of the hill in a cascade of flying embers, some of the young men following to make sure they didn't scatter too far. The boys who had undergone their initiation the night before tended the flames, proud in their new manhood, with the intricate spirals of the Spear Pattern pricked into the skin with woad, still raw and angry on their brows and chests. The chief priest of the tribe was chanting low over the flames, his brow crowned with a stag's antlers and his arms raised like the horned moon above him.

Licinius eyed him askance. "One holy man who doesn't care for Romans can cause more trouble to us than any ten warriors," he murmured to Justin. "They're the greatest nuisance in Britain, curse them."

Justin smiled at this mild term applied to the one force which had started more rebellions than any other. But he could understand why. There was a power in that low voice that was more than mere trappings.

The hill was crowded, not only with people from the village but with most of the neighboring clans as well. Justin saw Gwytha and Aeresius standing in a group near the farther fire, as well as a number of soldiers from the fort, some of them with their arms about native women. Technically, marriage was forbidden during their term of service, but that service was a long one and since the children would be made legitimate upon their father's discharge, many men married anyway. Among the officers, their marriages would receive social recognition as well.

The young men who had rounded up the animals returned, and the gathering settled down to the feasting part of the Feast of Beltane. The night was ordinary enough now, but while the priest was chanting his prayers to Lugh, silhouetted against the orange flames and the night sky, Justin had sensed what Licinius meant. Like the surgeon, and many who followed the Army, Justin made his prayers to Mithras, but he had felt a kinship there somewhere, as the tribe had given its thanks to the god who had given them this wonder of fire, produced out of dark nothing by the magic of the drill.

It was a gathering into which a handful of Romans would ordinarily have been wary of coming, but at Beltane, the feast of miracle and thanksgiving, all were welcome. Or, if not precisely welcome, at least no harm would be offered them. Someone handed them horns of sharp native mead and pieces of hot meat, and they stood on the edge of the crowd, watching.

"There are more here than usual this year," Licinius said. "Maybe they feel they need all the help from the god they can get after this winter."

"And maybe there was a council meeting before the feast," said Justin.

The flames had died to glowing embers now, and the young warriors were taking their wives by the hand to leap across them so that they would have sons in the year ahead. As they watched, a tall young man with a heavy golden bracelet clasped about either arm and a circlet of gold barely visible in his thick corn-colored hair pulled a girl out from among a group of women.

"I think you're right," Licinius said, as the laughing couple ran hand in hand to the fire. They leapt across it, the girl's blonde braids flying, and landed well to the far side. A great roar of approval went up from the tribesmen and someone shouted, "There'll be a son at the hearth before next Beltane!"

"That, my boy, is Vortrix."

Justin took a closer look as the couple came back to the crowd and the young man said something softly to an older man who was apparently the girl's father.

"So young?"

"Mmm. He's nineteen. But you have to remember that these people become warriors at fourteen," Licinius said. "So he's decided to marry. I think he's chosen well. That's Branwen, the daughter of the chieftain of the clan nearest us. Those were his villages we burned off last winter. A blood tie with Cathuil would be useful."

"I don't doubt it. How do you happen to know him?"

"You get to know all the local nobility when you've been out here a while. At times like tonight . . . and they occasionally consent to let me treat their illnesses when the priests give up. Though

I must admit they have more skill than you'd think. I'd give a good deal for a chance to sit down with a tame one and go over the local healing herbs."

Vortrix and the girl sat down, and his household warriors gathered around, shouting congratulations and cheerful advice, while one of his "hounds," the boys of the tribe who served in the King's hall, brought him a cup of mead.

"So every clan of the Brigantes will come to the bride feast," Justin murmured, "with probably a council beforehand. Now that's what *I'd* give something to be at. I don't quite trust friend Vortrix," Justin took a drink of mead, "for all old Lupus thinks he's so damn young."

"The god's greeting to you, Centurion. And you, Licinius the Surgeon," a voice said in his ear and Justin choked.

"And to you, Vortrix the King." Licinius also sounded as if he were about to strangle.

Justin turned round to find a fair-haired boy with a wolfskin cloak about his shoulders grinning cheerfully at him. Finn made a soft growling noise in his throat and moved a step closer. Finding that the High King was looking him carefully up and down, Justin pulled himself together and followed suit.

Vortrix was a tall man, half a head taller than Justin, and he looked down at him from a pair of eyes as crystal blue as a rain-washed lake. The golden fillet of the King glinted in the shining mane of hair which hung past his shoulders, and a massive golden torque was clasped about his throat. The blue spirals tattooed on his brow were visible also at the open neck of his shirt, which, like the short kilt he wore, was of some soft, finely dyed blue leather. His feet were encased in strong boots of wolf's hide, and from his belt, Justin noted, hung a sword of excellent workmanship. All in all, Vortrix made an impressive and dangerous figure, softened only by the smile beneath his luxuriant blond mustache.

Justin was surprised to find himself feeling a sudden liking for this boy who at the age of nineteen, with little more to go on than a closer right of blood and his own abilities, had won the kingship and the tribe from an older and more powerful kinsman. Also feeling that he now trusted him less than ever, Justin said pleasantly, "The sun and the moon on your path, Vortrix the King," and offered him good wishes on his forthcoming marriage.

"It is time I had a son to come after me," Vortrix said. "I set my house in order, you see."

"To what end, I wonder," Justin said softly, and suddenly found his eyes locked with those blue ones. It was like peering into the pool of an oracle, but what could be read from it was hidden in the depths.

And then the moment was past, and Vortrix was only a boy with the king's circlet on his head. "That there be no more disputes and no more regencies," he said. "My family have done with tearing each other's throats for this kingship."

"Then don't end by tearing your own throat with it," Justin found himself saying, and again Vortrix's eyes touched his and then slid away again, as if he too were puzzled by something.

They chatted of this and that for a while, like two dogs sizing each other up, and then Vortrix took his leave, saying that it grew late.

"Valé, Vortrix the King."

Vortrix smiled. "Valé, Centurion Corvus."

"Valé indeed," Licinius said as he left. "A pity he isn't a Roman or you a Briton. You'd like each other."

"I do, damn him," Justin said. "I wonder how he knew my name."

"I don't. You may not know it, my innocent, but you're one of the few officers in this Legion who poses any great threat to him."

"You mean I'm the only man save you who doesn't think his youth makes *him* no threat."

"It amounts to the same thing. That's his stock in trade where we're concerned. You went to the Legate after that patrol was cut up. News goes through the heather like the wind out here."

Justin had another brief vision of those clear blue eyes and the deceptive gentleness that lay in them. "Damn him. When will this bride feast be?"

"In a couple of weeks, most like."

"And trouble after that. Come on, it's an early morning for us, and any number of aching heads on sick parade from that mead, I should think."

They turned and began to work their way back down the hill, pausing to greet friends and acquaintances from the fort. Geta, his wound healed, was there; and Centurion Cassius, the tall dark-faced man who commanded the Fifth Cohort, laughing over some joke with a pair of legionaries and a wine seller from the town; and Favonius with a number of other young centurions, standing apart from the gathering, nonchalant and amused.

"He looks as if he's watching a play and wondering if the last act is going to be as bad as the first," said Justin, who had taken a not entirely rational dislike to the man.

"Yes, well, he's young yet," said Licinius, showing more tolerance than usual, perhaps under the influence of several horns of native mead.

"So is Vortrix."

The crowd was beginning to thin out, and they could see flashes of fire across the hillside and through the surrounding woods as the youngest warrior from each house thrust a torch into the flames or carefully placed a few coals in an earthen pot to carry the new fire back to light the hearth again. Two boys, fresh from their initiation, ran past them laughing, the fire streaming out behind them like comets' tails.

Catching sight of Gwytha and Aeresius among the knots of people moving back toward Eburacum, Licinius and Justin made their way over to them, Finn and Whitepaw loping on ahead. Aeresius carried a small pot of coals in one hand and gnawed contentedly on a piece of rib with the other.

Gwytha saw Justin and slipped round to Aeresius's other side to talk to him. She was wearing her best tunic of brilliant saffron bordered with scarlet, and her blue cloak was pinned with a bright bronze ring brooch. Her long hair, normally braided out of her way, fell in a cascade past her waist, turned to gold at the back by the fire. She looked very bright and cheerful, her blue eyes shining and her cheeks flushed with the fire and the brisk night wind.

"You look different tonight," Justin said.

She glanced up at him. "I am different. I remember my own people tonight. This is our night. I saw you talking with young Vortrix," she added.

"So you did, little Eyes-and-Ears. Your own people or the Brigantes?"

"Nay, then, what have Vortrix and his plans to do with me? I am Iceni, and not even that, now." She looked where the paths parted, the clans streaming back across the hillside, herself and Aeresius toward the fort.

"Still, the Iceni have been known to think of rebellion—occasionally."

Gwytha's eyes were sober now. "Yes, they took your Hispana to bits, didn't they? We were a great people until Rome took her price for *that*. I rather like young Vortrix, but I like you too, Centurion, for the same reasons, and I know you better. I am a woman, and, moreover, a slave. I don't know why you worry *what* I think."

Since Justin found he didn't know either, he merely requested her not to call him Centurion, it made him feel like a fool. He wondered what had prompted the unexpected admission that she liked him.

Over the next weeks, the cold muddy ground, soaked through with melted snow, dried finally into the springiness of new grass, setting the cavalry horses to frisking like colts in the pasture. The soldiers had left off their woolen mufflers and heavy, cross-gartered leggings and looked, as the Primus Pilus, commander of the First Cohort, remarked, more like Roman soldiers for a change and less like painted barbarians. The air was full of birds, even the fortress streets a-hop with them, spring-fat and important. And even Justin, heading for the Principia to put in his monthly transfer request, had decided that it could as well be done tomorrow, and picked up his hunting spear instead. He went alone, as he knew the country fairly well now, and had no intention of venturing outside Eburacum's patrol perimeter even with a guide.

Now he lay sprawled in the sun on the hill where the Beltane fires had burned, with Finn at his feet and his spear in his hand, and the wheeling curlews to watch for amusement. He didn't even much mind that he hadn't caught anything. It was very pleasant to lie here, with the men from the fort moving back and forth like scarlet dots in the distance, and watch someone else work. He scratched Finn's back idly with one sandaled foot and turned over in his mind the events of the past month.

Vortrix had had his wedding and his bride feast in the King's Hall at Isurium Brigantum some fifteen miles away, but after that very little more had been heard of him. He was certainly not at Isurium, in and out of which Roman officials went frequently, but no one was quite sure where he *had* gone, and there was a noticeable lack of men of fighting age in most of the nearby villages. Vortrix had packed up his warriors along with his bride and melted into the hills to the north.

To give him his due, the Legate had at least taken notice of this fact, although he was more inclined to put it down to the Brigantes' wish to avoid any further punitive action for last winter's attack, now that the roads were passable, than to their readying for war. Justin had argued that the time to deal with the Brigantes was now, before they could gather their strength, but the Legate remained unmoved. The Primus Pilus, a man of strict loyalty to his commander, might have had his own opinions, but he didn't voice them.

So they mended wall and waited, and the men remained as sloppy as ever. As long they looked reasonably decent on parade and gave no open trouble to their officers, most of the officers didn't care much what they did. Justin, who knew perfectly well that a transfer was unlikely to come through before fall, and in any case had too much conscience, wrestled mightily with his own cohort. They were slowly coming into line, especially the first century with which he had the most contact, and the second, whose centurion was a sober young man who had been more relieved than not to see Justin take over. But you couldn't, especially with the bad example of the rest of the Legion shining before them, reform overnight a whole cohort of men who had no great desire to be reformed. Still, they were developing a grudging respect for their mocking, sardonic commander.

"He looks like Hades himself when he's mad, with those damn yellow eyes of his," one of them remarked, watching Justin chewing out another century. "Especially if it's you he's mad at. But you can go to him when you're in trouble, and that's a fact."

"Aye, did you see him when Septimus broke his leg? Carried him up to the hospital himself, and mud all over his parade uniform. Most officers wouldn't take the time."

"He makes *me* nervous, is what. He knows too much."

"The Legate doesn't think so. I saw him coming out of the Principia with a face like fury and mad enough to spit."

"The Legate?"

"No, thickwit, the centurion."

"Well, I expect he hates this stinking hole as much as we do. They say he's been asking for transfer ever since he got here. Me, I hope he doesn't get it."

"Aye, there's no saying but he might think the same as us on a lot of matters. There's some of the officers do."

"Like Centurion Cassius? They're a poor lot. This one's different."

"How do you know?"

"You try any of your funny business on him, Drusus, and you'll find out soon enough."

"Oh, pack it up, all of you. Let's go and get drunk."

Justin, oblivious to this estimate of his character, lay drowsing on the hillside as the sun began to sink. The thudding on the roadway below had become a rolling thunder before he woke and heard it, and he sat up to see a cavalry scout flying at full gallop along the road from Isurium. He jumped up, whistled to Finn, and went headlong down the hill. Midway to the fort, he stopped and looked backward to the northwest. A cloud of black smoke rose from the signal fire at Isurium, and he could barely see another one, pale in the sunset, farther north. That would be Cataractonium.

IV

The March to
Cataractonium

BY THE TIME Justin reached the fort, the Legate, the Primus
Pilus, and several other senior officers were gathered around the
scout. He had dismounted from his horse, which stood stock-still,
flanks heaving and head low, until someone led it off to be walked
dry. A crowd of curious legionaries had collected, and the Optio
was endeavoring, with little success, to shoo them off about their
business.

"—Cataractonium," the cavalry scout was saying. "We beat them
off, but they'll be back. They came down from Vinovia. They
killed nearly every man there."

"How many?"

"Near the whole tribe by the look of it, and that devil Vortrix
at the head of them. They'll walk all over Cataractonium. They
only pulled off to regroup and let the stragglers from Vinovia
catch up."

At a word from the Legate, the Primus Pilus sent the man off
to the mess hall to be fed and turned back to the little group of
officers.

"Pack up. We march in the morning. Centurion Hilarion," the
Primus Pilus nodded at the thin, freckled commander of the Ninth

Cohort. "Take a relief column and get up there tonight. You," he motioned to the Optio, "send me the quartermaster."

So it had happened. Damn Vortrix and damn the Legate, and, now that he thought about it, damn the camp commander at Hippo Regius too. When he had seen to his men and given his orders for the morning, Justin went up to the hospital, where he found Licinius with his dark head bent over the lamp, calmly polishing his instruments.

"Evening, Justin. You look like death. Sit down."

"I'm just mad. This could have been stopped."

"Maybe. And then again, maybe not." He glanced at his junior surgeon, who was packing ointment into a case. "I'll finish up, Flavius. Go and get some sleep. We've an early start tomorrow."

"Yes, sir."

"And tell young Octavian he's to stay here and take care of anyone who brains himself with a catapult."

"He won't like it, sir."

"He's not required to like it, he's only an apprentice. He'll get his chance later. I can't leave you, I'll need you too badly."

"Yes, sir. Everything's nearly ready. There's only the linen to be packed. And your kit, of course."

"Justin," Licinius said slowly, when the boy had gone. "You liked Vortrix, didn't you?"

"That depends on what you mean," Justin said. "Let's say I have a good healthy respect for him."

"Could you kill him?" Licinius kept his eyes on the scalpel he was cleaning.

"I'm supposed to be a soldier, remember? That's what I'm here for. But I'm not likely to get the chance."

"Then make the chance. Look for him. He'll be in the thick of it, it's a matter of pride with them. Vortrix is the only thing that's holding the Brigantes together, and he's no one to come after him. Yet."

"That sounds strange, coming from you," Justin said. "I would have thought you were too much a surgeon."

"So would I," Licinius said shortly.

Something moved against Justin's feet and he looked down. Finn. He had forgotten him. "I'd better take him down to Aeresius," he said.

"All right, then. I'll see you in the morning."

The fort was buzzing with preparations as Justin turned off down the Via Praetoria under the shadow of the great gilded Eagle of the Legion where it shone pale in the torchlight. Men hurried to and fro about the baggage carts, and the cavalrymen turned out by troops to give their mounts a grooming and an extra feed of grain. A sentry at the gate was explaining to a highly indignant legionary that there were no passes that night, and somewhere in the distance the cook was loudly complaining that he couldn't put together that kind of provisioning in a few hours for the Emperor himself.

"Didn't you just hear me telling that one?" the harassed sentry demanded as Justin approached. "Absolutely no passes. Oh, sorry, sir. I didn't recognize you."

"That's all right." Justin returned his salute. "I'm only taking the dog back."

As he passed out of the gate, he saw that the town was as much in upheaval as the fort with the suddenness of the news. Men were coming back to the camp from all directions, having been found and firmly rounded up by the Watch. They were laughing, most of them, and seemed more pleased than otherwise to have something to do for a change. There was a fair-sized crowd of women about the gate, looking for a glimpse of their men, women whose men had not been out on pass when the orders came and who would consequently have no chance for farewells. One who carried a small, black-haired baby on her hip, Justin recognized: Manlius's wife. He wondered if she had found another man or if she were there out of some perverse habit.

Turning off the main street, he dodged past four legionaries emerging from a wine stall to the sound of one of the current marching songs of the Legion, rendered loudly and happily as they wove their way to the bridge:

> Lift a glass to the trumpet's song,
> The wine that makes the poor man strong!
>   We march, we march with the light,
>   So drink, my brothers, tonight!

Most of them appeared to have been taking this advice literally. Behind them came a centurion of the Watch, with an auxiliaryman in each hand. They were raising a song of their own in dreadful cacophany with the quartet in front of them.

"I wish you'd pipe down and sleep it off," the Watch officer said irritably.

"Yeah? Me, I wish I had a million sesterces and you had a turd in your pocket." The auxiliaryman saluted him and fell down.

When Justin reached the Head of Neptune, Gwytha was standing in the doorway, silhouetted against the lamplight. She smiled when she saw him.

"I thought perhaps you might be coming with the dog." She scratched Finn's ears and he yawned happily. "Come in, Centurion. I'll give you some food. I doubt you got dinner."

Justin followed her and sat down gratefully. He had spent the evening talking with his cohort, on the theory that commanders ought to be much in evidence when there was a battle on the way, and he was ravenous. When she brought him a bowl of stew, he devoured it hungrily, wiping the last of it from the bowl with a piece of bread. He sat back and smiled at her, wrapping his long fingers around the stem of his wine cup. "That was good. I felt as if I hadn't eaten in a week."

"And looked it. What happened? You were healthy enough when you came for the dog this morning."

"A combination of fatigue and nerves, I suppose. Trying to do two days' work in a couple of hours."

"Nerves?" Gwytha looked surprised, but he thought she was mocking him.

"Not that kind," he said defensively. "The kind that come from wanting to kick the first person in your path because you can't kick the one you'd really like to."

"Well, now you can go out and kick Vortrix, which is what you've been wanting to do all along, and teach him better manners."

Justin's fingers tightened around the wine cup. "That isn't true, you know."

Gwytha's face softened. "No, I know it isn't. I'm sorry." She sat down opposite him and put her hand out to his. "You'll break the stem if you keep that up."

He loosened his fingers and stared at them.

"When do you march?"

"At first light. A relief column went out tonight. We're lucky it's full moon."

"Is it permitted that I wish the Centurion well?"

He reached out and caught her hand again. "Of course. And—" he stumbled a little over the words, "—and my thanks for it."

"The sun and the moon on your path then, Justinius."

"And on yours, Gwytha," he said softly, standing up. He put his hands on her shoulders and stood looking down at her for a moment. "I had best get back," he said abruptly. "I must see to my men."

She walked to the door with him. "May the gods watch over you, Justinius."

He smiled. "Don't worry. They always have." And then, partly because the lamplight turned her hair to a misty aureole about her face and partly because he wondered if he could get away with it without catching another clip across the ear, he slipped an arm across her shoulders again and kissed her.

She didn't hit him, but she didn't respond either, merely standing perfectly still until he stepped back. Then, "For remembrance sake?" she asked.

"Not only."

"So. Valé, Centurion. Rome calls." She shut the door behind him.

Justin stood for a moment in the near daylight of the full moon, and then shook himself and started back for the fort. What in Mithras's name did he think he was doing, he wondered irritably. He'd known she was no one to play the lover with. And what's more, he liked her. But he'd never met anyone like her before, and she seemed capable of turning him into a perfect idiot. He put her out of his mind angrily and discovered, to his further annoyance, that it wasn't difficult. Every time he put anything out of his mind lately, the image of Vortrix came creeping in to fill the gap. There was no reason why the face of a boy with the High King's circlet on his head should pursue him like some British Nemesis, but somehow Vortrix and Britain were part and parcel of the same problem in his own troubled soul. Which brought up the question of how he could loathe Britain and yet feel something definitely stronger than his usual indifference for two of its people. On which side of liking this obsession with Vortrix lay, he wasn't sure.

He shook himself angrily and quickened his pace. As he came in through the gate someone far off in the cavalry barracks was whistling in untroubled anticipation of the morning, and Justin grabbed at the mood and tried to turn it to himself. Across the Via Principia, the wings of the Eagle of the Legion caught the moonlight along their back, but the staff was hidden in shadow so that it looked as if the thing had taken flight, and Justin felt the old, familiar shiver run down his spine as he watched it.

The light was just beginning to show above the horizon when they moved out the next morning, muffled in their cloaks against the dawn chill and stamping their feet in the mist. The officers returned from a last minute briefing in the Principia, and then the great gates were thrown open and the laden cohorts tramped through one by one. At the head of them all was the Eagle bearer in his lionskin hood, holding the golden form aloft above the column, and behind him the strength of the Legion: each man with sword and pilum—the deadly Roman javelin whose head extended down half its length and which could pierce a man at ninety feet—his shield slung across his back, and carrying, besides his weapons and the day's rations, tools for pitching camp and raising the earthworks. The Roman soldier was an apprentice of all trades.

Behind and to either side of the Legion marched the Auxiliaries and the cavalry, Spaniards and Gauls mostly, and bright in the war trappings of their homelands. Optios hurried back and forth, shouting orders and last minute instructions. Licinius, with the baggage train, supervised the loading of the last of his supplies onto the hospital wagons; while Justin, in marching gear, the scarlet fan of his helmet crest discarded, moved out at the head of his cohort and turned back to see the rest fall into line behind. Above them shone their own cohort standard with its number and the sea horse insignia of the Eighth. They went smartly to the sound of trumpets, in the steady twenty-mile-a-day march of the Legions, and as the last cohort passed, the baggage train fell in behind them, the tail end of a winding column of bronze and grey, with the scarlet cloaks of the officers showing like fire against the mist and early sun.

They raised a cheerful song on the road, the men seeming happier than not to be on the march, and halted before noon just south of Isurium. Justin dropped his kit thankfully. Even with the extra drilling, he had discovered that the winter had left him badly out of shape, but he knew from experience that the protesting muscles would soon toughen up again. They ought to make Cataractonium by early afternoon tomorrow. The relief column which had gone out the night before should be there tonight.

The sun was getting hot, but when the men had rested and eaten, they set out again. Passing through Isurium, Justin could feel the deadly stillness of the place. The magistrates and the Roman military officials conferred with the Legate as the column passed through. But there were no men of the Brigantes in the tribal capital. An occasional small child appeared at the doorway of a hut to watch them and was pulled sharply in again by its mother. The surrounding farms looked lifeless, and the only figure they saw in the fields as they passed was a woman, back bent to a hoe among the cabbages.

They halted again for the night, south of Cataractonium, having pushed on much farther than the usual day's march to get past a thick stretch of dense woodland where the risk of ambush was too great to make camp. Even so, the rolling purple swells of the moors were dangerous country when dealing with a people who had pinned their strategy on the quirks of the terrain even before Cassivellaunus had nearly driven the first Caesar mad trying to fight an enemy he couldn't find. Although the men were tired and they planned to move out again next morning, they threw up some hasty earthworks and posted double pickets. The Eagle and the cohort standards were mounted in the center where the Via Principia ran up to the Legate's command tent. All Army camps followed the same pattern, and no soldier was ever lost in an unfamiliar camp at night.

A scout came in to say that the Brigantes had attacked the garrison at Cataractonium again, and they were hard pressed. The relief column had arrived in time to circle to one side and push them back, but if they attacked again before the main body of the Army got there, Cataractonium's defenses couldn't hold. Scouts reported signs of the Brigantes massing again, but they practically turned into trees when you looked at them, damn them, and there was no saying.

When he had seen his men posted and fed, Justin got himself a plate of stew and sat down with it on the camp bed in his tent. After a few minutes Licinius joined him, still in marching kit with his instrument case hanging from his belt.

"How does it go?" The surgeon sat down beside Justin and began to eat also, stretching his stiff knee out before him.

"Well enough," Justin said. "The men are a little out of condition and there'll be some sore muscles in the morning, mine among them. But they'll work it off on the march."

"I only wish sore muscles were all I was going to have to deal with," Licinius said. "This is going to be no easy victory now."

"What in Mithras's name do you think I've been saying?" Justin inquired. "I was a bit surprised that it came *this* soon, though. I didn't think he could be ready this early. Perhaps friend Vortrix has made a mistake and overreached himself."

"Well, we'll find out tomorrow," Licinius said. "I only hope you're right. We do have one advantage over them, though."

Justin laughed. "Good. I was hoping we had."

"I'm serious. The Brigantes have their fields to tend and their sheep to shear, and the women can't do it alone. It cuts down on their strength, with the men knowing their farms are going to waste while they're gone."

"Whereas we're . . . uh, professionals, with nothing so mundane to distract us from the business of war. There's something rather disgustingly civilized about that."

Justin looked up as a shadow fell across the tent flap. It was Lepidus, his second in command.

"The watchword for tonight is 'Vinovia,' sir," he said, his sober young face showing more excitement than Justin had seen in it before.

"Thank you. Tell the men we break camp at first light."

"Yes, sir."

"We had best get some sleep," Justin said when Lepidus had gone. He stretched out on one side with his shield and sword in easy reach.

Licinius gathered up his dinner bowl and with a cheerful good night moved off to where Flavius and the orderlies had pitched the hospital tents.

Justin rolled over and closed his eyes, and a picture of Vortrix dancing on the howling ruin of Vinovia came unbidden to his mind. If they were too late, Cataractonium and its garrison would go the same way.

Justin was awake well before first light and was pacing aimlessly up and down when the sky began to pale. It was clear, and a little soft wind whisked through the heather. It was warm already; the day was going to be hot. Somewhere a cock crowed, and a bugle sounded reveille.

The men began to sit up, yawning and gathering their gear about them. A legionary who had been hauled in from a night on the town by the Watch, and who had consequently made yesterday's march with an excruciating hangover, opened one eye to the morning, said "Ugh," and rolled over again with his cloak about his ears. Lepidus prodded him with his vine staff.

"Come along, then. You'll feel better when you've had some food."

The legionary looked as if the mere thought of food was enough to send him straight across the River Styx, but he got to his feet with a baleful glance at his tormentor.

Justin got a couple of pieces of barley bannock and ate them while he reviewed his men. Camp was broken quickly, and the Legion moved out again, marching in battle order. As they neared Cataractonium, the distant, mournful sound of a war horn broke through the air, and was answered almost immediately by the high sweet note of a Roman trumpet. The Legate gave a quick signal and the Legion and Auxiliaries spread out to their assigned positions. Vortrix was going to try to stop them here, before they could join with the garrison at Cataractonium where they would have a more favorable position. It had been expected, and the battle plan had been worked out the night before with the help of auxiliary scouts who had slipped ahead of the main army to take stock of the countryside.

As Justin signaled his cohort into position behind the light-armed Auxiliaries, he could hear the drumlike sound that meant a mounted war host on the march, and then suddenly the rise opposite was topped by Vortrix's war band, headed by the chariot line, strung out along the ridge behind their blue-stained war shields, with the dawn sun glinting off shield boss and spear. They wore little save their weapons and the war paint on their skin, and they looked like a cohort of the demons of Ahriman.

Justin licked his lips and shifted his grip on his pilum staff. The scouts had reported that the relief column and what was left of the Cataractonium garrison were pinned down in the fort by one wing of the war band. They at least served the purpose there of distracting part of Vortrix's force, and if they could break through, or if

Vortrix was forced to call off the besieging wing to help fight the main army, they could strike to his rear.

There was a stirring along the British line, and the first wave of war chariots flowed like a stream in storm down the hill at auxiliary troops too light to withstand them. Justin caught sight of Vortrix braced in fighting stance behind a pair of roans driven by a slender man with a beautiful girl's face. The first rank of Auxiliaries hurled their spears and a number of horses went down under their chariots with a splintering crash, but the rest came charging on, the drivers maneuvering the light wicker frames with ease, sometimes running out, spear in hand, along the ridge pole, to strike as the chariot careened by.

Any formation which tried to withstand that onslaught would be shattered, but the Legions had long since learned the trick of fighting chariots. The Auxiliaries opened their ranks to let the deadly things pass through, and then closed behind them with an almost audible click. The chariots crashed hard against the main body of the Legion braced to meet them, and sent the first ranks reeling.

"Stand firm!" The Legion backed a pace and lunged forward, backed and lunged forward, and soon horses began to go down before the short, sharp swords of the foot soldiers. The air was filled with the screaming of the horses and the hot smell of blood as the chariot drivers pulled back to let the foot troops forward. Perhaps a third swung round to harry the Legion's flanks while the rest, drivers and warriors alike, sent their horses galloping for the rear, and moved up again to fight in the foot ranks.

Justin gripped his pilum harder and signaled his cohort forward, closing his ears to the sounds around him as the main body of the two armies came together. The sun was bright and already hot, and the air was full of blood as, for Justin, the battle narrowed down to the space of a few feet and the desperate struggle to move forward, with Lepidus to one side of him and the standard-bearer of the Eighth Cohort to the other. He abandoned his pilum and drew his sword when the press became too great to maneuver.

He raised his shield arm just in time to block a shortened spear thrust and drove the sword in under the shield of the man who had aimed it. The body, bright with blue war paint, crashed down at his feet. To one side, he saw his standard-bearer go down with a feather-decked war spear in his throat. He signaled behind him, and a soldier ran to catch up the sea horse standard and the wolfskin hood of its dead bearer, and the cohort moved forward again behind it. "Push 'em back, lads, and take 'em down!" Justin shouted. "We owe 'em a debt now for Vinucius!"

To the rear, cavalry trumpets sounded the Advance and the horsemen swept down on either side of the cohorts to guard their flanks from the still deadly chariots. If they could press them hard enough, Vortrix would be forced to call in his other wing and free the garrison at Cataractonium to move against his back.

Ahead, suddenly, Justin could see the High King himself, among his household warriors, the war paint startling against his pale hair. Justin stabbed with a sword that by now was as red as a helmet crest, and gained another foot. But then he was too busy to look up again, fighting for his life with a boy he had seen return from his initiation a month ago at Beltane. He was scarcely aware of killing him and turning to fight a new enemy, an older man with a flowing shock of steel grey hair and the heavy gold arm ring of a chieftain. Either he killed the chieftain or someone else did, Lepidus maybe, fighting at his shoulder, but suddenly he had time to look up in the dusty sunlight and see the young king no more than a yard away, pulling his reddened sword from the body of a legionary.

Vortrix blinked once as he recognized Justin, and raised his sword again. "Salvé, Centurion," he panted and lunged for his throat in the same breath.

Justin parried the first blow and struck back, but the young king blocked his thrust, and they pulled back and circled each other warily like two gladiators in the arena. Something burned brightly behind Vortrix's eyes as he feinted and leapt. Justin dodged, feeling as he did so the edge of Vortrix's sword along his ribs where it had sliced through his leather harness tunic on the downstroke. He thrust his blade in under the other's guard, but was thrown by the surprise of that sudden pain, and Vortrix brought his shield up in time to catch it. Justin saw the flicker in the blue eyes facing him above the bronze shield rim, and saw the blade flashing down again, aimed at the vulnerable spot above his breastplate. He twisted out from under it and struck back with all his strength before Vortrix could recover, sending the king staggering back.

But before he could move to press the advantage, one of Vortrix's household warriors, the slim, flaxen-haired man who had driven his chariot, leapt out at Justin from the chaos around them, slipping between him and the king. Justin turned to defend himself as two more warriors hurled themselves forward, and Lepidus moved up to protect his unguarded flank. By the time he had dealt with them, and the seemingly endless line of those who took their place, and could look around him again, Vortrix and his chariot driver were lost in the shifting battle.

The colors seemed unnaturally bright in the dust, the blue of the Brigantes' war paint and the scarlet of the Legions and the blood that was everywhere. And everywhere the howling fury of the battle roared. Justin took stock of his cohort and signaled them to move in and up as another wave of blue-stained warriors flung themselves against the Legion. Although he could see Vortrix nowhere, he could almost *feel* the presence of the young king in the battle around him, a presence compounded of fury and vengeance, and a will to conquer that was almost overwhelming. He shook his head and bade himself ignore it. A soldier who couldn't concentrate on the fight at hand soon had little need to concentrate on anything.

And still the Britons came on in wave after wave as Vortrix eventually pulled his besieging wing in from Cataractonium to throw its weight at the Legion.

Hilarion's troops and the remainder of the garrison, freed of the watchdog at their gates, began to move out and make their force felt at Vortrix's rear, as they joined with the auxiliary cavalry and archers. If Vortrix's line could stand against them, he stood a good chance of winning the day. If not—he would have to pull back soon while his war band was strong enough to break out of the encircling Legion.

As if sensing this, the Britons seemed to draw strength to redouble their thrust with a grim determination matched only by that of the Romans confronting them. The two lines wavered and held, wavered and held, and still the unbearable sun beat down, drenching the struggling figures below with sweat and dirt, and transforming the stench of blood in the air to a choking entity that enveloped them all.

Licinius, in a makeshift surgeon's camp to the rear, tended the wounded who came streaming back to him, and watched the cloud that rose on the far side of the hill with bitter eyes.

Centurion Hilarion, directing the relief column and the tattered remains of the men who had served at Cataractonium, rallied them for yet another push at the rear of the king's war band.

"For Vinovia, damn them!" And straight and true, the column drove like a knife into the war band's back.

Justin staggered a bit as he braced himself to meet the force of yet another blue-painted body, and realized that he was growing dizzy from the wound in his side. He struck desperately at the man who faced him, trying to shake off that strange heaviness whose meaning he knew too well. His adversary blocked the blow, but another sword came in where Justin's had failed, and the man's eyes widened suddenly as he fell backward. Lepidus, still at his side.

Justin pressed forward again, realizing as he did so, that it was easier now. Everywhere the legionaries were moving forward steadily with the Eagle of the Hispana winged and shining above their heads. The Brigantes were falling back!

"Hai! Vinovia! Push 'em, lads—hard now!" And the sea horse standard of the Eighth Cohort fought to the front of the press. The enemy moved more quickly now—Vortrix was getting his war band out while he could still break through the force at his rear. The little band from Cataractonium, with Hilarion grimly at their head, prepared to make a determined stand, while the cavalry began to move in pursuit, but the trumpets rang out loudly with the Halt, and they let the Brigantes go with a shout and a spear or two to hurry them on their way. It was just as well, Justin thought, survey-ing the Legion's losses and seeing the close formation the Britons kept even in retreat, shepherding their walking wounded with them as they went. They were beaten but not devastatingly so, and the Legion would do itself more harm than good in chasing them. Best to regroup and make an end of it at a time of their own choosing. He looked up at the sky and saw that it was still only midmorning. Then as he looked, it seemed to go from blue to black and he swayed dizzily.

"Are you all right, sir?"

Someone put an arm about his shoulders. It was Lepidus again. Justin opened his eyes to see his second in command, a bloody sword in one hand and his face streaked with dirt, looking at him anx-iously.

"Yes. It's not deep, I've only bled a lot. I have you to thank that it's not worse, I think."

"I had better get you to the surgeon."

"I'll be all right until he's seen to those that need him worse," Justin replied, and leaned against him as they joined the stream of men moving toward Cataractonium. The wounded were being loaded onto the hospital carts, and in the rear Licinius was already moving his temporary field hospital up to the Cataractonium surgeon's quarters. Justin looked bitterly at the number who lay still in the blood-soaked heather and the wreckage of disabled chariots. If it had been a victory at all, it had been a marginal one, with the bodies of the slain almost evenly divided between Briton and Roman. When he passed the body of the most junior centurion of his cohort, lying on his back with his eyes open and his throat cut nearly across, Justin turned away, sick.

"Are you sure you're all right, sir?" Lepidus asked again when they reached the fort, and looked so worried that Justin smiled.

"Yes, quite all right," he said, and the world promptly started to walk round him in circles. "I think perhaps I had better sit down, though," he added.

Lepidus helped him to where the less badly wounded were waiting. He went and got some linen from the Cataractonium camp surgeon and helped Justin bind it round his ribs to stop the blood, which had already slowed considerably as soon as he stopped moving.

"Mithras," Lepidus said, looking down at Justin's discarded armor where the blade had cut clean through the buckles of his breastplate and the leather tunic below it. "Who gave you that blow?"

"Vortrix the King."

Lepidus whistled admiringly, inspecting the cut. "Well, I'll just be taking his handiwork down to the armorer's and have it mended, that he doesn't get another chance."

Justin leaned his back against the wall and waited patiently for the world to turn itself right side up again. A depression, as unreasonable as it was enveloping, was settling around him. Unexpectedly, against all the odds of battle, he had actually come face to face with the High King—and he had failed. The fact that everyone else who had taken part in today's battle had failed as well made little difference. Justin was too much a soldier to repine because another man had beaten him in a swordfight. What was bothering him was the fact that he felt almost relieved to have missed his mark, as if there was something indefinable in Vortrix that he was loath to kill. The High King's face swam in and out of his weary delirium until

68

Flavius came out and cleaned his wound and bound it with fresh bandages, muttering as he did so that it was a good thing Lepidus had gone into the Centuriate because he would never be a surgeon. For a while Justin was occupied with remembering that it was beneath the dignity of a cohort commander to shriek when salve was rubbed into a wound that was no more than a bad gash. After that he lay back in the shade and watched the burial party set out under a sky already filled with dark, soaring shapes. A legionary with his cloak wrapped around his shoulder dropped down beside a little group to his right.

"Gods—Publius! I thought sure we'd lost you."

"Nay, then, I'm indestructible. Where's Servius?" The man looked around him.

"Out there," another man said bitterly, pointing in the direction the burial party had taken. "With the rut of a British chariot wheel across half his chest. And for what? For the Pax Romana, all glory to it, it won't bring Servius back. Curse it. And curse me for a fool for joining a Legion." He broke off as someone nudged him and motioned toward Justin. Then he spat and said, "Let him hear. If they cared enough about this hole to keep it half garrisoned . . . but no, so we fight double to make up the difference. Well, one of these days someone will decide he doesn't *want* to fight, and then where will the Pax Romana be?"

Justin, finding that his head had cleared, got up and went into the hospital, carefully pretending not to have heard. He diagnosed a case of battle nerves, and to make an issue of it so soon after the fighting would only make matters worse. His own nerves also were still uncomfortably on end.

Licinius looked up as he came in. His face was pale under his black hair except for a large daub of blood on one cheek where he had wiped his face with a scarlet hand. He had obviously been working for hours and looked on the point of exhaustion. The men were through when the battle was through, Justin reflected, but the surgeons often had to stay on their feet far into the night.

"I thought you were wounded," Licinius said.

"I'm not dead, if that's what you mean."

"You ought to be lying down."

"I'm all right. I thought I might be of use to you."

Licinius regarded him speculatively. "Very well, if you're so much at a loose end, come and help. At least you aren't squeamish.

It never ceases to amaze me how many men who can spend their time hacking each other to pieces turn green at the sight of blood in a hospital. Here, hold this, and give me some bandages."

He had been working steadily as he talked, and Justin obediently took the forceps and handed him the things he asked for. He felt more than a little light-headed, but looking about him he saw that Licinius hadn't been joking when he said he needed help. He spent the better part of five hours in the surgery, fetching and carrying, holding until he died the hand of a man for whom there was nothing to be done, helping to get a legionary whose arm was to be amputated as drunk as possible first on a mixture of wine and opium, and holding the lamp as he had done when Manlius died, while Licinius tried to save the arm of another. After he had watched Flavius a couple of times, he began to clean and bind the wounds of those only slightly hurt.

"Very good," Licinius said approvingly, watching him finish and tie a bandage into place. "We'll make a surgeon of you yet," and Justin felt more pleased with that than with anything else that had happened today.

Finally, when the worst of the work was done, the Cataractonium camp surgeon chased them out, saying that they had had a long day and a long march before it, and he would finish up. Licinius and Justin walked wearily over to the tent of one of the other cohort commanders where, now that the business of pitching camp was finished, postmortems on the day's proceedings were taking place.

"Hai, Licinius, Justin—sit down and eat. You look like you're about to collapse, the pair of you." It was Hilarion, the freckled, sandy-haired boy who commanded the Ninth Cohort and who had brought up the relief column. He passed them wine and a plate of bread and vegetables. "How was it with your cohort, Justin?"

"As well as with any part of the Legion, but they shook us up some. And yours?"

"Also well enough, under the circumstances. But we aren't through with them yet."

"It's in *my* mind that we should have chased them," Favonius said moodily, "once we had them in retreat."

"Ah now, that's where you're wrong," Hilarion said. "You can't fight the Briton that way. They were still in good order and like as not they'd have led the cavalry where they wanted it, and then we'd have no cavalry."

"That's the trouble with fighting an enemy who knows the country better than you do," Justin said. "He'll be running as if all the fiends of Tartarus were after him, and you giving chase like a hero, and then suddenly you'll look round to find you're in the middle of a marsh, and *he* may know where the firm ground is, but you don't."

"Or you'll chase a hundred of them into a dead-end valley," put in Geta, "and turn around to find another *five* hundred coming in after you. Or maybe the heather fired before you. Oh no, it doesn't pay to chase the Briton when he wants you to."

"What makes you so sure he wanted us to?" Favonius asked.

"I'm not, but the Brigantes know the country, and whether they wanted us or not, they'd know how to deal with us."

"I still think we should have gone after them when we had the chance," Favonius said. He stood up. "Well, I must go. My cohort's on sentry duty and I have to make rounds."

"Pray the gods *he* never gets a Legion," Hilarion said when he had gone. "He'd probably lead a grand charge for glory and go off a cliff."

"Nay, then," Geta said. "He's a conscientious man and he has courage. It's only that he will try to do everything by rote, with no thought beyond the surface. That and one other matter."

"And what is that?" Justin asked. Geta rarely joined in their conversations. He was older than the rest of them and had risen through the ranks to cohort level. Men with the ability to do that were rare, and Justin respected his opinions.

"He doesn't care enough for his men," Geta said. "He isn't cruel, or anything like that, mind, though maybe a bit overheavy with the vine staff; he's just . . . well, uninterested, as if they were pieces on a game board. I was a common rank-and-filer before I made the Centuriate, and I know what it means to morale if an officer cares for his men."

"That may be what's wrong in a lot of ways," Hilarion said. "If we go on blindly convinced of the invincibility of Rome, we may turn around one day to find that we haven't taken enough care to see that she stays that way."

"You mean the atttiude that Rome is unbeatable and that we will prevail, simply because we're Romans?" said Licinius.

"As it touches the Legion, I'm not sure I like that," Justin said, and then stopped to realize that he had caught himself regarding the loathsome Hispana as *his*.

"Nor I," Hilarion said. "Rome has come as far as she has because of her Army, no matter what the Senate may think to the contrary."

"And if the Army changes, Rome will change," said Justin.

Hilarion shifted position gingerly so as to avoid putting any pressure on a cut hand. "That kind of talk is tempting the gods. This campaign will come hard enough as it is."

Licinius stood up. "It's growing late. I advise you to postpone this philosophical discussion, especially you, Justin, if you don't wish to bleed to death. As for me, if I don't get some sleep I'll likely do murder in surgery tomorrow."

"Do you know when we march again?" Geta asked.

"No, but it'll be soon." Justin stood up also. "Vortrix isn't a man for half measures."

And that, as Hilarion remarked, left the Legion with a full measure of trouble.

V

Pax Romana

AS THINGS TURNED OUT, the next battle didn't come until
nearly a month later. The Legion was up and ready to march in
three days, which was later than the Legate wanted it and sooner
than the surgeons said it could be done, but, unexpectedly, Vortrix
neither came out to meet them nor mounted an attack elsewhere.
They chased him up into the hills for a bit, moving northward
through Corstopitum, but their scouts saw no sign of the Brigantes
other than the fact that foraging parties from the column invariably
discovered Vortrix had been there first.

"What in Hades is he doing?" Justin and Hilarion were making
the rounds of their sentry posts before turning in for the night.

"I don't know, but you can bet he's cooking up something evil."

But, oddly, for four weeks there was no sign of the war band.
The Legion took advantage of the time by sending a detachment
to leave the steadings around Isurium a smoking ruin and strength-
ening defenses in the northern forts. A replacement contingent of
troops from the south was sent to the murdered outpost at Vinovia,
and Cataractonium was brought almost up to its former strength.
But with the Legion not even up to its paper strength in the first
place, their resources were stretched thin elsewhere. They grew
daily more irritable and more scruffy, attempting to live off a land

populated by tribes singularly disinclined to have their cattle commandeered by Rome.

A cavalry scout had come in after a few days with word of some trouble to the north, and two weeks later a very hungry Pict, an outcast of his clan, traded some more definite information for a dinner.

Vortrix, he explained between bites of mutton, was having trouble with his war band. It seemed there was a slight disagreement as to who should command where, and several of his chieftains had been so foolhardy as to take the High King's youth as an assurance that they would get their way. There had been a confrontation, and Vortrix now seemed firmly in command, but in the meantime a raiding party from the north had been let slip by, and now Vortrix was busy chasing Picts. They were horse hungry, the outcast said, and had directed their efforts at the Brigantes' northern pastures where the new chariot horses were schooled.

It was unlikely that the Picts could stand against the war band long, but Vortrix needed those horses badly and the opinion in the Roman camp was that he wouldn't tackle Rome until he had them. There was some talk of catching him while he was busy with the Picts, but it was vetoed on the grounds that to pursue Vortrix that far north would stretch their manpower and supply lines dangerously thin. Besides, the Picts were just as likely to switch sides if given an opportunity of fighting Rome with the Brigantes' support, and the tribes who lay between the Brigantes' land and the Picts' were restless enough already.

So the outcast was given a new cloak and enlisted as a permanent spy (payment for information delivered only), and all the Legion saw of Vortrix as they pushed northward was a few skirmishes between rival scouting or foraging parties. The column kept close enough on the High King's trail to inconvenience him, but not close enough to risk an open battle with the Picts, who were, after all, outside Roman jurisdiction for the most part. They halted north of the auxiliary fort at Trimontium, among the birch and hazel woods and the billowing moors of the old northern province of Valentia, and waited.

"Well, we can fight the Picts or we can fight the Brigantes," Hilarion said, "but I don't fancy tackling both of them. Best to let them chew each other up as much as they can."

"Speaking of chewing," said Lepidus, eyeing his dinner plate with distaste, "if I see another piece of barley bannock, I think my mind will begin to go."

"It isn't that I mind so much," Justin said. "It's the things they put in it to make up for not having any barley."

"What do you suppose horse tastes like?" Hilarion fished a small, winged creature out of his wine cup and regarded it with disgust. "I draw the line at bugs."

"We're going to need the cavalry." Licinius pushed back the tent flap and dropped down beside them. "Good news, my blood-thirsty friends. That painted shadow we seem to have taken on as informer in chief was just in. It seems that Vortrix has sent the shadow's kinsmen scuttling off to the highlands and now he has his horses back."

"And he's coming our way with them," Justin murmured. "How nice."

"That means a camp meeting tomorrow night or I'm a German," Lepidus said.

"And a pep talk by the Legate," said Hilarion. "Standard order, I should think, on our chance to win a place in history."

"All neatly written out by his scribe," Justin added, looking down the beak of his long nose. "And you mustn't forget the bit about his long military service making the Empire great and safe for our mothers and sisters at home." He began to whistle a rude song about a Legate whose family took in some peculiar boarders while he was off at the wars.

"One of these days someone will switch the text on him," Hilarion said lazily, "and then he *will* be in the soup."

The other three looked at him for a moment in silent inspiration, and then Justin, whose tent they were in, sat up and began to rummage around in the chest behind him for the sheaf of papyrus he kept there. Centurion Hilarion possessed a talent for mimicking the hand of others, which, in the opinion of those who knew him, had yet to be properly exploited.

The next evening the Legion gathered in the makeshift parade ground, the field of a farmer who had taken one look at the approaching column and shot off into the hills with everything he could carry.

The Legate strode to the front of the group, cast an eye over the assembled troops, and pulled a roll of papyrus from his tunic. He invariably had his speeches written out beforehand. Some generals had that gift of impromptu exhortation for which the first Caesar had been so deservedly noted. Metius Lupus did not, and a scribe with the gift of oratory was his greatest asset.

"Soldiers of the Ninth Legion Hispana, Triumphalis, Macedonica . . .," he began in a voice pitched to reach the farthest ranks.

"We march toward a victory which will see the British rebellion crushed forever . . . which will see the power of Rome extended from one end of this land to the other . . . and see your names and that of this Legion enshrined forever in the glorious pages of history. Victory lies waiting . . . needing only your bravery and your faith in the gods and your general. I have never yet failed in my trust . . . I shall not do so now! Never have I shirked my duty! From the time when as aedile I worked to ban whorehouses and dog kennels from the city limits of Rome . . ."

There were a few unmilitary giggles from the officers' ranks and a loud cheer from one of the cohorts. The Legate paused for a moment and made a mental note to speak to his scribe. Since the editors of the speech had stuck strictly to fact, however, he forged ahead.

". . . my dedication has been indomitable, with the reward the generalship of this glorious Legion!" The Legate looked up dubiously, but the Centuriate of the Ninth had now regained its composure and maintained a blank expression.

"Faced with setbacks, we forge forward! Faced with losses, we prevail! Follow me unswervingly, and I will lead you to your greatest victory! Be steadfast as I have been in my devotion to the Eagles, as I have led Rome's bravest soldiers time and again to victory, as I have nurtured them as my own children, as I have upheld Rome's laws and discipline for the strength of all, working relentlessly to enforce the marriage restrictions and to curtail the use of foul language in the—" The Legate saw disaster leaping up at him from the page, and skipped hopefully to the next paragraph. The possibilities there were even worse. The Legate regarded the sheaf of papyrus as one who has inadvertently picked up an adder.

"The, uh, glory of the Legion and a place in history are in your hands," he said firmly. "We cannot help but be victorious." His mind remained obstinately blank of any further revelations. Seeing his Primus Pilus at his side, Metius Lupus gratefully turned the meeting over to him.

In a back row, the senior scribe regarded his general with horror and dismally contemplated the prospect of a posting to the Parthian front.

The war band was on the march, and this time there was no question of chasing Vortrix down or cutting him off before he could retreat to the hills again. The High King had dealt with his highland adversaries, and now he was spoiling for a fight with the Legion.

He would have preferred to have taken Eburacum, left with only a skeleton summer garrison, and let them try to take it back, but Roman communications were too good, and there was little chance of success with the Legion pressing at his back. So he settled for a fight in the open with the bulk of the Hispana. With the main Army scattered, he could acquire Eburacum when he felt like it. The southern Legions would think twice about marching against him, leaving the entire south undefended and maybe rising in rebellion behind them.

Justin and Hilarion stood on the crest of a little ridge, their cohorts already in position, and watched the war band streaming toward them. A morning of wearisome maneuvering had gained them the advantage of the higher ground, and the men, as Hilarion put it, looked quite chirpy about the prospect of another fight.

He turned to Justin, the wind lifting his sandy hair in little wisps about his face. "Stupendous-looking character, the young king, isn't he? All that blue and yellow. The Legate thinks he'd look nice in a triumphal procession."

"Whereas Vortrix merely thinks the Legate would look nice dead," Justin said. "Old Lupus is getting above himself. Picture Trajan letting a mere Legate steal his thunder. Triumphs are an old-fashioned Republican notion, my boy."

Justin eyed Vortrix, marking his position by the flame-colored border of his cloak rippling behind him as he surveyed the positioning of his war band from the vantage point of his chariot. The High King's corn-colored hair was bound back with a thong and the brilliant blue of his war paint cast an unearthly shadow across his face. Justin narrowed his eyes still further. Vortrix was looking at *him*.

Where the level land began to rise toward a gentle slope, the High King also narrowed his eyes. He could see the Legion strung out in a scarlet battle line across the hill, waiting for them. He also saw the beak-nosed centurion regarding him intently from beneath the rim of his helmet with approximately the same expression as the Legion's Eagle.

Vortrix grinned. The centurion marked his position, did he? He spoke softly to his chariot driver and regarded the battle line once more. The Legion was obviously waiting for him, with no intention of coming down and losing their advantage. So. He would go up.

Justin saw the king raise an arm in signal, and the trumpets and war horns clashed together in grim cacophony. Around him, he could feel the Legion steady and brace itself, and then it began. Again the chariots left their mark and were forced back by the short, sharp swords of the foot soldiers while the archers and cavalry harried them as they went and rained death on the outskirts of the war band.

As the last of the chariots pulled back across the bloody path they had cut in the front ranks of the Legion, the cohorts moved up, and this time Justin had no trouble finding Vortrix. The High King seemed to come straight for him, leaping from his chariot as the near horse went down to a Roman sword, his household guard scattered in the confusion of the first advance. As Justin parried a blow that would have taken off his head, he saw from the corner of his eye Lepidus drawn off in a frantic fight with a burly tribesman twice his size, but there was no time for anything but a fervent hope that the boy would survive.

Vortrix moved warily, with the timing of a born fighter, and Justin followed him with a deadly intentness. The High King's sword came flashing out of nowhere and struck not Justin, but a man of his cohort who had moved up to his side. Vortrix parried Justin's own blow as he pulled back his blade and thrust from below at Justin's ribs. Justin dropped his shield barely in time and pushed forward, striving to put his adversary off balance. The young king stepped back, recovered, and came on again.

Everywhere their struggle was mirrored in the contest between the war band and the Legion, while the sun, high and burning, took its toll of the strength of both sides. Behind Vortrix now was a solid phalanx of his warriors, and Justin moved his own cohort up to block the attack. As one by one their men dropped down around them, Justin and Vortrix exchanged blows, were separated by the press of battle, and were drawn again to each other as by a lodestone. It seemed to Justin that he had been fighting this grim, blue-eyed man for half his life.

In the end, though, the heavier arms of the Legion and the Brigantes' earlier losses to the Painted People took their toll. As the Brigantes began to fall back, Justin made a last desperate leap at the young king, his blade slicing deep into Vortrix's sword arm. Vortrix stumbled and one knee seemed suddenly to give way. He struck at Justin with his shield edge, catching him across the shins and sending him stumbling back. The High King's warriors moved to encircle Vortrix, but at a signal from Lepidus, the Eighth Cohort surged forward, driving them back over the bodies of their dead, and Vortrix went down among the feet of the advancing Legion.

Justin, recovering his footing, found himself caught up in the advance of his own men, and turned, blundering among them, back toward the still form of the High King. A gap opened for a moment in the ranks streaming by, and Vortrix twisted out from under the murderous mailed feet of the Legion and flung himself down behind the protection of an outcropping rock. A riderless cavalry horse, his eyes wide and terrified, galloped between them, sending a spray of dirt and foam into Justin's face. By the time he had passed, Vortrix had regained his footing and retreated further, his sword still clenched in a hand that was now scarlet with blood. Justin saw that he was making for a clump of brush and trees that marked the beginning of a wooded hill, and by the time he reached him, Vortrix had gained enough ground to put him at the edge of this slight refuge. He shifted his sword to his left hand, struck out at Justin, and backed a few feet further into the trees.

Justin, circling to get to the higher ground and cut him off, raised his sword for a blow that would have caught the High King through the heart if it had fallen. But as he struck, his foot caught in the discarded armor of one of his own men who had crawled away to die half hidden at the edge of a thicket.

Justin stumbled, righted himself, and saw that there had been no need for that blow. The High King lay on the ground before him, his sword still clenched in his one good hand, and blood pouring like a fountain from the wounded arm.

He had done it. One quick stroke to slit the High King's throat and the Brigantes would no longer be a danger. Ever. As Justin slid his dagger from his harness belt, he saw the blue eyes come open to watch him. *Hades.* Justin had a quick, horrible vision of cutting Vortrix's throat while Vortrix watched him.

"I shouldn't bother, Centurion," Vortrix said in a whisper. "I'll bleed to death anyway and save you the trouble."

Justin hesitated, watching the retreat now far below them rapidly becoming a rout. "I expect so."

The High King was naked except for a wolfskin fighting kilt, and Justin turned the dagger to his own tunic, hacking off a long strip. He set about applying a makeshift tourniquet to the High King's arm.

"Then to what purpose this?"

Justin, intent on his work, did not look up. "I've been around Licinius too long. I've no stomach for sitting by to watch men die. Besides, it's in my mind that you would be a welcome prisoner to the Legate. There, I think that has slowed the bleeding."

Vortrix still had the strength to look disgusted. "The Legate is a fool. The Legate might like me as a prisoner, but Rome would be better off to have me a corpse." His voice was so low that Justin had to turn his head to hear it, and the blue and ochre of the king's war paint stood out sharply against his ashen face. Even the golden hair was dulled with dust and sweat. He looked like a death mask.

"Why do you follow him?" Vortrix whispered.

"I don't. I follow the Eagles."

"And that is . . . different?"

"Very."

"And you go . . . where the Eagles go and serve . . . under whom they tell you?"

"Yes." Justin finished his work and sat back on his heels. After a moment he stood up and stripped off his armor, and slid it, covered with his leather harness tunic, under Vortrix's head.

"Thank you, Centurion." Vortrix looked up and caught Justin's eyes for a moment. He gave something that was halfway between a grin and a grimace. "Licinius the Surgeon is a . . . formidable influence."

Justin sat down again and propped his back against a tree. "He's very civilized, Licinius. Too much so for his own good."

"Civilization." Vortrix bared his teeth at the word. "Rome's gift to her colonies. Has it ever struck you, Centurion, that some of them would prefer to remain *un*civilized?"

"Forcibly."

Vortrix chuckled. "Then why do you follow your Eagles?"

"I'm a Roman," Justin said shortly. "That's all there is to it."

"A Roman. And is that all? No thought to gold or glory, Centurion?"

"Of course. A great deal of thought, in fact. But that's beside the other."

"And you love Rome, but not the way the rest do."

"As you love your Tribe, Vortrix the King."

"That, Centurion, is what . . . makes you dangerous. And also why I would . . . kill you, if I could."

"And that is what drew us always to each other in battle," Justin said after a moment.

"Aye . . . and in other ways, perhaps. And now I'm dying. But I tried. At least I'll have . . . that to know."

"So did I," Justin said, watching him. "Oh gods, so did I."

"Well, Centurion, you have won. No one but me can hold the Tribe together."

Justin eyed him appraisingly. "You have a remarkably swelled head," he said at last, "but I expect you're right. You'd best try to sleep now," he added. "You shouldn't be talking. You'll use up your strength." It was beginning to grow dark and, shivering in his uniform tunic, he began to build a fire, thinking wistfully of the roaring blaze in camp, his hooded cloak, also in camp, and his leather tunic, under Vortrix's head.

"Shouldn't you be taking your prisoner back to . . . the Legate?" Vortrix inquired.

"If I move you, you'll die," Justin said shortly.

But Vortrix was dying anyway and they both knew it.

The Brigantes were scattered and broken. Those who had escaped pursuit were moving wearily north and westward, away from the Roman Army and a rebellion that lay dead and bloody at their feet. Scattered as they were, it had not yet been borne in on many of them that they were leaderless.

To Lepidus, as he made the rounds of the cohort, taking count of their losses and stopping now and again to speak to one of the junior officers, the possibility that he might himself be leaderless was beginning to seem all too real. He thought of his last sight of his cohort commander, caught in the press around the fallen king. Justin should have been with the cohort in its advance, but he had not . . . and an enemy in retreat was often the deadliest of all. Licinius had sent an orderly to him, asking Lepidus for news of his friend, but he had been able to give him none. And Lepidus felt that the weight of Justin's mantle hung heavily on his shoulders.

Licinius, tending the wounded in the camp hospital, looked up as the orderly came in from the picket line where he had been seeing to injured horses.

"Did you see Centurion Corvus?" He pushed his black hair back from his forehead, leaving a streak of salve across it in the process.

"No, sir. Not since you last asked," the orderly said, giving every indication of being thoroughly tired of the subject.

It was a few moments before Licinius brought a flicker of pure panic under control. Surgeons did *not* panic, and Licinius had always been outspoken in his opinion that one who did was worthless. But Justin was his friend, which made a great deal of difference.

He finished bandaging the gashed leg he had stitched and looked around him. The worst of the work was done.

"Flavius!"

Flavius came away from the man he was treating. "Yes, sir?"

"See to the rest of them. I'm going out."

"But, sir—"

"You heard me." Licinius picked up a packet of ephedron, opium, some bandages, and his surgical kit. "You are perfectly capable of dealing with the ones that are left. And if you're not, it's time we found out about it," he snapped. "There's no place in the Eagles for a man who can't work under pressure." He snatched up his cloak and stalked out.

Flavius looked after him, a hurt expression on his face.

"Come then, young one, he didn't mean it," said the man whose arm he'd been cleaning. "He's had a hard day and a good friend gone missing."

"So have I had a hard day!" Flavius snapped.

The legionary raised his eyebrows. "Haven't we all?" he said, holding out his bleeding arm.

Flavius laughed and began to bandage it for him.

Licinius, lantern in hand, was methodically examining the bodies laid out for burial, holding the light to the face of any centurion's uniform he saw.

"Have they all been brought in?" he asked the legionary on duty as he came to the end.

"All that we saw, sir. Which isn't to say that there might not be one or two we missed. If you've a mind to check the battlefield, you'd best do it now. The birds'll be having a picnic."

Licinius repressed a shudder.

"Was you looking for anyone in particular, sir?"

"Centurion Corvus. Have you seen him?"

"The Eighth Cohort? The one with a lot of nose?"

"Yes!" Licinius snapped.

"Sorry, sir. Didn't know he was a friend of yours. No, *I* haven't seen him, but his men did say he was going at it with that heathen king of the Britons. You'd best try the battlefield, sir."

"Thank you." Licinius picked up his kit and set off down the hill. *Oh gods, Vortrix . . . and I . . . I told him to*, he thought miserably, picking his way down the slope.

He narrowed the lantern light to a thin beam and scanned the field. He saw no Roman armor among the scattered bodies of the Brigantes and was about to search further when he saw the thin glow of a small fire winking from the hill on the right, some two miles off. What in Hades? Licinius lengthened his stride to a trot and closed the lantern entirely.

As he neared the fire, he slowed and picked his way carefully. No telling who was using that fire, though by rights the Brigantes ought to be far to the north by now. A twig cracked under his foot and a figure in a scarlet tunic leapt up, a businesslike Roman short sword in one hand.

"Justin!" Licinius shouted joyfully and galloped up the hill.

"Licinius! What in the—"

"Looking for you, you fool," Licinius said irritably. "What in Hades are you doing? Camping out? I've had the whole Legion turned upside down looking for you. You'll no doubt be flattered to hear that the ghoul on the burial detail described you as the one with a lot of nose. What happened?"

"Over here, Licinius the Surgeon," said a faint voice from the shadows, and Licinius swung his lantern in the direction of the sound. "Great god Mithras," he said softly.

"The centurion isn't . . . as cold-blooded as he . . . thought," Vortrix said with difficulty. "He couldn't bring himself to . . . finish the job. He prefers . . . to let . . . the bleeding do . . . it for him."

"Could *you* kill a man while he watched you do it?" Justin muttered.

"No, I suppose not," Licinius said. He knelt down beside the High King and took out his kit.

"I could," Vortrix said.

"Could you?" Justin asked, with a trace of something like envy in his voice.

"Oh, yes," Vortrix said softly.

"Still, we'll never know, will we?" Justin said, half defensively.

"Yes, it will be . . . interesting . . . to see what Rome decides to do with me . . . if I live."

"You won't if you keep talking," Licinius said. "You have lost a great deal of blood. You may not live anyway."

"It is in my mind that it . . . might be just as well, Licinius the Surgeon," Vortrix said tiredly. "What's the going rate for fallen kings? I have no wish . . . to be . . . paraded for Rome's . . . amusement, until I'm—" He let out a cry as Licinius, who had been smearing the wound with salve, calmly began to stitch the edges together.

Vortrix tried to start up, then fell back against the makeshift pillow and was still.

"What have you done?"

"I believe the High King has fainted," Licinius said. He put his cloak over the still, naked form, and moved nearer the fire.

"Oh. Licinius, I—I couldn't."

"Oh, shut up," Licinius said. "No more could I."

"If I had killed him outright, it would have been different, but—"

"Justin, stop it! You sound like a schoolboy trying to explain why he let his butterfly samples go. He'll be just as out of commission as a prisoner as he would be dead. I think he's right, though. He won't be any happier for it."

"I know," Justin said miserably, looking at the still form across the fire.

"Well, if it's any comfort to you, it's nothing compared to what the British priests would have done to you in the same place. Now stay here and watch him. I'll send a couple of stretcher bearers for our royal prisoner." He started to stand up.

"I wouldn't," said a voice.

Licinius leapt to his feet. Old Cathuil, spear in hand, stood across the fire from them with a red-haired man of his clan and three of Vortrix's household warriors. Justin recognized the flaxen-haired chariot driver among them.

"Somehow your hunters missed us," Cathuil said. "No, Centurion, stay where you are." He leveled his war spear at Justin. "When we saw the High King was not with us, we stayed to find him. You should have killed him, Centurion."

"If you move him, it won't matter," Licinius said. "He'll die anyway."

"I'll not leave him as a mockery for the Romans," the chariot driver said to Cathuil, his face set.

Licinius shrugged. "Then take him and kill him."

"It's a risk we'll have to run," Cathuil answered. "I only wish we could take you as well. I'm thinking you would prove useful. But we cannot manage you and the Lord Vortrix at the same time. We'll have your tools, though, Licinius the Surgeon." He spoke to the other men in the language of the Britons, and one of them picked up Licinius's kit from where it lay beside the king. The chariot driver knelt beside Vortrix and gently wrapped Licinius's cloak around him while the other three kept a wary eye on the two Romans.

"And what will you do with us?" Justin asked. If he could get them to fight, something might be done.

"Leave you," Cathuil said. "It is a great pity, but we cannot risk losing one of us if we are to take the Lord Vortrix back safely."

Cathuil handed his spear to the red-haired warrior, while the others held theirs at the ready.

"Nay, lord, I will carry him," the chariot driver said.

"No," Cathuil answered. "I can tread as gently as you, Galt. And although it bites at my stomach to admit it, you are the stronger warrior. We will have need of your spear." He bent and picked up the king, staggering a bit. Cathuil was an old man, and the High King a heavy one, especially as deadweight.

"That arm will probably be useless if he lives," Licinius said. "What of the High King then?"

"Why, then, he will no longer be the High King," Cathuil said. Tribal law forbade a maimed man to hold the kingship. "But we take him anyway."

He turned and, with the others as a rearguard, moved softly into the trees.

Licinius and Justin looked at each other for a moment, weighing the chances of following them, then turned and started down the hill at a jog trot. Justin had only his short sword against five war spears, and Army surgeons carried nothing but a dagger. It was as well to be realistic.

"Come along, my boy," Licinius said. "This will take some explaining, but at least we can raise the alarm. I doubt they'll make it past our patrols."

But the High King and his escort sidestepped every patrol in their path. The only Roman who saw them was a legionary who, like Licinius, was out hunting a friend, and they left him with his throat cut in a highly professional manner. Except for his body, a three-days' combing of the countryside brought no trace of them.

Now Justin and Licinius crouched by the fire in a marching camp amidst the desolation which only an avenging army can wreak. After the High King was wounded, those members of the war band who had survived the battle had scattered, leaderless, and the Legion had exacted a toll in lives, burned steadings, and salted fields, which would leave the Brigantes scarred for some time to come.

"—and old Lupus has given me a dressing down and then forgiven me," Justin said with disgust. "Because he says he would much rather have had Vortrix for a prisoner—if I had managed to hang onto him."

"And so he would."

"If I hadn't been such a miserable coward and had killed him when I had the chance, we'd have no more trouble from them, ever," Justin said bitterly.

"For the gods' sake, Justin, leave off," Licinius said. "With the way you mangled his arm, I doubt he'll be king for long. Vortrix has plenty of relatives who would just love a chance to invoke tribal law and try their hand at being king themselves. That is, if they don't try to trade his hide to us in payment for this rising."

"I suppose you're right," Justin said. "How badly did I damage that arm?"

"Badly enough that he's lucky if he doesn't lose it."

The High King of the Brigantes lay on a bed of bracken covered with hides in a small hut on the outskirts of his family holding and fixed a furious blue eye on the priest of his clan.

"No, I say! You'll not take my arm off!"

"And if I don't, my Lord Vortrix, you'll be dead in a matter of days. I have seen the signs."

"And if you do, I'll not be your Lord Vortrix. No! I am the High King, and until I'm not, you'll do as I tell you, old man! Is that clear?'"

"Ah, you were a stubborn one, ever since you were a cub," the old priest said with some affection. "Would you rather be a dead king or a live and honored warrior?"

"A dead king," Vortrix said. "Now go away with your knives and let me sleep. Licinius the Surgeon did all that could be done."

"A Roman!" The old priest spat with great expression. "Like as not, he's poisoned you."

"We shall see, shall we not? I will send for you when it is time to pull the surgeon's stitches out."

"Have it your way. I only hope you may not die of it." The old man turned to go. At the doorway, he stopped and looked back. "If you live, you'll get no use from that arm."

Vortrix ignored him, lost in the dagger-sharp pain that seemed to run from his shoulder out to his fingers and beyond. He gritted his teeth and stared at the smoke-blackened ceiling of the hut until the old man had trudged away.

VI

Homecoming

"LOOK AT HIM, packing up for the winter." Hilarion laughed and pointed at a red squirrel watching them from behind an acorn almost too big for its mouth. "Time we were doing the same."

There was a hearty cheer from the cohort behind him, and "I know what I'd like to spend the winter with!" someone shouted amid much laughter. It was late afternoon and the Legion was marching back to Eburacum, heads up and at a smart pace as they came through the great gates, cavalry standards flapping in the breeze and the red crests of their helmets standing stiffly erect.

There was a throng about the gates, soldiers' women in their best clothes turned out to welcome back their men, wineshop keepers loudly praising the virtues of their establishments to an Army that had had a whole summer's campaign to work up a thirst, a crowd of curious townspeople, and Venus Julia, proprietress of Eburacum's only whorehouse (she knew how to deal with anyone who might be so unwise as to start another), resplendent in a lemon-colored mantle and amethyst eardrops and secure in the knowledge that a summer's campaign could be counted on to work up a thirst for other things than drink.

Justin saw Gwytha standing a little back from the road, in her best linen tunic, with her luxuriant hair neatly braided and her brass arm rings glinting in the sun. He wondered if she had come because, as she once told him half jokingly, all that red made a wonderful parade, or to drum up a little business for the Head of Neptune, or possibly to see him.

He had hardly thought of her all summer, but lately, on the march back to winter quarters, he had found her creeping into his mind again, and he wondered what welcome he was going to receive for the way he had said good-bye in the spring. He caught her eye and she grinned at him and gave a silent imitation of a Roman salute. Justin smiled back (as much recognition as he dared give while in marching order under the watchful eye of the Legate) and cocked his head back a bit more. At least she didn't seem to be mad at him.

The last of the baggage train clattered through the gates and the throng of townspeople began to disperse to make ready, in their fashion, for what promised to be a lively evening.

Justin went with the surgeon and the other senior officers to report in the Principia, where they were met by the unwelcome news that the Emperor had drafted yet another detachment from Britain to bolster his campaign in Parthia. A good part of it would come from the northern garrisons. By the time Justin had finished cursing and had dealt with his men and the subject of who should and should not receive passes for the evening, Licinius was not to be seen. Justin bathed and went down to the Head of Neptune, where he found the surgeon already romping with Whitepaw in the storeroom.

Finn let out a joyful yelp and launched himself headlong at Justin's chest. It was like being jumped on by a yearling colt, and Justin staggered back. "Down! Down, damn it, you horrible beast! Mithras, but you've grown!" He ran a hand along the dog's back and Finn wriggled happily.

"Here, I have brought you something." Justin took a heavy red leather collar from under his cloak. He fastened it around the dog's neck, and Finn pranced proudly out to show it to Gwytha. It was studded with heavy brass knobs and gave him a gay and rakish look.

"Yes, you look very fine," Gwytha said, moving a wine cup out of reach of his swinging tail. "He outgrew his other one long ago," she said to Justin. "No, stop that," she added as Finn danced ecstatically about Justin's legs. "You will make me spill the wine."

The shop was thronging with soldiers who overflowed loudly into the street.

"Come on, you horse," Justin said. "I'll take you outside where you can work off some of that energy." He whistled and Finn bounced obediently out at his heel.

Gwytha, taking a quick look over her shoulder to make sure Aeresius wasn't watching, ducked out after him. She took a deep breath of night air. "That's better. Aeresius will be mad enough to spit when he finds me gone, but if I don't get out for a while I'll begin to throw things. I've been pouring wine and dodging soldiers ever since your precious Army marched back today."

Justin laughed. "They've had a long campaign with little to show for it. It doesn't improve their manners."

"Obviously."

"Come for a walk with us, then. Walks are marvelous for improving the frame of mind."

"I daresay, but it won't improve Aeresius's. A short walk, then."

They set off down the street in a companionable silence, turning away from the boisterous crowd onto the path that skirted the river. If Gwytha remembered their last parting, she showed no sign of it. She was as self-contained and matter-of-fact as ever, and Justin found himself falling easily back into their old friendship. His fury at the loss of the latest detachment began to subside.

After a while Gwytha said, "I heard some tale about you and Vortrix . . . ."

"You heard some tale. I'd love to know who tells all the tales that people hear. Why didn't you ask Licinius?"

"There wasn't time. And I doubt he'd have told me," she added frankly.

"So do I," Justin said. "His taste for gossip is no match for yours, my girl."

"It isn't gossip if *you* tell me. Is he dead?"

"He wasn't when I saw him last, but he may be by now." Justin remembered the High King's still form as the old chieftain had borne it off through the woods, and there was a lonely, bitter taste in his mouth. Without quite meaning to, he found himself telling Gwytha what had happened.

"Oh, how horrible." Gwytha was silent for a moment. "I'm thinking that you will have had an evil time of it. I'm sorry."

"I did, and so am I," Justin said shortly. But it crossed his mind that most people would more likely have said "Oh, how horrible" and not meant at all what Gwytha had. She was a most perceptive girl, Gwytha.

"And what will the Legion do now?" she asked, obviously deciding that a change of subject was in order.

"Winter here, and next summer—I don't know. Probably an easy campaign to remind them we're still around. If there *are* any of us left after the Emperor gets through, that is." He whistled to Finn and they turned back toward the town again. "With any luck, my transfer will come through by then, and I can turn *that* problem over to some other poor fool."

"Do you hate it here that much?"

"I'm a soldier. I go where they send me. But as to this posting, I'd sooner dig ditches in Tartarus," he said frankly.

"It's a pity the rest of Rome doesn't feel the same way," she replied with equal candor, and he laughed.

"Amazing what a friendship we have built on mutual distrust, isn't it?" They came into the torchlit Street of Neptune. "Will you come out for a longer walk tomorrow when things settle down?"

She nodded and they turned through the door into the wineshop again.

"Oh, Mother!" Gwytha said guiltily, bumping into Aeresius in the doorway.

"And where in Hades have *you* been?—blast you, I'm coming—Oh, never mind. Get back to work!" He broke off, coughing, and Gwytha shot him a look of concern.

"He's had that cold all summer," she said. "I oughtn't to have gone off. He needs rest."

She hurried away to serve a group of auxiliarymen who had just come in, and Justin took himself off to a nearby table, calling after her that he wanted a cup of wine.

"Ah, Corvus. Sit down and join us." It was Cassius, commander of the Fifth Cohort. "How goes it, my lad?"

"It goes well enough," said Justin, who took the greatest possible exception to being addressed as "my lad" by a man he knew only slightly.

"It goes stinking rotten, you mean," said a legionary at the table, with more than grumpiness in his tone. Justin recognized him from his own cohort. "The centurion's right," the man went on moodily into his wine cup. "Things'll change when we've stood up for ourselves."

"That's enough, Drusus," Justin said quietly. He didn't care for the line the man was taking.

"Climb down off your high horse, Justin," Cassius said jokingly. "Everyone knows this Legion's a laughingstock."

"Oh?" Justin was getting a dangerous glint in his eyes.

"Come now," Cassius said. "You don't really think we'll get that detachment back, do you? Not unless we take a stand."

Gwytha brought Justin his wine and he waited until she was out of earshot before inquiring softly, "Exactly what are you getting at, Centurion Cassius?"

"Why nothing, my boy, except that everyone knows we'll be left to rot here unless someone does something about it. The Brigantes will keep trying, you know . . . or maybe the Pict. And we can't *all* get transferred." He winked at Drusus.

"And what did you have in mind, Cassius?" Justin asked.

"Why, whatever's needful," Cassius said, calling for another cup of wine.

"Aye, afore we all get our throats cut for something that's no business of ours," Drusus said.

Justin stood up, eyeing Cassius thoughtfully. "Centurion Cassius, if I were you, I would learn to keep my mouth closed before I crucified myself with it."

"Aw now, Centurion, we didn't mean no harm," Drusus said. "Just a friendly discussion as to what's to be done, that's all. I know an officer like yourself knows how we feel, sir."

"And what might you know about how your officers feel, Drusus? You will also mind your tongue, or it will be the worse for you. Now take yourself back to quarters before you end up in the guardhouse instead."

"But, sir—I haven't done anything!"

"I can always trump something up. Now get back to camp!"

"Weren't you a little hard on him, Corvus?" Cassius inquired when Drusus had departed grumbling. "An officer has to keep up appearances and all, but—"

"And as for you, you fathead—" Justin turned on him. "If I hear one more word out of you, I'll break your head. Are you *trying* to start trouble?"

"You seem to forget, Centurion, that I'm three cohorts senior to you," Cassius said.

"You try any more funny business with my men, and I'll see you're three months in hospital." He spotted Licinius across the room. "If you will excuse me, Centurion. I shall leave you with this thought: Stay the hell away from my men."

"The man's a rabble-rouser," Justin said next day when he had told Licinius about the incident. "I don't like him."

"What's he after?"

Justin, occupied with cleaning his armor, looked up over the edge of his breastplate. "I'm not sure. I'm not even sure he knows himself. I think he's one of these people who likes being subversive and going about dropping hints. It makes him feel daring and important and a hell of a fellow."

"Well, he'd best watch it, or he'll start something he can't stop," Licinius said. "This Legion's wobbly enough. All it needs is a few dangerous clowns like Cassius to give it a good push and it'll dissolve."

"Oh, Mithras. It's bad enough to be fighting the natives without fighting the damn Legion too. Why *don't* they either get enough men and equipment to garrison this country properly or pull out?"

"Because the Senate's either too complacent or hasn't got enough guts to buck the Emperor, that's why."

Justin stood up. "Well, the problems of the Empire will just have to get along without *me* for a while. I've got a date with a girl."

"Gwytha? I'd go carefully there if I were you," Licinius said.

"Don't worry, my intentions are as pure as snow . . . she's not the type. I only like her company."

"That's good. She's had a tough enough time, poor kid. I'll come with you. I want to look in on Aeresius. I don't like that cough of his."

Licinius had looked dubious when he met Justin and Gwytha at the wineshop door after their walk, but all he said was that Aeresius should be kept warm and he would be back the next day. He handed Gwytha a phial of medicine to give her master later in the evening.

But by the end of the month, it was obvious to anyone who saw him that there was something seriously the matter with Aeresius.

His face was drawn and he had grown thin and he spent most of his time, on Licinius's strict orders, wrapped in a blanket on his bed while Gwytha saw to the running of the shop.

As a result, Justin saw little of her. He thought she was worried, but when he did manage to snatch a moment's talk with her, she seemed to steer carefully away from the topic of Aeresius's health. As Justin had his own problems, and those of his repellent cohort on his mind, he didn't really notice Gwytha's peculiar reticence on the subject until the day when she turned a small, white face to him and said, "He's dying, Centurion, how should he be feeling?" and burst into tears.

When he tried to comfort her, she told him for the gods' sake to leave her alone, and ran into the storeroom. Justin stood looking after her helplessly for a moment, and then went to find Licinius.

The surgeon, when Justin finally tracked him down, was in the hospital cleaning instruments which, as far as Justin could tell, didn't need cleaning.

"He hasn't much longer, I think," Licinius said slowly when Justin told him what had happened. "He put it aside as nothing more than a cold for the better part of the summer. It's gone too far. I have done all I can. Everything. I drained the pleural cavity this morning in the hope . . . but it's a painful thing. I wonder now if I haven't only hurried it along for him." His voice was tired and the scalpel he was polishing was one which he had finished and set aside a moment before.

"Why didn't she tell me?" Justin was hurt. "I had thought we were friends, she and I. Why didn't *you* tell me?" he added accusingly.

"She wouldn't tell anyone, for fear Aeresius would hear of it," Licinius said.

"You mean he doesn't know?"

"No man ever really thinks he's dying, even if he has been told. She said if it were she, she would sooner it was something that came and was done with rather than something that she waited for," Licinius said. "And I thought perhaps she was right. I would rather have it that way myself, I think. But I shall know anyway. It's part of the job."

"I should want to know," Justin said. "And not be coddled and fooled by my womenfolk."

Licinius looked up at him. "Would you *really?*"

Justin was silent.

"Aye, one doesn't know, does one? Still, for Aeresius, I think this is best. I wanted to bring him here at first, where I could watch him, but she said would it make his chances any the better, and I had to say probably not. So Aeresius stays where he is, in the hope that he'll die in some sort of peace."

It was the changing time of year, when life went out in a flurry of fall leaves and the wild things of the wood dug deeper into their burrows and watched the last of the plentiful times whisk by on the wind. In the gold- and copper-colored woods of the High King's family holding, a pony trotted softly along a buried path, his hooves sending drifts of leaves fluttering about him. A warrior on the outskirts made as if to bar his way and then, recognizing the slight, flaxen-haired form of the rider, drew back again.

Galt halted at the hut of the healer priest, but sat for a long moment on the pony's back before he dropped to the ground and pushed aside the door hangings. It was the first time he had seen the High King since the day that he and the queen's father and brother had carried him into this same hut, unconscious and as close to death as any still-living man might be, and Galt was more than a little afraid of what he was going to find.

The High King lay with his face to the wall, but by the set of his neck and shoulders it was obvious that he was not sleeping, and his thoughts, too, practically shouted themselves aloud.

In the High King, Vortrix knew (and Galt knew) lay the power of his people, and they were the power in him. Therefore, the kingship must be held by an unblemished man, lest the diminishment of his powers diminish them as well. And yet, there was no one but him who, by the force of his own will, could hold the Tribe together. And what did that count for, he wondered, in the eyes of the god? He became aware of Galt watching him.

"Why have you come?"

"To see that you did not go away from us altogether," Galt said softly. He and the king were of the same age almost to the day. They had been closer than most brothers from the time they could walk, and Galt knew the High King's mind too well for comfort. If that arm should wither and die, the High King might well choose to die with it.

Vortrix kept his face resolutely to the wall, although Galt knew that the High King had known who stood in the doorway even before he had spoken. "It is my right," Vortrix said finally.

"If the time comes when you must exercise that right to a purpose, brother, I'll not stay your hand. But to take that road now . . . you throw your people to the wolves."

Vortrix was silent for a moment. Then slowly he turned to face the harper, and Galt flinched in spite of himself. The High King's face was pinched with the lean look that comes of much pain, and his bright eyes were clouded. The wounded arm, swathed and hidden in bandages, lay along the edge of the bed, and the white hand that trailed from those bandages was still and lifeless.

Galt knelt beside him as if he could somehow pull the High King back from the strange country in which he traveled. He stretched out a hand toward the bandages, but Vortrix's good arm came up suddenly and blocked the way.

"No! There are only two roads left for me to travel, brother, and until I know which I will take, no one sees that arm, not even the healer priest—he leaves the salve and I do for myself these days. And most especially not you, brother. I'll put no man at odds with the god for my sake."

For Galt's part, he would willingly have traded even his soul for the High King's peace, but being both more cynical and more practical than his brother, he knew that his insistence on that fact would only set a new demon to ride on the High King's back, and the gods knew he had enough of them already. So he stood, regretfully, his pale bleached hair and the cacophony of jewelry clattering at his wrists at odds with the seriousness in his face. "Then I expect the best service I can give you is to pacify your Council," he said lightly. "Old Cathuil rather likes being the High King's father-in-law. Between us we can hold them in check yet awhile." He sketched a formal bow, and then touched one hand lightly to the High King's forehead. "The god keep you in his hand."

To the south, it was raining, great dark drops that spattered upward when they hit the ground. Justin made his way back to the town after a day's hunting, with Finn prancing happily at his side, snapping at raindrops and smelling abominably of wet dog.

The Watch passed them in their evening rounds, their hooded

cloaks drawn over their heads and their mailed sandals clacking on the wet pavement. Finn waved his tail at them, his tongue lolling out between his teeth, and the last man eyed him nervously. Justin grinned. Finn was a very friendly dog, but that crocodile smile put people off.

He put a hand on the dog's collar. "No, fellow, I don't think they want to make friends." He pulled his cloak closer about him, and they turned into the Street of Neptune.

Lamplight shone from the windows of the wineshop, but the door was closed and the place looked unusually still for a rainy evening when anyone with sense would be in out of the wet, warding off chill with a cup of hot wine.

"We are closed tonight," Gwytha said as he opened the door. "Oh, it is you, Centurion. Come in, then." Her eyes and nose were red and she looked miserable.

"Gwytha, what is it?" he asked, flinging his cloak down by the fire. "Aeresius?"

Gwytha nodded and sniffled, a thoroughly unfeminine noise which somehow went straight to his heart. "He died . . . an hour ago."

"I . . . I don't have to tell you how sorry I am," Justin stuttered a bit. He never knew what to say at times like this, an incapacity which infuriated him. "He had no kin, had he? You'll be needing help with the burying and the shop. Please . . . tell me what I can do."

"That will be for the new owner to decide," Gwytha said in a small voice.

"New owner?" Justin hadn't thought of that.

"Aye. He . . . he owes a . . . a great deal of money to a wine merchant in the south. It was to have been paid from this winter's profits. Now he will have the shop instead."

"Couldn't you run the place and pay him? You've been doing it alone lately anyway."

"I?" Gwytha gave a strange, choking laugh. "I go with the shop, along with the tables and the wine jars."

Justin realized with horror that he had forgotten she was a slave. Aeresius had been kind enough, more an uncle than a master, but now it was unthinkable that she should go back to a life of being handed about from one master to another. Not Gwytha. It happened

97

all the time, of course, but for some irrational reason, Gwytha was different.

"But Aeresius would have wanted you freed," he stammered. "Didn't he do it?"

"He was unconscious."

"I see," Justin said slowly. "And he didn't know he was dying. Gwytha, *why* didn't you tell him?"

"Should I go to a man who has been good to me and tell him he is dying and, please, will he free me before he does?" Gwytha said bitterly.

"But it would have meant your freedom."

"Aeresius gave me all the freedom I've ever known since I was ten years old. I couldn't." She sounded tired and her voice was flat, as if worn out with weeping. "Anyway, it is done now. There's no way to go back and change things about."

"We'll see about that." He snatched up his cloak and turned for the door, telling Finn to stay. Gwytha watched him go, her face even more miserable than before. Then she turned back to her work.

Justin stepped out into the rain, which was now coming down in sheets, and tried to think. There must be something. A flicker of movement caught his eye and he turned to see a thin, familiar figure wandering aimlessly toward him down a side street and whistling softly to itself.

"Hai! Hilarion!" The figure stopped, peered at him, and ambled forward again. Justin saw that he was wearing nothing but his tunic, and his hair was plastered flat to his head. "What in Hades are you doing out like that?"

"Getting wet," Hilarion said mildly.

"Where's your cloak?"

"She threw me out. On my ear."

"Who did?"

"Claudia."

Justin found himself laughing. Hilarion was famous for his frequent and generally disastrous romances. "How did you lose your cloak?"

"Forgot it," Hilarion said. "In the, uh, heat of the moment. Didn't seem like a good time to go back and ask for it."

Justin regarded him suspiciously. "Are you drunk?"

"Not as drunk as I was, in all this rain. I recommend it highly to anyone who wants to sober up in a hurry." He peered at Justin. "What's the matter? You look like Jove with one thunderbolt left over."

Justin pulled the other man into a doorway out of the rain. That was exactly what he felt like. Damn Gwytha. She had no right to be such a self-sacrificing idiot. "Aeresius died," he told Hilarion.

"I'm sorry to hear that," Hilarion said. "I liked the man. What about Gwytha? Who's taking over the shop?"

Hilarion didn't have any trouble realizing Gwytha's position, Justin thought irritably. Nobody did, except himself. He was the idiot. But the fact that Gwytha wasn't free came up so infrequently, and was so unapparent, that he had hardly thought about it.

"That's just the trouble." He explained what had happened, and Hilarion swore softly and inquired what he was going to do.

"I don't know." Justin didn't stop to wonder why everyone seemed to think it was *his* responsibility to do something. "I can't buy her. She's worth too much." There was something unpleasant about discussing the price of Gwytha, but this was no time for a fit of gentlemanly airs and graces.

"And she can't either," he went on. "Aeresius would have let her go for the price of the debt he got for her, but this merchant won't."

"Maybe if we got together?" Hilarion suggested. "We all have a little money."

"Think of it, man. She's young and strong, she can read and write and keep books, and the gods know what all else."

"And good-looking to boot," Hilarion added.

"Yes, damn you, that too." Justin shied away from the thought of what a new master's reaction to that asset might be. "We haven't enough money between us to make up half of what he'd ask. If Aeresius had only freed her before he died . . . ." Justin let the words trail off. He looked at Hilarion, who looked back at him nervously.

"Justin—"

"Do you remember when we revised the Legate's speech last summer? You came so close to the scribe's hand, the poor fellow had Ahriman's own time getting off the hook with the Legate."

Hilarion's mouth twitched as he remembered his commander's now famous pep talk, but he said, "Oh, no. Absolutely not. Aeresius couldn't write above halfway anyhow. He'd have had a scribe do it for him, and they'll want to know which one. It'll be so awkward when no one comes forward."

"Not if he did it himself, so close before he died that he couldn't send for one. And Aeresius's writing was so bad you could do it standing on your head."

"I'm not going to do it at all. Justin, have you any idea what could happen to us?"

"Have *you* any idea what it would be like to be passed around like a piece of livestock, after you'd been practically free for a few years for the first time since you were ten?" he asked viciously. "Well, *have* you?"

Hilarion regarded him speculatively, his thin, freckled face thoughtful under his dripping hair. "No," he said after a moment, "I don't. But I have . . . a vivid imagination."

Hilarion sat back, pushing the sheet of papyrus away from him together with the few scraps of Aeresius's writing which they had been able to gather: a note of credit, an order for a pottery lamp from the legionary workshop, and a message to Justin saying that he and Gwytha had gone to the market and he would find the dogs shut in the storeroom.

"There," the boy said. "I think that will pass. I hope so, for our skins' sake. Now will you sit down?"

Justin snatched up the papyrus sheet and began to read. He had spent the past two hours alternately pacing the floor and sitting, drumming his ring on the table until Hilarion asked him to kindly get up and pace again, it was less distracting. He had also consumed a considerable quantity of wine, which Hilarion had given him in the hope, he said, of keeping him quiet, adding that forgery was not the easiest of tasks, especially with Justin peering over his shoulder every two minutes and pacing about like a penned wolf in the intervals.

" '. . . and because she has served me faithfully and well, I hereby free my serving woman, Gwytha, a woman of the Iceni, who came to me as a debt from Morgan the Trader,' " Justin read. "My boy, you have a great future ahead of you. Come on."

"Come on where?"

"To the magistrate, of course. I found this by Aeresius's bed when I went to pay my respects."

"Did you now? I hope the magistrate swallows it."

Justin raised an eyebrow. "I doubt he'll see fit to question a senior officer of the Legion."

The magistrate did not. Not when the senior officer was a man with Centurion Corvus's ability to pull rank. Justin refused to wait until morning, thinking of Gwytha alone in the wineshop with only the horror of a new master for company. Even Hilarion remarked as they were leaving the magistrate's house that he hadn't realized Justin was so adept at Favonius's "now-see-here-my-good-man" method of unnerving the lower orders, to which Justin replied airily that those tactics were occasionally useful.

They had certainly worked on the magistrate, a pleasant pink little man with a slight nervous twitch which was not in the least alleviated by Justin's hailing him out of bed and chiding him for not having conducted a search for the will himself. The magistrate had no intention of putting himself at outs with a cohort commander from the fortress that loomed in his own backyard just to please an unknown wine merchant from the south. He had said "Yes, sir" and "No, sir," the will certainly seemed to be in order, sir, and wasn't it lucky that the centurion had discovered it before any other steps had been taken in the matter of Aeresius's death? and had seemed not at all inclined to question the authenticity of the document.

By the time they reached the Street of Neptune, Justin, who was still a little drunk, was feeling exceedingly pleased with himself. Hilarion was beginning to think that they might get away with it after all. He had also been a little drunk when he had agreed to undertake the project, but the last couple of hours had sobered him up considerably. It was still raining.

Licinius was sitting with his arm around Gwytha's shoulders, unhappily trying to comfort her, when the two of them arrived. Justin felt mildly irritated that the girl seemed willing to accept the surgeon's comfort when she had so far spurned his own. He pulled off his cloak and flung it down by the brazier to dry, leaving his hair, the appearance of which was not improved by its being wet, hanging damply in his eyes.

Gwytha looked up and managed a small smile. "You look ghastly," she said.

"That's a fine way to talk to someone who's come all the way in this abominable rain to tell you you needn't worry about a new master," Justin said indignantly. "Here." He pulled Hilarion's handiwork, duly stamped with the official seals, from his tunic.

"What is it?"

"Aeresius's will."

Gwytha snatched it up and began to read, Licinius regarding the document with suspicion over her shoulder.

"Aeresius *couldn't* have . . . ." Her hands were shaking. "He was unconscious."

"We . . . uh, were hoping you wouldn't mention that to the magistrate," Hilarion said diffidently.

"Is this your doing?" Licinius inquired. "Justin, where did you get this? Justin!"

Justin, who by this time had reached that pleasant state of drunkenness combined with self-congratulation wherein it seemed silly not to continue, was pouring himself a cup of wine. "I sort of found it," he said over his shoulder, replacing the wine jug and laying a coin on the table for Aeresius's as yet unknown creditor. Then he got a look at Gwytha's face and set the cup down as well.

She had gone a dead, chalk white, like a plaster casting, beneath the bright red-brown of her hair. "I'm obliged to you, Centurion," she said, "for your care for my welfare. Oh, Mother, what am I going to do now?" She began to cry, choking, painful sobs that shook her whole body.

Justin was appalled. "Gwytha . . . oh, Gwytha, don't do that. What's the matter?"

Licinius regarded him with the expression he usually reserved for the most imbecilic of his patients. "Great god Mithras, what do you expect her to do? Aeresius didn't write that will and you know it. He'd have made some provision for her. Did either of the precious pair of you stop to think that freedom's not much use when you don't have anywhere to go? What are you going to do, send her back to the Iceni as a poor relation? If they didn't send her right back again?"

Justin was suddenly furious. Because he had given the girl her freedom, everyone now seemed to think him responsible for her future as well.

"Damn it, you wanted to be free! Well, now you are!"

"Thank you, Centurion." Gwytha turned on him a pair of blue

eyes intent with loathing. "I'm sure you feel very noble. Have you any suggestions as to how I'm going to live?"

"Couldn't you go on as you were?" Hilarion asked. "And work for the new owner, I mean?"

"He'd rather have a slave," Gwytha said bitterly. "It's cheaper. And he won't be here for months, with winter coming on. The magistrate's office will run the shop until then. And they aren't likely to waste their fee hiring any help."

"Justin—" Licinius began.

"Then sell yourself back to someone!" snapped Justin, who was rapidly working himself into a rage. *Damn* the girl.

"No." Gwytha spoke so softly he could hardly hear her. "If you had come to me first, I'd never have let you do it. But now that you have done it, I'm free, and I *can't* go back." She looked at him with such bitterness that he felt it drive like a knife into his stomach. "I'm free, Justinius. Do you know what that means? You've given me the only thing I ever wanted, and I have no way to keep it. But I won't go back. I'll die first."

Justin's anger deserted him. He was horribly afraid that she meant it.

"Gwytha, I'm sorry. I'm so sorry. Please forgive me." He dropped down on his knees beside her and took her hands, but she pulled them back and turned her head away. He felt desolate. What had he done, with his damned interfering conceit and his vicious tongue? "I'm sorry," he repeated, and had an acute vision of his mother informing him tartly that being sorry was no doubt nice for his conscience, but it didn't do much good for the person he had hurt. He was seized with a terror that this girl would go on hating him for the rest of her life. "Gwytha, please look at me."

There was so much misery in his voice that she turned around. Her eyes met his for a moment, and she began to cry again, with her head, this time, on Justin's shoulder.

"Hilarion—" Justin looked up at him helplessly— "can we do another page? Leaving the shop to her?"

The boy looked unhappy, but he shook his head. "Oh, no. You've already got me in a fair way to being cashiered. Gwytha's one thing, but I'm not going to steal a whole wineshop."

"He has a point," Licinius observed. "You've already taken one highly suspicious will to the magistrate. How were you planning to explain just happening to find another one?"

Justin sat still as the enormity of the situation broke against him like a wave. Gwytha was still crying, but silently, her whole body shaking in his arms. He had done this. Somehow he had to undo it. Through the haze of wine and torn emotions, only one idea came to him. He pulled the girl closer before he spoke. "Well, then, marry me."

She flinched and jerked her head up.

"Gwytha, do you hate me that much?" he asked.

"No, Centurion." She held his eyes for a moment, but he couldn't tell what thoughts lay in those bright depths.

"Gwytha, please," he went on desperately. "I know I'm not much of a prize, but I'd try to be a good husband to you. I got you into this—"

Across the table, Licinius and Hilarion regarded them with horror.

"And you feel it's your duty to marry me to get me out again?" she asked.

"No," he said finally. "It's all I *can* do for you."

Gwytha's face was impassive, the barriers raised once more. "All right, Centurion," she said.

VII

Wedding Feast

JUSTIN WOKE THE NEXT AFTERNOON in the grey winter light with a violent headache and a vivid recollection of the previous night.

He still had one day's leave left (having no relatives in Britain, he had chosen to spend his leave in camp, loafing) and he was going to use it to get married. Not strictly according to the letter of the law, but a marriage made in service was socially binding, and for Justin there could be no half measure. He had a sudden desire to start screaming and to keep it up until they came and got him and tied him up.

Licinius, coming to collect him half an hour later, found him resolutely shaving instead. The surgeon had come prepared to make a stab at putting a stop to this idiocy, but he didn't think he had much chance, and he had also put on his parade uniform.

Justin laid down the razor when he saw him and managed a smile. "You look very fine. And yes, I remember what I did last night."

"Justin, are you sure you—"

"And yes, I do intend to go through with it." He picked up a comb and concentrated on his cowlick. "And no, there doesn't seem to be any graceful way to change my mind now, does there? If it's any help, I know I was drunk last night—my head feels like death—but even cold sober with a hangover, I can't think of anything else I could have done."

"You won't get that transfer if you go through with this, you know." The surgeon's dark face was serious.

Justin looked at him bleakly. "Are you under the impression that I don't know that?"

"Couldn't you have just offered to take care of her? Men have taken mistresses before now, you know."

"So have I, if it comes to that. Gwytha's just not the type. I tried once, did I ever tell you? She caught me a clout that left my ears ringing. It wouldn't work, Licinius. I'd feel like a lecherous old senator fondling a thirteen-year-old every time I touched her." He twisted his scarf about his neck and knotted it carefully.

Licinius's lip twitched, but he knew Justin well enough to know when there was no point in arguing. At least he was fond of the girl. He only hoped that wouldn't make matters worse.

"What is your mother going to say?"

"She's going to have a fit," Justin said. "But I don't want Gwytha to know that. I'll handle Mama."

From what Licinius knew of Justin's mother, she was going to take a good deal of handling. She was extremely fond of her son, and Justin was too fond of her to lie to her. She was not going to receive well the news that her son, in a fit of gallantry, had married a slave. All he said, however, was, "Well, if you're determined, we had best get going."

Justin flung his gold and scarlet parade cloak around his shoulders, and they set out for the magistrate's house. A fine rain was still falling.

The magistrate was inclined to be amused. He wasn't overly fond of Romans, especially Romans who woke him up at night acting like Caesar. So that was why the centurion was in such a hurry about the will, he reflected, as they went through the short ceremony, though he couldn't see why he wanted to go and marry the girl. It was going to cause an unholy stink in the centurion's family. Still, marriages of this sort could always be hushed up, if you had enough money. He didn't suppose they did, though, or the bridegroom wouldn't be in the Army. The centurion, he noted with a certain grim amusement, looked as panic-stricken as a horse at gelding time.

The bride, on the other hand, went through with the business stoically. Whatever she was thinking, it didn't show in her face, and she kept her voice to the monotone of a child reciting a lesson in Greek. But she had bound her hair up Roman fashion, and she wore the Roman bride's traditional flame-colored veil—whether in a desire to please him or in mockery, Justin couldn't tell.

When it was over, Licinius and Hilarion lifted her over the threshold of the little house which Hilarion, with some difficulty and a great deal of bribery, had found for them that morning. And then, looking embarrassed, they left them alone.

Justin ran his eyes over the house. It was constructed in Roman style, and had been built by a young tribune who had seen no need to be uncomfortable while putting in his obligatory year with the military. The central room, the atrium, was rectangular in shape, with a somewhat dingy pool in the center and walls of painted plaster. Of the two longer walls, one was windowed and faced onto a garden with flower beds which had been laid down under mulch, and, near the gate, a single tree, winter bare in the drizzling rain. What it would turn out to be when it budded in the spring, Justin hadn't the faintest idea. The opposite wall was frescoed with a pleasant oceanic scene of nereids and dolphins, and the tiled floor was checkered in a pattern of blue and white. The other walls were of plain painted plaster, and there was a niche in one for the household gods, small figures in bronze, the wedding gift of Licinius. The room was furnished at one end with several chairs and a small desk, and at the other with a dining alcove of couches and a central table. Ranged around the atrium were a small bedroom, servant's room, and a kitchen and storeroom. A hypocaust beneath the floor warmed the main house and the little bathhouse and latrine at the back, with the addition of a three-legged brazier in the atrium.

The house was a bit down at the heels now, Justin decided upon finishing his inspection, but the construction was good and it could be made comfortable.

"Thank goodness," he said. "I was afraid we'd have to make do with much worse on such short notice. I wonder how Hilarion did it."

"I don't know, but I expect he'll send you an account," Gwytha said. She had flung her veil back from her face and was looking about her with uncertainty. "I expect you owe him a great deal of money," she added with a frankness that made Justin laugh.

"I don't doubt it. But nothing for you to worry about," he added. "I've a good many months' pay accumulated, with nothing to spend it on." He put an arm around her hesitantly. "I'm afraid I'll be rather an absent husband, but I'll be with you whenever I'm off duty, and you'll have Finn to keep you company." The big dog paused in his exploration of the house to wag his tail at his name. "As soon as I get a chance, I'll find a good serving woman for you so you won't be left alone so much."

"Nay, then, I can see to the household myself. You forget it's what I'm used to."

"Well, you're going to have one anyway," he said, ignoring this. "I don't want you left alone nights that I'm gone. Anyway, a fine thing it would be if I let my wife scrub floors . . . and Vesta knows they need it."

"You mean I'm to learn to live like a lady, Centurion?"

"Precisely. *Must* you call me Centurion?"

"I . . . I had got used to calling you Justinius. Now it seems a little strange."

"I suppose it does. I've gone from friend to husband rather suddenly, haven't I?" He smiled at her. "Try Justin then. It's shorter."

Gwytha was silent and looked, for once, as if she didn't know what to say. Neither had as yet made any mention of the reason for their marriage, and both seemed grimly determined not to.

He came over and pushed her gently into a chair and settled himself at her feet. "Try and get used to me. I'll do my best."

"I know you will," she said softly. "You always do. It's just that I'm hoping you won't be hating it."

"I promise you I won't. It's you that's more likely to have cause to regret. I've gotten the best end of the bargain, I'm thinking." He leaned his head against her leg, wearily, because although he could not say it, he *was* hating it . . . hating her, and himself, and the malevolent Fates which had seen him posted to Britain and the ruin of everything he had ever wanted. And then he felt her begin to shake and saw that she was crying again. Conscience-stricken, because this was a reaction he had never seen in Gwytha until lately, he stood up again, taking her by the hand. "Come. We're both feeling strange, I think. We're going to collect Finn and go for a long walk, the way we used to. It's stopped raining." *And will that make everything to be as it was?* a small voice inside him said.

Hilarion, seeing them walking up the hill, shook his head despondently, but by the time they returned to the house an hour later, they found themselves slipping unconsciously into their old untroubled friendship. And Justin had managed to kiss his new wife twice. The first time, he had felt her stiffen, but the second time she was calm. They stopped and ate meat pasties in a food stall in the town, because there was nothing in the house, and then walked slowly home, Finn gamboling ahead along the rain-washed road.

Their first night together was compounded of small awkwardnesses all the same. They sat late beside the little pool in the atrium, carefully talking of nothing in particular, while the nereids simpered at them from the wall, until Justin, tongue-tied and embarrassed, had finally held out his hand to her and said, "Come, then," and led her into the bedroom.

Gwytha silently and obediently pulled her tunic over her head, and Justin, seeing the shape of her breasts and the flat curve of her belly in the flickering light, felt the one thing that he had never expected—he wanted her. Wanted her so badly that it almost sent him reeling.

He reached forward and gently pulled the pins from her hair, bathing his hands in it as it came cascading down about her shoulders. She touched his face hesitantly, then moved to curl herself on the rough blankets of the bed, watching him.

Justin, in that strange halfway sensation between embarrassment and desire, dropped his belt on the floor and pulled his own tunic off, tousling his hair and lending a vulnerable quality to an otherwise formidable body. He was lean and tanned and muscled . . . crisscrossed here and there with scars, but alive and vital, as if distilled in him was the essence of his ancestry—the men who, one after the other, had fought for their place in the Empire. Fought . . . and loved.

He slipped onto the bed beside her, by now throbbing with desire for her, both surprised and afraid that this woman stirred him as she did. He kissed her lightly and, shaking, slid one hand down to cup her breast. She must feel the desire in his touch, and Justin thought that an answering throb ran through her own body as his hand slipped softly between her thighs. He stroked her gently for a moment, his own desire so tautly controlled that his muscles seemed to be screaming, then softly slid his fingers inside her. She made no protest, and Justin, knowing he could bridle this longing no longer, turned and in one motion thrust deep inside her.

It was awkward all the same. Gwytha, as he had thought, was not inexperienced, but she lay perfectly still beneath him, as if even here her barriers held good, while Justin found himself pulled into a mounting passion that suddenly burst in a series of almost unendurable waves that left him spent and shaken.

When it was over he put his arms around Gwytha and held her close for a moment, and it seemed to him as if his eyes were wet, and he wept. But Gwytha kissed him, turned on her side, and, as far as Justin could tell, dropped into sleep.

Justin lay awake then, propped on one elbow, watching the patterns the moonlight made in her hair. It was not the first time he had fallen asleep with one hand tangled in a girl's long hair, but it had always been a lighthearted thing, for the pure joy of it. None of them had ever moved him as this unlooked-for wife had done . . . nor scared him quite as much. If she had been in his bed for sheer pleasure, or from love . . . but Gwytha had married in sheer desperation, and it stood between them. He wondered if she had *ever* taken a man from choice and, with this unhappy thought in mind, lay down to sleep.

When he woke in the morning, she was not there. He wondered if she had packed and run (back to her people, maybe) before he smelled mutton broiling in the kitchen.

Gwytha was turning barley cakes on the stove with one hand and tending the mutton with the other when he came in.

She looked up at him. "Did you think I had run off?"

Justin hadn't known he was that transparent. "No, I was only wondering where you came by the mutton. There was nothing here last night but a few sacks of meal. You must have been up early."

"Early enough for a trip to the butcher. And see, there is honey for the cakes, too."

"Quite a breakfast. You're certainly an improvement over Pausanius." Pausanius was the head cook of the officers' mess, renowned for his ability to ruin anything.

"Well," Gwytha said, dropping cakes onto a plate, "it will have to serve for a wedding feast. You'll be back to Pausanius soon enough." She untied her apron and sat down to eat with him. Her hair, he noticed, was back in its neat braids.

When Justin had swallowed the last mouthful of mutton and barley cake and wiped the honey from his hands and mouth, he stood up reluctantly. He was due back at duty, and no matter what he said, it would be an awkward parting. "I must go. I don't know whether I can get back tonight or not, but I will tomorrow. In the meantime, do whatever you think needs doing to the house. There's money in the purse by the bed." Finn, finishing a bowl of scraps, looked up expectantly and wagged his tail. "No, old fellow, you can't come."

"By tomorrow, I'll have the place so you won't know it," Gwytha said, brisk and apparently cheerful. "I wonder when was the last time anyone cleaned the atrium floor."

He came to kiss her good-bye, but she was scrubbing her pots and pans and spoke to him over her shoulder. He turned away again, feeling foolish, and let himself out into the garden, shutting the door firmly in Finn's hopeful face.

As he turned into the Principia to report back for duty, the Optio at the door stopped him. "The Legate wants to see you, Centurion Corvus," he said, with a good deal of sympathy behind this ominous statement.

Well, he had been expecting it. The news must be all over camp by now. Justin braced himself and headed for the Legate's office.

The Legate was not pleased. He was, he implied, a busy man with better things to do than rescue senior centurions from disastrous marriages. However, as he also strove for a reputation as a good fellow, he began by inquiring jovially if Justin had had to go so far as to marry the girl.

"Yes, sir. It wasn't that sort of an affair."

"Your family is not going to be pleased, you know. Nor, for that matter, am I."

"I was afraid you wouldn't be, sir." Justin held himself stiffly at attention.

"Not afraid enough to stop you, I notice. You're a hotheaded young fool, Centurion. Well, a marriage in service is easy enough to get out of, but it doesn't look well, all the same. Not for a cohort officer."

"I assure you, sir, I have no desire to get out of it."

"That's just as bad," the Legate snapped. "Either way, it's going to cause a scandal. If you couldn't just bed the wench, you should have left her alone. A senior centurion has no business flaunting his amours in public."

"I wasn't aware, sir, that marrying a woman constituted flaunting one's amours," Justin said, gritting his teeth. He couldn't afford open war with the Legate.

"It does when she's a slave out of a wineshop. If you're so infatuated with the girl, why in Hades couldn't you wait until you were out of service?"

"I think you forget my wife's position, sir."

"Forget her position?" The Legate was beginning to splutter. "Damn it, how could I?" He looked grimly at Justin. "I'd boot you from here to the most godforsaken outpost in Britain for this, except that I'd have to say why, and I'd prefer not to have it thought that my officers make a habit of marrying slaves. And I can't dissolve a marriage I can't even legally recognize. But I think you'll find, Centurion Corvus, that you've done no good to your career. I hope your . . . *wife* is worth it, because that transfer you want so much isn't coming through!"

Justin flinched. He had known that, of course, but he had been keeping it pushed to the back of his mind. "I know, sir," he said with as much matter-of-factness as he could muster.

"Well, much joy may you have of it," the Legate said. "You are dismissed, Centurion. Get back to your duties."

Justin saluted and left, avoiding the Optio's heavy, sympathetic face. He had been right in hoping that Metius Lupus's concern for appearances would keep the Legate from posting him off to the north of nowhere, but it would be a long time, if ever, before he could hope for promotional transfer to another province, or even another Legion. The prospect of his life loomed miserably before him . . . a shattered career in a green, unfriendly land, with a Legion that was only one step shy of a rabble . . . .

He walked on, wrapped in unhappiness and paying little attention to where he was going, until a voice shook him out of his lovely misery. It was Favonius.

"Hai, Justin, the most determined man in the Empire! I never thought I'd live to see our Gwytha say yes to anyone!"

"Ah, now, he offered more than anyone did before," laughed Sylvanus, who was second in command to Favonius and inclined to take his cue from him.

"Aye, that he did. Tell me, have you broken the news to your mother?" Martius, who commanded the Sixth Cohort, inquired. They clustered around him, laughing.

Justin was silent and Favonius intervened.

"Be quiet, you two. This is a serious matter. You've got to get yourself out of this, Justin. The news is all over camp. If you need money—I'm sure the girl would be glad of it—I could—"

Justin turned on him. "I have just finished telling the Legate that I have no wish to 'get out of this' and I will tell you the same thing and it will be the last time!"

Favonius blinked at him. "You can't be serious. A slave out of a wineshop? Just as well marry one of Venus Julia's girls."

"One more word out of you about my *wife*, Favonius, and I'll knock all your teeth down your throat and spoil your pretty voice."

Justin drew back a fist as if to get a head start on this plan.

"You can't do it, Corvus," Martius said. "You'll disgrace the whole Legion. We won't stand for it."

"And you—!" Justin turned to face him.

"Justin!"

He swung around to confront this new voice, intent on murdering someone, and stopped. It was Hilarion, carrying a large bundle under one arm.

"From what I heard, the Legion seems to be disgracing *itself*, Martius," Hilarion said mildly. "If I were you, I'd tuck my tongue back in my mouth before I tripped on it." He handed the bundle to Justin. It was a blanket of gleaming grey wolfskin lined with bright bright red and blue checkered wool. "It's a wedding present," he said. "I'm sorry I didn't give it to you yesterday, but you didn't give us much notice."

It was an open declaration of the side he stood on, and Justin was grateful. "Thank you. Gwytha will like it."

Favonius opened his mouth to speak and Hilarion decided that things had gone far enough. He didn't want Justin hauled up for beating a fellow officer to a bloody pulp. "I really came to find you, Favonius," he said. "One of your centurions has gone and stuck his finger in a catapult and they want you to send someone out to replace him. I think he's broken it. Come on, Justin, we're both on wall-building duty today. We can leave this off in your quarters on the way."

He steered Justin firmly past the other three and off toward the officers' block. "Whatever you do, try not to push Favonius's face in," he said when they were out of earshot. "Granted it's a face that could use it, but you'll just make matters worse."

"I know," Justin said. "I'm afraid you've made yourself three enemies, though."

"Oh, well, I never did have much use for Favonius and company. They are to gentlemen as a cart horse is to the Emperor. Still, you'll have a lot of that to put up with."

"And I've got to put a stop to it now, if I'm ever going to."

"Well, just try to do your fighting verbally," Hilarion said. "And let your friends help you where they can. I think you've got more friends than you know."

When Justin marched into the mess hall that night, his hair still clinging damply around his ears after a solitary splash in the bath-house, it appeared that Hilarion was right.

He had considered going back to Gwytha and the house in town, but had changed his mind. Facing the other officers at mess was something that had to be done sooner or later, and better sooner. He was going to give no one any cause to say that Centurion Corvus was ashamed of his wife, although his self-confidence was not bolstered by the knowledge that his marriage was one which he himself would have condemned strongly had it been made by a centurion of his own cohort. And he wasn't entirely sure that he wanted to face Gwytha tonight either.

He entered the mess hall in an antagonistic mood, determined to keep the peace if he could and to break someone's head if he couldn't. As he came in the door, a group who had only too obviously been waiting for him swept him off to sit with them.

Licinius was there, and Hilarion, whom he had expected, and Lepidus, of whom he had not been quite sure. Justin, always ruthlessly veracious, had been inclined to put Lepidus's liking for him down to a sense of duty and a bit of hero worship for a commanding officer, and he was faintly surprised to find that it ran deeper than that. Even more unsettling was the discovery of Geta at his elbow. Separated from the other senior officers by the unbridgeable gulf of class and from the common soldiers by his rank, Geta had, so far as Justin knew, no real friends in the Legion. To Justin he had never shown anything more than a passing respect. Certainly he had never given any indication of a willingness to declare war on the rest of the Centuriate for his sake.

But there he was, cracking a friendly joke, and next to him was young Flavius, Licinius's junior surgeon. That Licinius might have ordered him there crossed Justin's mind, but Licinius didn't work that way. And if Flavius's presence had been Licinius's idea, Octavian, the surgeon's apprentice, would have been there as well. He was not.

So Flavius, too, was there from friendship and it made Justin feel a little guilty. Always slow to make friends, he had left no one behind him on the Rhine or in Africa that he much missed, and in the Hispana it was only to Licinius and Hilarion that he would speak freely on some matters. He had tried to be a compassionate commander to Lepidus, and to Flavius and Geta he had given friendliness but never friendship. Now he found that in the Legion he hated so much there were five men willing to risk their standing with the rest for his sake, three of them without even any idea of why he had gotten himself in this mess in the first place.

He was still mulling this over as they hauled him off and sat him down near the end of the table, one on either side of him, two across from him, and Licinius like a watchdog at the end.

Justin looked around him and grinned. "So, you look out for my welfare."

Across the table Lepidus grinned back at him. "No, sir. We merely show where we stand."

"Hmmm." Justin cracked open an egg. "I see. I'm quite capable of defending myself against the likes of Martius, you know."

"We know," Licinus said drily. "That's precisely what we're worried about, you idiot."

"I take it your aim is not so much to protect me from outraged public opinion in the person of Martius, as to save me from myself?"

"Precisely. Public opinion will die down in time, but if you punch it in the nose in the meantime, it'll take a lot longer. And make things uncomfortable for Gwytha as well."

Justin was silent. He hadn't thought of that. "Very well, I'll endeavor to, uh, restrain myself. But there are some things I can't let go by."

"No. Can't." Geta spoke for the first time. "Just don't go lookin' for 'em, that's all."

"I'll be good," he promised solemnly. "And . . . my thanks to the five of you. I know what you're doing and I appreciate it."

"Nothing of the sort, sir," Flavius said. "Can't let those idiots set themselves up as the custodians of everybody else's behavior. If they were as grand as they think they are, I don't imagine they'd be centurions in Britain," he added.

The Legate, hearing the laughter from Justin's table, glanced in their direction and was glad he had decided not to take further measures in the matter. Corvus had more friends than he thought, and it would have been sure to cause a great deal of undesirable talk. Unlike Justin, he did not acquit Licinius of having ordered Flavius's attendance but that did nothing to lessen its importance in his eyes. Although he did not like to admit it, the senior surgeon made him nervous.

His friends' good intentions managed to keep Justin out of trouble for three days. He occupied them with combing a few more kinks out of his cohort—in case anyone should feel himself privileged to comment on his commander's marriage—and with finding a serving woman for Gwytha.

After talking to several prospects, he settled on Januaria, a round amiable woman with glass drops in her ears, who had been nurse to a family who had moved to a drier climate for the sake of the father's health. As the last child had recently married, they had decided against taking Januaria with them. Bereft without something to mother, she took to Gwytha on sight and treated her with the same high-handed affection she had had for her former charges.

Gwytha balked at first, but succumbed rapidly to Januaria's mother hen instincts. When she had pointed out testily that she had gotten along without a nursemaid since the slavers had come when she was ten, Januaria's dark eyes had brimmed with tears and she had said, poor lamb, then it was high time she had someone to look after her. Gwytha gave up.

Finn's affection had been instantly won by a largesse of bones, and his respect by a firm refusal to let him sleep on the furniture.

Januaria allowed Gwytha to do such housework as she considered proper for a lady, and the rest she did herself. When Gwytha went marketing, Januaria accompanied her, basket in hand, and using her wide person to clear a passage through the street.

Not for nothing had Januaria been nurse to a gentleman's children, and anyone thinking to make remarks to Gwytha on the subject of her recent marriage would, upon taking one look at that imposing figure, have changed his mind. All in all, Justin thought that he was leaving his new household in good hands.

Januaria was of the same opinion, and also that it was high time my lady learned to behave as befitted her station in life—this when she caught Gwytha cleaning out the pool in the atrium.

Gwytha pointed out that as a freedwoman her station in life was far below that of her housekeeper, who had been free all her life.

Januaria was indignant. "And you a chief's daughter! I was born British and I'll die British, the Mother be praised, and so will you. The Roman may be master here now, but that doesn't change what we were born!"

"Nor what we've become," Gwytha said, turning back to her scrubbing.

"It's what you're born that counts, my lady," Januaria said tartly, "and I'll thank you to remember it. Now give me that scrubbing brush and take yourself off to your loom. I'll not have the centurion finding I've been letting you scrub out pools."

Justin she tended to regard as something only slightly less omniscient than the Delphic Oracle in all circumstances and when Gwytha, somewhat irritated at this apparently blind faith in her husband's powers of judgment, remarked that the circumstances of his marriage hardly argued a cool head in a crisis, Januaria answered firmly that the centurion had behaved exactly as a gentleman should, and would hear no further argument on the matter.

She rapidly became a power in the household, exercising over her new family and its friends the same domination she had had over her late charges. Hilarion and Lepidus she treated much as she had her former master's schoolboy sons, with more regard for their youth than their rank—when she spoke of "the centurion" it was always Justin she meant.

Aside from Justin, only Licinius commanded Januaria's deference.

Him she regarded with an admiration approaching awe. The ability to save a man's life through medicine was to her a gift close to the powers of the gods.

Under her domination the little household settled down, at least on the surface, to something approaching domestic tranquility. Justin, under the watchful eyes of his friends, also appeared to settle back into the old routine.

On the fourth day of this uneasy peace, Favonius, with the lack of good sense which only a firm conviction of being in the right can bring, tackled Justin again on the subject of putting an end to his marriage, and a much-tried Justin picked him up and pitched him in a horse trough.

He then strode off to the bathhouse, leaving Lepidus, who had been coming to report, to help the spluttering victim to his feet.

Favonius was furious, but being thrown in a horse trough was very different from being punched in the jaw, and he retained enough care for his dignity not to take the matter to his superiors. Thereafter the disapproving element decided that Centurion Corvus was incapable of being reasoned with, and simply ostracized him.

Justin made it clear that this arrangement was to him the most agreeable one possible, but the armed truce did little to help the already strained relationship among the officers of the Ninth.

VIII

Hilarion

IT WAS CLEAR AND COLD IN THE NORTH, and the afternoon light hung like amber in the bare branches of the trees as a cloak-wrapped figure slipped through the door hangings and into the snow-enshrouded wood.

Pausing at the crest of the nearest hill, Vortrix looked back once over his shoulder and then crouched carefully in the snow. He took a deep breath and, steadying himself with his good arm, reached out with the other for a small branch lying at his feet. He lifted it a bit, not with the grip of his fingers, but by slipping them under it until the branch rolled onto his palm. He straightened his back and brought the piece of wood higher, wincing as the movement pulled at the crimson scar on his forearm and twisted it until he almost yelped.

He let the branch back down again, rocked back on his heels and regarded it grimly. A twig cracked behind him, and he swung around, balancing on his good arm, to find the old priest of his clan panting with the exertion of making his way up the hill and looking, Vortrix thought, like a mother hen with one lame chick.

"My Lord Vortrix, what are you doing?"

"Sitting on this hill, as you can see, and hoping to be left alone for a change. Can't I come out for some air if I've a mind to?"

"No, not without telling me where you're going, you can't," said the old priest with a surprising amount of spirit. "You may be the High King, my young lord, but you're sick all the same. If you ask me, it's a miracle that you've lived at all, and you've no right to worry me half to death by disappearing."

"And if I had told you, you would have come with me, now would you not?" Vortrix inquired softly, his blue eyes taking on that dangerous gleam which at another time the old priest would have heeded. "And maybe, just maybe," Vortrix went on, "I might have wished to be to myself, and to think, without you to come chattering in my ear with your opinions and your potions."

The old man came closer and narrowed his eyes suspiciously. "It is in my mind that that is not all you've been doing. You're sweating like a horse. If you've been trying to use that arm, my lord, you're a bigger fool than I thought."

"Oh, *is* it so? I have as much use of my arm as I have need of, old man!" He picked up the stick with his bad hand and flung it furiously in the old man's face.

The old priest had seen Vortrix in a rage enough times to know when it was prudent to let a matter drop. He turned and clambered unhappily back down the hill. Still, the boy had more use from that arm than he had thought.

Behind him, the High King lay in the snow, clutching his maimed arm, his face running with tears and contorted with the agony of trying not to scream.

The winter that blanketed Britain lay with a lighter hand on the lands of the south, and Justin's mother was propped on a couch in her elegant little house at Antium, decorated only with the lightest of fashionable wraps. She clutched a letter in one frail hand and fanned herself with the other. She looked at the letter again and lay back and closed her eyes.

"That boy will drive me to my grave," she announced weakly. "Take that thing away and bring me a cup of wine," she added to the maid who was hovering distractedly at her side, attempting to thrust a perfume flask under her mistress's nose. "I'm not going to faint, you silly woman. Oh, that boy . . . ."

Julia Valeria did not ordinarily allow herself to become agitated about anything—it upset the careful balance of her facial muscles and consequently restored some of the years which she painstakingly removed every morning at her dressing table—but she felt that this was a special occasion.

She was a fond mother but not an overpowering one. Having launched her only son on a respectable career which could, with the intelligence and ability which he was held to possess, lead to great things, she was content to sit back and concentrate on her own life for a change. Following a soldier husband all over the Empire had been a trying sort of life for a woman of her temperament, and although she had mourned her husband's passing, she had been only too happy to return to civilian life. Her husband's will, plus a small inheritance of her own, had been sufficient to allow a single woman to live in a comfortably fashionable style, if she practiced a few economies where they didn't show. Providing for a growing son had been something of a strain on the budget, and although she missed him, it had been a definite financial relief when Justin was old enough to embark on a career. She had done without a great many things for the better part of a year to establish him as she thought fit, and had then sat back to enjoy herself.

Judging by his letters and a few flying visits home, he had seemed to be very happy in the Army—just like his father—and to be rising rapidly. She couldn't for the life of her understand this desire to go careening all over the world, living in the most uncomfortable fashion and letting barbarians throw spears at you. Influential friends said, however, that they had heard good things of Justin and predicted a brilliant career for him. The arena episode at Hippo Regius and his subsequent demotion had worried her, but the same influential friends had said that it merely showed he had spirit, and it would do him no harm to cool his heels in Britain for a year. They promised a few good words in the right places when the time came, and, all in all, it looked as though Justin was going to be a credit to her.

And now this. His whole career brought to a sliding stop all because of a pretty little barbarian (now that she thought of it, he hadn't even said she was pretty) and Justin's idiotic sense of responsibility. If he'd just consent to give the girl a nice present and send her packing . . . . Julia Valeria gave that idea no more than passing consideration. It was obvious from his letter that he had no intention of doing any such thing, and she knew her son too well to have any illusions about his changing his mind. Pigheaded, just like his father, with a conscience that cropped up at the most uncomfortable times . . . .

There were only two possibilities—to brazen it out or to somehow conceal his wife's background from general knowledge—and she had neither social position nor money enough to get away with either one. This was clearly beyond the scope of even the most influential of friends, unless she should suddenly strike up a close friendship with the Emperor, she thought disgustedly. She would give an extra large offering to every god she could think of, but she didn't see how they could help much either, unless they could manage to strike the wretched girl dead of a plague.

She opened her eyes to find the maid again hovering at her side with a cup of wine. "Marcus Claudius the praetor has called, lady. Shall I send him in?"

"No! Tell him I can't see him. Tell him I've been taken ill. Tell him I've fallen into fits, I don't care, but I can't possibly see anybody now. I shall go away and become a priestess and live on an island with a herd of goats . . . I shall . . . oh, I don't know what I'm going to do. Go mad, probably. And what am I going to tell old Vehilius Gratus? We've been talking about his daughter for Justin ever since . . . send the man away and bring me something to write with immediately."

The maid brought her writing implements and she scribbled a number of short notes to anyone she could think of who might help. Why had she sent the praetor away? As the most influential of her friends, there might be *something* he could do.

"Have these taken round at once and get me my chair. I'm going out."

My baby, she thought mournfully, reflecting on Justin as a chubby, beaming infant, being sick on her best stola. Justin as a small boy, falling out of a tree onto a visiting senator. Justin as a twelve-year-old with a collection of frogs that escaped one night in the middle of a banquet. All these disasters were somehow very endearing at a distance.

"That awful girl . . . she probably wears trousers or something. She'll probably feed him on barley gruel and sour milk or whatever it is they eat in Britain . . . and *what* am I going to tell old Gratus?"

* * *

Justin trudged wearily home through the late January snow with a letter from his mother under his tunic. She was taken aback, but wanted him to do whatever he felt was right, but was he sure this *was* the right thing, and what would he like her to tell their friends? Of course she wanted to do just as he wished, but it was going to be a little difficult. Did women really wear trousers in Britain and did he think he could get her used to wearing a tunica? On the whole, her letter read much as he had expected—horrified, determined not to alienate him by letting him know it, and with a strong undercurrent of hysteria running through the whole. It was a pity he couldn't show it to Gwytha. It would tell her more about his mother than Justin could ever hope to, and the bit about the trousers would amuse her. But it would also bring home to her exactly what marrying her had meant to him. She knew that, of course, but there was no point in throwing it in her face. It seemed to be always topmost in her mind anyway, he thought sadly. Alone with him, she invariably did everything he asked, but it was as if the soul was gone out of her, or locked behind a door to which he had no key.

So the letter stayed in his tunic when he came in at noon and stood damply steaming in front of the brazier in the atrium. He had something else in his tunic, though, and he pulled it out as Gwytha got up to take his cloak. Januaria was hobnobbing with a crony down the street.

"I . . . I brought you something." He handed her a little bag of silk and watched her as she opened it and took out a pair of gold eardrops shaped like stags' heads.

There was a flash of pure happiness in her face as she stood turning them over in her hand. "I've never had anything half so fine," she breathed, and then unexpectedly she kissed him.

"I thought they were pretty," he said and paused, somewhat at a loss for words. He hadn't expected them to please her so. The words, when they came, proved to be the wrong ones. "They're the badge of my family."

"Oh." Gwytha stepped back. "I . . . I must see to the baking," she said in a queer voice. "And . . . and thank you. They *are* very nice." She fled into the kitchen.

Justin listened for a minute, but he didn't hear any noise from the kitchen. Whatever she was doing in there, it wasn't baking.

Oh, damnation! He snatched up his cloak. He couldn't even make a guilt offering—he *had* been thinking about his mother's letter when he bought them—without having her see through it. Why did she have to be so damn sensitive?

In the storeroom, Gwytha sat miserably on a sack of flour, staring at the eardrops. Why did he have to make gestures? The front door slammed hard, and she rose and went back to the atrium. Fighting tears, she set her loom to clicking back and forth, a lulling rhythmic sound to blank out, at least for the moment, the bitter memory of Justin's face as he swore by his own gods to live with her forever.

She forced her mind to drift with the chatter of the loom, but the carefully circumscribed paths of her daydream shifted invariably to forbidden ways . . . the image of her mother, in her corner by the hearth, constantly weaving—a cloak for Gwytha's father, or *his* father, or one of Gwytha's brothers—and Gwytha herself, with a little loom of her own, practicing her patterns on a smaller piece.

Now, after thirteen years of slavery in the Roman world, she sat at her own loom and wove a cloak for a Roman husband. It was a deep, military scarlet, edged in dark gold, and the gold thread, she had thought when she selected it, would set off his eyes . . . golden eyes, bright and changeable as a hawk's . . . .

Januaria returned, rabbit in hand, to begin dinner, and Gwytha banished her husband's falconlike good looks from her mind, trying to set it spinning on less bitter pathways.

An infuriated howl from the garden roused her. Januaria, she knew, was masterminding the rabbit in the kitchen, so she pulled her cloak around her shoulders and let herself out, to find the grey and white cat who had wormed his way into Januaria's affections in the last few weeks and had apparently decided to take up permanent residence, indignantly cleaning a shower of snow from his ears.

"Sorry. I seem to have started an avalanche." Hilarion perched, legs dangling like a friendly spider, on the wall above.

Gwytha scooped up the cat and peered up at him. "What are you doing up there?"

Hilarion produced a snowball from under his cloak with a faintly embarrassed air. "Lepidus," he said. "I saw him coming this way. You must think I'm about eight years old."

"Not at all," Gwytha said cordially. "Nine at the least. You *are* bored, aren't you?"

"Extremely. Justin's teaching his catapult crew to spell his name out in rocks or something, and Licinius is consorting with an Egyptian potion peddler who looks like a beetle and is full of a lot of large talk about the influence of the stars. He's always hoping to find out about a new disease."

"Don't you mean a new cure?"

"Oh, Licinius isn't particular. The scientific mind, you know. He's writing a book. Can I come in? This snow is beginning to soak through my clothes."

"Come along then, and Januaria will find something to warm you." She was grateful for the interruption.

Hilarion scrambled down and followed Gwytha into the house, making his apologies to the cat, who glared at him balefully but allowed himself to be scratched between the ears. Gwytha called to Januaria and sent her to the storeroom to fetch wine while Hilarion flopped down beside the brazier and eyed the loom admiringly.

"For Justin?"

"Yes. His old one is wearing thin."

"I envy him," Hilarion said. "My mother has *my* wife all picked out," he added, and favored her with a brief, unflattering picture of the young lady in question.

"Shall you marry her?" Gwytha set the loom clicking again.

"Not for worlds. I've told my mother so, but she will keep thinking I'll come round when I'm older. She'll get the idea eventually."

"Poor girl," Gwytha said. "I hope then that some other man may ask for her."

"Is it so important, to be married?" Hilarion asked.

"It is for a woman," she said grimly. "What has she to do else?"

"That must not be overly pleasant. To *have* to be married, I mean." Hilarion was startled. He had never really considered the girl's side of the question before.

"It depends on whom you marry, I expect. In my tribe, a girl's father gives her where he chooses, although many are willing to listen to her preferences in the matter. And at the least she gets a man who wants *her*." There was a bite to her voice on the last sentence, he thought, but it faded out again. "Is it the same in Rome?"

"I expect so. I don't really know much about Rome. Most of us don't come from there, you know. Roman citizens are scattered from one end of the Empire to the other."

"And yet I think you all count it as home?"

"In one way, yes. I think it's the place that you're born that you want to go back to in the end, but Rome is—it's hard to explain. It's the center of things. In one way, it *is* the Empire."

Gwytha was silent a moment. "That is an idea, I think, that my people would do well to learn," she said slowly. "That no matter what single tribe goes down, what is important is that the land as a whole should survive. If we cannot learn unity, we will never win over any invader, and the next one, maybe, will be worse than Rome."

"That's very advanced thinking," Hilarion commented.

"It's what Justin says of this war. If you are going to do a thing, do it quickly and right. Otherwise nothing survives at the end."

" 'Justin says,' " Hilarion grinned at her. "You sound more like a wife all the time." She was silent, and he saw that he had touched a wound. "Feeling a little strange about it all?"

"How could I not? Hilarion, *you* know why he married me."

Hilarion searched for some sentiment of comfort and found that it did not come easily to mind. "Do you know," he said finally, "I rather think most new married people feel that way. There aren't that many marriages for love, you know, even among Justin's folk and mine. Less maybe—look at my mother's plans for me. And Justin told me once, *his* mother had a bride all selected for him. If she's anything like mine, he made a good bargain, getting you. At least you and Justin are fond of each other . . . there are lots who don't even have that."

Gwytha didn't say anything, and somehow Hilarion felt that he had still said the wrong thing. He sat watching her fingers as they wove their intricate pattern of red and gold across the loom, and a certain amount of light burst upon him. "Gwytha, you can box my ears for me if I'm out of line, but . . . was there ever anyone else but Justin?"

Gwytha kept her eyes on her loom, but her answer came clear and sad over the click of the shuttles. "None that I loved . . . no."

The sun came out that afternoon, giving a white gloss to the world, but Justin, supervising his cohort at drill and keeping a wary eye on the catapult practice going on behind him, found himself impervious to the beauty of the world. He was occupied with gloomily wondering whether he should buy Gwytha something else, a real present, for its own sake, not like those damned eardrops, or whether that would just make matters worse. And why in Hades, he thought viciously, had he tied himself to a woman who could never forgive him for having married her in the first place?

He was jerked out of this train of thought by an oath and a scuffle from the parade ground. One of the men, apparently also with other things on his mind, had turned right instead of left and snarled up his whole century.

"Very impressive," Justin said, advancing on the traffic jam. "Remind me to leave this century behind next time we march. I've no desire to have a pilum flung at me by one of my own men. Do any of you know what you're doing, or do you just make it up as you go along?"

"I'm sorry, sir," the junior centurion in charge began, looking nervously at his cohort commander.

"It was me, sir," said a penitent voice from the rear of the tangle. "I did it. I think I turned wrong. It won't happen again, sir." The culprit was easy to spot, a wiry, barrel-chested legionary who stood a good head above the rest of his century.

"Who is it? Clemens? Ah, yes. Well, I appreciate your admitting being the cause of this monumental mess, but you've just let yourself in for extra drill, you know. All right, Centurion, take them round again, double time, until they get it right. *All* of them. The whole century shouldn't come apart just because one man's dreaming."

"It's getting close to dinner, sir," the young centurion said.

"Well, then they'd better learn it quickly, hadn't they? Otherwise they'll get awfully hungry." He went back to his position at the edge of the field.

"Whoo, I thought you were for it, Clemens," said one of the soldiers, watching the centurion out of the corner of his eye.

"So did I. He's a queer one, though." Clemens considered his commander with furrowed brow. "I tell you this," he said at last. "I'd sooner have him on my side than not."

"Aye, well, likely you did right. Lying's the thing he won't put up with, they say. He's the old school, he is."

Justin, who was not privileged to hear this conversation, wondered just how irritated they'd be by the extra drill. Enough to get it right the first time, he hoped. He was cold and he wanted *his* dinner.

All the same, when Justin finally got home (they had *not* got it right the first time) he had another little silk-wrapped packet in his hand. He stepped into the atrium to find his wife curled on a couch, dispensing wine and sweet cakes to Hilarion and Licinius who were lounging at her side, and laughing at whatever story Hilarion had been telling her.

Justin held the silken bag out to her hesitantly. "I thought you might like these better," he said, apprehensive of her reaction to this somewhat clumsy apology, and also hoping fervently that this time she would not see through him. He himself was all too aware that the new gift was a penance for his previous mistake.

Gwytha gave him a startled look and pulled out a pair of amber bracelets. "Justin—"

"He's been selling passes again," Hilarion observed to Licinius. He eyed the bracelets. "You'll look as fine as the Empress in those."

"Please take them," Justin said.

"There was no need." She looked unhappily at the bracelets, and Justin wondered if she too was a little embarrassed about those eardrops.

"Of course there wasn't," he said tiredly. "They're a present."

"They are beautiful."

"Well, put them on then, and let's see how they look." He could feel an edge of exasperation creeping into his voice and tried to quell it.

Gwytha must have heard it too, for she slipped the bracelets on obediently. Hilarion nodded at her with approval, and she smiled shyly. "Hilarion says they'll become me," she said. "I don't think we can argue with his taste in these matters."

Justin wondered what in Hades had been going on all afternoon and why Hilarion seemed to be eyeing his wife with such transparent concern, but he shrugged it off. Everything Gwytha did these days baffled him anyway.

Hilarion wasn't sure what was going on either, but he had the feeling that a crisis had been averted, and thankfully resumed the story he had been telling. Gwytha gave a shout of laughter at the end of the tale, and Justin watched her sadly, wishing he could call up that mood in her. Still, if she couldn't make a friend of him, he was glad at least that she had others. And her laughter was good to hear.

"Play something for us, Gwytha," he said suddenly.

"All right." She took up her harp. "Happy or sad, think you?"

Justin realized that he only wanted to hear her voice, so he shrugged and said, "You choose." He closed his eyes and let the sound sweep over him, while she watched him, surprised, as she sang:

> The winter sun sets early now;
> It glints along the snowbank there,
> And through the fire's smoky breath,
> It tints our spear points bright as death,
> And turns to gold the king's grey hair.

Her clear voice floated through the room . . . an old song of her people, born of an old war and an old king long forgotten.

> He is come, a last resort,
> To council table with his kin.
> Across that table Alun stands,
> And Evan with his bloody hands,
> And counts the men he knows for him.

> Death blows on the wind here where
> MacBrendan sits among his brood;
> Silent as the rest are fed,
> His cup untouched, he will not shed
> Their blood nor eat their food.

> We followed him in our wild youth's flight,
> When war was to our liking,
> And earned for each a golden band,
> Cattle and our wives and land,
> For thirty years of fighting.

> Now come his sons to claim their share:
> At smell of blood the jackals rise.
> Our foemen's huts are rent and burned,
> Their farms and fields to wildwood turned,
> Yet still the swift-wing war spear flies.

And so we keep our watch upon
Alun's eyes and nervous hands,
For death lies in a knife blade hid,
And it comes to feast unbid,
As this last dark council ends.

It was a song with the fine-drawn strength of a bowstring, and
the old harper that had made it lived again for a space in Gwytha's
voice. The mood she created caught more than Justin in it.

"Brr," Hilarion said when she had finished. "Now there's a tune
to give a healthy man the creeps."

"It is a song of my own people," Gwytha said, laying the harp
in her lap. "Still, I could not sing it for them," she sighed. "Among
my people, it is not permitted for women to make such music."

"Then your people have lost much," Justin said softly.

Licinius smiled. "Give us 'The Courting of Claudia,' Gwytha.
That's more in Hilarion's line."

Hilarion's face reddened, but he grinned appreciatively as Gwytha
struck up a lively, mocking tune of two rival suitors and the setbacks
they suffered, ending with the winning of Claudia by a man who
appeared not to want her in the least.

"That's women for you," Hilarion said mournfully. "Bring them
sweets and perfume and they fall over themselves chasing the fellow
who's not interested."

"On the contrary," Justin said grimly, "that's strategy. Never
wear your heart on your sleeve. It gets trod on."

Gwytha looked at him oddly, and the other two watched them in
uncomfortable silence until Licinius gave them an abrupt change of
subject.

"I came to talk to you, Justin," he said. "And you also," he
nodded at Hilarion. "I've been hearing some highly unpleasant
things in my surgery when my patients apparently overlooked my
presence. How do things stand in your cohorts?"

"Well enough among most of the men," Hilarion said. "There
are a few—I suppose there always are—who are talking rather large
and loud."

"I think I'm finally beginning to make some headway with mine,"
Justin said, "although I've had to crack down on a couple, like
Drusus. I rather fancy *our* cohorts are in better shape than most, but

that may be just vanity. Still, I've heard some things from men in other cohorts that I *wouldn't* stand for."

"No more would I," Hilarion said. "Though I dislike putting a man in the guardhouse for saying old Lupus is an idiot when I've been thinking it myself."

"Two distinctions seem to have escaped you," Licinius said drily. "One is that you haven't been holding those views in public with an eye to stirring up trouble. And the other is that no matter how mistaken you think Lupus is, you obey his orders and you'll go on obeying them. Can you say that for the rest of the Legion?"

"For most of *my* men, I think, yes, at the moment," Justin said. "I'm not so sure about the rest of the Legion. They're spoiling for a fight of some kind. I just hope they'll be satisfied with fighting the Brigantes. I think they would be if they could do it properly."

"I think also that the right man could bring them round," Hilarion said. "They're not that far gone yet. But the best *we* can do is keep our own men in line."

"This should never have been allowed to get started in the first place," Justin said. "It's a damn sight easier to prevent than it is to stop it once it's started. And if we had any brains, we'd take every warrior the Brigantes have left and ship them off to the Auxiliaries in Parthia—before they can pull themselves back together." Justin made a disgusted noise in his throat.

"Will we, do you think?" Hilarion asked.

"No."

"Why not?"

"Because they're very sorry now that they were bad boys and are being very good and paying their taxes and behaving themselves like the good little barbarians that they are, and after all, our job here is to keep the peace."

It was only too obvious what was the source of this speech, and Hilarion said indignantly, "But surely after last summer— the man's got to have changed his mind. We can't go on just spanking them and sending them to bed without their supper indefinitely."

"I think he will, though," Gwytha said.

"But why?" Hilarion looked startled. His experience of women did not cover any who took an intelligent part in military conversations.

"He is a man who does not like to . . . take chances." She looked thoughtful. "And he does not understand Britain. I think he feels they will . . . will give up and turn to something else."

"You're a better judge of character than I gave you credit for," Licinius said. "What do you think of Vortrix?"

"It always comes back to Vortrix, doesn't it? I don't know. I think he is . . . dangerous. He has too much charm, too many men who would follow him across the Rubicon—or the Styx—without question. If he still lives." She glanced at Justin.

Justin was silent. He had the uncomfortable sensation that if Vortrix were dead he would know it. "This isn't getting us any-where," he said abruptly. "We have enough to do with our own cohorts without trying to run the whole Legion singlehanded."

And enough elsewhere as well, he thought, looking at Gwytha. He knew, sadly, that her laughter and her outspokenness would last only until their guests had gone.

On an impulse, he asked them to stay for dinner.

It was a wakeful night, moon-washed and shining, when Licinius and Hilarion left the house. The surgeon raised a hand in farewell and started up toward the hospital to make a final check. It was quieter there now that Justin didn't come so often to talk, and Licinius found that he missed him.

As always, he took his comfort from the countryside, watching the black knots of trees whispering in the wind. He was more than half in love with Britain, he thought. A strange, compelling country. Like Justin, he had hated it when he first came. Now . . . there was something here that drew him. But he was lonely for someone with whom to share the moonlight and the trees. Only Hilarion, of the three of them, seemed to be heart-whole, he thought, and tonight he had wondered about him. But perhaps it was only the restless night.

Hilarion picked his way through the icy wheel ruts in the street and glanced down the narrow alley that led to Cordaella's garden gate. He had been considering her as a likely successor to Claudia, and there wasn't really a thing wrong with her. In fact, there were a great many things right. Her figure was opulent, her tastes were not, and her virtue was almost nil. Somehow he just didn't seem interested. The truth was, he acknowledged ruefully, he had

Gwytha on his mind. It would be nice to have a wife to bring presents to, if she were someone like Gwytha, not his mother's selection, a pudgy eight-year-old with a passion for cream cakes which threatened to spoil her face as well as her figure in a few more years. "I simply can't marry her," he said aloud. "Mother will just have to think of something else to do with her. I shall rise to be Emperor," he added, repeating a childhood formula, "and then I can do what I like."

He kicked suddenly at a clod of dirty snow and turned down Cordaella's alley. There was a light in her window, and she might even be alone.

In their own window, Justin and Gwytha too stood looking at the night. It seemed a live thing, rustling in the garden. An owl floated by on silvered wings, and they watched it drift past in silence, as if the gentle mood that still lingered was too fragile to break with words.

"Do you know," Gwytha said finally, "I think that's going to be an apple tree. It has the right shape."

Justin didn't answer, but took her words as he thought perhaps she had meant them and slipped an arm around her shoulders. The grey and white tomcat went prowling along the wall, intent on his own amours, and Justin, with a silent grin, took his wife by the hand with like intent.

He felt that same ache and longing which seemed always to come to him with Gwytha at night, and as always, she lay still and let him do what he wished. But this night, instead of turning away to sleep, she closed her eyes with her head on his shoulder and his arm around her. In a while he tried to slide it out from under her, and she stirred and wrapped her own arms around him in her sleep.

So Justin lay still, his arm slowly growing numb beneath her, and held to him, if only for this one night, a new and unknown thing.

IX

The Music Maker

VORTRIX LOOKED UP, frowning, his eyes narrowed against the sudden sunlight. "What do you want?"

A small white hand jerked the door hangings back. "A word or two with my lord," said an icy voice.

"Branwen!" He turned his mangled arm away from her. "Were you not told to bide with your women?"

She advanced on him like a large golden thunderstorm. "My women!" she said furiously. "I began to wonder if I was not like the maid of the story who marries a monster and knows it not, since she never sees him!"

"I am not much to look at," he said drily. "And I have other things on my mind just now. And—" he stopped short.

"*And?*" One small slipper beat an irritated tattoo on the floor.

"And I would not have my woman see me shamed!" he flared at her, holding out his arm. "Look, then! Look well, if you will! I cannot use it! When I do, I faint like a maid with the pain. Now you have seen. Go away."

The thunderstorm vanished. "Let me look." She pulled the curtains back again and tugged him into the winter sunlight. "So. Someone caught you a fine blow, did he not?" Vortrix pushed her away.

134

"How much can you do with it?" she inquired practically, seeming to take no offense.

He picked up a large wooden ball from the bench where he had sat, lifted it, touched his shoulder with it, and set it down again, his face contorted. "That," he said, breathing hard.

"It is a good beginning," Branwen said. "I did not know. I was told only that you were wounded. My father knows, does he not? That old priest who made me a sour face when I came in, he knows! But me—me, I am queen of the Brigantes for the good it does me— no one tells *me!*"

"No one tells anyone!" Vortrix snapped. "Not even your father and the healer priest know for sure. I do not give up the kingship so easily. There are too many of my loving family who would be pleased beyond bearing to invoke the law if they knew."

"Me among them, I suppose?"

"Nay, but a woman's tongue—"

"Mother of us all, what do you think I am, a chattering serving wench? I am your *wife!* I leapt the Beltane fires with you not a year ago! Of what does my lord suspect me, conspiring to wed your cousin and set him in your place?"

"*No!* It must come to a test and I need time. That is why I have set it about that I am still sick with the wound fever. All the same, I would have you remember that I am king," he added softly. "Never think to rule *me*, lady."

"Treat me as your queen and I'll not try."

Vortrix eyed her consideringly. "Come then," he said roughly and pulled her to him. "Branwen, I am sorry," he said into her hair.

"Then I am sorry too." She was still stiff. "It may chance that I can help you exercise that arm."

"That is possible." A smile twitched under the corners of his blond mustache. "At all events, it is comfortable to have you here."

Vortrix lay back on the bed, eyeing his queen as she brushed the tangles from her hair. He grinned to himself. Well, that was one thing he could still do with his arm. Branwen looked up from her hairbrush and grinned back. It occurred to him that he wasn't really sure how much he knew about this tall, golden girl he had taken to wife, perhaps half for her father's position and half for her beauty and her wide hips. Vortrix needed sons, and as soon as possible, if the same squabbling that took place when his father died was not to undo his own work after him.

"Do you really want to know what's going on?" he asked suddenly.

"Of course I do," Branwen replied, placidly brushing her hair. "And you, you wear yourself thin with being alone and with having no man who knows your heart."

"No. I will not burden Galt with a knowledge that might set his conscience at odds with his love for me. And I know of no man save him that I would trust completely. And one other, perhaps, if things had fallen differently."

"And who is that one?"

Vortrix gritted his teeth as he shifted position on the bed. "He gave me this," he said, holding up his bad arm.

Branwen was silent for a moment. Then she came and sat on the floor by the bed. "You are too young to have been so long alone. It's cruel."

"I have survived. My loving family has tried, and yet . . . I survive."

"When Arviragus your father died, Dubric who should have been regent took the throne instead. And when Dubric died and Rhiada his brother would have ruled, the clans spoke for *you*, not for Rhiada or Cawdor his son. So much I know. No more."

"The wolves are waiting. If I let loose my grip just once, they will pull me down and everything I would do."

"Cawdor is a wolf?"

"In full cry. Remember how he tried to win the war band to him last year. *That* cost us sore."

"You should have killed him."

"So says Galt. But there are others. And none of them can hold the Brigantes as one people except me. And if we are not one people, we will be no people. Rome will scatter us. But will they see that, stupid old men? No, they blether about their home fields and who will look after them when they take the war trail. Or they fight among each other over who has precedence or who does not send his fair share of men to the war band."

"Now they also fight over whether or not the High King has the use of his arm," Branwen said.

"How long can your father hold them in check?"

"Yet awhile. But you must show yourself soon." She reached out to touch his arm and looked him in the eye. "It may not heal, you know."

It was dusk when Branwen slipped out, leaving Vortrix asleep, in the company of a nightmare full of wolves. When she returned, she informed the old priest curtly that she was here to stay and he might as well get used to the idea. He departed, muttering and scandalized, and the High King's lady settled herself grimly in front of the hearth, a dagger in her lap and fire in her eye.

Unlike the previous year's, this winter was a mild one, and two days later the High King professed himself far enough recovered to walk in the winter sun. Beside him went Branwen like a large golden shadow, smiling, placid, and watchful, her arm linked through his bad one, and chatting of new hangings in the Great Hall for the benefit of any nearby ears.

"Crowded, isn't it?" Vortrix murmured. The courtyard was fuller than usual of people who had no business to be there. "Dawid!" he called, and a small form skittered across the snow and bowed. One of Vortrix's "hounds," the grandson of old Cathuil, and Branwen's nephew.

"My lord." He beamed. "I'm . . . I'm so glad to see you well."

"Thank you," Vortrix said gravely. "You must credit your aunt with that. A most excellent nurse. Go you and find me Cathuil your grandsire."

"Yes, my lord." The boy hesitated. "My lord?"

"Yes, Dawid?"

"Some of your Council, my lord. And—others. They *all* want to see you."

Vortrix turned to look at Branwen, and then, like a pair of golden hawks, they both turned to look at the figures gathered in the courtyard.

"I have every intention of indulging them," said the king.

The Great Hall was crowded. The High King's family holding was not so large as the King's Hall at Isurium Brigantum, but it had the advantage of being less accessible to the Roman kind, tucked away in a defensive position high in the hills. And it was peopled with folk who had served the High King's family for generations, an advantage grimly noted by the High King's Lords of Council.

The Council Lords were all there tonight, as well as the other tribal lords who had gathered at the start of winter to see whether the High King lived or died, and who remained still camped in and about the High King's hall. Cathuil, with his rheumatism bundled against the night in a wolfskin cloak and leggings, was there in his official position as chief Council Lord and father-in-law of the High King, and unofficially to serve as watchdog on the rest of them. If Vortrix's arm did not heal, Cathuil would support tribal law and a new king. The king was god for the Tribe, and a maimed god brought ill for his people. But until the matter was clear one way or the other, the young king was going to have his chance.

Red-haired Donal, Branwen's brother and the father of Dawid . . . . Dependable and unimaginative, he had helped his father carry the High King's inert form back that night, deposited him with the healer priest, and asked no questions.

On the other side of the hall, Galt, leader of the king's household warriors, whose feminine airs and graces belied a magic with horses and a silken feel of danger that few had the nerve to challenge. Resplendent in a red cloak and golden arm rings that clinked musically as he moved, Galt circulated among the throng, showing off his new harp and keeping a careful eye on anyone he thought might be unwise enough to start anything. Cawdor, for instance, his reddish hair braided and tied back, warming his hands at the hearth and carefully keeping his eyes on nothing in particular, while noticing everything. Or Berec, who had been a hound in Dubric's household. Or Conor, who had ever an eye to the main chance. Or even Talhaiere, chief priest of the Tribe, who would wield his not inconsiderable power with the clans against any king whose actions might call down the god's wrath.

Galt ran his fingers along the harp strings, picking out a few shimmering notes, and strolled over to prop himself against the wall and play with the beginnings of a tune, one ear cocked toward the talk between Berec and Conor.

"—never any use from that arm," Berec was saying. "A maimed man to lead us. It will anger the god and he will lead us *all* to hell."

"The law is quite clear on that, of course," Conor murmured. "If, of course, he is truly maimed."

"No man survives a wound like that with a whole arm. Better they had left him to the Romans."

"And left the way open for—whom?"

"There are others with as good a right as Vortrix. Other men who are whole."

Conor smiled sweetly. "Then I would give those other men a piece of advice. If they are strong enough, let them take the king-ship now, before the god becomes offended—or the High King's arm can heal."

"The High King's arm is strong enough to take that other man's head off." Galt spoke aloud to no one in particular, and Berec whirled around.

"It is an offense to—"

"It is an offense to the High King to talk treason in his own hall! The man who does so may find more fight on his hands than he wants, friend adder-tongue." Galt slid his hand down to the dagger at his gilded belt and Berec turned furiously away.

Cawdor, who had been observing, took Berec by the arm and said something to him in a low voice, and Berec moved toward a gathering of tribal lords from the westernmost settlements.

There was a stirring from the far end of the Great Hall and an icy blast of wind preceded the High King into his council.

Vortrix's eyes were as coldly blue as the wind which sent the smoke from the hearth whirling upward, and his golden hair hung loose under the deeper gold of the circlet that crowned it. Gold shone bright around his neck and arms and he wore the sword which had belonged to the High King his father before him. As he reached the hearth he stopped and coldly surveyed the room. The smoke-grey wool of his shirt and breeches blended with the fire's smoke and he looked grim and inhuman, a winter king born of the ice and snow and the howling wind outside. His eyes traveled slowly around the hall, noting Cathuil, grey as an old watchdog and grim-faced, softening as they reached Galt, and turning brittle again as he saw Cawdor bowing gravely before him.

Vortrix bent to retrieve a small twig, smoldering at one end, which had rolled from the hearth, and pitched it into the heart of the fire with his wounded arm. There was a murmuring behind him and, satisfied with the effect he had created, he strode to the end of the hall and seated himself there, nodding to Cathuil to proceed.

The old Council Lord raised his hand for a silence that was already there, as, their murmuring stilled, they waited for the High King to speak.

For a long moment, Vortrix merely sat and watched them, hawk-wise, until Berec began to fidget and even Talhaiere looked uncomfortable, although the talk was none of his doing. Conor merely seemed amused.

"It pleases me to see so many of my spear brothers in my hall," Vortrix said, "but it troubles me somewhat that concern for my welfare should so long have kept you from your fields and hearths. I am sure the wolf guard has need of every spear, even though the Mother has blessed us with a lighter winter than our last. We must take council quickly and then I must let you go."

"Go back to what?" a voice cried. "My steading burned, my sons dead—what have I to return to?"

Vortrix's voice was gentler. "I also grieve to see so many of my brothers missing. We must hope to have learned a lesson in unity from this summer's losses. While we quarreled among ourselves, the Painted People were let to slip by our guard. While we fought them, the Romans gathered strength." He eyed Cawdor for an instant, then turned again to the old man. "And yet, we must go on. We have no choice if we are not to live all our days with Rome's hand on our necks."

There was a murmur of assent, and the old man slowly straightened himself. "Aye, lord. I would not see my sons' sons chattel on their own land."

"And whom will you follow in this battle?" a voice murmured from the shadows.

"Aye, I canna send more men to a war band that will ride leaderless," a voice from the back of the hall spoke up. It was Duncan, stocky and greying, a veteran of many war trails, whose steading lay far to the north and west.

"Aye, what of a leader with an arm he cannot use?" Berec took up the cry.

"You saw him use it not five minutes ago!" Cathuil roared.

"To pick up a twig, no more," Cawdor's smooth voice interrupted. "The question is, how *much* use has the High King of his arm? You cannot lead a war band with a twig."

"It is the law!" Berec shouted. "Remember the law, my brothers!"

"*Enough!*" Vortrix was standing, blazing with fury, sword in hand. "Am I a chariot horse for sale that you discuss me among yourselves in my own hall? You, Berec . . . and you, Cawdor . . . you've tried this before and are lucky to have the breath still in you—do you question my right to hold the kingship? It is mine by right of blood—and mine by right of battle—and *I . . . will . . . not . . . let . . . it . . . go!* See, I hold it—thus!" He raised the sword in his right hand. "If you think you can take it from me, cousin, then try—*Now!*"

Cathuil drew in his breath sharply. What did the young fool think he was doing? That arm would never hold. Oh, fool!

Could he use it, Galt wondered, or couldn't he? If he couldn't, he was taking a superb risk! Galt almost laughed at the beauty of it— what was behind the door, the lady or the serpent? With a bad arm, Vortrix didn't stand a chance. But Vortrix with two good arms was capable of dealing with Cawdor, or Berec . . . or even Conor . . . and Cawdor knew it. He had clamored for a test and Vortrix had offered him one, with a vengeance. But the price was high if he was wrong. Galt eyed Vortrix speculatively. That arm had looked bad enough the night he had helped old Cathuil steal the High King away from under the Romans' noses, and he still remembered their last conversation in the hut of the healer priest. Galt knew there was a crimson scar the length of the High King's arm hidden under his shirt sleeve. But it was the muscle under the scar that mattered.

Vortrix advanced a step toward Cawdor, the sword blade shining in the torchlight, his eyes blazing like a demon. "So! Who would sit in the High King's place? You, Cawdor?"

Cawdor fidgeted with the jewel in his cloak pin, remembering. "Nay, I do not dispute you, kinsman. Later, should that arm fail you, we shall see."

"Fool!" Conor murmured.

Vortrix sheathed his sword, hoping the trembling in his grip went unnoticed. "Let you bear witness, my brothers, that I have offered the test that was called for. Is there any other who disputes the High King's right?"

"Nay," Duncan spoke up. "It is proved." The old lord stomped to the front of the hall. "The man who willna back up his own words is none that I'd be following." He shot a contemptuous glance at Cawdor and stalked back to his place. "I am the king's man."

Cathuil breathed a sigh of relief. Duncan's steading was small, but the old warrior's word counted for much. Conor played silently with his dagger hilt. Cawdor was capable of stirring up trouble, but never of holding the Tribe under him. Fool not to have taken the thing when it was offered him. Vortrix's arm was no good—Conor was almost sure of that. Well, when the test did come, it did not have to be Cawdor who sat in the High King's place. Conor also had descent from the royal line, through his mother's blood, which was the old way and not entirely dead.

The old way was the way of the Mother, of the dark things of the earth, when the Queen was ruler and goddess both for her tribe, and each king died in ritual battle with his successor, a blood sacrifice to the Mother that the land might be fruitful and peaceful. When the tall golden people had come overseas from Gaul when the world was young, they had brought with them new ways, and the influence of the Mother had given way somewhat to the way of the Light, of Lugh Shining Spear, and the sacrificial death of the king had become a willing gift in time of great need, not a ritual slaughter. But the Mother held much sway still, especially among the Painted People and their left-hand kin, the little dark folk. Among the golden people, she was strongest in the women, and in the dark and secret places of a man's mind. But descent in the female line remained a valid claim to the kingship, and Conor knew it, though he had no mind to rule as a seven-year king himself. It was merely the place to start.

Vortrix was seated again, dealing with plans for the spring. A vengeance-hungry Legion was not his only problem; the Painted People showed signs of moving south again, and as reports began to come in from the northernmost clans the picture looked grimmer than ever.

Generations ago, the Painted People had been pushed gradually northward by the settlements of the Brigantes and their kin, where they had mingled with the little dark folk who had been there before them, and where they remained a thorn in the flesh as much to the golden people as to the Roman kind. The Romans had slaughtered them by the thousands thirty years before, but now it seemed that they had gathered their strength and were ready to push southward again, toward their old domains. The untimely raid on the tribal horseruns had been only the beginning. The Brigantes, caught between the Painted People and the garrison at Eburacum, had need to make peace with one or the other. And the High King knew there was only one choice.

Vortrix beckoned to Galt and lowered his voice as the household captain dropped to one knee in front of him. "So, my friend, it is good to see you."

Galt smiled. "And to see you, my lord. I have ever a soft spot for a man who takes a risk."

"It may be that we must take a bigger one yet, brother."

The moon hung low over the heathered hills, a round, fat moon that shed a watery gleam on the rocks and new spring grasses in the rider's path. The light changed almost constantly with the clouds which shifted now across the moon's face, and now away again, but there was enough to see by . . . and to ride by, for a man who knew the country.

He rode silently, his cloak huddled around him against the damp wind which blew from the north, and draped so as to give extra protection to the harp bag on his shoulders. An owl swooped low across the trail and the pony pitched and shied.

"Steady, little brother." The rider ran a slim hand along the pony's neck and spoke softly in his ear. "We'll talk to stranger things than owls this trip, I'm thinking."

The pony tossed his head and snorted, and the two moved northward through the wet night.

With dawn, they came to a little stream bubbling down over the rocks, and then to a hill steading half hidden by the encircling heather. Horse and rider drew wearily to a halt as an old woman emerged from the hut. She fixed them with a malevolent eye and made a sign with her hands.

"Good morning, old mother," Galt said. "May the gods look well on you."

"Huh!" She turned toward the hut and spoke to someone inside, then turned back to the visitor with no further comment.

There was a bustling inside the hut, and presently she was reinforced by a man of almost equal antiquity and two others much younger. Grandsons, perhaps. They were small, dark people, the lingering remnants of the people who had inhabited this land before the Brigantes and their kin had come with new weapons and new gods and swept the little dark folk into the wind like so many leaves.

"The sun and the moon on your path. May I enter?" Galt spoke carefully. Much was said of the little dark folk's magic, and while Galt generally remained a sceptic in such matters, he had a healthy respect for the powers of the hill people.

One of the younger men stepped forward. "I am Dree. What does the golden harper want with our house?"

"A place by your hearth to sleep this day. We have run all night, my horse and I. And a guide for the trail north at sundown."

"Have you the true music in you, harper?"

Galt smiled. "Some men say so. The god's gift is not for me to claim for myself."

Dree exchanged glances with his brother, who stood leaning on his spear shaft, and then motioned for Galt to dismount. "Come you in to the hearth then, harper. We will see to your horse. When you have slept perhaps you will wake your harp for us."

"That gladly," Galt said. "My thanks to you and your kinfolk." He followed the small dark man into the hut and settled himself on the bedplace that was shown him. There was a small stirring among the hill people, then they settled to the business of the day, ignoring their guest.

Galt sunk himself deeper into the pile of furs and bracken, firmly ignoring their smell, which was ripe and well aged. At his movement, the old woman eyed him darkly and then returned to her cook pots, muttering.

"Brother, the things I do for thee," Galt murmured to himself, tucking his forearm between his nose and a particularly redolent wolf skin.

Galt had been the High King's sworn man since their boyhood together in Dubric's usurping household, where the king had prudently kept his nephew under his eye. It had been Galt who had shared Vortrix's bitter tears and fury at his humiliation, Galt who had solemnly sworn a brother's bond with him when they were ten. They had gone through the dark and awesome ceremony of initiation together, and when the time was right, the bond was fulfilled in blood as Galt rode at the head of the war band that put Vortrix on the High King's throne and Rhiada on a bier beside his brother's.

Dubric, dead of a lingering infection in a wolf-bitten hand, Rhiada, dead three days later on the edge of Vortrix's sword . . . . Vortrix had stood watching the flames rise from the bodies, and then turned to Galt beside him.

"There will be an end now to kin killing kin," Vortrix had said, and Galt had kept his silence. But on the fringe of the spear brothers he could see Cawdor, bitter-eyed, watching his father's body burn. However loath the High King was to shed more kinsmen's blood, the time would come when he would have to, or see an end to all hope of the unity which would be their one telling point against Rome. Rome was losing that capacity to fight as one man which had been her bulwark. If the Tribe could learn it, and turn it against her . . . .

Galt slept until late afternoon, when he woke to find his four hosts regarding him unblinkingly from across the hearth. His fingers went to the harp bag and what it contained, and he sighed softly as he drew it out from under his cloak. "My thanks to this house for the place at your hearth," he murmured, sitting up and stretching himself. "I have slept well."

"That is good," Dree said. "The harper will honor our house by eating with us before he goes. And perhaps by waking the music in that bag he guards so carefully."

"She has borne me good company on many long trails." Galt laid his hand on the harp bag with affection. "I would be honored to wake her music for the house of Dree."

This exchange of courtesies completed, he accepted the bowl of stew and barley bannock which the old woman brought him. There was a slightly odd taste about the broth . . . not unpleasant, but different. Galt remembered the old women's stories of his childhood, of how a man ate of the little dark folk's food and was forever bound to them, and of his return to his own people to find them long dead and a hundred years gone by in the wind. He shrugged and continued his meal. *Not* to eat would have been an insult too great to be erased, and he was going to need the dark folk's good will. Without it he would have little need to worry about his possible bewitchment.

145

The stew was rich and satisfying, and he finished the last of it, then laid the bowl aside and drew his harp carefully from its bag. He ran his fingers along the strings in a questioning trill . . . the old music? It seemed appropriate.

Galt began to play, calling up the deep and stirring music that pulled at the heart . . . the old music of his Tribe, born centuries ago from the songs of the little dark folk when they were kings in the land. Dree and his brother sat silent, their eyes reflecting the shining sounds that filled the room, while the old woman stirred and cocked her head at the sound, and the grandsire, secluded in his deafness, fixed his eyes on the hands of the harper and seemed to draw the music from them.

Presently Galt began to sing, a lament at first, low and mournful, then changing with the music to a great striding sound that called down the very hounds of war and gloried in their coursing. He brought forth again the high and far-off days when the gods themselves came down on the horses of the sky and fought beside their mortal armies.

Galt's eyes were fixed on some distant space, and his face lay shadowed while the light of the cook fire danced in the white gold of his hair. No longer mortal, he was Music, and the sound that he called forth enveloped them all.

When he had finished, there was silence.

At last Dree said, "It has been long since I heard the ancient music made thus. Truly the golden people have bred a harper of the old ways."

Galt shook off the trance such music always laid on him and smiled. "Nay, then, merely a harper who loves his craft. Have you not such among your own people?"

"Aye, though these days they are few. But it was our music before ever the golden people came overseas. Or did you not know?"

"I knew. But the love of the music opens many doors." He slid the harp gently back in its bag and gathered his cloak about him.

"The sun is low, and I must be on my road." He looked at Dree. "I ask guidance of you."

"For the sake of the music, I will take you so far and no farther," Dree said. "But there are those who will serve after me, if I ask it."

"And will you?"

"That depends on why the harper rides north at night."

"No harm to you and yours. I have eaten your food and I swear it."

"I begin to see," Dree said, "but it is all one to us. Come then."

Outside the hut, Galt found his pony fed and bridled. He swung up and followed as Dree, barefoot and fleet, slipped like a shadow into the heather.

X

Birthright

EBURACUM WAS HUDDLED UNDER a sullen March drizzle as Gwytha picked her way across the camp, and the sentries squelched miserably from puddle to puddle, casting curses according to their nationality on a government unfeeling enough to send its subjects to drown by degrees in a marsh.

In the hospital, Flavius, perched on a surgery table, was happily singing a ditty about the shores of sunny Italy for the annoyance of the senior surgeon and his patients.

Seeing Gwytha in the doorway, he stopped his song, forestalling one of the more robust patients who was apparently preparing to stuff a bandage down his throat.

Licinius looked up from the unfortunate whose boil he was engaged in lancing and raised his dark brows at her. "Child, you're soaked to the skin. You've no business being out in this. Were you looking for Justin?"

"No, I came to see you."

At this, the owner of the boil, finding himself exhibited in a most undignified position before an unknown female, raised his voice in protest.

"It won't take me a minute to lance this," Licinius said, eliciting a further protest from his prisoner. "If you don't mind waiting . . . uh, perhaps in my office?"

She nodded and left Licinius to his victim. There was a howl of outrage as the surgeon applied his scalpel to the problem, and a few minutes later he joined her in the hospital office, wiping his hands and looking, she thought, indecently amused.

"Poor Balin. He's suffering as much from wounded pride as boils on the backside." He settled himself behind the desk. "What's Januaria doing to let you run around in the rain like this?"

"It never ceases to amaze me," Gwytha said drily, "what a hothouse flower I've become in the last few months. Licinius, I've *slept* in the rain."

"I suppose so. But there's no necessity for you to do it now. Unless, of course, it's a matter of pride."

"Oh, shut up," she said affectionately.

Licinius hesitated. It seemed as good a time as any. "Don't be too reluctant to accept the things Justin can give you. He needs to be able to, you know."

Gwytha studied her hands. "I . . . yes, you're right. But what about me? I must have some dignity left to me. It's bad enough knowing what this marriage has done to his life without feeling like a complete charity case."

"If you insist on *acting* like a charity case, and a grudging one at that, you'll do him far more harm than you did by marrying him. And as to that, I'm not sure you may not be a good thing for Justin. He has a great need of someone to love, I think."

"It should have been one of his own . . . and it would have been —except for me. Now he's trapped."

"And so were you or you wouldn't have married him. Don't think I don't know that. But I'm not sure . . . Gwytha, who knows how the gods work these things out? It may be that this marriage is what should have been. At any rate, you'll do better by acting as if it is . . . learn to love him, if you can. And let him love you."

Gwytha looked pale against the dark folds of her mantle. "Licinius, my friend, I would give . . . more than you know, for that to happen. But it has never occurred to me that it was possible."

Licinius was taken aback. Poor child, no wonder she had been having such a tough time of it. If the two of them would just let the barriers down . . . .

"Oh, I think it is, you know," he said, and smiled at her. "If not now, then in time . . . if *you* give it a chance. There is a bond between you that I think is stronger than you know."

Gwytha twisted at a fold of her mantle. "Very well, Licinius. If you, who know him better than anyone, say so, then I will try." Some of the weariness left her face and she laughed at him. "How very fatherly you sound."

"Yes, well, you make me feel old. Now tell me why you've come trudging up here in the rain, instead of biding at home like the lady you're supposed to be and letting me come to you."

"I didn't particularly want Januaria to know about it. Or Justin either, for that matter."

"Are you sick?"

"Only in the mornings," she said grimly.

Licinius started to laugh. "Well! That's a pleasant piece of news. You had me worried for a minute."

"*I* wasn't feeling very pleasant about it on the way up here. It looks a little less formidable now. But Licinius, I know Justin—this will tie him to me forever . . . and if he—"

"If you know Justin, then you know that he considers himself tied to you forever now. So for the gods' sake, woman, try to make it a pleasure to him!"

"But—"

Licinius stood up. "Come along, my girl, we're going to find out for sure. Then I'll argue with you."

"Well, I'm as sure as I can be," Licinius said, helping Gwytha to sit up on the table in the examining room. He dragged a chair over and sat facing her. "Probably about the end of October from what you've told me." He reached for the little records folder he had carried with him from the office, and made some notations. Then he pointed the quill at his patient. "Now let's get one thing straight —the first thing you're going to do is to tell Justin."

"Not yet." There was a stubborn set to Gwytha's mouth that belied her youthful appearance as she sat swinging her bare legs against the table edge.

"If you don't, I will," Licinius said firmly. "That's a promise. This is Justin's child as well as yours, and you have no right to deny it to him even for a few months. If you'll start treating your-self as his wife, and not an accident, you'll do fine."

"I don't want to be fussed over. And I don't want him worried about me when he's gone. He'll have enough on his mind with the Legion." She leaned down and began to pull on her boots.

Licinius looked exasperated. "My dear girl, Justin isn't stupid. He's going to notice your being sick. And I think you're going to be one of those women who show their pregnancy early. As to being fussed over, I shall give strict orders that you're not to be, if *you'll* promise to behave and do as I tell you."

Gwytha finished tying on her boots and then cocked her head up at him. "Very well, Licinius, it seems I haven't any choice."

"Indeed you don't. Now come back to the office with me and I'll give you something to warm you, and more advice than you want."

She got up and followed him back down the corridor, past patients' cubicles, and storerooms filled with bandages and blankets, and pots of ointments scenting the air with myriad unappetizing smells. An orderly leaning on a mop and contemplating the far wall drove it hurriedly into his bucket as Licinius appeared, and began mopping the floor with commendable energy. The senior surgeon had what the orderly considered an obsession with cleanliness, and he searched for hidden dirt with the zeal of a housewife.

"I should lend you Januaria," Gwytha murmured as they passed.

"I should kick him in the rear," the surgeon retorted in a voice pitched to reach the unfortunate orderly.

He led her into his office, stowed the records folder away, and produced a jug of wine and two green glass cups.

"Here. I keep this for special occasions. Or days when I've talked to one idiot too many."

"And which is this?" she inquired, accepting the cup.

"Special occasion. I'd like to have children myself someday. Now, then. You are to have plenty of meat, milk, fruits, and vegetables. Moderate exercise is good for you . . . you like walking, keep it up. I don't imagine I have to tell you you are *not* to lift anything heavy. I probably *do* have to tell you not to worry about your fig-ure. A little extra weight won't hurt you. If you get too vain, you'll only shortchange the child."

"Very well, I shall get as fat as Januaria if you tell me to—*She'll* be in a high old mood. With a new babe to mother, maybe she'll stop trying to mother *me*."

"Don't bet on it until after the babe is born." They both laughed. "But I *will* tell her that you'll do better if you aren't coddled too much." He pushed the curtain aside and peered out at the grey sky. "It seems to have stopped raining for the moment, so wrap up and take yourself home before it starts up again. I'll want to check you over again in about a month, but *I* will come to see *you*. Clear?"

"Yes, I will behave."

"Good girl. Tell Justin tonight, mind."

He watched her go, wondering if his advice about Justin had made any impression. He hoped to Hades it had. Justin was getting a fine-drawn look about him that Licinius didn't like. If Gwytha couldn't forget about the circumstances of her marriage and get on with the business of making it work, her husband was going to explode somewhere. And Licinius rated his friend's explosive capacity rather high . . . .

As Gwytha made her way back through the sodden fortress, she looked about her from a new perspective . . . barracks and granaries, drill hall and armorer's shop lay in orderly rows along roads as straight as an arrow's flight. It had always seemed a sharp-cornered world and alien to her kind. But now she was truly of the Roman world, bound to it by a half-Roman babe.

It had saddened her, in the long bitter years of slavery, even those she had spent with Aeresius, that she would never have a husband and children at the hearth. Now, unexpectedly, she had both . . . Licinius had seemed to think it a good thing . . . .

A scarlet-cloaked figure on the west rampart called out and waved to her, and she waved back. Hilarion, posting his sentries. She smiled reminiscently at his description of the bride his mother had selected for him ("pleasingly plump and terrifyingly stupid") . . . perhaps Justin was not so badly off, after all . . . . Then, seeing another face she recognized heading her way, she turned down a side street and made for the fortress gate by the long way round. She had no desire to outface Favonius right now.

In the wet streets below the ramparts she paused and stared at an elaborately carved cradle outside a woodworker's shop. But then it began to rain again, big fat drops that spattered on the ground, and the shopkeeper cursed and pulled his wares inside. She moved on, again taking stock of the Roman conquest as it appeared in these streets . . . the togaed officials of the city, the columns of the basilica, the steady rounds of the Watch, even the Roman ringlets adorning Venus Julia's "girls" who were gathered languidly under the portico of her establishment to watch the passing traffic and drum up a little business for a rainy afternoon. Gwytha fingered her own long braids . . . perhaps she would try that style. *That* ought to give Justin a shock.

As she turned up the street toward their house, Januaria emerged from the doorway, hands on her hips and scouting the neighborhood for her wayward mistress.

"There you are, my lady!" She came galloping forward, a spare cloak under her arm. "You're wet!" she exclaimed indignantly, engulfing Gwytha in its folds. "Come in the house this minute before you catch a cold!"

"All right, all right." Gwytha was laughing. "Only leave off wrapping me up like a bundle. I can't see!" She hurried into the house under Januaria's protective wing, and was ushered firmly into the bedroom to strip off her wet tunic.

"*And* your shift, my lady. You're wet to the skin. *What* the centurion will say, I *don't* know!"

"I doubt that she dissolves in water," Justin observed mildly from his seat beside the brazier. "All the same, get into something dry and come sit by the fire with me."

Januaria bustled out to the kitchen to dry her wet clothes on the hearth, the grey and white cat leaping happily after the trailing end of the mantle. Gwytha slipped into a dry shift and, on impulse, got out her best tunic. She settled herself at the dressing table, unbraided her hair, and combed it up into a knot on her head. Then, remembering Licinius's comment, she picked up the little pouch containing the stag's-head eardrops.

The last gesture made, she presented herself, combed and dried, to her husband.

He blinked when he saw the eardrops, but he didn't say anything, merely gesturing to the empty chair beside him.

She plopped down in it and stuck her toes out to the heat of the brazier. "I'm sorry to be back so late. I hope I haven't spoiled Januaria's dinner."

"So far as I can tell, the only thing getting spoiled around here is me. Januaria stuffs me like a goose with the best cooking I've had since I joined the Army, and you go trudging around in the rain while I toast my toes by the fire. What were you up to, by the way?"

Gwytha fidgeted with the folds of her tunic, then gave him a sideways look. "More than you'll be liking, maybe."

He leaned forward, intent now, and a shadow of concern slid over his face. "You're worried, aren't you? Gwytha, I'm *not* going to bite you."

She looked rueful. "That's what Licinius said. I wasn't going to tell you yet, but he made me promise."

"What in Hades has Licinius got to do with anything? For the gods' sake, Gwytha, get on with it, you're giving me fits."

Gwytha took a deep breath. "I'm carrying your child," she said as fast as she could, and then sat back, the worst of the telling over.

There was a moment's silence. Justin ran a hand through his hair and looked around the room, apparently assimilating this new complication. "Well," he said at last, "we might have expected it. Under the circumstances."

"Well, *I* didn't expect it!" Gwytha was indignant. "And you needn't laugh at me. It . . . just never occurred to me."

At this Justin began to laugh in earnest, his yellow eyes crinkled shut and one hard brown hand beating an exultant tattoo on the arm of his chair. Gwytha eyed him dubiously. "We shall never do anything like other people," he explained between shouts of laughter. "We might as well quit trying!"

"Then you're not upset?"

"I'm in shock. But don't worry, it's very pleasant." Seeing the doubt still in her face, he sobered and pulled her gently onto his lap. "Indeed I am pleased," he whispered and his arms tightened about her shoulders. More and more this world became his own, he mused, unconsciously echoing Gwytha's thought. Now he would have a child of this world. It seemed that, however unwillingly, he had come home.

"Dear Mama,"
Justin wrote at his desk in the atrium while the nereids regarded him in arch flirtation from the wall,

"I have a piece of news for you which may not best please you, as I don't fancy you'd counted on having to think of yourself as a grandmother for some years yet. All the same, you'd better brace yourself.

"We are going to have a child sometime in the end of October, or so Licinius says. And in case you're wondering what the senior legionary surgeon is doing playing midwife, he vented his opinion long and loud on the subject of 'old witches who couldn't deliver a letter safely' and who treated complications by waving a dead chicken over their victim's head. He then favored us with a wealth of statistics on the mortality rate for infants and mothers as a result of this barbarous attitude, and informed us that if he was in camp, he would deliver the child himself; and if he wasn't, he would tell Januaria exactly what to do and put the fear of the gods in her to see that she did it.

"Licinius is ahead of his time, I fear. He talks of the medical profession reforming its entire attitude toward childbirth, and is laughed down heartily whenever he expounds on this notion. But I can't help thinking of the two babes you lost before I was born, and the one you lost after, when we nearly lost *you* as well. No parent should have to live with that kind of grief unnecessarily. I am glad Gwytha will have Licinius to look after her.

"About Gwytha . . . when my posting here is over, or I have my next long leave, I would like to bring her to see you. I haven't mentioned this to Gwytha yet, as I suspect she would dig in her heels against the idea as much as you would. But it would please me greatly to see the two of you friends. Moreover, I think it important for the family now, because of the babe.

"And now, some things I have not told Gwytha, although I am sure she knows them well enough . . . I know that my marriage has been a grief to you. It was, in a way, a grief to me at first . . . and also to Gwytha; put yourself, if you can, in her place, and I think you will see that. But lately things seem different, and I begin to feel that perhaps this marriage has brought me something I would not have found elsewhere. Perhaps it is this land, that I hated so bitterly at first, and which now seems more and more a part of me. Perhaps it is Gwytha herself, to whom I find myself drawn more strongly than I would have suspected. Perhaps it is the babe that binds the two of us together, me to her world and she to mine.

I don't really know . . . but unexpectedly, I find myself content. Knowing that you love me, I ask that you be content for me."

Justin put down his pen and rested his chin in his hands. The late afternoon sun, making a rare appearance, sifted in through the window; he watched the dust specks dancing in it, and wondered when and how the change had begun to happen. In him, perhaps from the beginning, when he had found the idea of Gwytha as some stranger's property unbearable. In Gwytha it had seemed to stem from the coming of the baby . . . but somehow there was more to it than that. At any rate, something had drawn the tension from the air, leaving them still in an awkward state, but with more comfort than he had known since Aeresius died.

Finn, lying in companionable silence at his feet, lifted his head and scented the air, and Justin glanced out the window to see Januaria returning laden from her marketing. On her arm was a covered wicker basket, and from her other hand hung a string bag redolent of fish. Behind her pranced the grey and white cat, whiskers atwitch and eyes on the cloth-wrapped parcel in the bag. Finn heaved himself to his feet and Justin clutched at the inkpot and papers as the desk rocked with his passing . . . Finn never remembered that he was taller than that table. Justin was taking up his pen again when an eldritch howl split the air, echoed by cries of human indignation. He leapt to his feet and reached the kitchen door just in time to see a grey and white shape, teeth clenched in triumph on a fishhead, streak along the shelves, and Finn, lunging frantically in pursuit, bring down the flour bin.

"Typhon take you!" Januaria, emerging from the storeroom with a new broom, began to sweep clean, and the cat, sailing like a flying squirrel over Finn's head, hit the floor and dived between Justin's legs into the atrium. Justin prudently flattened himself against the doorpost as Finn hurtled by. The cat swarmed up the shuttles of Gwytha's loom and stood swaying on the topmost bar, and Justin watched in paralyzed horror as Finn hurled himself after him, landing squarely on both cat and loom.

Gwytha, sorting linens in the bedroom, turned around to see a cat fly by the doorway three feet off the ground, followed, as she watched in fascination, by her loom, which came shuddering down across the doorstep. An upheaval seemed to be taking place beneath the half-woven fabric on the frame, while Justin, across the room, was apparently having a fit of some kind. Gwytha dropped her linens in indignation as Finn heaved himself free of the loom, a square of weaving flying from his collar like a cavalry pennant. Cat and dog together flew out the open window and Gwytha, giving chase, collided with her husband in the doorway. Together they stumbled down the wet path, came afoul of a slippery stretch of mud, and fetched up against the trunk of the apple tree in whose topmost branches the grey and white cat was consuming the fish-head.

Side by side in a mud puddle, they sat and looked at each other. "No, Finn, let him go," Justin said weakly to the dog still hopefully launching himself heavenward. "Gwytha, my dear, your loom . . . I *am* sorry . . . in fact I'm prostrate with apology." He touched his forehead to the ground, eastern fashion, at her feet.

"Justin, get up, you'll get mud in your hair."

"If you could have seen Januaria swinging at that cat with a broom . . . and you! Going down the path on your backside!"

Gwytha began to chuckle. "That wasn't half the view we had of you, with your tunic up over your ears."

Suddenly they were clutching each other in laughter, while the muddy water soaked through their clothes and a passing nurse and her small charge regarded them from the garden gate.

At last Justin stood up and pulled Gwytha to her feet, and Hilarion, strolling in some minutes later, found them helping Januaria restore order to the kitchen, where the remains of the fish, returned to its string bag, hung suspended from the ceiling. He cast a wary glance about the room.

Justin and Gwytha exchanged looks and burst out laughing again, while Januaria explained with dignity the cause of their merriment. "And a fine sight they were, rolling about in the mud with that hulking great dog."

Gwytha grinned at him. "Januaria feels we've disgraced ourselves. And my poor loom . . . ."

The loom was standing again, but it listed drunkenly to the left. Hilarion ambled over to inspect it. "I wish I'd been here," he murmured appreciatively. "Where are the culprits?"

"Making themselves scarce." Justin heaved a collection of broken crockery into the trash bin. "Let us retire to the atrium and leave Januaria her kitchen before she takes a broom to *us*."

Hilarion settled himself in a chair and stretched his legs out comfortably. He was obviously big with news.

"Had you something particular on your mind," Justin inquired, ducking back to the kitchen for a jug of wine, "or were you just passing by?"

"Just passing by," Hilarion grinned at him. "I'll make *myself* scarce if you like."

"Certainly not." Gwytha drew up two more chairs.

"You can help us throttle the cat," Justin added. "Have you come from camp?"

"Mmm. Did you know the Governor's coming out?"

"I heard a story to that effect."

"Confirmed. He'll be here next week. Full-scale parade and all the trimmings."

"And does this mean—" Gwytha leaned forward to pour the wine "—that he will maybe be making some changes?"

"More men, you mean?" Hilarion was doubtful. "They've posted out some replacement cavalry. Not enough, though, and it's heavy foot troops we really need. Still, I doubt he could send them if he wanted to. The south is undermanned as well, and with more cities to patrol."

"No, they'll have to come from the Emperor," Justin said. "But all the same, we have to have them. This visit may be a step in that direction."

"Has he got enough influence to sway the Emperor, do you think?" Hilarion asked.

"I doubt anyone does, as long as the campaign in Parthia goes on. Still, we'll plead our case and see what happens. Stay and eat with us, Hilarion, if you'll excuse the fish."

A brisk little wind was blowing as the Ninth Legion Hispana assembled on the parade ground, rank upon rank of scarlet helmet crests and burnished armor winking in the sun, ten cohorts strong, each man with sword and dagger in their sheaths and pilum held at attention. The breeze ruffled the horsehair crests and flicked at the hems of their cloaks, and tickled at noses that didn't dare sneeze. It did, however, as Justin murmured to Lepidus, blow the flies away.

Scrubbed and polished, he stood at the head of his cohort, the seahorse standard gleaming beside him. To either side of the Legion were ranged the Auxiliaries, dark-browed Syrian archers, and the cavalries of Spain and Gaul with their banners shivering in the breeze. And at the head of them all loomed the Eagle of the Ninth, silver wings swept back as if to lift upon the wind.

There was a stirring about the commander's platform, and then the trumpets sang out, the Optios saluted smartly, and Marcus Appius Bradua, Governor of Britain, marched up to the platform with the Legate of the Ninth.

He raised his hand and the cheer went up, ragged at first, then gaining momentum; but always, Justin thought, listening, with an underlying current that echoed the dissatisfaction that lay beneath the polished bronze and brave show of the Ninth on parade. As the roaring died away, the trumpets sounded again and the whole Legion turned as one in parade formation, up, down, and around, coming back to rest with a flourish and the triumphant note of trumpets.

Justin, keeping a wary eye on his cohort, saw that they kept pace well for the most part, stepping out the drill with precision. They were, he thought with some pride, a far cry from the cohort he had first taken over. A fumble and a wrong turn in one of the lead cohorts sent a ripple of confusion eddying around it, but their officer barked an order and the guilty century righted itself. "Someone's for it," Lepidus murmured, making the precise quarter turn that signaled the second century of the Eighth Cohort to its closing formation.

The Governor turned to congratulate the Legate, and the Legion passed in review before him and out through the parade ground gates. Gwytha, from her vantage point among the crowd, watched them go . . . first, the Eagle of the Hispana, frozen in flight above his gilded wreaths of honor, then the Primus Pilus at the head of the First, with all the bronze and scarlet glory of his cohort behind him. Familiar faces and strange ones, heads up and stern under their helmet rims . . . Favonius with the Third, polished and shining, swaggering a bit . . . the commander of the Fourth, the one that had fumbled during drill, looking surly . . . Martius at the head of the Sixth . . . then the Eighth, with Justin, yellow eyes shadowed by his helmet rim and nose jutting unmistakably from under it. This was where he belonged, she thought, watching them swing past . . . where her babe, too, would belong if it were a boy. Strange to think

of watching a Roman son march out with a Roman Legion . . . .
The last of Justin's cohort passed, and her attention was caught up
by the Ninth Cohort, with Hilarion looking far older than the boy
who had sat talking in the atrium last night, his freckled face made
serious by a cohort commander's helmet, his thin frame no longer
gawky but dangerous in burnished steel.

The Auxiliary cavalry clattered by, their horses full of bounce
in the morning breeze, frisking behind their standard-bearer. And
the Army Medical Corps, Licinius with his junior surgeon and ap-
prentices in full dress uniform. They looked as solemn as the rest,
but she thought the senior surgeon winked at her as they passed. She
stood watching until the last of the column had marched to the barracks, their solemnity decreasing with their distance from the parade
ground and in anticipation of the games and celebration attendant
on a Governor's visit.

Justin had drawn street patrol duty (consisting, as he said, of preventing the populace from murdering each other in sheer high spirits), but Licinius and Hilarion found her and took her off with them
to watch the Governor's procession to the arena and the games in
his honor. They had changed out of their full dress kits and looked
much their normal selves as they escorted her through the throng
of mingled legionaries and townsfolk. Justin, on the other hand, posting his men along the opposite side of the street, was beginning to
look exasperated. The Governor was taking his time and the crowd
was getting restive with the exuberance of the first good celebration
to come their way after a long, dull winter. The townsfolk had
turned out in their festival best, and the merchants were doing a
thriving business, hawking everything from hot pastries to cures for
catarrh. Urchins with bunches of April flowers and trays of dried
figs zigzagged through the spectators with pleas to "buy something for the lady." A strolling snake charmer, his unsavory pets
stowed in a basket on his head, offered to perform for coins thrown
his way, and Venus Julia's girls, rigged out in their spring best,
strolled giggling through the throng, making eyes at susceptible
males. Hilarion, Justin noted, was buying his wife figs.

There was a flurry of hoof beats and the first riders in the Governor's escort appeared, troops from the Second Augusta and the
Twentieth Valeria Victrix who had ridden north with him, followed by an honor guard of the Ninth. Governor Bradua, chat-

ting amiably with Metius Lupus, rode in state behind them. He acknowledged the cheers of the crowd with a gentle wave of his hand. There was a stirring behind Justin as two young townsmen exchanged a rude joke. He fixed them with a firm eye and they looked abashed. Then from somewhere in the crowd a rock came flying over their heads and clattered at the feet of the Governor's horse. The stallion leapt and curvetted, and the Legate, purple with fury, shouted an order to Justin. His men turned with leveled pilums against the crowd, and it lapsed into tense silence as the procession resumed its progress.

Gwytha, watching nervously from across the street, saw Justin haul a ragged child out of the crowd. Faced with the spears of the soldiers, the boy seemed to disintegrate with terror.

"He give me a penny to do it," the child wailed. "The man did, a penny!" He exhibited the evidence in a grubby paw.

"What man?"

"I don't know! A big man. Oh, please, let me go, I didn't mean no harm!"

Justin knelt down and looked him in the eye. "You're lucky you aren't older, my boy. As it is, I think you're too young to be much of a threat to the Empire. Now you tell me what man gave you a penny."

"One o' them." The child pointed at the soldiers still lining the street.

"Are you sure?"

"No . . . but he was like 'em." The child tugged at Justin's grip on his forearm. "I didn't mean no harm."

"No, but I'll be bound someone else did," Justin muttered. He turned the child over his knee and gave him a swift smack. "That's for throwing rocks at your betters, even for a penny. Now take yourself off."

He stood up and surveyed the crowd. There would be precious little chance of finding the man with the penny. In uniform, one legionary would look very much like another to a seven-year-old. He swore and turned back. "All right, move along. The parade's over. And remember that this kind of thing does none of us any good."

The crowd melted away like smoke and Justin made his way over to Gwytha and his friends. "It's going to be a long day."

"Was that what it looked like?" Licinius asked.

"Mmmm. One of ours. Damn them!"

"This is hardly going to dispose the Governor in our favor," Hilarion said. "Any idea who it was?"

"No. 'A man gave him a penny.'"

"Justin, this is serious."

"Don't I know it. I just hope it doesn't give some other damn idiot any ideas."

Justin returned to the house in town late that night, tired and disgruntled. Gwytha was curled on a couch in the atrium, a pool of light from the oil lamp casting her face into sharp relief. She opened one eye as the door opened, closed it again, sat up, and stretched. Slowly both eyes opened, and she gazed at him foggily.

"What time is it?"

"Well into the third watch." He dragged his breastplate over his head and flung it in the corner. "What are you doing still up?"

"I wanted to be sure you were all right."

"What did you think was going to happen to me?"

"How should I know what your precious Legion is going to do? But you talked as if there might be trouble."

"There's trouble enough when a man of the Legion commissions a rock for the Governor. If he'd been caught that would have been the end of him. As it is, things aren't going to be very pleasant for any of us. We've all drawn double duty for a month."

"Was there any more trouble?"

"No, they're all tucked safe in their little beds," he said disgustedly. Justin had spent a trying night collaring drunks, settling financial disputes between the wine-sellers and their customers, and separating legionaries who wanted to punch each other's noses out of sheer exuberance. In between he had overseen the search for "the man with the penny." His shin ached where it had been kicked in the process of breaking up a fight between one of Venus Julia's girls and a local competitor; he was tired, and he wanted to go to bed.

Gwytha held out her hand, and he let her lead him into the bedroom, sitting docilely while she unbuckled his sandals and stripped his tunic over his head. She pushed him gently down on the bed and curled up beside him. Next to her soft warmth, he found the prospect of an uninterrupted month in barracks long and bleak. Stirring, he wrapped an arm around her and pulled her close. As always, the same wild longing took him as he cradled her.

Gwytha turned her eyes to his, caught them, as if searching for something . . . and then suddenly it was as if a door had opened and set free a longing in her to match his own. She ran her hands along his body and smiled in delight as she felt his response. And then, her eyes still on his own, she pulled him down to her.

Gwytha had been a compliant and agreeable bed partner from the first, but always her own emotions had been held in reserve, and Justin had known that the wild and dark desire which always took him when he lay with her was not something which she shared. Lately it had seemed that that reserve had begun to thaw . . . and now suddenly it was washed away on a wild spring flood of emotions so strong he could watch their changes in her eyes. He pressed deeper inside her, his eyes locked hungrily on hers, and the joy on her face as she felt and mirrored his throbbing want of her was blinding.

Exultantly, he laughed and gripped her harder, and together his hard, scarred body and her soft one rolled entwined, and Justin knew for the first time the satisfaction of giving over his whole soul to one whose soul came flying out to meet him.

As their mounting passion pulled them higher, he felt he could not bear to lose this wonder yet, and he sat up and back, astride her. For the first time she took her eyes from his and lowered them to watch his body join with hers. He reached out his hands to the upturned tips of her breasts, feeling them harden between his fingers, until she reached up to him with her eyes and brought him down to her again.

And suddenly the desire that drove him was longing no more, but the joy of the one half as it comes together with the other. And thus, deep in each other's eyes, they mounted the peaks of the world together, and lay at last spent at the gates of Paradise.

A bitter wind from the north rustled in the streets, scattering the night's debris, and the grey dawn hung in the trees as a shivering bugler made his way across the Principia and blew an icy reveille.

In the house below the walls, the light of the forgotten oil lamp shone where two sleeping figures lay still entwined.

XI

The Spring of
Many Horses

THE MEADOW WAS alive with new foals. Bays and duns and blacks, they frisked about their placid dams, heels high in the air, sending up showers of pebbles and tufts of new grass. Galt, leaning his arms on the stone wall that fenced in the lower end of the little valley, watched them with approval. He nodded his satisfaction at Ewan, the grey-haired horseman who schooled the chariot herd.

"Aye, they be a good lot." Ewan scratched his chin and followed the careening foals with an approving eye. He was a taciturn man who spoke more freely to his beloved horses than to his fellow tribesmen, and Galt privately suspected that the old trainer thought him a frivolous fellow. But since Galt's skill with horses was near the equal of Ewan's own, he had the old man's grudging respect.

Of the mares taken in the Painted People's raid, all but two had been recovered, and the herd had been augmented by twenty more sturdy brood mares and as many promising two- and three-year-olds as Vortrix had been able to buy. The additions had been made quietly, bought singly for the most part, with no mention of a purchase on the High King's behalf.

"How many could be war-trained in, say, a year, think you?" Galt asked.

"Of our own stock, all of this year's two-year-olds, and they're the biggest lot we've had yet. You might put some of this season's yearlings in, but it's not a thing I'd advise," he added drily.

"Nor I, friend, unless it's do or die." Galt knew well the price of taking an untrained horse into battle, and it generally came high. "What of the new stock?"

Ewan scratched his head. "Early days yet, Lord Galt. I've not had time to work with all of them yet, and some of them with bad habits already, no doubt. 'Tis best we breed our own when we can."

Galt smiled. "Ewan, if you can come up with a way to breed a three-year-old in a year, the Mother herself has indeed smiled on you."

"Hmmmph. A year, is it? He's mad."

"A year, perhaps more. But better we were ready, eh? Come now, what can be done with the new stock in a year?"

"See for yourself, then." He turned and walked away down the lane, bowlegged and irascible. He led the way to a paddock where a young tribesman was schooling one of the newcomers. The stallion was a dark steel grey color, wicked as a sword blade, and a full hand higher than any of the horse herd. He circled, ears flattened, at the end of his lead line and appeared to be barely under control.

"That's one of your precious 'finds'," Ewan spat. "Three years old and evil as a demon."

"Ah, you beauty." Galt took in the fine head and powerful shoulders, and the fire in the dark eyes. A war-horse out of legend, that one. "Where did he come from?"

"Away to south. He's had bad treatment, I'm thinking, and now he hates the lot of us."

"Is he trainable?"

"By one man maybe. If there was one with the time and skill to do it."

At a signal from the young trainer, the stallion halted his gallop and stood quivering as the boy approached. Suddenly there was a flash of hooves and the trainer was rolling frantically out from under the plunging horse.

"The devil!" Ewan was over the paddock fence in a second, with Galt behind him. The horse reared and came down hard on the trainer's legs, and there was the sickening crunch of bone.

"See to the lad!" Galt yelled to Ewan, grabbing for the lead line as the horse raised his great forequarters up again in panic. Galt caught the line just below the halter, and before the powerful neck muscles could shake him, he had caught a handful of the flying mane and leapt on the horse's back. The stallion screamed and plunged, while Galt, the lead line still in his hand, strove to pull the grey head around.

Ewan caught the injured trainer under the shoulders and dragged him out of the paddock while the stallion kicked and twisted to rid himself of the terrifying creature who clung to his back. Galt, one hand wrapped in the grey mane, increased the pressure on the lead line with the other, hoping the stallion wouldn't tangle his forelegs in the flying end of it and bring himself down. Slowly his frantic plunging began to move in an ever-narrowing circle, as Galt pulled his head steadily around to the left . . . and finally, with his muzzle almost against his shoulder, the grey stallion stood still, shivering in panic and terror.

Gently Galt stroked the quivering shoulders. "Someone has put the fear in you well, brother, and it would take longer than I can give you to show you different." He slipped down from the stallion's back, a careful grip on the lead line, and led him to the far gate where the paddock opened onto the brood mares' meadow. "Is there another stallion with them now?" he called to Ewan.

Ewan looked up from the splint he was fashioning. "Nay, the old boy's on t'other side o' hill. And old he is, too. Are you thinking what I am?"

Galt opened the paddock gate and slipped the halter from the grey head. The stallion stood stock-still. "Go on, then, brother," Galt said softly. "It's a better life than I can give you. And mayhap someday I'll drive your sons instead." Suddenly the stallion shot like a streak through the open gate. Galt closed it behind him, watching sadly the grey form flying in freedom down the hillside.

Then he turned his back, and together he and Ewan gently carried the injured boy up the hill to the house.

Taking the homeward trail, Galt looked about him wistfully. Ewan's tally sticks were tucked in his saddlebags, a full record of the number of brood mares, foals, yearlings, and older horses in the herd. In his head he carried Ewan's estimate of how many chariot-trained he could provide in a year's time . . . and the memory of

Ewan's parting comment: "You'd do better to stay here wi' me, young harper. Any man may carry a spear . . . but you've a rare way wi' a horse."

He could see the grey stallion below him in the meadow, head up against the wind, guarding his mares and his newfound freedom. Rounding the hill, he came to another little valley pasture, and the old bay stallion, among his mares, recognized him and whickered as he rode by. Galt had spent most of his childhood summers here in the horse runs, and the old stallion was a friend. He stopped to rub the bay nose thrust across the fence, and searched his saddle for a piece of sweetcake to give him. The stallion whuffled appreciatively in Galt's ear, slobbering sweetcake down his collar, and the harper laughed.

"Yes, I'm sorry to have cut you out with some of your mares, old friend, but Grey Brother will sire fine colts for the herd." He gave the old stallion a final pat and remounted, turning his horse's nose homeward again. It was pleasant and peaceful to the soul here with the frisking colts and the cool green hills. Maybe when there was peace for the Tribe again, he would come back.

He moved on, through familiar territory now, far different from the roads he had ridden north two months ago, and came, as the sun fell on the next day, to the High King's northern hall. A crowd of urchins was rolling happily in the dirt with a half-grown litter of puppies as he turned through the gates. One of them, seeing him, detached himself from the melee, shook off a cloud of dust, and galloped ecstatically to the harper's side.

"You are back, sir!" He turned a pair of shining eyes on the older man. "Come and hear what I have learned to play! The High King my uncle said I might play in the hall the night you came home if you permitted!"

Galt slid down from his horse and hoisted Dawid into the saddle. "Steady, youngling. I will listen very soon, but first I have business with Lord Vortrix." He unstrapped a long, awkward bundle wrapped in hides. "Take Nighthawk here and give him water—but not too much, mind—and then put him in the paddock for me."

The boy rode off happily, his short legs dangling from his perch, pausing only long enough to exhibit himself to the envy of his earthbound companions. Galt turned up the steps of the High King's hall.

Inside, the hearth fire was smoking abominably, and Galt peered through the murk to find the High King seated well out of the draft. Old Cathuil was with him, looking sternly at the small "hound" who was frantically trying to keep the wet wood under control.

Galt plunged coughing through the cloud and knelt before Vortrix. "My lord has need of a drier place to store his wood," he murmured, clasping the High King's hand in greeting.

Vortrix smiled. "Even kings get holes in their roofs, brother. There now, young one, leave it be. There's nothing you can do." The boy bowed and scampered off, and Vortrix turned to Galt. "How was thy trail, brother?"

Galt took the hide-wrapped bundle and unwrapped it carefully. Then he sat back on his heels and looked at Vortrix while Cathuil whistled softly under his breath. It lay on a bed of wolf skin, wicked and gleaming: a six-foot spear, deadly sharp at the blade, and collared with a ring of white swan's feathers.

After a moment Galt handed Vortrix the tally sticks and began to speak of the horse herd, but again and again their eyes came back to the war spear at their feet.

"A dangerous game," Cathuil said once, and again there was silence.

And once Galt flicked a finger along the haft. "It may bite us still," was all he said.

Finally the High King rose to his feet, bent and reached his right arm down for the spear. He hesitated, and whether it was for the wound in his arm or the deadly life in the spear, neither man could tell. Then, with one swift movement, he grasped the haft and raised the spear upright. "Call the Council," he said.

Branwen took stock of her reflection in the polished bronze of the mirror, while one of her women plaited her blonde hair into two neat braids, each ending in a little gold sheath at the tip. Her body was still as slim as ever, and she had arranged her girdle to best advantage to show it. With luck there would be no need for anyone to know about the child she carried for another two months. She dismissed the waiting woman and turned sideways to the mirror, looking for the telltale rounding of the belly she had seen in other women. Not yet.

Vortrix knew—she had told him as soon as she was sure, and if necessary, he would send her home to her father and brother rather than let anyone know the High King's queen was with child while there was yet any doubt of the High King's right to rule. Too many of the tribal lords would rebel at the prospect of another regency and the division and civil war it might bring with it. If she, and the unborn babe with her, should meet with an accident, there would be many, even among the loyal lords, who would breathe a sigh of relief. And some, like Cawdor, would have no compunction about killing her outright. Even if the babe was a girl, she would remain a potential source of dangerous descendants.

The curtain in the doorway fluttered and the High King burst through it, shattering her grim reverie. "Come, it's time we were in the hall."

"To face such of your Council as have arrived?"

His eyes were dancing. "I'll have a thing or two to show my Council," he said. "Look." He pulled his sword from its sheath and executed a pass against an imaginary opponent. Another pass, and then another, and the sword slipped from his grasp. Branwen bent to pick it up, but he was ahead of her, retrieving it with his left hand and slipping it into the sheath.

"You see, it is healing," he said, and only the two of them knew what that progress had cost him in hours spent forcing pain-twisted muscles to move at his will. He slipped an arm around her gently. "By summer's end there will be no more need to bluff."

"If it is truly healing, until then I can bluff as well as you." She let him lead her to the door. "Do you speak to your Council tonight?"

"Nay, not until they are all here. I will discuss this matter once and no more. Besides," he smiled as, golden head by golden head, they paced sedately up the hall to the High King's table, "I have more important matters to attend to tonight. Young Dawid makes his debut as a harper."

All the same, he took silent stock of those present, as the hounds who served the High King's hall scurried about with flagons and platters, and the four-footed hounds who lay beside their masters' chairs followed them with hopeful eyes.

Cathuil was there, of course, a grey bulwark seated beside the queen, and, farther down the hall, her brother Donal, Dawid's father, who had driven in that night. Galt, to the High King's other side, appeared unconcerned with anything save his protégé, who was pouring mead at the far end of the table and looking as if he might drop the whole flagon out of sheer nerves at any moment. But Vortrix was well aware that when his blood brother seemed unconcerned, he was most likely to be dangerous.

Conor was there, quietly watching the High King eat his meal, and Cawdor, sulkily eating his own across the room. Talhaiere, impressive in his priestly robes, was talking quietly with Cathuil. They had been boys together and saw eye to eye on certain matters. Berec would arrive in the morning, though no one, except perhaps Cawdor, seemed to miss his presence at the moment. Duncan would most likely be there by late afternoon tomorrow.

Those present seemed content to wait for the morrow to discover why the High King had called them in. For the moment, the mead flowed freely, and the sacrifice of some of the High King's best spring lambs did not go unappreciated. As the meal was ending, the boys came out to dance the Spear Dance for the assembled lords, its wild, sweeping music and flying spear points catching them all up in the exultation of the hunt . . . or the battle, depending on the interpretation the dancers wished to give it. Tonight the battle aspect of the ancient dance of the Tribe was most evident, and its effect on the watchers was not lost on Vortrix who had had a private word with the leader of the dance earlier in the day. Enmeshed in the sound and the pattern of the dancers, they shifted in their chairs, some unconsciously fingering sword hilt or dagger. It was the Dance of Death, of bloody victory and the end of the enemy, blotted out like a candle flame to rise no more, while the Tribe danced singing on the grave. Few men could watch a spear dance such as this one without emotion. Of them all, only Conor sat unmoved, his unwavering eyes fixed on the High King, and curiosity in his gaze.

The dance ended in a flash of spear points and a shout of triumph, and then the dancers were only the High King's hounds again.

Vortrix beckoned to the youngest of them, a freckled urchin with bright blue eyes and ears like a jug. "Go and fetch young Dawid. Tell him he may bring his harp."

The boy nodded and scampered around the edge of the hall to the group of boys at the far end. "I hope your harp's in tune," he whispered, grinning at Dawid. "The High King wants you." Dawid took the harp from the bag he had hung on the wall behind him, and started, heart pounding, for the head of the hall, while behind him two of the older boys suppressed the message bearer ruthlessly for lack of respect for his elders.

"I am told you have the music in you," Vortrix said. "Will you wake your harp for us?"

Galt, seeing that his protégé was becoming more petrified by the moment, smiled reassuringly and murmured to him, "Indeed, *I* have told him so, and I'm sure you wouldn't wish to cast us *both* into disrepute."

Dawid smiled and took his cue. "I shall endeavor not to do so," he said with such an inflection of Galt at his driest that the others laughed.

"You have taught your pupil well, Galt."

"A harper needs many things besides his music. Keeping his head in a crisis is but one of them."

Dawid took the old harp lovingly from its bag and ran his fingers along the strings, letting the music wash away his nervousness. The Council Lords and their retinues settled back to listen. The blue-eyed urchin, undaunted, dusted himself off and perched, legs a-swing, on the end of the boys' table, while the other boys also fell silent in anticipation. The gift of music was a great thing, and few men were blessed with it. It was a source of pride to them all that the master harper saw that gift in Dawid.

The wooden frame was oiled and rubbed to a glow as soft as candlelight, and the strings were shining and alive with the music in them. Slowly, as Dawid touched them, the music began to emerge, a song as old as the golden people themselves, of a daughter of the Sky Folk who loved a mortal king and gave up her powers and her free world of wind and clouds to be his queen. In the end she died, as mortals will, and her sisters mourned their lost one, seeing her always in the faces of her children from generation to generation. In time her descendants forgot that ever they had a foremother from the Sky Folk, but the wind and rain remember her still and sigh for their lost sister when a mortal with her likeness passes by.

As Dawid drew the last note from the strings, it hung in the air like the voice of the wind, and even the High King sat in silence until it had faded past hearing.

171

Then he lifted his brows at Galt, who nodded. Vortrix leaned forward. "Do you wish to be a harper, little brother?"

"Oh yes, sir!" Dawid looked from one to the other, eyes shining.

"Then if Galt will take you for pupil, you are excused from housekeeping chores that you may have time to learn your craft. But you must not let your training with your spear brothers suffer. The Tribe has need of warriors, and I am told you show promise there also."

"Yes, sir. I promise."

Then Galt also leaned forward, taking from his wrist an ancient and finely wrought band of red gold. "This was given me by a very great old man, who woke the music in *me*. I would have you wear it if you will come to me as fosterling." Dawid hesitated, and Galt added gently, "I have spoken to your father, and you have his blessing."

"Th-thank you, sir. I will come, and gladly." The boy took the armband and slipped it on his own, pushing it high up on the fore-arm for safety.

Galt touched him on the shoulder. "Very well, youngling. We will talk later." The High King nodded his dismissal, and Dawid picked up his harp and made his way slowly down the hall to the gleeful approval of the boys' table. Their congratulations were tinged with envy for one excused from the housekeeping chores which were part of their duties and overseen with a firm hand by the women of the king's house, but there was no real malice in it; a harper in their midst promised to enliven their lives considerably.

Dawid gave his father a look of gratitude as he passed, although custom forbade his speaking to him now. They would find each other when the evening was over. Donal watched him go with a pride that was tinged with bewilderment. He himself lacked any ear for even the simplest music. It had been a source of wonder to him, ever since Galt had first spoken of it, that he had sired a harper.

The night was getting cold, and a biting wind whistled in the rooftree and set the torches to sputtering. Two of the boys threw more wood (now mercifully dried) on the fire, and the women of the house came out to dance. Galt pulled his own harp from the bag and took up an accompaniment to the drumbeat kept by a brown-haired girl with braids almost as long as she was. The women's robes swirled about them and their golden jewelry caught the torchlight as they whirled and leapt, their feet as light upon the rushes as swallows in the wind. Branwen, tall and golden as a shaft of sunlight, danced at their lead, taking the line in intricate formation around and through the trailing dancers. Unlike the Spear Dance, theirs was a dance of new beginnings, of the kernel in the corn, the bud within a winter tree and the promise of a babe unborn. Vortrix, watching his wife spin by him, arms outstretched, thought perhaps she wove a double meaning in her steps. If so, it was meant for none but him; Branwen could indeed bluff as well as he. He had done well when he took old Cathuil's daughter.

And the spirit of rebirth, which the dance wove around them all, served to end the evening on the note he wanted.

"And so we are to continue to bleed ourselves dry to put grain in Rome's storehouses?" Berec turned furiously to Vortrix where he sat in the great oaken chair at the head of the Council Hall.

"That is right, Berec," Vortrix said quietly, "and the man who does not will answer to me." He was dressed in his best, in a robe of sleek furs and the golden torque of the High King around his neck. His boots were of the soft leather worn only indoors, pricked and patterned with blue woad in much the same fashion as the spiral tattoos on his face and chest. His golden hair, brushed and shining, hung loose over his shoulders, brilliant against the dark back of his chair. He was impressive to look at, but beneath the finery was still the warrior—patient, watchful, and dangerous.

"So we put our necks meekly into the Romans' yoke and plough where they bid us?"

"For the time being, Berec, you will plough where *I* bid you."

Conor, who had been making much of studying the toe of his right boot during this exchange, now looked up. "I would suggest that we hear the whole of Lord Vortrix's plans before we brangle about the part of them," he said.

"Aye." Duncan, stiff from the long journey, shifted in his seat by the fire. "I have driven far for this council, at the High King's word, and it is he I will hear."

Vortrix murmured something to one of his household and the man slipped from the room. "I know as well as you that no High King may rule without the consent of the Council. But that consent, once given, may not be withdrawn at your caprice. I am king and *I will rule*, and that will end the matter." He leaned forward, his hands gripped tight on the arms of his chair, and looked at them one by one. "By the Spear of Lugh, can you not see? We must be *one* people, or we will be *no* people . . . we will go down before the Romans as the little dark folk went down before our fathers' fathers."

There was silence for a moment, and then the priest Talhaiere spoke for the first time, in the low voice of one accustomed to be heard in silence. "The High King speaks the truth, for I have seen it in the night sky . . . and there are yet worse wolves than Rome. The time has come for us to learn to hunt together."

"And think you not that there will be no payment for this lesson," Vortrix said. "I have sent to Eri the trader that we must have all of the new blades that he can bring us this season. And so now we must pay double tribute for our hunting—to Eri for the blades we need and to Rome for the time."

"And what of those who have paid already, in burned steadings and slaughtered cattle?" Donal's voice was bitter, and Vortrix knew well what the Legion had left behind it of Donal's hall.

"They must give what they can, brother, and we will ask no more. If we are to be as one, we must pay as one." He pulled the torque from his neck and sent it clattering to the floor. "Thus we will pay if need be."

"This is insane," Cawdor said.

"Nay, it is good trading." Vortrix stripped off his arm rings and the circlet from his head, and sent them spinning after the torque. There was a moment of uneasy silence, and then Galt stepped forward and pulled his own jewels from him. With a wry smile of farewell, he added them to the pile.

"All my vanity, stripped away so easily," he murmured, and the others began to laugh.

But the crowning touch was provided by Branwen. Choosing her moment well, she had entered the hall unnoticed, and now she marched to its center, clad in the plainest of her gowns, to spill her dower chest upon the floor, a little rain of gold. Behind her came her women, carrying finely worked cloth and furs, and jewels of their own. When the last bolt of cloth was stacked in the middle of the hall and the last eardrop had rolled down the little pile of gold and come to rest against the shining torque of the High King, Branwen turned to the Council Lords and raised her brows.

"Can your women not do as well?" she inquired, and then, gathering her ladies about her, she swept from the hall again, a commanding figure in a plain grey gown.

Donal, looking less grim, grinned at her as she passed, and.she winked at him, never breaking her stride. Still smiling, he pulled an enameled brooch, his only piece of jewelry, from his cloak, and laid it with the rest. The little vixen! He'd be willing to bet she and her lord had thought that one out beforehand.

All the same, it had its effect. One by one, some eager, some shamefaced, the Council Lords came forward and made their gifts . . . Cathuil's golden arm rings and topaz-studded brooch . . . Duncan's silver belt buckle . . . Conor's amber necklace and heavy golden ring . . . Cawdor's rings and eardrops, and—when Galt looked at him pointedly—a little jeweled dagger in a wrist sheath; Berec, with a beautifully worked bracelet of enameled copper links and a cloak pin of red gold. Then the warriors of Vortrix's house, with armbands and collars of copper and bronze, and a few precious bits of gold. Even the small jug-eared boy who was tending the fire scrambled up and pulled off a tiny drop of amber on a chain. "It came to me from my mother's mother," he said, his homely freckled countenance upturned to the High King, "and she is dead now. Better that you have it."

And last of all, Talhaiere, stately in his snow white robes, and carrying the golden diadem of the sun that was the mark of his priesthood. He laid it gently with the rest and whispered over it a ritual none but he could hear, running his gnarled fingers lightly over the surface of the sun, as if to seal its outline in his mind.

"Father, this is not necessary," Vortrix said gently, but Talhaiere shook his head and smiled.

"Nay, its power lay in the Mystery within it, and I have called it forth again. The rest is but metal."

"May it not still be used to bring ill upon us?" Donal asked.

"It shall be melted and cast, and the last of its light shall go out in that fire."

"I cannot say I like it all the same," Cathuil said.

Talhaiere came and stood by him. "Cathuil, we hunted together from our boyhood, and we are brothers still, for all that our paths have taken different ways. Cannot you believe me when I tell you that it is but a trinket now, the outward trappings of a Mystery too great to be captured in a piece of gold?"

Cathuil nodded and Talhaiere swung round to face the others. "It is fitting that it be sent to save us, for if we cannot stem the Roman tide, *all* our old ways will be taken from us, and we shall die. It is as simple as that." He took his seat again, and his face regained its usual expression of serenity, but Galt, seated beside him, heard the priest mutter into his snowy beard, "Superstitious old fool."

Cathuil's inaudible comment substituted the adjective "pompous," but otherwise it echoed that of his old friend. Thus they remained in charity with one another. And when Galt had made his report on the horse herd and the financing of Eri's goods, and when the next installment of tribute had been worked out, the two came forward together to pledge themselves, and such of their households as would follow, to the High King's service.

Vortrix, knowing that there would be few in those two households who would dare *not* follow, thanked them gravely and proceeded to accept the pledges of the rest of the Council.

"I am the king's man." "The king's man." Donal and Duncan bowed and moved on.

"Yours, brother." Galt knelt gracefully before him, but his eyes were grave.

"I am the king's man in this matter. So I swear." Conor, who could afford to wait.

"The *king's* man," pledged Cawdor, with subtle emphasis.

"The king's man."

"So now we hunt as one," Duncan said when it was over. "But we have chased this wolf before and found him overstrong. This is our last chance to make a kill, I think."

"I did not speak of the Tribe alone." Vortrix rose and took the white-collared Pictish spear from its bed, and the shadow he cast towered on the wall behind him. "This time, *Britain* hunts as one."

XII

Trimontium

IN THE HIGH PEAKS the snow was melting, and the little streams danced and bubbled down the hillside to the sea. The stream beds were alive with minnows and crayfish, and water bugs skated leisurely on the surface. The banks were cool and green under the trees, thick with maidenhair and hartstongue. In deeper waters, the fish were waking from a winter sleep, rising idly to the bait of the persistent. The wolves paid less attention to the pastures of man, and turned their noses to the forest where their prey was growing fat again. Everywhere was the drone of bees, and the air was wild with birds.

In Eburacum the Legate's rosebush was blooming, and green shoots were coming up in the kitchen gardens where the "on report" list labored with hoe and trowel.

It was spring and the world was out and about again. Swallows swooped and twittered in the portico, and the scent of honeysuckle mingled with the fresh and fishy odor of the market stalls and the briny smell of oysters in their tanks. Justin and Gwytha, coming in from the walks they snatched in Justin's few off-duty hours after the Governor's departure, bought oysters by the plateful, consuming them raw and washing them down with flasks of cheap sour wine from the stall across the road, while Finn wheedled bones from his tame butcher in the next street.

Licinius, beset by an inclination to lie in the new grass and count clouds, was irked to find himself counting spring colds instead; while Flavius was no happier to be counting bandages while spring rolled by outside his window.

Hilarion, who had drawn extra duty for the Governor's rock along with the rest of the Legion, was forced to curtail his promising romance with Cordaella, and then to abandon it entirely when she took her favors and her free time elsewhere. Ruefully he watched a parade of hairy calves march by on the drill field and thought of Cordaella's plump white ones.

Lepidus, afflicted with an unexpected case of spring madness, got into a brawl with another centurion in a wineshop and drew a dressing down and three days confined to quarters from Justin, who then went back to his own room and laughed himself sick at the memory of his staid second in command, helmet hanging over his one unblackened eye, trying to explain that he thought it was about a girl, sir, but he wasn't sure. No, he didn't think the other centurion was either.

Gwytha, with the Legion on a month's punishment, spent much of her time with Januaria now. But after the night of the Governor's visit, she was content to wait, and the cold, sinking feeling she used to get when she thought of Justin and their marriage was gone. In gratitude for Licinius's unasked-for marital advice, she took his medical advice religiously, eating as she was told and walking for miles over the spring countryside with Finn beside her, waving his plumed tail above the tall grass. Since Licinius was also doing extra duty, she would often stop and pick up Whitepaw as well.

Whitepaw was still quartered at the Head of Neptune, now under new management. The owner had arrived early in the spring, and there had been a sticky moment when he had inquired as to Gwytha's whereabouts. But since the shop itself was enough to cover Aeresius's debt to him, and as he had no wish to tangle with the tall, dark-browed centurion who informed him curtly that the wench was now his wife, he decided to let well enough alone. He intended selling the shop anyway as soon as a buyer could be found, and any effort to reclaim Gwytha which kept him stuck in a dump like Eburacum town for a minute longer than necessary was, as he told his junior partner, not worth her price.

He looked curiously at the freedwoman the first time she came
for Whitepaw. He remembered her vaguely from the time, a year
ago, when he had supervised the delivery of a shipment to Aeresius
. . . a tall British wench in an outlandish blue and saffron checkered
tunic and two long brown braids wrapped in deerhide. This, however, was a Roman lady, taller than most, but with a graceful car-
riage, and clad in a tunic and mantle of soft blue wool worked with
a pattern of white vine leaves at the hem. She was shod in soft
leather boots of a deeper blue, and the brown hair was now coiled
in an intricate knot on her head, the front trimmed short and arranged to fall in soft curls about her forehead. She wore a pair of
gold eardrops cast in the same stag's-head pattern as her centurion's
signet ring, and her cheeks and lips had a rosy glow that bespoke
skillful use of a paint pot. She was also, he thought, with child.

She gave a soft whistle that brought Whitepaw hurtling from
the storeroom, thanked the shop owner gravely, and turned back
down the road, the two dogs racing exuberantly ahead. The pro-
prietor watched her go, saw the junior surgeon from the fort wave
and call out to her and a thin, freckled centurion with a stubborn
chin stop and speak affectionately. Apparently she had other cham-
pions than her beak-nosed husband. Nor did her new and elegant
image altogether erase from his mind a picture of the wench clout-
ing a drunken legionary halfway across the wineshop. All in all, he
thought he had been wise.

But Gwytha, for all her air of assurance, had thirteen years of
slavery behind her, and it had left its mark. She breathed a sigh
of relief when the shop was sold to a time-expired soldier come
back from a Rhenish Legion, who knew nothing of her story.

Meantime the Legion, grumbling, worked out its month's punishment and was almost immediately ordered out on patrol. Justin's
cohort went with them.

"It's not fair!" Gwytha clung to him the night before they
marched, her soft hair falling about his face. "We've had so little
time. Just when—"

"I know. Just when things were happy between us." He kissed
her and settled her head in the crook of his arm. "It won't be long.
I'll be back before the babe is born."

"I was so happy, even when you couldn't get home. Now I'm
afraid."

"I doubt I'm in much danger this trip. The Brigantes are paying their taxes and behaving like little gentlemen. Even old Cathuil has rebuilt and moved back to his hall. He even comes into Isurium sometimes to show us how law-abiding he is." Suddenly he sounded disgusted. "They're too good to be true, of course. *Why* won't the Emperor leave Parthia alone and save the provinces he's got?"

"He thinks he can hold it all, I expect. But I think he puts too great a distance between Rome and the edge of her Empire." She propped herself up on one elbow. "Justin, I would like to see Rome sometime."

"Well, then you shall. But you surprise me."

"It's a part of you . . . and of our child. And now I suppose I'm a part of it. Tell me about Rome."

Justin closed his eyes, remembering. "Lovely. A city of marble. It shines. At a distance anyway. Close up it has its horrors, like any other city, I suppose. But it's beautiful all the same. The mother of us all."

"Would you live there?"

"Perhaps for a while, for the excitement of it. Not forever. Gwytha—"

"Yes?"

"Would you like to go back to *your* people? You said once that you would never go back . . . but now, with me, and the babe?"

"I don't know. I would like to see my mother again . . . but I don't know that she would like to see me. She lost a child of the Iceni. Would she want back a grown woman with a Roman lord?"

"Would they hate me so much?"

"Perhaps. They might even hate me. There is no love for Rome among my people. I don't imagine *your* mother is overjoyed either," she added drily.

"She'll come round. Does it bother you still?"

"Not as it did. You are the other half of my heart, and you have learned to love me. Nothing else is as important." She touched his face lightly, tracing the ridge of his brow and the angle of his nose.

"If we're lucky, the babe won't inherit *that*," he murmured, looking at her like a cat through half-closed lids. He pulled her into his arms again. "Think about it. We could go south this winter when I have leave. Your world is part of *me* now. I would like to see it."

She sighed and snuggled against him, and the need of her, as strong as ever, overcame him. He rolled over, pinning her beneath him. Her legs opened and closed around him hungrily as he took her.

In the morning, he marched out with his cohort and two others, north toward Cataractonium. From there they would branch westward to Alauna and Luguvallium, then east along the northern frontier, and sweep north and west again through the outpost forts of the old province of Valentia. They would return again through Luguvallium, south and east to the main northern road above Eburacum. Another detachment under the Primus Pilus would make the southern sweep through Lindum and back, a shorter tour by half. The Legate with the northern detachment, and the Primus Pilus with the southern, would inspect the marching camps and outpost forts, drop off replacements, collect those whose tour of frontier duty had expired, and further the good behavior of the Brigantes by, as Justin said, "letting them know we have our beady eye on them."

Gwytha watched until the last tail of the baggage train rattled out of sight, and then turned back to the house to help Januaria with her baking. Finn drooped dejectedly at her heel.

"You miss him too, don't you?" Finn pressed his muzzle mournfully against her chest, and Gwytha rubbed the grey head. "Come, then, I'll find you a bone."

Finn followed her into the kitchen where the grey and white cat spat at him from the cupboard. Taking the bone gently in his jaws, he retreated to the atrium to worry it in dignified silence.

Feeling much the same, Gwytha took out her bread pans. The sun flowed through the window, making bright pools on the floor; everywhere was the scent of roses and honeysuckle, and a nightingale was running through his repertoire in the garden. It was a glory of a late spring day, and the house had never felt so bereft.

To Justin, in a miserably uncomfortable marching camp on the Alauna road, the world was also very empty. His life seemed to have turned itself around of late, and there were parts of it he didn't know how to tackle.

The matter of Gwytha's people, for instance. Should he have let well enough alone, or would they accept her . . . and if they didn't, how much would that hurt her? The Iceni had no fondness for Romans, least of all the Ninth Legion. This had been forcibly demonstrated over fifty years ago when their warrior queen Boudicca had led an uprising that all but destroyed the Legion. Two thousand men were slaughtered, along with the citizens of Camulodunum, Verulamium, and Londinium. Then an avenging force drawn from two other Legions had marched in and laid waste the country of the Iceni until all that was left of a once-great people were a few scattered and leaderless villages. There would be little love there for an officer of the Eagles.

A bugle shrilled reveille outside his tent. "Go blow your damn horn someplace else," a voice muttered from a tent across the road, and Justin pulled himself out of the cramped camp bed, feeling in the semidark for his sandals. They were on the march again today, north toward the frontier which marked the sphere of Roman domination. Taxes were demanded, and occasionally paid, from the tribes of Valentia to the north, but since the frontier had been pulled back such requests were more often ignored than not. Once, when Agricola commanded in Britain, the Eagles had pacified the land as far north as the fortress of Inchtuthil in Pict country. Under their war leader Calgacus, the Picts had brought thirty thousand men against the Eagles, and their defeat by Agricola's army at Mons Graupius had broken the Picts in two. But then Agricola had been recalled to Rome, and the Emperor Domitian, troubled by war in Germany, had pulled the Second Adiutrix out of Britain.

The combination had been fatal. Within four years, the lack of manpower had forced the evacuation of the legionary fortress at Inchtuthil. And slowly, as a new generation of men grew up among the Picts and boys whose fathers had died at Mons Graupius came to manhood, the Roman frontier fell back and back, under a steady pressure of ambushes and raids, too undermanned to mount a campaign of reconquest. Now the Army patrolled the north only when, like last summer, there was an immediate danger to be dealt with. This summer's sweep would take them only as far as Trimontium, little more than a day's march north of the Segedunum-Luguvallium frontier line.

The territory of the Brigantes extended north of that line, but most of their holdings lay below it. There were rebuilt steadings and newly planted fields everywhere. Taxes and good manners were much in evidence. As for Vortrix, his family holding lay northward in the lowlands, and there he was presumably lying low.

Justin tightened the straps of his breastplate, crammed his helmet gloomily on his head, and went out to inspect his cohort.

Ten days later he was squelching through the mud at Vindolanda, one of the least delightful of a string of rundown frontier fortifications. It was raining, as it had been ever since they had reached the frontier. They had been rained on in camp, rained on throughout the march, and now they were being rained on through holes in the roof. The summer rain came down in sheets from the north, and up from the south on a howling wind, slamming together over the frontier and pouring buckets on the ground below. The Army got a cold, the cavalry horses got thrush, and everyone got heartily sick of Vindolanda. It was understandable that postings to the frontier were generally of short duration.

The commanders of the northern forts reported no martial activity among the Brigantes, and taxes were coming in from the northern holdings as well as the southern. There was more likely to be trouble from the Picts, in their opinion; the blue bandits were raiding farther and farther south, preying almost indiscriminately on Roman settlements and British alike. The Selgovae, who were kin to the Brigantes and whose land lay between them and the Picts, were quiet, although it was known to be unhealthy to linger in their territory too lightly armed. And when were they going to get some reinforcements?

Everywhere the story was the same. The auxiliary garrisons of the northern forts were desperately thin of men, and their discipline in the harsh conditions of the frontier, and without strong leadership from the Legion, was deteriorating rapidly. The Legate gave orders for shoring up the worst of the problems, and moved on.

"This used to be a rearward fortress. Now it becomes an outpost." Justin was perched on the rampart of Trimontium, where he and Licinius had spent the evening with the Legate and the rest of his senior officers discussing the situation in the north with the garrison commander. Originally built to hold a full Legion, Trimontium had been garrisoned only with a small body of Auxiliaries since the Eagles had pulled back from the north. Its red sandstone ramparts shone huge and lonely in the moonlight beneath the three peaks which gave the fort its name, and small insect noises drifted up from the grass below.

"Aye, and we'll end up pulling back from this too, in time, if they don't bring in someone to stop the rot."

"When I was posted here, I thought we could," Justin said. "Now

I begin to wonder if anyone can. Or am I becoming like the rest of them? I know I *care* what happens, and not for the Legion only."

"Britain exerts a strong pull," Licinius said. "I remember telling you when you were first posted here. Now you begin to understand."

"I understand that we are all that holds this island free of sea raiders, or the next invasion. Without the Eagles and the Fleet, the sea raiders would grow bolder and the tribes would be pushed aside as they pushed the dark folk. If we had another Agricola, we could make this island a fortress *no one* could conquer."

"Including Rome. That may well have occurred to the Emperor too, you know. It would be too easy for a British Governor to name himself Caesar and stand off the best that Rome could throw at him. I doubt we'll get the chance."

"All the same, the Eagles *must* endure here, or there will be a burning like has never been seen. Bah! I sound like Cassandra." He kicked against the stone wall of the parapet.

A lantern came swinging along the walkway and the sentry paused and regarded them dubiously. "Sorry, sirs, I didn't recognize you. Whatever are you doing up here?"

"Admiring the view," Justin said.

"Aye, well, you'd best be getting back to your camp. It's going to rain like Hades."

"How can you tell?" Licinius looked at the sky, star-strewn with only a light wisp of cloud across it.

"You get to know, out here. It'll be coming down by the pailful in an hour."

"Judging by the weather so far, I imagine he's right," Licinius said, getting to his feet. "Come along; it's a good two miles to camp, and I've no mind to swim it."

The Legion had been put to use repairing the Trimontium road on the march north, and had consequently installed itself where the work was, in a small marching camp to the south. They would be barracked at Trimontium the next night to conduct repairs on the fortress itself (the present garrison was too small to do more than keep it operational) before heading across the mountains to the western outpost stations.

Licinius, who had made the same patrol sweep before, two years ago, was disquieted by the evidence of disrepair and suspicious that it was not entirely due to lack of men. This impression was heightened during their stay by the large number of tribesmen, men of the Selgovae, who frequented the fortress apparently unchallenged. The Legate didn't like it either, and ordered the commander sharply to shape up his security, or be prepared to get a very nasty surprise one day. The commander assured him earnestly that he would do so.

"In a pig's ear," Justin said. "Hasn't Lupus got sense enough to realize the garrison's probably making a very tidy profit in trade and paying for it by bending rules?"

"If he does, he doesn't think they'll risk getting knifed in the back for it. The other possibility probably hasn't occurred to him."

"Which is?"

"That Trimontium is the Selgovae's hidden asset," Licinius said shortly.

"Do you think they're that far gone?"

"I hope there's never a rising up here, or we'll find out."

"They ought to be replaced."

"What with? Do you honestly think the other Auxiliaries are in any better shape? And we can't spare a legionary cohort."

"Then we'd better pray to Mithras that the north stays quiet."

Licinius looked at him. "That's not a bad idea, taken literally," he said.

By common consent they turned their steps toward the temple of Mithras outside the Trimontium walls. The mystery of the Mithraic sect was not one which was often discussed even between initiates, and they walked in silence, their thoughts shared but unvoiced. There was no formal ritual scheduled that day and no vestments to add solemnity to their service, but helm and breastplate were fitting garb in which to worship the god of soldiers.

The temple, built by a long-ago commander at Trimontium, was small and cavelike, with a double row of benches lining the nave. At the far end, flanked by the twin torchbearers of light and darkness, was the carved relief of a great bull, his head bent back before the knife of the man who rode him . . . Mithras, the Guide and Mediator, whose word was Light.

As initiates of the soldier's degree, Justin and Licinius were not permitted the sanctum opposite the altars but were free to enter the main temple at any time. And Mithraism was a sect whose initiates formed their own priesthood.

It was dark, with only a small window to light the altars of the Bull-Slayer, and they stood still a moment to accustom their eyes to the dimness. Then Justin began the invocation, his armor washed with a faint gleam from the window as he moved before the altars.

"Oh, Mithras, Unconquered Sun, Redeemer—"

"Grant us thy aid and intercession—" Licinius also stepped forward.

"And take our pleas before the Lord of Boundless Time."

"As you slew the Bull for our sakes—" Justin raised his dagger to the altar.

"Take now our Sacrifice, freely given—"

"And grant us strength."

They knelt, side by side, and in the absence of the Wine and Sacrifice, pricked each the other's forefinger and rubbed the blood along the stone edge of the altar. Then, eyes fixed on the face of the god, they made their vows in silence. The cloud cover shifted and the little window gleamed golden, shining on breastplate and helm and softening the shadows of their faces.

"Mithras, Lord of Armies, grant us victory."

They rose and, giving homage at the place of the Father, made their way out into the light.

A week later, the repairs at Trimontium completed, and the freedom of the Selgovae about the fort curtailed on the Legate's order, they were on the march again, this time southwest across the mountains to the outpost of Castra Exploratorum, there to receive the official surrender of the High King of the Brigantes.

Treaty had been made the previous summer with Cathuil as the High King's agent, the king himself being too near death to be moved. The Legate, with the testimony of Justin and Licinius as to Vortrix's wound, had accepted that, but demanded a personal appearance in future by Vortrix (or his successor) as part of the bargain.

He had considered demanding Vortrix's hide as well, but since the Legion couldn't wield enough force to ensure that the new king would be of their choosing, he had decided against it. A new king might forget his allegiance to Rome as speedily as Vortrix had; whereas Vortrix with a bad arm afforded a source of internal dispute which might be used to break the tribe apart. Castra Exploratorum was the nearest fort to the High King's hall, and a number of the extra troops the Legate had brought with him would be staying there, much to their dismay.

It was a dismal place for a surrender. Built by Agricola in the heyday of his drive north, Castra Exploratorum now marked the northwest outpost of Rome. The turf and grey stone ramparts were solid, but there was a bleakness about the place. The commander's quarters, in which the Legate was installed, were dark and full of unused rooms where cobwebs hung in ropes from the ceiling. The Optio had taken one horrified look at the state of the Principia and ordered it scrubbed from top to bottom. Now the legionaries and Exploratorum's auxiliary garrison stood at attention in the grey afternoon light, lining the road the High King would take, while the Legate and his senior officers awaited him in the Principia.

Justin, scrubbed and polished in full dress kit, stood uncomfortably in the row of officers posted behind the Legate's chair. There was a clamor of hooves and horns, and five chariots swept through the open gates. The mist was coming down already, and it wreathed about the horses' fetlocks and gave a ghostly image to the light wicker chariots careening behind them. In the lead, behind a team as grey as the mist, rode the High King. His driver, who carried a harp bag slung from his shoulders, was the same slim warrior with the girl's face that Justin remembered from the battle of Cataractonium.

Vortrix was dressed in a wolfskin cloak, and boots and breeches of soft grey leather. Even his eyes seemed to reflect the mist, and only his hair, shining palely about his face, gave testament that he was not indeed a being created from the grey air.

As the chariots came to a halt, he vaulted down and, with his driver and two of his household guard, strode forward to make his service to the Legate. His face was grim, and as cold as stone, and Justin could imagine what this afternoon was costing him. The High King knelt to Rome, in the person of the Legate, and his eyes caught Justin's. Only then, as yellow eyes met blue across the top of Rome's helmet crest did a trace of emotion cross his face. What emotion, Justin could not be sure. The light in the blue-grey eyes flickered once, and then he was looking down again as the Legate pronounced the terms: so much in tribute, so many men for the Auxiliaries, so much in indemnity.

Vortrix nodded and, in the lilting accent of the British, asked truce and pardon for the war band. The Legate also nodded, seals and signatures were affixed, and it was done.

Vortrix and his spear brothers turned in silence from the Principia, wheeled their chariots in the road, and were gone. This time the High King drove his own team, shaking them out to their full stride until the chariot rocked and bounced over the roadway and his blond hair streamed out behind him like a torch. The last ray of sunlight winked and went behind the hill, and the five chariots vanished into the forest, the thickening mist deadening even the sound of their passing.

The Legion came back to Eburacum in August sunlight, through fields thick with rabbits, popping out of the wild grasses like puppets, ears at attention.

There was news of some sort in the air as Justin followed the other officers into the Principia to report. The men were standing about in groups of two and three talking softly as Centurion Geta came up to him, his wrinkled face even more sober than usual.

"You won't have heard yet," he said. Geta had gone with the Primus Pilus on the southern patrol and had returned almost a month ago.

"What's going on?" Justin asked in an undertone. (The Legate preferred official announcements to come from him without any preliminary gossip.) "Something big, it looks like."

"The Emperor's dead," Geta said.

"How?" This could mean a good deal of trouble.

"Natural causes, I believe. For a change," he added with a bit of a smile. "We only heard last night."

"And who to succeed?"

"Hadrian, they say."

"Well, that's good, then. There'll be no sword-made Emperors with their eye to the purple while Hadrian's wearing it. What is—" He broke off as the Legate coughed and strode to the front of the room.

"Officers of the Ninth," he began portentously, and Justin braced himself. The Legate was a politician of the old school and could hardly be expected to pass over the chance to deliver himself of a lengthy speech on the virtues of the new Emperor and a flattering eulogy of the dead one. The two were fortunately not incompatible (it was always awkward if they were, trying to combine pleasing the living power with proper respect for the dead one), since Trajan had been his successor's foster father. Still further lengthening the speech was the fact that the Tribunes of the Legion, whose year was almost up, were both present, giving the Legate some cause to hope that the gist of his remarks might reach the ears of the new Emperor.

Justin eventually made his escape to see his men settled in barracks. The whole fort was rippling with excitement and speculation. A new emperor could mean new postings, new policies, new favorites. . . .

"Don't be an ass. He'll pay no more mind to us stuck up here at the world's end than Trajan did."

"Aye . . . go out and get killed for a damn rotten province that's not worth a denarius, that's what we're good for!"

"Maybe things will change now."

"Sure, and pigs can fly. There's only one way to change anything here—"

"Shut up, here comes the commander!"

Justin fielded questions, gave out all the information he could, and departed with the admonition that while the proclamation of a new Caesar would mean games in his honor, bonuses, and other largesse, none of these would be forthcoming to any man of his who did not behave with the circumspection of a Vestal Virgin.

"There will be no 'man with a penny' among my cohort, and if I catch him, I'll put his penny where he won't like it."

"Hear that? You better watch your ass, Drusus," one of them laughed as Justin left.

"Nay, it wasn't me," Drusus said sulkily. "'Twas one of Centurion Cassius's. Not but what a rock's less than they deserve."

"Oh enough, go to bed. Me, I intend to enjoy the handouts. I hope the Emperor's generous. I've got my eye on a little Egyptian piece. . . ."

The body of Trajan, uncaring, lay in state at Selinous while Hadrian took stock of his Empire.

As Justin turned in the garden gate, the door of the house flew open, and a figure far rounder than he remembered came hurtling down the path and into his arms. He held her for a moment, smiling down into her eyes, while Finn danced hysterically around them.

"I knew you'd be a while in camp, so I didn't come up," she said.

"There are rumors flying all over. Is it true? And I have missed you!"

"I have missed you too, and yes, it's true, little Eyes-and-Ears. Your sources are accurate as usual. The Emperor is dead."

"And what of the new one?"

In the house, he piled his armor in the corner and stretched out gratefully. "Hadrian? I don't know. He's a soldier. As good a man as any from what I hear. I suppose we must wait and see." He pulled her down on the couch with him and kissed her. "You're getting fat, my girl."

Gwytha gave a little hoot of laughter, her eyes dancing. "Yes, it kicks me now, and very hard too. They say that means a boy."

"Hmm. I suppose 'their' guess is as good as anyone's. Are you well? I want Licinius to look at you again."

"I am very well, and Licinius has other things to do than play midwife. But I'll see him this week if you like." She buried her face against the hard muscles of his forearm. "I am so glad to have you home."

Januaria, returning from an information-gathering tour of the town, quietly collected Justin's gear to stow it in the bedroom, and left them thus until dinner.

The meal was a special effort on Januaria's part, her own welcome-home to the centurion, a miraculous array of milk-fed veal, peas, pastries, and summer fruit. The evenings were warm in mid-August, and afterward they sat companionably under the portico in the long twilight, listening to the sounds of river traffic and the tramp of the Watch. Gwytha was giving herself eyestrain over a pair of tiny boots while Justin polished a summer's rust from the blade of his hunting spear. Finn, who knew what that meant, stretched his great paws out and thumped his tail on the paving stones.

After a while they were joined by Licinius and then Hilarion, drawn by the murmur of voices and the open gate. The surgeon kissed Gwytha on the cheek and inquired after her progress while Hilarion perched on a chair opposite and regarded the domestic setting wistfully. Inevitably, as with all conversation that night, the talk turned to Hadrian, the unknown quantity, and now the ruler of them all.

"And what will the new Caesar do now?" Gwytha asked.

"No one knows yet," Hilarion said. "One would think he would feel somewhat bound to keep to his foster father's policies, at least at first. But they say he's pulling back the boundaries in the east. All hell's broken loose in Egypt and Mesopotamia. Trajan overreached himself, I think. But it's early days yet."

"And will that mean more troops free for Britain?"

"Not for a while yet, I shouldn't think," Justin said. "Things are scrambled all over the Empire. Eventually maybe." *Too late maybe*, he thought, but he didn't say it.

Gwytha snipped off a thread. "A year ago I would have said the fewer Romans in Britain the better. Now I suppose I am become one. At any rate, I begin to think differently."

"About Rome or about Britain?" Hilarion asked.

"I love this country as you love Rome . . . or your Eagles. This is *my* land. But I begin to see that Justin is right. Always there have been wars among the tribes. And before, there were wars between us and the dark people. My people came from Gaul . . . in the north, they came overseas from Eire. In between, we battle the sea raiders and the Northmen. Someday they too may decide to settle and begin raiding land instead of gold. And then they will push us out as we pushed the dark people. Rome could make us one people, strong enough to hold our land against them."

"But you would still be ruled by Rome."

"I have seen what the sea raiders do. They burn and kill for the joy of it. Of the two, I prefer Rome."

"A pity young Vortrix doesn't."

"Vortrix thinks he can unite the land himself, but I think that day will not come in his lifetime. I think also that when it does come, it will be Rome with Britain. We cannot go back and shut our island off. Rome is too big to be ignored. And there are worse things than Rome."

"You're right, of course. But how flattering." Justin eyed her slyly. "I've always wanted to be regarded as a necessary evil."

Gwytha grinned back at him and made a rude gesture very few Roman ladies would have known, and the seriousness dissolved in their laughter.

August faded to September, and September to October, with no further word of the new Emperor's activities other than confirmation of the rumor that he was indeed pulling back the eastern frontier of the Empire. The games in his honor lasted all through September, and Licinius spent much of his time with the black eyes and broken heads of exuberant legionaries with largesse to spend and fine fall weather to spend it in. Venus Julia did a thriving business, and the wineshops and beer stalls laid in extra casks. The harvest celebrations of the tribes and the approach of Samhain added to the festival atmosphere.

Gwytha's baby was born, as predicted, two days before Samhain, the Night of the Dead, when the world made ready for winter and the shades of the dead walked free in it, bringing good fortune to those of their descendants who honored them properly.

"Get the centurion! And Licinius the Surgeon!" Januaria took one look at Gwytha and sent a village urchin scurrying through drifts of fallen leaves up the road to the fort.

"I'm all right," Gwytha gasped.

"Of course you are, my dear, but it's as much as my life is worth not to send for the surgeon. He's told me so often enough. Now you lie still and hang onto me, there's my good girl."

Licinius came in half an hour, brisk, professional, and comforting. But Justin was on duty, and by the time he could get away, it was over.

He came flying down the road, still in armor, terrified at the idea that something might go wrong, only to be met at the door by Licinius. At the sight of the surgeon, blood-spattered and weary, Justin turned white.

"There's always blood at a birthing, you idiot," Licinius said. "Januaria, come in here! Give this man his baby before he faints."

She bustled in and Justin found himself holding a small howling bundle with a wrinkled monkey's face.

"They all look like that when they're born," Licinius said, laughing. "That's your son, Justin. He'll improve with age, I assure you."

"Nonsense! He is very beautiful." Januaria took the baby away indignantly. "You are dirty, Centurion. Go and wash and then you may hold him again."

Justin shook himself out of his state of shock. "Gwytha?"

"Asleep," Licinius said. "You may go and look for yourself, but don't wake her."

"Thank you. I . . . Licinius, don't go yet. Get Januaria to give you something to drink. I won't be long." He walked slowly into the bedroom and stood looking down at his wife. She was asleep, her brow beaded with sweat and her face weary. The linens had been changed, and her brown hair spilled out on the white pillow in a wave. He pulled the covers up around her, and she opened her eyes.

"He *is* going to have your nose," she said, smiling up at him, and then she was asleep again.

XIII

Aurelius Rufus

HADRIAN HAD DONE SOMETHING after all. Seated at a makeshift desk in a marching camp in Syria on his way to Nicomedia, he had taken a long hard look at the map of the Empire, the record of Rome's domination of barbarian tribes and ancient civilizations alike. Then he had taken pen and ink and inscribed his orders in sweeping lines on the map itself. And the Parthian campaign was over.

Then, his grey face austere in the twilight, he had begun his work of reassignment . . . .

". . . To Britain as Governor, Q. Pompeius Falco, reassigned from Lower Moesia . . . .

". . . To Legio IX Hispana, Aurelius Rufus, as Legate . . . ."

And privately to both of them, "Get up there and stop the rot."

The Optio's hammer rang sharp in the morning air, and Justin paused to read the proclamation. He had just come from a briefing in the Legate's office where the change of command had been announced. Metius Lupus had served nearly five years with the Ninth and was more than happy to be recalled. He had merely announced that the new commander would be arriving within the month, and dismissed them. Now, feet propped on his desk and hands clasped behind his head, he was hoping that the weather would hold clear for a winter crossing to Gaul, the first leg of a pleasant journey back to Rome.

Q. Pompeius Falco . . . Aurelius Rufus . . . names on a proclamation, unknown or known only by hearsay. But something was being done! And Justin had heard that weakened lines were being strengthened elsewhere in the Empire, and the eastern rebellions summarily dealt with. It was a beginning, and Justin turned home with a lighter mind than he had had in some time.

The situation had grown worse than ever over the autumn months. The bonuses and games in Hadrian's honor had carried spirits on a high tide for a while, but then the celebration was over, leaving flat dissatisfaction. The restlessness had begun to grow again as the boredom of the winter months progressed. The "on report" list was lengthy with cases of malingering and outright insubordination, each incident seeming to trigger another. There were a frightening number of cases of brawling, and one horror of an incident in which a legionary had tried to knife his centurion and been killed by him instead. The centurion, whose nerve was completely blown, had hastily been posted elsewhere and as little noise made of the incident as possible, but the blow to morale had been shattering.

Justin and Hilarion, wrestling with their own men, found it harder and harder to maintain effective discipline in the face of other cohorts that were growing dangerously out of control. Even Favonius and Martius were plainly growing worried, but the months of neglect had already done their work, and they found that their commands had become precarious. The legionary who had been killed by his own centurion had been of Martius's cohort, and Martius's other officers walked gingerly now.

"I feel as if I'm picnicking on Vesuvius," Justin said to Licinius. But the disintegrating morale of Eburacum Fortress could not quite destroy the solace he found with Gwytha and the baby in the house below the walls.

Young Justin—Marcellus Justinius Corvus, for Justin's father— was now two months old, a golden-skinned baby with Gwytha's red brown hair and eyes that were gradually changing to the amber color of his father's.

Justin was as proud of him as any new father could be, and was content to spend his evenings lounging beside the cradle, watching him wave his fat baby legs in the air and discover his toes. Gwytha too seemed to have a softer, rounder look to her, although she said disgustedly, eyeing her waistline in the mirror, that came from all the weight Licinius had told her to gain. Justin wrote Julia Valeria a glowing description of her grandson, sent it off by military post, and was rewarded by the return of a letter much softened in tone from her last one and the gift of a fine shawl of pale green wool to swaddle small Justin in.

He had just dropped both package and letter on his bed in the barracks (this letter he *would* show to Gwytha) and was about to strip off his armor and head for the bathhouse when there was a commotion on the ramparts, and the young centurion in charge of the sentries came flying down the steps in a shower of snow. Justin shrugged his breastplate back on as an Optio pounded on his door. He caught up his helmet and joined the crowd heading for the main gate.

The transport *Nausicaä*, the same one which had brought Justin to Britain, was nosing her way up the river, oars dipping to the beat of the hortator's mallet and an honor guard of troops standing at attention on the deck. A short, spare man with greying hair and a lined but not unhumorous face stood leaning on a staff in the bow. A dark-haired girl of about nineteen stood beside him, one arm draped affectionately about his shoulders. Her figure was muffled in a cloak, but the hood had fallen back to show a cascade of black ringlets ruffled by the wind. On the deck, a tall, sober-looking man and a plump, middle-aged woman bustled about giving orders to a half dozen marines wrestling with as many trunks and boxes.

The *Nausicaä* nosed expertly up to the dock, and the Captain of Marines signaled to make her secure. The grey-haired man nodded approvingly.

"A most pleasant passage, Captain, especially for midwinter. I trust you will be able to join me at dinner tonight."

"Thank you, sir. I should be honored." The captain saluted and stood at attention as the honor guard marched briskly down the ramp, followed by his passengers. Metius Lupus stood on the dock to greet them, and Justin slipped in among the senior officers gathered behind him.

"I trust you had a pleasant crossing."

"Indeed, most enjoyable," Aurelius Rufus smiled, and one or two of his guard winced slightly. The Channel seas were rough in January, and the new Legate's delight in ocean voyages was evidently unshared. He beckoned to the girl, and she slipped an arm through his. "My daughter, Felicia."

Justin looked at her curiously as she made her compliments to Metius Lupus. He had heard that Aurelius Rufus, a widower, took his household with him wherever he was posted. Her skin was a fine, soft gold with a tinge of pink in the cheeks which might or might not be her own, and her eyes a soft, deep brown. She wore a pair of coral eardrops of a style suitable for a young, unmarried lady, and her cloak and boots were of the serviceable traveling sort. Metius Lupus escorted the pair of them up the dock and presented the senior officers of the Ninth.

". . . Claudius Galba, Primus Pilus of the First . . . Fulvius Martius, with the Sixth Cohort . . . Lucius Favonius, who commands the Third . . . Justinius Corvus, commander of the Eighth . . . Gaius Licinius, Senior Surgeon . . . Marcus Hilarion, with the Ninth. . . ."

Behind them the tall man, who was evidently a servant, dealt with the luggage with the firm hand of one who was used to uprooting his household on short notice.

"No, no, no, are you mad? There is wine in that crate, and you heave it about like hay bales!"

"Take that trunk first." The plump woman directed two of the luggage carriers to a mountainous leather case. "My lady will wish a clean gown." She fluttered up the dock, shooing her transport ahead like reluctant chicks.

Aurelius Rufus, pacing beside his daughter, gave Eburacum Fortress the once-over and did not look impressed. However, the senior surgeon and the cohort commanders, as well as the retiring Legate, were invited to join him at dinner that night. Metius Lupus had insisted that the new Legate install his family in the Praetorium immediately, moving his own bachelor household to rooms in the officers' quarters. Formal change of command would take place the next day, and Metius Lupus would depart gratefully on the *Nausicaä*.

Justin, polished and shining, joined Licinius and the little group of senior centurions heading nervously for the Praetorium. The captain of the *Nausicaä* fell into step beside him as they reached the courtyard.

"Didn't you take transport with me sometime back, Centurion? I seem to remember you."

Justin laughed. "I'm sure you do. I was sick all over your deck."

"Ah, yes. You elected to travel north by road, I recall."

"I merely chose the lesser of two evils. I hope the Legate's stomach was stronger than mine."

"Oh, yes, he enjoyed himself thoroughly." The captain smiled reminiscently. "Said he'd been fond of thunderstorms since he was a boy, and invited his escort up on deck to watch. They, uh, declined."

"What's he like? As a commander, I mean?"

"Hard to say. I command on my own ship, so I don't know what it would be like serving under him. The escort seemed to like him well enough. His daughter dotes on him, and vice versa. And the servants seem happy—that's often a good sign."

The elderly majordomo, whose name turned out to be Theodore, swung the doors open at their approach, divested them of their cloaks, and led the way to the dining room. The trunks and boxes had either been unpacked or stowed out of sight, and both Legates and Felicia awaited them, the men in uniform and Felicia in her semiformal best.

She took little part in the dinner conversation which consisted mainly of the situation at Eburacum and the news from Rome, but she listened attentively, friendly brown eyes resting on each speaker in turn. Aurelius Rufus had produced an excellent dinner on short notice (Justin decided that Theodore must be invaluable to him), set out his best wine, and encouraged conversation. He himself had little to say, content to form a few opinions from the tone of each man's talk.

"So there you have it," Metius Lupus sighed, "and I wish you good luck to the work."

"So, of course, do we all," Cassius murmured, and the look which the surgeon and two of the cohort commanders gave him was not lost on the Legate.

With the fruit and cheese, talk turned from the military to more diverse matters, and Felicia began to add a comment now and then, in a soft, clear voice. When Licinius murmured a complicated and rather vulgar pun in Greek to her father, she capped it happily, and he blushed.

"I beg your pardon, my lady. I didn't realize—"

"Of course you didn't or you wouldn't have said it, and then I should have missed it. Don't look so worried, my friend. I have lived with the Army all my life, and I'm not easily upset. Why do you think I travel with my father? It's the only way I know to acquire an education in the world."

"I should have warned you," the Legate said, stretching out his arm for an apple. "My daughter has not had the normal schooling for a girl of her age. We decided it between us long ago, when her mother died, that we would both be happier if she traveled with me."

"You didn't feel the Army was rather a rough life for a girl?" Favonius asked.

"She also speaks Syrian, Aramaic, and several Gallic dialects, hunts like Diana, and rides like a Centaur. I fully expect her to be conversant with the local British tongues within six months."

"Papa, you're embarrassing! Here, let me do that, and brag about something else."

The Legate gave up wrestling with an apple far too small for the grip of his hands, and handed her the fruit and a little knife. "I merely wish these gentlemen, and hence the men under their commands, to be warned. I might add that she also uses a dagger expertly. In fact, she used it on a drunken Gaul who attempted to, uh, take liberties with her person. The camp surgeon managed to patch him up, but he has walked oddly ever since."

Felicia chuckled but kept her eyes on the small spiral of peel unwinding from the apple. "The only thing I occasionally miss is the company of other women. I've always thought it a pity that the Army discourages marriage. I've never felt I was a distraction to my father."

"My dear, we could hardly have every soldier in the Army trailing a wife and children and mountains of baggage along with him. I get away with it because I am the only one. The others must shift their families about as best they can."

"Well, not all the men perhaps, but I do think the officers ought to be allowed their wives in camp. That would provide me with enough company, I think. I assure you my motives are entirely selfish." She dropped the apple peel back into the bowl, neatly removed the core, and presented the fruit to her father with a little bow.

"Perhaps, my dear, but I can hardly rewrite the regulations for your own sweet sake."

"Of course, some officers marry where they're stationed," Martius said, a shade too loudly.

"Shut up, you idiot," Licinius hissed.

"Why, I think the lady ought to know what kind of women officers are likely to marry on campaign." Martius raised his goblet to his lips unsteadily, slopping a trickle of wine down his wrist. "She might change her mind about having them in camp."

"One more word out of you, Centurion Martius, and I'll rearrange your face!" Hilarion made as if to make this offer good.

"Knock it off, both of you." Justin sounded weary, as if he had heard it all before.

"My officers do not fight at table, especially not *my* table," the Legate said quietly, while Felicia sat startled, feeling a little guilty for having stirred up what appeared to be an old grudge. "Now what is all this?"

"I *did* marry out here, sir," Justin said, "although the Army doesn't recognize it, of course. Any more than they recognized my father's . . . or any of you who come from Army families." He ran his eye over the officers reclining about the table. "What these gentlemen object to is the fact that my wife is a freedwoman."

"She sold wine—and other things, no doubt—in a shop in the town," Martius said.

"Now see here, Martius—" This appeared to be a bit much even for Favonius.

"Dunno why he had to marry her," Martius laughed. "She'd 'a been happy enough with a necklace and a kiss good night."

"That'll do! Lay off the wine, will you?" Favonius removed his goblet, and Martius sat staring sulkily at his plate.

"I'm afraid most of it's true," Metius Lupus sighed. "I tried to dissuade him. . . ."

"My wife is of the Iceni," Justin said, "and wellborn in her tribe. When she was ten, a Gaulish slaver found her alone. And don't think it couldn't happen to any of us, in a wild country where

Rome's protection would do us little good. Her last master was a time-expired man of the Ninth who kept a wineshop called the Head of Neptune. He freed her when he died."

"And you married her?" Felicia asked.

"She had no one but me. Her people would not be likely to want a grown woman, with her past, back. All the girls of her year would have husbands and children by now—" (*What man of the Iceni would ask for me now?*) "—What would she do? The Britons can be very harsh. And she had no way to live in Eburacum. There are few men who would hire a freedwoman when there are slaves in plenty."

"You took her from pity?"

"No. I loved her."

"Then you did right," Felicia said.

"Good girl!"

Felicia looked at Licinius, startled, and realized that he had not meant her to hear his comment.

"Then let us make an end of the subject," Aurelius Rufus said. "As the centurion has said, I can't recognize his marriage, therefore it does not concern me . . . or any of you. I don't care if my men are wed to she-apes, as long as they perform their duties. They might do better than some I've seen, at that."

Martius retrieved his goblet and subsided into a glum silence. Favonius tipped the contents of his finger bowl into it when his compatriot wasn't looking, and Theodore, who had formed his own conclusions already, saw to it that the centurion's next glass was well watered.

The conversation moved on again, carefully, to other subjects, but after the last course of small, hot sweets had been served the officers began to yawn and take their leave. Martius left under his friend's guidance and Cassius alone. The others filtered out in twos and threes. As Justin was bidding his host good night, flanked by Licinius and Hilarion, Felicia took his hand and smiled.

"Your wife must be a lovely lady indeed, Centurion Corvus, to have so many defenders." She glanced at Licinius and Hilarion. "I should like to meet her."

"Thank you," Justin said gravely. "I rather think she would like you too."

The sky was clear and cold as black glass as they walked back to quarters, and the diamond pinpoints of the stars flickered in its bowl. Justin had recovered his temper and was trading rude rhymes with Hilarion while Licinius walked in silence, apparently wrestling with some private puzzle. The two centurions turned into the officers' quarters, making the night hideous by rendering the last of their impromptu rhymes in song, while Licinius walked on toward the hospital to make a final round. One of his patients had relieved his boredom the night before by attempting to smuggle in one of Venus Julia's girls, to the delight of one and all; he had succeeded in rebreaking his healing arm, and the senior surgeon was in no mood for a repeat performance.

The entire Legion, and a good part of the town as well, assembled for the change of command in the morning. Afterward, Justin found Felicia waiting for him outside the parade ground, wrapped in a pale yellow cloak with a soft green border that could only have been bought in Rome, and her black ringlets dancing in the wind.

"I have come to make you keep your promise to introduce me to your wife," she said, taking his arm. Justin led her to where Gwytha and Januaria were standing, with small Justin swaddled in blankets and clasped to Januaria's massive bosom. He made the requested introduction and stood back to see how they would take to each other.

The contrast between the two women was immense. Gwytha, tall and stately and unmistakably British even in her Roman finery, seemed to tower over the shorter, fine-boned daughter of the Legate. Where Gwytha was white-skinned, Felicia's complexion was honey-colored, and her hair seemed to take naturally to the curls which Gwytha's luxuriant mane abandoned at the slightest mist. They seemed to accept each other on the instant, however, and Justin realized that Gwytha too might have been lonely for the company of a woman her own age. The interview ended with an invitation to lunch on Felicia's part and a pleased, if nervous, acceptance on Gwytha's.

"I like her," Gwytha said, strolling back to the house on Justin's arm. The Legion had been excused from duty for the rest of the day in honor of the new Legate. If they knew what was good for them, however, they would gather to give the retiring one a fitting send-off.

The *Nausicaä* was loading cargo at the dock, and the Optio was already supervising the stowing of the Legate's trunks. A harassed-looking legionary was trying to persuade the Legate's horse down the ramp into the hold, assisted by cheers and advice from the crowd on the dock.

"Yes, I liked her too," Justin said. "A most extraordinary girl." He favored her with the Legate's description of his daughter.

"It seems that what she really burns to do is drive a chariot," Gwytha said. "Perhaps I'll rent one and teach her."

Justin looked surprised. "I didn't know you could."

"I was taught as a child. Among my people, the women also learn to fight, against the time when every spear might be needed. But it is only in great need that the king calls out the women, or puts his mares in the chariot line."

When they reached the house, Januaria began to set out a lunch, and Gwytha put the baby to her breast, where he sucked greedily and with much noise.

"Small pig," said an approving voice from the doorway. "If all your babes are as healthy as that one you'll have more family than Justin can support." Licinius pulled a parcel from his tunic front. "Here. I have brought him a present."

The baby eyed the small leather cat curiously but refused to be distracted from his meal.

"I had it from a British trader who came in this morning," Licinius said. "He had a cargo I didn't care for."

"What cargo?" Justin asked.

"He covered it up quickly enough as soon as I began poking about, but it was a shipment of Gaulish blades. And it was *not* for sale."

"Not to us at any rate, you mean. As I recall, there was an injunction against buying weapons in that treaty young Vortrix signed. If he *is* getting them sub rosa, the Legate had better know about it."

"He does. He was digesting that news along with a report that the Picts seem to be up to something in the north, when I left him. My trader friend was gone by the time they could send for him for questioning. Probably hightailed it out of here as soon as I turned the corner. He wasn't too happy about my seeing those blades."

"There is talk in the town already of the Painted People," Gwytha said. "Will there be trouble again this spring?"

"Perhaps." Justin was noncommittal.

She jumped to her feet clutching the baby. "Justin, I am no man's fool!" she flashed. "Now tell me the truth!"

Justin sighed. "Very well, yes, there will likely be trouble, if not this year, then the next . . . and if not with the Brigantes, then with the Picts. There have been rebellions already in the eastern Empire, and one seems to breed another. I suspect our new Legate was sent to try to pull this Legion together before it happens."

The necessity for major action was brought home forcibly a few nights later. Justin, grown restless while Gwytha was occupied with the baby, flung his cloak about him, looked at Finn asleep by the brazier, and went out alone for a walk.

Wandering through the streets, he passed many of the legionaries from the fort, come into town to watch a cockfight or buy a pot of rubbing oil for sore muscles . . . and many just to cap off a day's work with a night's amusement. Down a side street, behind the glow of an open doorway, someone was singing, accompanied by the stamp of feet and the drumming of cups on the tabletop, and an occasional request to shut up and give the world some peace.

Justin turned and headed in that direction. He had no other place in particular to go, and the noise was growing louder and more quarrelsome. He had the feeling there would be trouble in a minute. Perhaps the presence of an officer would put a damper on their spirits.

When he reached the doorway, he saw the wineshop keeper, with a worried expression, refusing to serve anything more to a truculent-looking legionary in a torn tunic.

"You've had enough. I know you, Junius, and you fight when you're drunk. Go along now, before your yelling has the Watch in here."

"You used to march with the Eagles yourself, Varus," another man said. "Since when do you refuse a brother his right to a drink?"

"Since he becomes too drunk to need any more," Justin said, coming in under the lintel.

Junius turned around to stare at the newcomer. "Has the centurion any more sage advice?"

"Just this. Take yourself back to barracks and soak your head to cool it off if you don't want to be spending the night in the guard-house."

"You heard the centurion," Varus said.

"Aye, we heard him. It so happens that *we* don't happen to agree."

"Drink while you can," someone shouted. "We're going to be ordered out before spring, didn't you know?"

"As soon as we've mended the precious walls so the precious tribunes can wait it out in comfort!"

"Then we're off to teach the Pict a lesson. Only you can't teach the Pict a lesson because he hasn't any manners!"

"He doesn't know it's not polite to attack a Roman!"

This sally was greeted with shouts of laughter and someone grabbed a wineskin from the counter and began passing it around.

"So we've got to go and show him that we're gentlemen even if he isn't, by fighting one to three!"

"That will *do!*" Justin snapped.

"What's going on here?" Another centurion ducked into the wineshop beside Justin.

"One of us to three of him! Don't it stir your blood, sir?" one of the legionaries laughed, trying to push Varus out of the way to get at the wine behind the counter.

"Judge for yourself," Justin muttered to the man beside him. "There'll be a brawl if this isn't stopped."

"Here, you," Varus said, collaring the man and shoving him toward the door, "I told you to get out and I meant it!"

One of the others jumped him, waving the wineskin happily over his head, and in a moment the whole shop was a shambles of overturned chairs and flying crockery.

"Ah, would you now?" Justin pulled the man off Varus and heaved him out the door, where he landed with a thud in the gutter and came charging back again. The other centurion fended him off, and Justin began trying to separate the others, who were indiscriminately hitting each other as well as the shopkeeper.

The three of them had managed to dispose of several of the combatants, most of whom were too drunk to throw a punch with much accuracy, when someone picked out the tramp of boots coming down the alleyway.

"The Watch!"

There was a break in the scuffling as most of the participants dived for the door. They weren't quite so drunk that they wanted to take on the whole force of the Watch who, having split up so as to come in by both the front and back ways, were waiting for them as they came out. There was a brief spate of shouting and curses as the officer in charge barked an order, but it was quickly silenced. The officer of the Watch came inside and grabbed a man who had been crouching beneath one of the tables by the collar of his tunic.

"I'll be taking him with me, if you don't mind. Gods," he said, looking about him, "the place looks as if you'd taken an ax to it. You shouldn't have let them drink so much, Varus."

"It wasn't my idea," Varus said as the officer went out again, taking a considerably sobered legionary with him. After a moment, Justin could see their lanterns weaving back down the street, and the footsteps died out in the distance.

The young centurion who had come in earlier turned to him. "Centurion Corvus, isn't it?" he said, holding a fold of his cloak against a cut cheek. "I'm Albinus. I'm to take the Fourth Cohort."

"Yes, I think I remember you." A number of replacement postings had arrived on the *Nausicaä* with the new Legate.

"I heard the noise and thought it sounded like trouble."

"So did I, and it was. You had better get up to the surgery and get that cut seen to. If Licinius isn't on duty, one of his men will be."

Justin stayed a few minutes, helping Varus repair the worst of the damage, and then wandered out into the street again. It was growing late and Gwytha would be worried. On the way back he passed a shop which displayed oils and perfumes and, in one corner, a tray of toys in bronze and clay. One in particular caught his eye. It was a small figure of a dog, shaggy and long-legged, with its head raised in a comically expectant manner. It looked like Finn begging sticks to chase, and Justin asked the shopkeeper how much it was.

"Fifty sesterces, sir. See the excellent modeling of the hair. A very fine piece of work which I bought only last week from a western bronzesmith."

"Yes, never mind, I'll take it." Justin put the money on the counter.

"Can I show the centurion anything else? Perfume for his lady?"

"No, only the dog." He slipped the little figure into his tunic and turned back toward the house again, wrapping his woolen cloak about him. The night was growing colder, and flakes of snow were beginning to drift down around him, driven on an increasing wind. Metius Lupus was likely to have an exciting voyage home.

He knocked at the main door of the house and immediately heard the bar slide back. Gwytha stood in the doorway with a lamp in her hand.

"I was getting worried about you." She held the lamp closer to his face. "Where were you? And what in the Mother's name were you doing while you were there? You've torn your tunic and there's blood all over your hand."

"Brawling in a wineshop," Justin said shortly. "Don't worry, it's only partly mine. I was helping another centurion break up a tavern brawl and someone's teeth got the worst of it. Poor man, he'd only just been posted here . . . he got a lovely welcome." He dropped down on the couch and reached inside his tunic. "I bought something. Ostensibly for small Justin."

"Oh, it looks just like him!" Finn came up, sniffed his replica and snorted in disgust when it did not appear to be edible.

"I got it from a perfume seller who deals in oddments on the side." He laughed. "I didn't realize what a sight I looked. He must have thought I was mad."

There was another knock at the door, and Justin opened it to find Licinius standing grumpily in the snow, instrument case in hand.

"I hear you've been trying to save the honor of Rome single-handed."

"If we hadn't done something, they'd have demolished the place. They were in a foul mood."

"So I gathered from young Albinus. When he said you'd laid your knuckles open, I left him to Flavius . . . didn't figure you'd have the brains to know you should have it seen to."

"They're just grazed."

"On someone's teeth?"

"Yes."

"It may interest you to know," Licinius said, unpacking a clean cloth and a jar of salve, "that a human bite is far more dangerous than a sword cut. If that gets infected, you'll regret it."

"Very well." Justin held out his hand obediently.

"Are you off duty tonight?"

"Yes, but I expect the Legate will want me in the morning. There're upwards of ten men in the guardhouse for that escapade, and fighting with an officer is a serious matter, the other problem aside."

"I don't imagine Varus was exactly amused either," Licinius said, applying salve.

Aurelius Rufus, newly appointed Legate of the Ninth, was even less pleased. As Justin entered, he looked up from a stack of papyrus rolls he had been inspecting. His helmet, with its crest of eagle feathers, lay beside him on the desk.

"Ah, Centurion Corvus. I understand you were involved in that . . . uh, altercation at the Blue Swan last night."

"Yes, sir, I was."

"How did you happen to be there?"

"It sounded like trouble brewing, and I thought if an officer were there they might behave themselves."

"Apparently you were wrong."

"I'm afraid so. I think it was beyond stopping at that point."

"Well, you seem to have made a good try at any rate, you and Albinus. There was, I believe, some rather undesirable talk as well, which Albinus only heard the tail of. Would you care to explain that?"

"There wasn't much. Only some wild remarks about fighting three to one. Nothing you could put your finger on, just a feeling that wasn't good."

"Ah, yes, that makes it difficult. All the same, I think we'll give those men a little harsher punishment than usual, in the hope they'll remember to hold their tongues in the future. As it happens—" Rufus stared dreamily out the window, as if the matter were of little importance to him—"I've heard something of the same already . . . concerning some of my officers. Would you know anything about that?"

"Only that there has been talk all over about being undermanned, and the discipline has been let slip."

"That much I could tell. I think I will be able to get us some reinforcements, but that alone is not going to solve the problem." He turned to look at Justin. "I'm tired of moving around the edge of this, like a cat at a puddle. So—young Albinus is new to the Legion and has had no time to get mixed up in treason. Of you I know little except that you have a British wife, had a skirmish with Vortrix and let him get away, are accounted hot-tempered . . . and also that your cohort is in better shape than most. In short, I find you an enigma, Centurion."

"And if I were to say that I have had no hand in treason, but that Metius Lupus has let things slide so far that I have trouble stopping it even in my own cohort?"

The Legate's gaze traveled speculatively over Justin's face and came to rest on his eyes.

Justin found himself getting irritated. "The Legate may believe me or not, as he pleases."

"Do you know, I rather think I do, all other evidence considered." He picked up his helmet and studied the crest of it. "Sit down, Centurion Corvus," he said after a moment. "Now that we have settled that matter, there are a few other things I would ask you."

Justin pulled a stool over obediently and sat.

"This talk that goes on, this smell in the wind, this feeling of yours —of what *precisely* does it consist?"

"I'm not sure I can be certain, sir. As far as I can tell, they complain, as I said, of being undermanned, and left to rot here by Rome. The talk is mainly that we would do better to let the Brigantes have the land if they want it so badly, rather than fight at those odds. And I think the odds are by way of being an excuse. I think it's probably rather than fight at all."

"An unattractive lot. the Ninth Hispana, but then I'm new to it. Where did you hear this?"

"From a lot of loose talk, and some conversations not meant for my ears I imagine. Some of them, I regret to say, among my own men. And, I'm afraid, an officer or two."

"Yes, well, I think I have a fair idea who they are. I suppose the fools think to sit in our fortress and let the Britons come to us, and the north look out for itself."

"I rather think so, sir, yes."

"In Typhon's name, don't they know that if the Luguvallium-Segedunum line goes, we go, and if we go, so does the whole province? See," he pulled a map from the record chest behind him. "Here we are, and there is Deva, and Isca Silurum. The Brigantes are here, and here and here." He swept his hand northward from Eburacum across the whole width of the map. "The Twentieth Valeria Victrix are at Deva to the west, and the Second Augusta at Isca to the southwest. Without us, the Brigantes would have a clean path all the way to the southeast, if they wanted it. And then the Picts are here and here and anywhere else you care to name, probably including under the table. And they'd like nothing better than to shove us right out of Britain. Already they have driven us nearly out of Valentia."

He sat rubbing the small rough place beneath his chin where his helmet strap had left a callus. A career soldier, this Legate, with long years behind him in the Eagles. "To my mind, Centurion, the Pict is a greater danger than any. He has learned to bide his time."

"Will we have the men to stop him, sir?"

"We can slow him down at any rate. But it will mean leaving Eburacum with nothing but a skeleton garrison to hold it. That garrison will have to be one I can rely on. And that means a flogging for the man who makes me think I can't. I am desperate enough that I would even resort to decimation if I thought it would make the remainder more trustworthy than the whole."

Justin shuddered in spite of himself. Decimation was the harshest punishment that could be meted out to an army . . . the death of one man in every ten, called out from the ranks in front of his brothers.

His reaction did not escape the Legate. "I fear it would not serve our purpose," he said, "but it would be as well if the camp remembered the possibilities. Now, Centurion, I want some more precise information."

"Very well, then. When you get those reinforcements, change over the garrison at Trimontium."

"Indeed? You paint an unpleasant picture, Centurion."

"I—" Justin broke off as the Optio appeared in the doorway, ashen-faced.

"What is it?" the Legate snapped.

"There's been another stabbing, sir . . . Centurion Martius. He's dead."

XIV

The Hand on the Knife

AURELIUS RUFUS TOOK A DEEP BREATH and exhaled slowly. "How long ago?"

"Not more than five minutes, sir. Licinius is with him, but Martius was dead by the time he got there. Licinius says the knife likely killed him right off."

The Legate looked at Justin. "Well, Centurion Corvus, at least we know *you* didn't do it," he said grimly. "That's a blessing."

"We have the man that did, sir," the Optio said. "One of his own."

"Poor fool," the Legate said softly, and Justin wasn't sure whether he referred to the murderer or the murdered. He rose and picked up his helmet. "Come along, Centurion Corvus, I want you."

Martius lay in the shadow of the drill hall, his scarlet uniform cloak spread over him like a pall of blood. Licinius was scrubbing his hands with a fistful of snow that fell in pink splotches at his feet. A silent circle of legionaries stood waiting for the Legate . . . grim-faced men of Martius's cohort, and Favonius with his face twisted in grief. A ploughed-up path through the new snow showed where a man had been half dragged, half carried to the guardhouse. The circle opened as the Legate approached, with Justin and the Optio behind him. They stood, shifting and wary-eyed, while Aurelius Rufus looked down at the still form beneath the cloak.

Finally he spoke. "Where is the man that has done this?"

"In the guardhouse, sir," one of the junior centurions spoke up.

"Very well. He will be executed in the morning, after he has had time to make a better peace with himself than he gave his commander. Who saw what happened?"

"It happened so fast, sir," the young centurion said. "There was a mix-up in the drill, and Centurion Martius stopped us as we came out of the hall and said to go back and do it again. Then Tullius yelled something at him and the commander gave him a month's 'on report.' Then he turned to go and Tullius jumped him. It was over in a second."

"And Tullius?"

"He just stood there, as if he didn't know where he was. He kept talking about Pertinax. He was the one who tried to knife Centurion Galen and got killed. I think he thought he was getting the man who killed his friend. Galen was riding Pertinax pretty hard when it happened, and I think Tullius blamed him for it . . . he's been strange ever since."

The Legate looked him in the eye. "This cohort is a danger to itself and to the Legion. I would break it if I could spare the men."

"Yes, sir."

"Failing that, it is my opinion that it should not go leaderless for even a day. Therefore, I am assigning Centurion Corvus to the Sixth, as of right now. Centurion, who is your second?"

"Lepidus, sir. A good officer."

"Very well, Centurion Lepidus will command the Eighth until a replacement can be posted. Centurion Corvus, Tullius is to be executed tomorrow morning. As for the rest of them, deal with them as you see fit, but get this cohort in shape if you have to flog every man in it." He turned on his heel and marched toward the Principia.

Justin, equally grim-faced, surveyed his new command. "Very well, take your commander to the hospital and see that his body is properly cared for. I want it done by men of his cohort. After that, I want every man in it on parade. I will arrange an exchange for any who are assigned duty today, but I want every man there, including any on sick parade who are well enough to move. Is that clear?"

"Yes, sir." The centurion signaled to those who were standing nearby, and silently they took up the body of Martius and bore it away.

Only Licinius and Favonius remained, watching the blood sink into the snow. Justin turned to Favonius. "He was your friend. I am sorry."

Favonius's face was haggard and his eyes were a little wild. "It is judgement," he said. "On us, on this Legion . . . the gods turn their backs. . . ." He trailed off, looking in the direction they had borne Martius's body. "I wish you joy of your new command, Corvus," he said bitterly, and turned to follow them, a stumbling, pathetic figure, enveloped in his grief.

"Dear gods, what are we come to?" Licinius spoke for the first time, still rubbing his hands with snow, as if to rid them of the mark of a dead commander.

"I don't know," Justin said. "We're at the edge of the cliff, I think. I wonder if we can draw back in time. Here, you!" he called to one of the crowd still standing, wide-eyed with curiosity, some ten paces away. "Bring some dirt and cover the blood." He looked at Licinius. "I must go and talk to Tullius. Will you come?"

Licinius nodded, and together they followed the recently trampled path already partially obscured by new snow.

They found Tullius sitting on the cot in his cell, staring blankly at the floor. Justin questioned him gently, then angrily, and finally with something akin to despair, but elicited only a stuttering plea to the shade of Pertinax to accept the vengeance he had bought him. As for Justin and Licinius, he seemed not even to see them, although he moaned in terror when Justin told him, as gently as he could, what was going to happen. Finally they left him, and he roused himself at their parting to spit in their path.

It was in no good frame of mind that Justin turned out for parade that afternoon. He had found Lepidus, briefed him, and left him to handle things as well as he might. It was a lousy way to get your first cohort.

Now Justin faced his own new command, the promotion back to Sixth that he had been wanting ever since he'd made an ass of himself in the arena at Hippo Regius. It was a lousy way to get that, too.

The men were sullen and untidy, and they watched him suspiciously, wary that the hand of punishment might reach out for more than Tullius. But they were all there, as ordered, even a few from sick parade, nursing colds or strained tendons. Justin kept his voice dispassionate as he called them all the names he could think of, apparently including one or two they hadn't heard before. When that was done, he informed them that the next time he saw them they were to be clean, polished, and nothing short of reverent in their attitude toward their officers.

"I agree with the Legate. If we had the men to spare, I would break this cohort and start again from the ground, rather than try to repair a rotten thing. And it can still be done if you push me too far. Perhaps you might find you like that less than you like the Eagles. But I will not command a disgrace. I will command a cohort of the Eagles or nothing. You will do well to remember it.

"I have made exchange with the other cohorts to pull you off duty for this parade. It was not to reward you with a day's leave, so you will use the rest of the afternoon to make sacrifice to the shade of the man you murdered, for you are all guilty of that, though it was Tullius who held the knife. Be glad you will not pay the price he is going to," he added grimly, and fought down a sick feeling in his stomach.

With that he dismissed them, holding back only the centurions of the cohort. With them he was somewhat gentler, knowing that their jobs could not have been easy under Martius's command. Some of them seemed good men, if worn down with fighting uphill against their men and their cohort commander both. Others were of the same breed as their dead commander . . . careless of discipline, but with no great care for the men under them, weaker of spirit than was normal for the Centuriate. It had been a long time since Rome had sent her best men to Britain, Justin thought. The recruiting standards of the Ninth had fallen also, with the difficulty of finding men willing to serve in a Legion considered unlucky since first Boudicca had shamed and slaughtered it, and then Agricola had barely saved it from a second loss. And now this. Justin began to feel as if he was standing on the heaving edge of a bog.

They executed Tullius in the morning, with every man of the Ninth Hispana paraded to watch. Death by stoning, the ancient punishment for mutiny. Tullius, clad only in his white undertunic, came docilely between an eight-man guard to be chained to the post in the center of the execution ground, but his eyes stared in terror at the death that waited.

The sky was nearly as dark as night, the sun obscured by rolling banks of black cloud broken only by the jagged lines of lightning that spat within them. The grim, impersonal orders of the Primus Pilus were covered by the heavy boom of thunder, and the air was thick and oppressive.

The execution squad, drawn by lots from the condemned man's own century, flinched like wild things pursued by shadows and looked, Justin thought, as if they would like to turn the stones on him instead. It was a grisly business and Justin, sick at his stomach, could only be glad when the Primus Pilus gave the order to the spear men, releasing the broken body of Tullius from its agony.

In the end, one man of the execution squad knelt down and was sick in the snow, and Justin quelled the writhing in his own stomach as he and Licinius certified the death and Tullius's name was stricken from the legionary rolls with a single grim notation. At Justin's signal, they rolled the stones from the feet of the mangled form and bore it to a shallow grave at the corner of the field while the black clouds rolled and swelled like a living thing above them.

The rest of the day continued in the same nightmare fashion, with one half of Justin's new cohort demoralized and trembling and the other plainly blaming him for the death of their comrade.

It was evening before he could drag himself, bone-weary, to the house in the town. Gwytha, seeing his face, silently handed him a cold dinner and kept her questions to herself. She could imagine what the past two days had been like with very little trouble, anyway. She herself had spent them repeating over and over to herself, why Justin? why Justin? Why not anyone but Justin to have that accursed cohort? But to Justin she said nothing, merely offering him the solace of her arms, and then trying to sleep while she knew he lay awake staring at the ceiling.

The next morning he had a visitor, a sallow-faced man of his new command. He sidled in under Januaria's disapproving glance, but she obeyed Justin's standing order that his men were always to be admitted and presented him to her master in the atrium.

"Yes? What do you wish?"

The man laid a parcel on the desk at Justin's elbow. "My woman bade me bring you this," he said. "As a welcome to the new commander, like. We had a lamb die newly born, a big lamb that was late in the coming, and the meat was more than enough for us, with me usually up to the fort. We thought maybe you and your lady would do us the honor to accept it."

"That was kind of you and your woman." Justin handed the parcel to Januaria. Judging by the looks of him, Justin doubted that he owned any sheep or that, having managed to buy—or more likely to steal—a lamb, he would offer a part of it to his centurion without an excellent reason. "How goes it with the cohort this morning?" he inquired.

"It goes as well as it might," the man said. Phaedrus, that was his name, Justin remembered. "What with the commander, and—and yesterday morning and all, and—"

"And, Phaedrus? Tell me."

"Well, with the Brigantes last summer, and now the Picts, they say, talking rebellion, and maybe even the little dark people too, unless they're just a fairy tale, like some men say—myself, *I* haven't seen them—but a lot of the men don't like it, sir, thinking we would better leave the north to them as seems to want it so bad, 'stead of lose the men in trying to stop what maybe can't be stopped."

"That," said Justin sharply, "is not for the men to decide."

"Aye, true enough, sir." The legionary watched him, taking stock, from under a shock of matted hair. "But they do say in camp as how maybe some of the officers might think the same way, given the choice."

"Well, they had better not say it around those officers, or they might get an unpleasant surprise," Justin snapped. Phaedrus didn't *look* overly surprised, he noted, merely as if he had got the information he was seeking. "You may go," he continued, before the man could say anything else. "And see that you wash that tunic before you report back for duty. It looks as if you'd rubbed down a horse with it."

"Yes, sir." The man backed toward the door.

"And, Phaedrus—"

He halted, looking nervously at Justin.

"My thanks to you and your woman for the lamb."

Phaedrus departed hastily. Justin sat looking after him. He wondered just how far Martius had let things go. Too far for him, at any rate, poor man.

"Gwytha," he said, as she appeared and settled herself at her loom, "if Phaedrus should show his face again, and I rather think he won't, tell him he had best lose himself in the ranks before I notice him."

"What did he want?"

"To tell me a tale about a gift of some lamb and to sound out my views on certain matters."

"Oh. And did he find out what he wanted to know?" Her face was worried, but she kept her eyes on the flying shuttles of the loom.

"Not precisely what he *wanted* to know, no, but I trust his own views have been somewhat clarified. Martius was a bigger fool than I thought, I'm afraid, though I'd swear he wasn't mixed up in treason. Still, we may as well use the lamb, for the expenditure of which I imagine Phaedrus is now cursing himself."

"Well, at least he will think twice before he tries that trick again," she commented. "Lambs can't be that easy to come by."

"That was what I thought. I thanked him very nicely for it when he left."

She fetched the parcel from the kitchen and started to laugh. "And see, he has given us the best part."

"Well, I hope it gives him to think," Justin said, "but I doubt it. I may have put the fear of the gods into Phaedrus at least, but it's no more than on the surface. Meanwhile they put the fear of the gods in *me*, with their quarreling and their laziness, while the Brigantes lay in a stock of good Gaulish blades and wait."

He pulled his breastplate on over the harness skirt of leather and bronze and stood for her to buckle it for him. He hefted his centurion's vine staff. "I may have to start *knocking* some better sense into their heads, but I'd as soon not. I've had my fill of that."

. . . Dark clouds and the crack of lightning, and he and Licinius standing over the mangled body of Tullius . . .

"My job is to mend bodies, not break them!" Licinius had said savagely, gouging his signature across the official death certificate.

That scene was still uppermost in the surgeon's mind the next morning, and while Justin was entertaining Phaedrus, Licinius was bitterly polishing his instruments for the third time, sick and ashamed, of himself and his Legion.

He didn't hear the light step on the hospital floor until she was beside him, and he looked up, startled, at the Legate's daughter.

"I would like you to look at Theodore's hand." She gestured to the slave standing a deferent four paces behind her. "He has poured boiling fat on it, and it looks bad to me. He refused to come and see you, so I have brought him myself."

"I have assured my mistress that the matter is negligible," Theodore said.

"Hmmm." Licinius put his instruments away. "Let me have a look." The slave stretched out a scarlet left hand with obvious reluctance. "Well, you won't die of it, but it's as well to be careful of infection with burns. I'll give you some salve for it." He produced a small clay pot sealed with wax. "Rub it with this twice a day, and make very sure you keep it clean."

"Indeed, sir." Theodore looked with distaste at the unguent pot.

"Theodore is a Greek. I'm afraid he has no very great opinion of the state of Roman medicine," Felicia murmured.

"The Army Medical Corps does a damn sight more good than most!" Licinius snapped. "If you don't believe me, neglect that hand. If you see any red streaks running up toward the shoulder, let me know, and I'll come and take the arm off."

Theodore eyed the surgeon with new respect, and Felicia started laughing. "Very well, Theodore, you may go. And see that you do as the surgeon bids you.

"I think," she added when he had gone, "that you are one of the few people ever to make an impression on Theodore."

"Hmmm." Licinius reached for his instrument case again.

"Do you know, those look quite clean to me. Would you be willing to put them up long enough to show me your hospital?"

His black brows flew up in eloquent surprise, but after a moment he laid the case down again. "Very well, if you like."

She paced silently beside him, her soft boots whispering on the stone floor, but after they had toured the operating room and the dispensary, she turned to him. "You are troubled, I think. Would it be better if we did this another time?"

Licinius ran his hand through his black hair and looked at her apologetically. "No. I am being a clot, and I am sorry. Yesterday's business has been much on my mind, and it has made me vile company."

"Yes, I expect it would. My father also." She laid a hand on his arm and kept it there a moment. "I am sorry. You had to attest the death, I expect. Was it very bad?"

"Have you ever seen one?"

"No. I saw a man flogged once. My father felt that if I was going to follow the Army I should know that such things happen. It was bad enough." She read the bitter pain in his face and knew that this had been worse yet. And because she could think of no other way to soothe the pain, she put her arms around him, and he bowed his dark head to her shoulder.

Justin, strolling with his wife to shake off the horror which still hung on him, nudged her and pointed up the road where a light two-horse chariot came clip-clopping down a side street toward the livery stable. Guiding the team was Felicia, her black curls tangled by the breeze.

"I think you're too late. It appears that one of our local beaux has already offered his services." Then his brows rose as she leaned forward and the other dark head came into view. "Light of the Sun—Licinius!"

In the chariot, Felicia, her cheeks flushed with the cold, was proudly showing off her mastery of the afternoon's lesson while Licinius watched with a look Justin had never before seen on his friend's face.

When Januaria, whose spies were everywhere, reported that this outing was repeated the following day, Justin began to be worried. Licinius had never shown more than an occasional physical interest in girls, remaining seemingly wholly heart-free if perhaps a trifle lonely for it. If his heart was touched now, he was in for a rough crossing. Aurelius Rufus would look in no friendly fashion on a mere Army surgeon.

This observation was not lost on Licinius either. Some two weeks later, he sat propped against a young birch tree, with the chariot ponies unbridled and tethered nearby, sourly watching Felicia threading a wreath of brown winter grasses reclaimed from the snow. "I suppose you realize my life was almost blissfully uncomplicated until you came along," he said at last.

She looked at him from her perch on a dry rock. "You might as well come and sit by me," she said. "You'll be soaking your backside to the skin sitting there in the wet like that."

He rose and sat down again beside her, drawing the folds of his cloak around them both. She reached up and placed the finished wreath on his head. "Not even the Emperor has a finer," she said, adjusting the angle until it tipped rakishly across one eyebrow. She drew a silver hand mirror from the folds of her own cloak and showed him his reflection.

"My dear girl, I know perfectly well what an ass I look in that thing. You needn't exhibit the effect to me."

"Very well, I'll put it away. You know, I'm afraid Papa isn't going to care for this."

"Mithras! I suppose you think that hadn't occurred to me. Well, there's not a damned thing I can do about it except avoid you like the pit of Ahriman."

"Licinius, no!"

"I can't marry you, and I can't bear it this way much longer. I can't marry anyone while I'm in the Army, and I don't suppose you want to wait another ten years for me."

"But Centurion Corvus—"

"Justin didn't marry a Legate's daughter. You know perfectly well you wouldn't be allowed to contract an Army marriage, and I wouldn't let you if you could. In any case, your father wouldn't have me. Use your head, Felicia!"

She shook her head, and the pearl drops in her ears, and those that hung from the gold fillet in her hair, were set to jigging like snowdrops against her black curls. "Licinius, listen to me! I have followed my father's Legion since I was a child, and I might have married long ago if I had a taste for the easy life. I'm not a ten-year-old in love with the bugler!"

He chuckled. "*Were* you in love with the bugler?"

"Oh, yes, when Papa was in Syria with the Third Gallica. He was *very* handsome, tall and blond with a lovely bristly mustache, and he used to let me play his bugle."

"Ah, true love!"

"Now see here, you're getting me off the track." She put her hands on either side of his face so that he could not turn away. "Since I have been grown, there has never been one man I wanted . . . save you. I am not going to say, 'Ah, the Fates deny us!' and cry a little, and then go and think of something else."

Licinius pulled away from her, shuddering, and bowed his head in his hands. "Give me strength!" Then he sat up again and gripped her hard by the shoulders, the gentle note gone from his voice. "Now *you* listen to *me!* I resigned myself long ago to an uneventful retirement raising horses somewhere to the south; alone, because I never met a woman I could love and I would not make some woman's life a burden to her because I didn't love her. Lonely because of that, maybe, but content. And now you come, all silk and pearls and laughter, and take me in your arms when I am hurt past bearing, and now I love you! And where do you fit on a British horse farm, and where do I fit in your world? And the gods help me, what am I going to do? I am sick with wanting you!" He flung himself up off the rock and set about bridling the chariot ponies.

But when he had finished, and turned to see her still sitting on the rock, turning the fallen wreath of dead grasses between her hands, he began to shake again. And then, without meaning to, he was beside her and his arms were hard around her waist.

And then it began to snow again, and he bundled her into the chariot and wheeled the horses straight down the hill.

It had been a late winter, but with that day's snow it arrived in earnest. It fell from then on, drifting deep about the barracks and granaries, freezing in the ruts of cart wheels and falling endlessly, blindly, smothering the world in a powdery blanket that stretched for miles.

There were days that were fair enough for travel, but Justin, wrestling with the rot at the heart of Martius's cohort, could not be spared, and so Gwytha's mind was made up for her concerning a winter's visit to the Iceni.

Aurelius Rufus, gloomily checking over the rosters in the Principia, made the interesting discovery that the Ninth was even farther below its paper strength than he had been told. Worse yet, there were no suitable replacements for the officers he felt were unreliable. Cassius was top priority. There wasn't anything he could put his finger on, but the Legate was an experienced enough soldier to know trouble when he saw it, even under a cohort commander's helmet. Favonius, shaken to his soul by the death of Martius, might either pull himself around and be the better for it, or break altogether. Young Lepidus was doing well enough with the Eighth, which Justin had almost got whipped ·into shape before his transfer, but Lepidus was a good year away from his own cohort in the normal course of things and had less experience than the Legate liked. Hilarion's Ninth Cohort was shaping as well as possible under the circumstances, as was the Seventh under Geta. But young Albinus was having Ahriman's own time with the Fourth, which had been under the command of its second for almost a year before his posting. The Tenth was a demoralized mess, and the Legate had managed to get its centurion transferred elsewhere, leaving command with the second, who showed more sense and was ready for promotion. The Second Cohort was so far down from its paper strength and showed such promise of being real trouble that the Legate had lumped it together with the First under the command of the Primus Pilus, Claudius Galba, where they remained a surly thorn in the flesh, but would at least have an eye kept on them.

The auxiliary cohorts in the northern forts were under strength as well, the more so now that the Vinovia garrison had had to be made up from among the other units stationed in the north. The southern detachments sent in during the last rising had since been recalled. And Justin's remarks about the Trimontium garrison had given the Legate cause to doubt the Auxiliaries' stability as well.

It was well after dinner when he finished his rundown of the rosters, accompanied by a growling stomach and a splitting headache. He drew forth a clean papyrus and then pushed it away again, scraping his chair back across the tile floor.

There was another matter he had to attend to before the night grew too late, and he might as well see what the hospital could offer for his headache while he was at it.

A light in the surgery sent a hazy gleam through the drifting snow as he reached the door, and he entered to find the senior surgeon redressing a feverish-looking leg wound in one of the small wards.

Licinius glanced up from his work and nodded, but didn't speak until he had finished. "There, that should help. You paid a high price for your wolf skin, my friend."

The soldier looked up at him. "Aye, too high, I'm thinking. I'm not going to lose it, am I?"

"I don't think so, if you behave yourself and take care of it." Licinius tipped the contents of a phial into an earthenware cup and handed it to the boy. "Here, drink this, and get some sleep."

He turned to the Legate and ushered him across the hall into his office. "I regret keeping you waiting, sir, but the boy was in pain and it wouldn't keep." He offered the commander a chair.

"Commendable. What have you got for pains in the head?"

"A moment, sir." He disappeared down the hall to the dispensary and returned with a small ampule of powder. He drew out the green glass cups and a flask of wine and shook the contents of the ampule into one of them. Licinius handed it to the Legate with a small bow.

He took a sip. "Thank you, that is vile. I trust this won't put me to sleep? I have several matters yet to finish up tonight."

Licinius sat down again. "No, sir, it's purely a painkiller. If you take too much of it, it'll knock you out, but not the amount I've given you."

"I doubt if I *could* drink more of this than was necessary." He swallowed the rest of it at a gulp and coughed. Licinius refilled his cup, this time with wine alone. "Thank you. An excellent wine, when unadulterated."

A smile tugged at the surgeon's mouth, and he refilled his own cup. "To the Army." He raised it in mock salute.

Aurelius Rufus sat back in his chair. "Tell me, what are you doing in the Medical Corps? You've got 'Centuriate' stamped all over you."

"I have a bad knee. Oh, I get around all right, but it wouldn't hold up on the parade ground, and you'll find when we march that it doesn't hold up there either. The hospital mules and I are old acquaintances."

"Then why the Army at all?"

"The Eagles are in my family . . . it seemed the natural thing. And then, the Army is the best teaching hospital in the world. Most advances in surgery come out of the Medical Corps."

There was a small silence while the two regarded each other in the lamplight, their faces equally unhappy. Finally the Legate spoke again. "I expect you know why I came up here, instead of sending for you to my quarters."

Licinius nodded. "I suppose it's no good my saying I didn't think this up to tear myself apart on purpose."

The Legate's voice was gentle, but there was, when he came to the point, steel in it. "All the same, my friend, you're on the road going nowhere. Get off *before* you tear yourself apart, and my daughter with you." He rose and gathered his cloak around him. "A word to the wise." And he was gone.

In his office, the Legate reached again for the papyrus roll. As well to tackle this one now, too. It was a grimly private communication, and once posted, there would be no record copy for the

Legion's files. Stop up the rot, they had said. Well, they had better send him something to stop it up *with*. . . .

The lamp burned low, and the wind had come up and was howling like a wolf in the courtyard outside, by the time Theodore came looking for him with a flagon of hot spiced wine.

"It is nearly the third watch, Master."

"I know. I will be home directly." He drank it while he finished . . . three letters, almost identical, to the newly appointed Governor Falco, to the Senate, and to the Caesar of Rome.

". . . unless we have more men . . . regretfully inform you . . . the hand on the knife is likely to be our own."

XV

The Hearth Fight

THE COUNCIL MOUND WAS A white bulk rising solitary above the flames. It was dark-of-the-moon, and the only illumination came from the spit and flare of the torches as they fought with the mist in the circle below the ancient barrow. Full in the glare, head high, stood a dun stallion tethered to a peg in the ground where his hooves had trod a dark circle in the snow. Outside the circle of torchlight, disembodied in the mist, a sea of faces stretched back into the trees. The feeling of something coming loomed heavy in the air, and suddenly, though no man had marked their passing, an antlered form sprang up from the top of the mound, and another figure that began as a man but ended with the curve of a stallion's crest appeared amid the torches.

The men outside the fire held their breath and waited while farther back in the trees two knots of warriors stood detached. In the center of one the face of a grey-eyed chieftain stood out from the rest, beneath a head of hair that burnt like molten copper down his back. His eyes were fixed on the naked, stallion-crested form among the torches, as if he knew what was to come. In the midst of the second group, a slight, dark-haired man with tattooed patterns thick on his skin and a circle of twisted gold on his head eyed the

Horse Man with something akin to hatred.

And then the stallion-crested figure raised a shining knife and a scream tore through the stillness with a defiance that lingered after the great golden body of the horse had come crashing down in the snow at the feet of the Slayer.

As the sound died away in the mist, the antlered figure on the Council Mound raised its arms to the night sky. Below, naked except for the horse mask on his head, Vortrix the High King of the Brigantes held up the silver blade above the body of the great stallion whose blood would seal the Binding.

At a sign from the antlered form of Talhaiere on the Council Mound, a second horned figure stepped forward and raised a small swaddled shape before the gathering. The baby woke and began to howl as Vortrix dipped a thumb into the blood that ran from the stallion's throat and inscribed two intersecting curves on the child's forehead.

"Look well, my brothers, look well. I, Vortrix, son of Arviragus and High King to the People of the Brigantes, give my firstborn into the keeping of the Tribe, that he may grow wise in our ways against the day that he shall come after me. By the Shining Spear I vow it."

"Look well, my children," Talhaiere repeated. "Look well. The Tribe accepts Bran, son of Vortrix, into its house, and returns him to his mother's keeping until such time as he takes his place as warrior among us."

"By the Shining Spear we vow it!" The words came from a thousand throats ringed around the torchlight.

Then Talhaiere himself stepped down from the mound and took the babe, making the sign of the Spear Lord over him, and there was a great roar of approval from the Tribe, as they beat their spears against their shields.

"Who speaks for the cub?" Talhaiere threw back his head, hidden in the red deer mask, and surveyed the gathering.

"I, Cathuil, father of the mother, speak for him, that he may go in peace with the Mother of us all." He crushed a tuft of corn above the baby's chest, and the riven grain drifted down around him to the earth.

"I, the Hound of the Father, speak for the cub, that he may bear his spear in the sunlight, and the Lord look well on him." Galt too

stepped into the circle and touched the baby lightly on the forehead
with his spear point.

There was another shout of approval, and the watchers drew back
to form an alleyway between them. Galt and Cathuil plucked the
nearest torches from their stands and led the way through the opening. Then all around the circle men took up the remaining torches
and the procession flowed like a stream of light through the white
forest. Vortrix and Talhaiere bore the child between them, and
when Talhaiere whispered to him, the babe ceased his wailing and
reached out for the thongs that dangled from the red deer mask. Behind them came the warriors of the king's house, and streaming out
behind, the clan chieftains and their warriors, and finally the boys
who would come to manhood in the spring, proudly bearing their
spears in the men's ranks this night.

As the procession passed, the two groups of strangers fell into
step beside the Horse Man, the sprigs of evergreen in their belts
showing red in the torch flare.

He turned his head in greeting to both, but did not speak. The
time for that would come when he had put away the stallion-
crested mask of the Slayer.

As they approached the king's hall, Branwen came out, her hair
flowing loose about her shoulders in token to the Mother. She held
out her arms to take the child from Horse Man and Deer Man, and
bore him back into the hall, the men of the gathering thronging
after her, for the feast which would follow the Binding of a
king's son. The two masked figures moved away into the darkness.
When they reappeared some minutes later the mystery was gone,
and it was Talhaiere the High Priest and Vortrix the High King
who took their places in the hall.

Branwen took the babe away to feed it, and Vortrix watched her,
smiling, until she had passed through the curtained doorway. He
was glad that it had not been necessary to send her south to her
father to wait for the babe. By the time her pregnancy had begun
to show on her, the fight was over, and he no longer feared the
stab of pain that would take him unexpectedly, sending his sword
clattering to the floor. None but Branwen knew what that fight
had cost him, the hours of searing pain, forcing himself to work
the arm more each day, frantic lest he should have to choose between the chance of a knife in the dark or sending his wife and

babe to bide within striking distance of Rome, and maybe not being able to get them back before Rome took notice of them.

He flexed his hand and smiled a small wolf-smile. There had been no more talk of maimed kings among the Tribe since the day he had sent a throw spear whistling half an inch past Cawdor's ear and made him a guest gift of the grey goose it had pierced cleanly through the throat.

Now the time had come to seal the next hunting. "It is good for a man to have a son to come after him," he said, nodding at the red-haired chieftain on his right, and the young spear bearer behind him, who was marked with the chieftain's features and flaming hair.

"Aye, it was a good kill and a clean one. The Shining One will look well on your cub." Brendan, War Lord of the Selgovae, nodded his head in approval. Except for the copper hair, he had much the same stamp as Vortrix, and indeed the Selgovae were close kin to the High King's tribe. He was a golden warrior, some ten years older than the young king, grey-eyed, with pale skin lightly freckled by the sun, and the shining torque of the High Lord around his throat. The spear patterns on his face and breast had faded to a soft grey-blue in the years since his initiation, but his hands and arms were those of a man still in his prime.

"And what of the Mother? Is there no honor to her in all of this?" The second chieftain gestured at the thronging hall.

"The women make the mysteries of the Mother, as they always have," Vortrix said cheerfully, "but among the spear band, aye, and the women in it as well, our foremost prayers are to Lugh."

The chieftain shifted in his chair as if uncomfortable. He was smaller than the other two, with dark hair and eyes, the stamp of the native folk with whom his tribe had intermingled. And, like all the tribes of the Painted People, he was blue with woad almost from head to toe. He was very beautiful to look at, but there was something alien there, and he seemed to sense the difference as well.

"Come, Dergdian," Talhaiere put in, seeing his discomfort, "because the Caledones make their first prayers to Earth Mother and we and our kin make ours to the Shining One does not mean that we cannot hunt together in this thing. Our folk were still kin to yours, you know, when the world was young."

"Aye, belike," Dergdian said, twitching at the folds of his kilt, "but I had not heard that the Brigantes had so far left the old ways that a maimed king was not an insult to Earth Mother and the Shining One alike."

"What?" Vortrix whipped round so fast that the golden hair hung for a second in the air behind him like a cloud.

"There is talk in the heather of an arm that is not healed and cannot hold a spear," Dergdian said quietly, looking him straight on. "If this is so, there will be no hosting until the Brigantes have crowned an unblemished king."

Vortrix's eyes were cold and furious. "And you, Brendan? Is there talk in the heather you hunt in also?"

"Aye, there is talk. But I had thought to wait and see for myself before I gave tongue to it. I saw you make the Sacrifice tonight, and the kill was clean. But a knife to slit a horse's throat is not a sword to cut a man's."

Vortrix scraped his chair back and stood full in the torchlight as he stripped his shirt off over his head. "There, look well!" He held out his right arm, so that the firelight played along the twisted scar. "Ugly, is it not? But still strong enough to slay a ferret. Watch and you shall see!"

Silence fell as the High King spoke, and for a long moment there was only the drifting smoke from the hearth and the almost visible fury that seemed to radiate from the half-naked figure of the king. Then he leapt over the table, landing cat-footed on the dancing floor below.

"Dawid! Bring me my sword and Cawdor my kinsman's." The boy scurried off and Vortrix turned to face his cousin. "I had thought to put an end to the bloodletting in our family, and so I did not kill you when I could, even when you would have taken the High King's crown and set it on your own head! But stopped up at one run, you turn to another—aye, I know whose tongue this talk in the heather has behind it. Did you think to force the matter as the price of alliance?"

Cawdor stood also, his eyes gleaming dangerously. "And have I not as much right to the kingship as you, cousin? I who am son to Rhiada whom you murdered? *And* a whole man!"

"We shall see, shall we not?" Vortrix said softly. "Come you out, then, and find out."

"Do you make formal challenge?" Cawdor's face was confident—the price for the maker of such a challenge, if he won, was higher than most men were willing to pay. Then he found himself looking into the demon light that flared behind the High King's eyes, and went cold.

"I do." Vortrix took the sword that Dawid held out to him.

"You know what you must do—after?" Talhaiere asked him gently.

"Aye, Father, I know." To kill a man at such a gathering was forbidden. Only by making challenge, and accepting the three-day purification which followed it, was such a fight permitted. And the purification was not pleasant.

But the challenge was not a thing which could be refused, and Cawdor came forth slowly, taking his sword from Dawid without looking at him. Berec followed, white-faced, to take his cloak and shirt, and to tie Cawdor's hair back from his face.

Then Galt also leapt lightly across the table, to tie the king's hair back for him. "The Shining One go with you, brother," he murmured. "I do not think the price he asks will be overhigh."

"In any case, it is mine to pay," Vortrix said. "The more fool I that I did not listen to you earlier." He handed Galt the plain bronze fillet from his hair, replacement for the gold one that had gone in payment for time and new blades. Galt took it and moved back among the tables, while on the floor Vortrix and Cawdor circled in deadly silence.

Branwen returned to the hall just then, and Galt caught her in the doorway, leading her out of Vortrix's line of sight. "Hush and be still, lady. He needs no distractions."

"And I am not needing you to tell me that," she returned, and he half smiled and made a little bow to her.

At the High Table, Brendan and the Caledonian chieftain watched tensely. For himself, Brendan had no wish to make an alliance with Cawdor in the High King's place. Too much rode on the strength of the leader.

Dergdian watched with a different eye—there was much in this combat that came close to home. But for him, when the time came, the outcome would be foreordained. To fight to hold your throne, and win—there must be a glory in that that he would never know. For a king of the Caledones to do such a thing would surely bring the wrath of the Goddess on them all, and she was the giver of plague and famine as well as fruition and plenty. No, Dergdian's death would be the life of his tribe, and there was glory in that, too.

"Vortrix's time will come," Brendan murmured to him, seeing the way his thoughts lay. "As it does to us all. But not, I think, tonight."

"How do you know?"

"Because we choose our own time, when the need is there—and he does not choose."

In the circle of the dance floor the two figures, stripped to the waist, with the blue spirals bright against the pale skin over the heart, stepped round each other, measuring, in a pattern that might have come straight from ancient ritual. Then Cawdor lunged and brought his blade down hard toward the base of the king's neck, and the dance became a deadly, chancy thing that was ritual no longer. Vortrix brought his own blade up against the blow, flinging the man back from him, and drove it straight for Cawdor's heart. Cawdor too parried and they circled briefly once more, the fire and torch flare shining on their hair and setting their shadows to leaping huge against the wall, like the painted warriors of the old days who danced on the rocks of the Council Mound. The scar on the High King's forearm flamed as red as the fire, but still the muscles held. Cawdor licked his lips and lunged again, and the High King's sword flickered up to stop the blade.

"The God speed thy knife, brother," Galt whispered from his place in the corner beside the queen, and she looked up startled at the fervor in his voice.

"If the God will listen to any man in this thing, I am thinking it will be you," she said, and his arm came round and gripped her about the waist, an unexpectedly steadying comfort from a man so lightly built. They had had but a wary regard for one another in the days since Vortrix's marriage, the High King's queen and his blood brother, but now suddenly they were one on the outskirts of this battle.

Vortrix moved slowly forward, angling Cawdor back before he had a chance to realize that three more steps would take him to the edge of the hearth with its firepit glowing red and raised a full foot above the floor. Vortrix feinted with his sword and a streak of pain ran down his arm, but there was no lessening of its strength. And Cawdor took another step back.

"Mine, cousin," Vortrix hissed. "Did I not say it was mine by right of blood?"

"You lost that right," Cawdor spat at him, breathing hard, "the night the Roman healer mended your arm and you forsook your call!"

"My call was not yet . . . nor is it now! *I* choose, Cawdor! And —your own call comes!" He swung his sword out and down in an arc that flickered past Cawdor's guard and caught him on the thigh, slicing bone deep before Cawdor could recover.

Cawdor stumbled to his knees, his back against the burning of the hearth fire, as the blood gushed up from his leg. Righting himself unsteadily on his good leg, he raised his sword against the High King's blow—a second too late. And the blade came down in a wicked, shining arc that took him through the throat.

And it was over. Cawdor lay with his head lolled back in the ashes of the hearth and the fire mirrored in the blood that ran glistening down his breast. Vortrix flung his own sword from him and knelt to pull his kinsman from the flames.

Talhaiere stepped forward, but he shook him off. "Give me a moment, old father." He turned to face the allied kings.

"I am thinking that this is a poor welcome to Council, and I am sorry for it. But I must leave you now. If you will but bide in the company of my queen and Galt my spear brother, we may yet speak of our hunting . . . in three days' time."

He nodded to Talhaiere and walked before the old priest to the door, pausing only to speak to Berec as he passed. "See that he is well buried, and the grave mound raised aright." And then he was gone, and there was only black night to be seen through the door of the hall.

The next day was the Midwinter Festival, but to Branwen, nursing small Bran in her chambers, it was a desolation of a day. The previous evening's feasting had limped along after its spectacular interruption, out of courtesy to the allied chieftains, but the empty chairs at the High Table loomed bleakly among the festival makers, and the dancers wove the pattern of the Spear Dance well away from the hearth.

Berec had picked up Cawdor's body and borne it alone out into the snow and mist. After a moment, Galt shrugged his shoulders and followed him. It was not fitting that Berec should prepare his spear brother's body for the pyre alone, and it seemed that no one wished to be mentioned to the High King afterward as the man who had helped. Galt, knowing his king better than most, had no such qualms.

Branwen was left alone to play host as best she might, and it was no easy going. The spectre of death—Cawdor's, and possibly that of the hoped-for alliance—hung over them all, and she was grateful when the warriors began to yawn and beckon for their spear bearers. Galt, leaving Berec to his vigil, returned in time to help her escort Brendan, Dergdian, and their respective entourages to the Guest Hall, and bid them welcome to the next day's festival.

As if by common consent, when the queen turned toward her own quarters Galt followed and she beckoned him in.

"Thank you, Merin. I will take him now."

The brown-haired girl who had played the drum for the women's dance on the night that Vortrix had come to her laughing and sword in hand put the babe in her arms and withdrew.

"She is of an age to make some man a fine wife," Branwen said. "But I'm thinking there will be many of our women who will never see a husband's hearth when this hunting is over."

"Would you have her go to a free lord of the Tribe or to a serf of Rome?" Galt inquired. She gestured to the chair opposite and he settled himself in it and curled one foot up catwise.

"A free lord certainly. But I am not so sure that a serf of the Roman kind is not better than no husband at all. Bah! I talk like a woman!" She laid the babe back in his cradle and curled up in her own chair, facing him. "I thought I had learned not to."

Galt raised an eyebrow. "You surprise me."

"I surprise myself at times since I was wed to the king. One learns to . . . adapt."

He smiled, a flickering cat-smile that matched the fluid grace of his movements. "I am thinking that the king's hound and the king's woman have yet something to learn of each other. And now, get some sleep if you can."

But Branwen found sleep a long time in coming.

Galt came again the next morning and gripped her shoulder in comfort before going to take his place at the Midwinter worship. "I am thinking you will have spent an evil night. Rest, lady. The thing was necessary, and he did not grudge the price."

But she knew little of the Lord of the Shining Spear, even

though the women raised their own dance to him when they took the war trail, and the unknown is always the most fearful.

Talhaiere also came to her chambers and, seeing the way her mind went, said gently, "There are mysteries that I may not speak of to you, but remember this—he never asks anything of a man without reason, or which that man cannot endure. Come now. Give the small lord to your women and take your place at the gathering. If the king can bear his part, then you must bear yours. That too is part of the price."

She rose and, calling for Merin to take the child, followed him out to where a trampled path ran through the snow to the field on the far side of the Council Mound. The Midwinter Fires that would be beacon-bright at nightfall shone like pale flowers against the dazzle of the sun. The clans of the Tribe were gathered in a splash of bright plaids and checkered cloaks around an oval track in the meadow, its sides banked high with cleared snow. Already the lithe wickerwork-and-leather chariots were gathered at the starting stone for the high point of the day's festivities, the Midwinter Race. Race day was flexible, moving with the weather, but this year it had held fine, and the race would be run on Midwinter Day itself.

Her father's team, steel grey with a flurry of snow-dappling down their rumps, pranced and fidgeted in the crisp air, their breath standing in little puffs about their nostrils. In the chariot, making a last check of the leather bindings that supported the frame, was her brother Donal, resplendent in a blue-bordered cloak of the same russet color as his hair. Brendan's team, a milk white pair almost invisible against the snow, threw up dainty heads with the small pricked ears that spoke of Arab blood, while the chieftain himself settled into the driver's place.

Team by team they filed onto the track . . . Dergdian, also driving his own team of bays . . . Duncan's blacks, driven by a blond boy who looked almost too young to be a charioteer. (Galt had said he showed much promise, she remembered, and that his youth was deceiving.)

And then a familiar pair of roans frisked down the narrow ramp that led to the track and she drew in her breath until she caught sight of the driver—Galt, driving the High King's horses instead of his own.

He frequently served as the king's charioteer in battle, for the two fought best as a team, but when it came to the race, they had always matched their horses against each other, and Galt's were accounted a favorite in any race he entered. This, then, was his own gift to his brother . . . a way perhaps of drawing him up from the dark night that enclosed him.

She turned her head to the white bulk of the Council Mound among the trees on the hill. Somewhere in the cavern beneath it, she knew, the High King made his penance alone.

It seemed harsh payment for a death well deserved, but it was a necessary law of the Tribe, that no man might fear to speak his mind at Council. Without invoking challenge, the payment for Cawdor's death would have been the killer's own life, High King or no.

"Come." Talhaiere took her by the arm again and led her to the high-backed chair draped with wolf skins that was the queen's place at the festival. The teams were lined up across the course now, and the starter raised the long bronze trumpet to his lips, as the horses twitched in anticipation. At the first note, they were off, the whippy little chariots springing like live things under their drivers' feet at every rise in the ground. Donal, in the inside position, gained the first lead, while Galt, midway down the line between the unknown quantities, Dergdian and Brendan, maneuvered for space to make his move. They rounded the first bend in a flying skein, and the pack began to take shape. Donal, still in the lead, hard-pressed by Duncan's young charioteer ("The young fool, he's pushing them too early!" she heard Cathuil grumble beside her) . . . Dergdian drawing forward, his blue-stained arms bright against the snow . . . and Galt, still feeling his way through the gap between the Caledonian chief and the Lord of the Selgovae who hung close on his flank. Behind and before, the six other teams that made up the race were strung out in a flying V like winter geese.

Into the third turn, the dapple greys were falling back while the black team flew before them like dark smoke . . . the fourth turn, and the blacks led still, pursued by the triple threat of Galt behind the High King's roans and the allied chieftains to either side of him. Cathuil's dapples had fallen behind the black team, and the two drivers between them had seized the chance to move forward, trapping Donal behind them, with the sharp-cut edge of the course on one side and the flying tail of the pack on the other. Cathuil's curses rang bitterly in the icy air.

At the fifth turn, the second and third teams were slackening, and Duncan's blacks catapulted forward across their path, into the inside position, with Dergdian's bays a nose behind. A length behind them thundered the High King's roans, and on the roans' right flank still hung the snow-colored team of the War Lord of the Selgovae.

"Fly then, my beauties, fly then, oh sons of Light!" Galt, bent forward, whispered to his team and the roans leaned into the traces and flew like the Wild Hunt into the bend.

Then, careening round the sixth turn, the near horse of the black team stumbled on a loose stone, and Dergdian's bays catapulted past him before he could recover, with the roan team in their wake. Brendan's Arabs, jockeying for position, ran afoul of a trailing harness strap thrown loose by the jolt to the blacks' chariot, and before Brendan could pull them up, the two teams were entangled in a snaking coil of leather.

The blond charioteer gave one glance over his shoulder and pulled his team up hard. They slowed, shaking their heads and fighting the pressure on the reins, and the boy leapt out along the pole to hack at the trailing strap with his dagger. Behind him the white team stumbled, panicking, while Brendan strove to keep them aligned with the chariot ahead. If they plunged to the side, they would bring both chariots down.

The trace parted just in time, as the off horse of the Arab team went crashing down, and Brendan hauled back on the near one's reins with all his strength. The blond charioteer leapt back to his place again and, seeing that the white team was free, shook out the reins and gave the blacks their heads. It was plain that it was too late. The two lead teams were a good six lengths ahead and coming into the next-to-last turn. Duncan, watching, gritted his teeth but kept silent. No charioteer worthy of the name would have risked hurt to his own or another's team for the sake of a race.

The white team was up again, apparently unhurt, and now all eyes were on the leaders, separated by no more than a head as they rounded the seventh turn. Galt was crooning to the red team in a singsong of encouragement, and they flicked their ears back to the sound and gave one more burst of speed. Slowly, in the last turn, they narrowed the gap to half a head and then less and, coming into the straight, hurled themselves past the flying forefeet of the bays as the racekeeper's arm flashed down.

There was a roar of approval from the crowd, and jubilant demands for bets to be paid off, as the teams slowed their pace and circled the track at a trot. The roans were first up the ramp, their red tails frisking in the sunlight and looking well pleased with themselves. Galt drove them straight up the aisle to the queen's chair, where they dipped their heads to her and then spoiled the effect by whuffling against the breast of her gown for the barley cake they knew she sometimes carried for them.

"No, no, my friends, I am carrying no sticky cakes in my best gown," she laughed, putting the winners' wreaths of evergreen about their necks. "Content you with this."

"They ran well, considering that Sundown is young and new to the race." Galt leapt down from his place and knelt before her for his own wreath, and she smiled as she set it on the pale head. "The king's woman has learned another thing of the king's hound," she murmured. "There is a great kindness in him." He shook his head and looked embarrassed, so she said no more and nodded at him to rise.

He backed the team down the aisle, which was too narrow for the chariot to turn, stopping in the press of congratulations to speak to Duncan's young driver.

"That was well driven, lad. I am sorry to have a victory at your expense. We must match old Duncan's team to *my* blacks someday, for the sport of it. I'm thinking it would be a rare race."

The boy's dejected face split into a grin. "Aye, that would be fine." He stood back to let the red team pass with worship writ large on his face.

Dergdian also came to offer congratulations, his face more alive than Galt had seen it before, with the joy of the race still in it. The Caledonian chief was a horseman with few equals. Brendan too came forward, having made sure that his team had suffered no hurt.

"That was an ill piece of luck," Galt said.

"I must find the lad and speak with him," Brendan said. "If he had not been quick with his dagger, I'd have more than hurt pride to grieve me now." He glanced to where the white stallions, legs miraculously unbroken, were being walked cool.

"There is food for feasting, and far less noise, in my quarters," Galt said as the three shouldered their way through the holiday throng. "When I have seen the High King's horses stabled, I will be the High King's hound again, at Your Graces' service." He bowed and took his leave.

"A trusted hound indeed," Dergdian said, looking after him.

"And one to be reckoned with. I'm thinking young Vortrix's fox-haired kinsman lived as long as he did because that hound was leashed. There's a danger in that pretty face I'd as soon not have turned toward *me*."

The pretty face, when it appeared again at the private Council of Alliance, was somber. "There will be an ill mood in the air when the merrymaking has worn off," he said, flinging his cloak onto the bed and drawing a chair toward the others at the fire. "Already there is talk that the alliance will not stand and the thing cannot be done alone."

"Perhaps the Lord of the Brigantes should have thought of that before he slew a man at Council," Brendan said.

"It should have been done long ago," Galt said frankly, "at a time when the price did not come so high. But remember, he has seen the Royal Family murder each other one by one, and so he promised himself that there would be no more. I think even Cawdor was surprised when he broke that vow."

He called out through the curtained doorway, and swept a litter of harness straps and broken harp strings from the table as his spear bearer appeared with a platter of steaming boar's meat and a pitcher of beer with three flagons hanging from hooks round its mouth. When the boy had gone, Galt poured beer for the allied lords and then looked them straight in the eye.

"It will not wait," he said flatly. "You made the first council with me last winter. Now perforce you must make this one also."

Two mornings later Branwen, huddled alone beneath the piled furs on the bed, was awakened by an icy touch on her bare shoulder. She sat up, shrieking at the imagined culmination of all her nightmares, and was confronted instead by the face of the High King, chalk white and haggard. He was clad only in a fighting kilt of grey wolf skin, and there were fresh scars radiating in a sunburst across his chest. A faint trace of dried blood, missed in the Cleansing, ran from the center of the pattern down across his belly.

"Nay, I am no demon." He smiled, but she could see that he was weaving on his feet. She thrust the tumbled hair back from her face and reached out to him.

"You are cold to the bone!"

"Aye, bitter cold." He shivered, and she thought that the cold he spoke of had little to do with the winter frost.

"Then come you in with me." She pulled him down to her and wrapped them both in the soft furs, cradling his head on her breast.

"I cannot stay longer than to let you warm me. I must find Galt."

"Hush, it is well. They had to call Council in your absence, but it went well, I think, and Galt will still be sleeping now. Was it very evil?"

"Not evil, no, but . . . bad enough. And now there must be no more talk of it, else I speak of forbidden things because I am tired and you are warm and comforting. I knew the price beforehand, and I have paid it. Let that be an end to it." He settled himself deeper against her breast, and a shudder ran through him like a tremor in the earth. Then it seemed to her that he slept, but after a moment he roused himself to whisper, "What of the small cub?"

"He is sleeping, which is what he mostly does when he is not eating like a pig. And he took no chill at the Binding, as I had feared he might. Midwinter is no time to take a babe out in the snow."

"Branwen, it was necessary."

"Aye, I know it was, with things as they are. And see, he has taken no harm from it, and I was foolish. It seems the Mother and the Shining One both have smiled on our cub."

He stirred and wrapped one arm around her tightly. "And on me, when they sent me Branwen Cathuil's-daughter to my wife." His eyes fluttered shut and, seeing that he was on the edge of sleep, she gently pulled the thongs from his hair, letting it fall in a golden wave across her breast to mingle with her own.

But when she woke, she found herself alone again. Vortrix, with his cloak pulled around his shoulders, stood leaning in the outer doorway, talking softly with Galt's young spear bearer.

He dismissed the boy and padded lightly across the floor to pull a shirt and breeches from the clothes chest. "Go back to sleep," he said, seeing that her eyes were open. "I'll only be as far as the Guest Hall."

She nodded drowsily and obeyed, as he caught up his sword and the king's circlet and slipped out into the courtyard.

By midmorning there was much bustle between the King's Hall and the Guest Hall, small boys scurrying here and there with trays and pitchers and older boys doing messenger service, loping through the outer buildings, heads popping through doorways. "Have you seen my Lord Cathuil?" "King Brendan wants his spear bearer. Where have they put the boys?" "Lord Galt says if you don't get him something to drink there'll be murder done." "Good Lord, who set an infant to tend the kitchen? Give me that, child, I'll show you how."

In the midst of the confusion the clan chieftains came and went, summoned to the Guest Hall one by one to make their reports, with Talhaiere among them, stately in his white robes.

From the Guest Hall could be heard frequent spates of shouting, followed by the thump of an emphatic fist on the table.

The women also hurried to and fro, overseeing preparations for the feast that night. "A proper feast," Branwen said tiredly, with her sleeves rolled up, spreading fresh rushes on the floor, "with the High King to sit at it, thank the Mother. If they don't murder each other first," she added, as angry voices broke out again across the courtyard.

"It is only the small matters they are ironing out now," Talhaiere smiled, stepping deftly around a pail of dirty water, "but they make for much shouting. The rest was settled peaceably enough this morning."

By midafternoon the shouting had died to an occasional burst of raised voices, and the last clan chief had made his appearance before the four figures seated around the table.

Galt emerged first, looking tired and bedraggled, and took himself off to his quarters. He reappeared some two hours later looking his usual fine self, decked in the few trinkets that had not gone to the war chest and with his flaxen hair freshly bleached for the occasion.

Vortrix also, when he stepped from the Guest Hall with Dergdian and Brendan beside him, looked bone-weary, and also made his excuses and retired to his chambers where he flung himself down on the bed and drew the covers up over his ears. Brendan and Dergdian gathered their warriors to them, and there was much quiet conferencing before they too went to make ready for the evening's celebration.

Branwen made one last tour of the hall, evicted a small boy who had gone to sleep under one of the tables, and called her women to her chambers. She sat back wearily while they dressed her hair, amid much fluttering and hushing lest they disturb the High King asleep in the adjoining room.

For the next two hours quiet reigned, as the whole court made ready for the night; and then, as dark fell, it blazed into life again. Torches wove to and fro in the darkness, streaming through all the courts of the king's holding toward the Great Hall; the men in kilts or breeches and shirts of soft dyed leather and brightly checkered woolens, the women in flowing gowns of the same materials, with the glint of bronze and gold and bright enamel round their necks and arms. The children, as always, set to make themselves useful, tended the fires with much importance and added the final touches to the tables in the hall. Dogs of all varieties paced at their masters' heels, those on their home turf eyeing the dogs of the visitors with open suspicion, making it clear that their masters had but to give the word and they would show the interlopers a thing or two.

Brendan's warriors mingled freely with the men of the Brigantes, trading jokes and tall tales amid shouts of laughter. The Selgovae were old allies, and there had been much intermarrying among the two tribes as well. The blue-stained men of the Caledones held themselves aloof, although the High King's men, in the expansive mood that always prevailed at a great feast, set themselves to be friendly. But it had taken much negotiation to hammer an ancient enmity into a new alliance, and in some ways it was uneasy still. Only an undying hatred of the Romans bound the northern tribe to this new friendship.

The three kings made an entrance together, set by Vortrix with a showman's timing for the moment when the dried herbs that the boys tossed on the fire to sweeten the air sent the flames shooting up in a burst of light. Brendan, in a kilt and shirt of dark green leather, with red gold encircling his throat and upper arms, and running almost invisibly through his flaming hair; Dergdian, clad in woolen checkered bright blue and black, with a fine red thread running through it, and his shouders draped in a scarlet cloak held at the throat by a huge brooch of amber-studded gold. His dark hair was braided back with thongs of soft red leather and the fresh stain of woad stood out sharp against his fair skin.

And finally Vortrix, his golden hair streaming down his shoulders, the raw scars hidden beneath the winter white of his shirt, and his russet kilt belted with a bronze-studded circle of leather and a bronze buckle that curved into the form of a leaping horse. His eyes were wolf-bright under a fringe of pale lashes, and he carried the bronze fillet on his head as regally as any golden one. Come from three days in the presence of the Shining One himself, he stood on the edge of the fire glow, enveloped in a haze of smoke and light, and even Dergdian's warriors looked on him in awe.

Then the fire sank down again, young Dawid scurried up with three flagons foaming with the best beer, and the moment was over. The allied kings took their places at the High Table and the evening's concentration turned itself to the feast, the revellers doing their best to make up for the grimness of that other feast two nights before. In this they seemed likely to succeed, and the hall was loud with laughter and bragging, and tales of great battles in the high and far-off days when the world was young and the golden people were its kings. A light snow had begun again outside, but the hall was warm with the fire and the press of bodies and the flying feet of the dancers. After a while, Galt took up his harp and made a song of one of the old tales of the coastwise tribes, about a woman who mated with a man of the seal people and bore him a son, and how she cursed him when he came back years later and took the child away to his half kin, and how the curse flew home on the spear of her hunter husband, striking both the seal man and her son.

There were shouts of approval and requests for other songs equally well known among the tribes, but Galt just shook his head and, taking his harp, drew a stool close by the glimmer of the sinking fire. Eyes closed, he began to make a new music, born of the new alliance . . . a battle music to be remembered by the sons of the sons of the men who sat there, with the brightness of a spear point and the keen edge of death and victory in it. His slender hands danced along the strings, and the sounds of chariots thundering down a valley and the clash of armies could be heard, and the high sweet note of trumpets. The bleached hair and bright jewelry and the brilliant green and saffron of his kilt, faded in the firelight, and it was Music who sat there, as blinding as the sun, and wove them all in its spell.

When morning came, the shadow of that singing still lingered in the air, underlying the excitement that rippled through the courtyard. The holiday mood was gone, and a tense expectancy gave every face the sharp, eager look of a hound about to be unleashed.

There was a rattle and thunder from the stables, and the chariots of the Selgovae swept through the courtyard, sunlight glinting from harness rings and wheel hubs, Brendan at their head, his hair streaming out like a wind-borne fire.

Behind them careened the horses of the Caledones, with Dergdian at the center, shadowed by the lithe, wicked length of a feather-decked war spear.

The great gates were flung open, and the road north lay snow-dappled before them, blinding white in the winter sun. The chariots wheeled and poured through the gates as the allied chiefs leaned down to pluck two flaming torches from the gateposts.

XVI

A Spring Too Early

Come you bold fellows and join the Ar-mee,
To slaughter the Pict and the heathen Parsee—

Someone was singing in the street outside the armorer's shop, his
cheerful voice cleaving the morning stillness.

And maybe, just maybe (the chances are small)
But maybe you'll rise to be Emperor of all!

Roma, far Roma, we list to your call,
Townsmen of Italy and farmers from Gaul.
We've bought you an Empire from Britain to Crete,
With the boils on our backsides and the sores on our feet!

The song in its heyday had enjoyed a popularity throughout the
Army, and Justin, lounging in the armorer's shop while a loose
rivet was pounded back in his helmet, poked his head through the
doorway and joined in. The last time he had heard it was before
setting out from Lambaesis under the hot sun, on a summer's campaign.

244

So take up your pilum and shield and your sword,
And fly with the Eagles to fame and reward!
But remember, young fellow, ere glory you seek,
A recruiting centurion will lie like a Greek!

Come you bold fellows and join the Ar-mee,
To slaughter the Pict and the heathen Parsee,
And maybe, just maybe (the chances are small)
But maybe you'll rise to be Emperor of all!

Some of us turn home with twenty years pay
At the end of the long march, and—some of us stay.
So when you have climbed to the Emperor's throne,
Remember the Eagles who'll never fly home!

"I haven't sung that since Africa," Justin said, when they had finished with a last rousing chorus that rattled the roof tiles.

The dark young auxiliary officer, punching a new hole in a bridle strap, looked up and grinned at him. "Glad to have you join in, chief," he said. (The auxiliary cavalry, being mostly rugged individualists, had scant respect for the regular Legions.)

"You've a good voice."

"Oh, aye, all the Silures are accounted good singers."

"Silures? Then what are you doing in the Asturian Horse?"

"Oh, that's a long story." He tried the new hole in the bridle buckle and seemed satisfied with it. "My mother, you see, she married a man from the Second Legion, and when he was shifted to Spain, she followed him, more fool she."

"An officer?" Legionaries were seldom bounced from Legion to Legion as the centurions were.

"Oh, aye, and killed right off, so there she was, stuck, with me on the way. But she did well enough. Married an Asturian who didn't mind bein' presented with a family two months after the weddin'. So here's me, in the Asturian Horse."

"Why not a Legion? I expect you'd have qualified."

"Nay, I never had a taste for goin' too much by the book. My Asturians now, they're a handful, but they're one o' the best troops in the unit. 'Course, I've known a lot of 'em since we were boys, and sometimes it's a help."

Justin held out a hand. "I'm Justinius Corvus, Sixth Cohort."

"Ah, you'll be the poor devil they threw to Martius's sharks. I'm Owen Lucullus—and there's a good half-and-half name for you."

And typical of the Army as a whole, Justin thought. British mother, provincial Roman father, Spanish stepfather, and now come full circle back to Britain with thirty headstrong Asturians in his charge.

"How long have you been out here?"

"Posted last year, with more of us to follow, so they said. Me, I haven't seen 'em yet."

"Well, we'd better have them soon."

"Aye, we had, or we'll have the little painted bandits stealin' the horses out from under our arses." He paused and his ears pricked up. "And speakin' o' that, who's the one trailin' round with Cunory the Hunter? I've never seen him before."

Justin turned to look where the cavalry man was pointing. Cunory, taking advantage of a light winter to make an early tour, was unloading skins in front of the soldiers' barracks and haggling cheerfully over their price. Behind him, holding the pack ponies' bridles, was a slight, dark man in a nondescript cloak and checkered breeches. He was tattooed in brilliant patterns over every visible inch of skin.

"I don't know him either," Justin said, "but Picts make me nervous just now. Still, we can't keep out every native hunter that comes to sell skins . . . ."

"He's probably only a henchman of Cunory's," Owen said, rising. "Otherwise he'd be busy enough in the north, most like. Still, it won't do to have him lounge about and count noses, will it? I'll just be having a word with Cunory. The sun and the moon on your path, chief." He picked up his bridle and ambled over to the group collecting around the hunters.

"And I'll be having a word with the Legate," Justin murmured. The armorer called him in to collect his helmet, and he strolled up toward the Principia, dangling it by the strap. In the courtyard he paused and settled it on his head before proceeding into the Legate's office.

"There's a Pict trailing round with Cunory the Hunter that you might like to talk to—sir," he added, saluting. (Consorting with Owen seemed to be contagious.)

"Indeed." Aurelius Rufus nodded to the Optio who was presenting a duty roster for his inspection. "Please make it so."

"And now," he said, when the Optio had gone on his errand, "I thought Cunory hunted solo. Kindly tell me all."

"That's all I know, sir. But I've an idea that if you sent for Decurion Owen Lucullus of the Asturian Horse—I don't know which troop—he would probably be able to tell you by now."

The Pict, when questioned, protested vehemently that he was just a wanderer, one of the many of his kind who for one reason or another (sometimes shady, sometimes not) broke away from his tribe and sought another life elsewhere. He had merely contracted his services to Cunory for the season for the price of his meals and a little loose change at the end of it.

Cunory, Owen said, substantiated the story as far as he could. The Painted One was a good hunter, as were all of his kind, and had much skill with the pack ponies. He brought in more skins than the price of his hire. Therefore the bargain was sealed. He would no doubt be off again in the spring—the Pict never stuck to hired labor for long.

"I'm thinking Cunory speaks the truth as he sees it," Owen added, the mended bridle still jingling from his hand. "But then, it's probably all one to Cunory anywise. His home ground is a good ways south of here."

The upshot was that the Legate ordered Cunory and his painted companion out of Eburacum Fortress and Eburacum town, and told them that for their skins' sake they had best *stay* out. "Nay, I am told that Cunory the Hunter has always done well by the Legions," he added when Cunory indignantly protested this decree, "but there is too much unrest in the heather just now for me to take a chance. Come to me in a year when there has been no rising, and your pony driver has had no hand in it, and I will apologize."

Cunory shrugged his shoulders and departed, remarking that he had sold the better part of his skins anyway.

And Justin invited Owen to lunch.

"You've a fine house, chief," Owen said cheerfully, as they turned in the garden gate with the apple tree hanging winter-bare and snow-flecked above it.

Inside they found more company than Justin had bargained for. Januaria bustled about with trays of sweets and boiled eggs and winter fruit while Felicia sat toasting her toes at the brazier, her dark curls tumbled about her face, and her back hair braided in a British fashion of which her father would undoubtedly have disapproved. Beside her sat Licinius, apparently inspecting a flaw in the tile, and glowering like a fiend.

Gwytha and Hilarion, in the dining alcove, were making much of the grey and white cat, and looking greatly embarrassed.

"Justin, *dear!*" Gwytha leapt up from her couch as if it had suddenly become red-hot and embraced him warmly. "I invited her to lunch," she whispered frantically in his ear. "I had no idea Licinius would pick today to look in on small Justin—he's as healthy as a hound puppy and Licinius knows it! If it hadn't been for Hilarion stopping by, I should have crawled into the storeroom and pretended I was a bag of apples and let them murder each other, or whatever it is they're going to do!"

"Dear Lord!" Justin said fervently. And then, remembering his guest, "Let me present to you Decurion Owen Lucullus, of the Asturian Horse. I've invited him to lunch as well."

"The sun and the moon on the path of the woman of the house," Owen said gallantly in the British tongue.

Gwytha smiled and held out her hand. "You've the wrong coloring for a Briton, but the face—"

Owen raised one black, flyaway eyebrow, and bowed. "Me father, good lady. The face is me mother's—of the Silures, to the south."

Gwytha laughed and called into the kitchen to Januaria. "In any case, Decurion, you are welcome. Will you drink with us?"

"Aye, and gladly. What ails yon couple in the corner?" he asked, regarding them with curiosity.

"Thwarted love," she hissed in her own language, and he also laughed.

"It's no laughing matter," Hilarion said grimly, striding over to be introduced. "If something isn't done, we're going to need a new surgeon. Licinius is at the end of his tether."

"Well, I don't know what you think *I* can do about it," Gwytha said practically. The grey and white cat, offended at the loss of his lap, stalked into the kitchen in search of consolation, and an uneasy silence fell as the couple in the corner came forward to make their compliments.

"We've decided to mind our manners," Felicia said frankly, allowing Justin to present Owen Lucullus to her. "Gwytha, my dear, I'm behaving terribly, and I do apologize. So, I expect, does Licinius."

"So I do," Licinius said. "Hallo, Justin. I'm afraid you've got rather a houseful."

"Not at all," Justin murmured idiotically, viewing the foot which Disaster had stuck in his door with alarm.

The black eyebrow had flown up again when Justin presented Felicia, with all her names, to Owen, but the cavalry man managed admirably to stifle the various remarks which Justin imagined came first to his lips.

Fortune, in the ample person of Januaria, chose that moment to appear with a plate of seasoned meats wrapped in pastry, and the six fell upon them gratefully. When they had eaten, the talk turned by common consent to the situation in the north and the possibility of real trouble come spring.

Licinius, Hilarion, and Justin, already used to Gwytha, were not overly surprised when the Legate's daughter took an animated and intelligent part in the talk of fortifications and night fighting, and the best possible garrisoning of their thin ranks to cover all strategic forts. To Owen Lucullus, however, this was obviously a novelty, and Justin guessed that his mother, for all her marriage to an officer of the Eagles, had concentrated her attention upon her husband's person rather than his profession.

"Well, I hope to Hades we get some reinforcements in time," was the general tenor of the remarks, and Felicia pushed the black curls back from her face and looked at them soberly.

"They have been requested, you know," she said. "I expect I'm telling tales out of school because there's no saying what Hadrian may do, but I'd prefer you didn't think my father was an idiot."

"My dear girl, there's no question of that," Justin said.

"On the contrary, he's merely a poor man who's been handed a den full of wolves and told to make them into lap dogs," Owen said. "Me, I don't envy him the task."

"How do matters stand with the Auxiliaries?" Felicia asked.

"For my troop, and most of the others who are fairly new to Britain, well enough. But there are a lot who are rotten like a bad apple with being undermanned and posted to the frontier too long. I wouldn't answer for the cavalry of the outpost forts either. The last lot I saw through here had rust in their bridles and burrs in their tails, and I didn't like the look of 'em."

"No more do we all," Licinius said, rising from his couch. "Gwytha dear, the gods keep you. Justin, I must go. I have an infected leg in surgery that wants looking at." He glanced bleakly at Felicia but made no comment.

After a moment, though, she also stood up. "I'll come and help," she said. "Cybele knows I've had enough practice over the years."

The two went out together, and the other four looked after them dubiously. Januaria, evidently sharing their sentiments, was heard to mutter "Poor young babies" from her post in the kitchen. The idea of anyone's regarding the Legion's self-sufficient senior surgeon as a "poor young baby" amused Justin to the point that he burst out laughing, and the tension dissolved as the others joined in.

"Well, he is then," Gwytha said when she had stopped spluttering. "We all are from time to time, and Licinius helped *me* over it—" she smiled at Justin and rubbed a small hand along his knee—"and the gods know I owe him one."

"My dear, I'm afraid there is little you can do. I doubt the Legate would thank you for playing Cupid."

Gwytha was forced to admit the justice of this observation, but in her own newfound happiness she was galled to see it denied Licinius. When the men had left, she sat and mulled over the conversation of the afternoon.

"Felicia, you *cannot!*" A picture of herself expounding mightily came first to mind.

"And *why* can I not?" Felicia's chin was set in a stubborn line. "Centurion Corvus married in the face of much to-do—and I've heard all the tales of *that*, so you needn't look embarrassed—and you are as wellborn in your tribe as I am in mine."

"The to-do was raised by *his* people, not mine, and it crops up still. Justin told me about the dinner at the Praetorium after he had a chance to cool down. And Martius is dead, poor man. But at least Justin had only his own people to fight, and not mine as well."

"Well, Licinius will have only *my* people to fight," Felicia had said practically.

"His people and your people are the same . . . only yours are a good four steps upward from his. And that's your problem. There are times when it's easier to unite one folk with another than to bridge the gap that runs down the middle of the same folk."

"I can recall saying as much," Licinius had interjected as he strode in the door. "I have come to see the babe," he added, but his baleful glance was drawn to Felicia as a moth is to a lamp.

And so they had sat and stared at each other, or the floor, for the better part of the afternoon.

Now, in the surgery, she worked silently beside him as he tended the boy's wolf-bitten leg. It irritated him that his patient, who had been startled and wary at her first appearance in the hospital, now seemed to take her presence for granted, trading jokes with her like an old comrade and telling stories of his boyhood in Spain. Felicia, Licinius discovered, had worked in camp hospitals before, in the bloody aftermath of battles when every hand was needed. He had told her once that if she weren't a woman she would have made a good surgeon, and had thought for a moment that she was going to spit at him. It was not a remark he had repeated.

There had been no further comment from the Legate who knew his daughter well enough to realize that her continued visits to the hospital, and the chariot-driving lessons, were mostly on her initiative. Had it not been for her effort to see him, Licinius would merely have retreated into miserable solitude and suffered from afar. As it was, the Legate quietly made up his mind to transfer the surgeon to another posting as soon as was practical, which would be after this summer's campaign. With a Pict rising in the wind, Aurelius Rufus had no intention of replacing a man who was accounted to be one of the best surgeons in the Army; and once the Legion marched, Licinius would have precious little opportunity for courting.

"There," Licinius said, pinning the last bandage in place. "That leg is healing nicely. If you're lucky, you'll be fit to march in a couple of months."

"My thanks," the legionary said wryly, and Licinius laughed and dropped into a chair, running his fingers over his own leg.

"Pulled a muscle, have you?"

"No, merely an old knee trouble. It's been flaring up of late."

"What do you do for it?" Felicia asked, kneeling down to look.

"There's an operation that helps sometimes, if it hasn't gone too far, but it's chancy. And I can hardly do it on myself. The only man I'd trust to tackle it is stationed in Moesia, which isn't much help."

"But you should have it seen to."

"Oh, I get by. It mostly bothers me when I overwork it." The legionary yawned, and Licinius stood up again. "Come along, my girl, this man needs his rest."

"Oh, aye, I'd be fearsome disappointed if I didn't get to let the Pict take a shot at me," the legionary called after them, grinning.

"Where are we going?" Felicia inquired.

"As far as the first empty bed," Licinius said, gritting his teeth. "And then you are going to get me a cup of wine and some pain-killer from the dispensary. I can't walk on this thing."

She got one shoulder under his arm and half carried him to an empty room where he dropped white-faced onto the bed. He told her what he wanted, and she bustled off to fetch it while he lay back against the pillow.

"Licinius, you have got to have that seen to," she said, as he shook the powder into his wine and swallowed it.

"Well, I'm in no condition to hike to Moesia," he said. "And in any case, it will go back in if I rest it." He leaned up and kissed her. "Now take yourself off before your father comes looking for my hide."

Watching him strolling toward the bathhouse the next evening with Justin and Hilarion, she decided he was right about his knee. And then her attention was distracted even from Licinius, when she walked into her father's study to find him perusing a newly arrived despatch, its edges heavy with official seals. He looked up as she entered and held out his hand to her.

"What is it, Papa?"

"The Fates, thinly disguised as the Emperor Hadrian. Here, child, you might as well read it. It will be public knowledge the minute I can make it so."

She took the sheet and studied it. ". . . reinforcements . . . detachment of Legio VI Victrix . . . cavalry support . . . within the month . . . hold until then . . . Imperator Caesar Traianus Hadrianus Augustus."

"At least when we march, it won't be in this pitiful condition."

"But you will march. And I'll be left here with Theodore and Calpurnia."

"My dear child, it happens every campaign. Hmmm, I see. Now there are two of us to grieve over. I am not unsympathetic, but you are going to have to put the man out of your mind, and you know it as well as I do."

"I know nothing of the sort, but there is no point in arguing the matter with you now, and I *do* see that." She kissed him on the forehead and handed him back the despatch.

Aurelius Rufus sat looking after her. There would be no point in arguing the matter later either. Licinius was going to be tending some other Legion's sword cuts.

In the meantime . . . He called for the Optio, and began drafting an official announcement.

"Not that it will make much difference to those bastards," Justin said to Hilarion after the officers' briefing. "But at least we can intersperse them with a few good men." He was still wrestling with Martius's legacy, a cohort composed half of sullen, rebellious troops and half of men who were well and truly frightened, with a few barracks lawyers and professional malingerers thrown in for good measure. He had tried everything from speeches to a liberal application of the vine staff and various forms of "on report" punishment. He thought he was making headway here and there, but it was slow going. It had taken him two years to get his old Eighth Cohort into shape, and he had not had much more than two months with this one. The detachment from the Sixth Victrix was desperately needed, for the bolstering of both physical strength and morale, and for the example they would provide of properly disciplined troops. With luck, a little might rub off on the Hispana.

The Legate also awaited the reinforcements impatiently. It was never easy to fit a last minute detachment in with an existing army, and he wanted a chance to get the kinks out *before* the last minute. Also (although this had not been part of his official announcement) there was an extra cohort centurion coming out, a replacement for Centurion Cassius, and him the Legate wanted desperately. Knowing that his rabble of a cohort would support him (more fools they), Cassius was treading a very thin line these days, and his second wasn't much better. His replacement, when it happened, would have to be swift and without warning, or the cohort could get out of hand.

In one way or another, the whole fort was marking time as despatch followed despatch to chronicle the progress of the reinforcing detachment and its cavalry Auxiliaries.

And then, in the space of one warm late March day, the single bud on the apple tree became thousands, and the snow trickled away into the ground. It was spring, spring come too early and as deadly as a flower with poison at its center. And the reinforcements were dangerously overdue.

With the capriciousness of nature, while the spring sun shone on northern Britain, the mother of storms hovered over Gesoriacum, bogging down the supply trains, swamping the smaller craft in harbor, and setting even the great transports riding at anchor to pitching. The port commander at Gesoriacum had half his men at work reinforcing the sea wall and battling the storm to draw the light craft into safer berths. When the commander of the Victrix detachment asked him how long he thought it would be before they could cross, he stood him in the doorway of his office to watch the rain coming down in sheets over the white foam of the Channel. Rutupiae Light, visible on a clear day, was hidden behind that raging wall of water. Even over the roar of the storm, the cavalry horses in the transit barns behind them could be heard having hysterics.

"All the same, my orders are to sail immediately," the Victrix officer said stubbornly.

"Not from my port, you won't," the Gesoriacum commander retorted, rain plastering his forelock flat to his forehead and running in rivulets down from his helmet. "If you want to drown yourself, just go and take a dive off the sea wall there. That way you won't be taking good ships with you. Listen to them," he added as a handful of cavalrymen raced across the cobbles to the transit barn while the neighing and kicking increased frantically. "If for some reason the storm didn't get you, those damn horses would kick the ship apart. Horse transport's hard enough in good weather. I'm not sending a bunch of hysterical brutes across the Channel in *this!*"

"How if I take them down the coast to Grannona and embark from there? It's a longer crossing, but it might be quicker than waiting out the storm."

"And have the storm follow you down the coast as like as not. Look, lad, your supply train hasn't even caught up with you yet. You've got to *feed* these troops once you get them across, you know. *And* you'll have a longer road by land that way."

A flash of lightning illuminated them both, setting their faces in sharp relief under their dripping helmets. Then the Victrix officer shrugged and turned back into the port commander's office.

"All right, we'll wait at least until the supply train catches up, if you'll give me your word you'll give the order to transport the minute the sea is calm enough to try it."

"Don't worry. You'll cross as soon as possible. I get no kick having the lot of you quartered here, eating your heads off on *my* supplies and asking me about the weather every five minutes."

The Victrix officer stalked out again, this time remembering his cloak, and turned, head down, through the driving rain for the transit barracks where his legionaries and auxiliarymen were crowded twelve to a room.

In Eburacum the birds were singing, the sun was warm and beneficent, and the cavalry horses tossed up their heads and frisked their tails at morning drill, their winter coats falling away in tufts that blew across the parade ground and piled up like cobwebs in the corners of their stalls.

Justin, walking with Gwytha and small Justin in the spring warmth, was among the first to see the grim grey beacon to the north. The baby, tucked in a shawl under his arm, was giggling and making futile grabs at Finn's comical face as it rose, fringed in a feathering of grey whiskers, before his field of vision. Justin, watching the wolfhound's leaping antics, followed his progress upward and stopped, caught by the billowing cloud on the northern horizon. Closer, as his vision narrowed, another cloud came into focus, and closer still, the barely discernible glow of yet another beacon fire beneath an even larger and more ominous billow of smoke.

"Mithras, God!" He dumped the baby in Gwytha's startled arms and caught Finn by the collar. "Home, you, with your mistress! Gwytha, take the baby and get home! No, I'll be there, I promise," he added as she started to protest. He flung himself away and went leaping down the slope to the road below.

Gwytha, her protest cut short, saw the billowing black signal in the north. She caught up the baby and, whistling Finn to her heel, ran down the track to the town. Januaria met her at the door, big with news, but Gwytha shook her aside.

"I have seen it. I must feed the child, but when I have done, come you and take him. Justin will be back tonight, before . . . before they march . . . I will wait for him."

"They will march?" Januaria hovered in concern.

"Yes, they will march. The Eagles will fly, as Justin would say, and the gods help us, they are so few."

"Oh, my lady—" Januaria took the baby from her, her substantial bulk heaving with distress. "You shouldn't be alone. Let me send for the Lady Felicia. She also—"

Gwytha turned a white, distracted face toward the housekeeper. "Yes, she also has a parting to endure, but let it wait til morning. No," she added as Januaria looked likely to protest. "It will keep til morning. Justin has said he'll be back, and he does not give his word lightly. And I expect Licinius will be looking for Felicia. Better that she find him than me."

She ran a hand lightly over the baby's brow (he had gone to sleep in Januaria's comforting embrace). "Take small Justin and put him to bed. He can eat later . . . and I will wake him when his father comes. Yes, wake him. It will do him no harm, and he will remember . . . remember . . . ." She trailed off and sat down to wait, huddled in the chair by the window.

In the Praetorium, Felicia also sat and waited, curled up on a couch in the bright little bedroom of her private quarters. It was a cheerful room, with a painted wall on which a troop of dancers cavorted to the piping of a trio of small fauns, but this afternoon the dancers failed to lift her spirits as they usually did. Her father, she knew, was closeted with his senior staff in his office in the Principia, and it would be nightfall before he had a moment for her. As for Licinius, he might or might not come looking for her when he left the briefing.

She rose and paced to the window. The whole camp was in an uproar, and she could see heads bobbing by past the garden wall, amid shouted orders and the tramp of marching feet. Despatch riders came and went from the Principia, and even Theodore in the kitchen was in what for him amounted to a tizzy.

She waited until she saw a group of senior officers pass by in the twilight and then pulled her cloak around her shoulders. Her father was still sitting at his desk in the Principia when she got there. His face looked tired in the greying light, and older than she could remember ever seeing it.

"Well, my dear, it's come. There's an allied war band of Picts and Brigantes heading south, with the Selgovae thrown in for good measure."

"But your reinforcements—"

"Can't wait for them. If we don't stop this in the north it will be too late. They will have to catch up as best they can. I'm not leaving much of a garrison here, but enough for safety. I've put Centurion Hilarion in charge of it. He didn't like it, of course, but I have to have someone reliable here. And his cohort's among the least likely to give trouble under another commander. I'm taking most of *it* with me, needless to say." He paused and beckoned her to him, pulling her down on his lap the way he used to do when she was small.

"Oh, Papa."

"Now listen to me, Felicia. I have made arrangements for you and the servants to be sent south if it seems necessary."

"Papa—"

"I said, *if* it seems necessary, and I don't think it will be. But if it is, you are to go—understood?"

"Do I have a choice?"

"No."

"All right, Papa." She put her head down on his shoulder, and he hugged her to him for a moment.

"Good. Now take yourself off home. At least we'll have dinner together. I've given Centurion Corvus leave to spend the night with his wife. Somebody might as well enjoy himself tonight."

Outside, Hilarion said much the same thing as he stalked grumpily along beside Justin. "It certainly won't be me! Left behind like a nursemaid—and my cohort marching without me."

"Well, I expect he's left you bits of it," Justin said consolingly.

"Very funny."

They stopped outside the officers' quarters and Justin turned sober. "See here, Hilarion, I'm just as glad it's you that's commanding the garrison. There's something I want to ask you."

"Anything."

"It's Gwytha."

"Oh." Hilarion's thin, freckled face looked uncomfortable and he fidgeted with the leather kilt of his harness tunic.

"If anything happens to me, I want you to look after her."

"Justin—"

"You've been a good friend to us ever since we married," Justin went on, ignoring the other man's discomfort, "and I know how you feel about her."

"Justin, I never—" Hilarion was obviously appalled.

"No, you ass, I know you haven't. Just—if something happens to me, see that she's all right. Take her to my mother at Antium, or—anything else that seems appropriate to you." He reached out and hugged the other man to him, and then he was gone, heading down the road to the town gate.

Hilarion stood looking after him a moment, his friendly countenance turned somber. Then he turned in the door to his own quarters, to work out the garrison duty of the handful of troops that would be left to him.

By the time it was full dark, preparations for the march were well in train. The supply carts were loading, extra weapons were inventoried and checked out from the armory, and everywhere the centurions, the backbone of the Eagles, were checking and rechecking their fit-for-duty lists, and reporting upward to their cohort commanders and thence to the Primus Pilus, and finally the Legate. In the horse barns and the auxiliary barracks, the decurions of the cavalry and light troops were carrying out much the same procedure, as name after name was ticked off on the rosters, weapons were inspected, and last minute hitches either got round or rolled over. The machinery of the Army was in full swing, with the well-oiled precision that had carried the boundaries of the Empire farther and farther with each succeeding generation, and even the troublemakers seemed caught up in it for the moment.

Cooks, armorers, supply masters, and clerks each fell neatly into his allotted slot, while the common legionary put a final polish to his helmet, removed the scarlet crest that was strictly for parade use, and executed a frantic search for the new pilum point he had meant to affix last week.

The major excitement of the evening occurred when the senior surgeon of the Legion, supervising the loading of the hospital wagons by torchlight, leapt up to the top of one to tighten a strap that seemed faulty to him, leapt back down and, as his feet touched the ground, turned pale and fainted.

"He *what?*" The Legate flung himself off the couch, dropping his napkin in his half-finished plate, as the Optio made his breathless announcement from the doorway. Theodore hovered behind him, furious at the intrusion.

"I regret, sir, that the gentleman felt the matter would not keep," he ventured as Aurelius Rufus stalked past him, yelling for his cloak and helmet.

"You're damn right it won't keep!" He slammed his helmet down on his head, even its crest of eagle feathers apparently quivering with rage. "There's a whole damn army of Britons heading this way, and my senior surgeon puts his *knee* out?"

He reached the hospital to find Licinius, awake and glowering, propped up in bed with young Flavius applying a poultice to his knee. The surgeon winced as the hot linen was wrapped round his leg. "It won't do any good, you young idiot. The only thing that helps is to stay off the damn thing. Get me a place in one of the hospital wagons and let me rest it for a few days and I'll be all right."

"Don't be stupid—sir," Flavius replied grimly, tending to the poultice. "You aren't going anywhere. I've told Octavian to get his gear together. He was in great good spirits over that, I can tell you. He hasn't been on a campaign since he finished training."

"If you think," Licinius said, grimacing as Flavius gave a final tightening to the poultice and pushed a pin through the top layer, "that I am going to stay here like an old woman with arthritis while you and that ham-handed young butcher look after *my* Legion, you have another think coming!"

"Drink this and shut up." Flavius handed him a pottery cup. "The Legate's coming."

"Good! We'll see whether *he* wants me left behind or not."

"He doesn't," an irritated voice said from the doorway, "but he doesn't see much help for it. Can you walk on that thing?"

"Not at the moment, no."

"In the morning?"

"No."

"That settles it. You—" He motioned to Flavius. "Clear out. You've just been promoted—for the duration."

"It only needs a few more days, sir," Licinius said, as Flavius packed up his kit and left.

"Is that the truth?"

"No."

"I thought as much. Now see here—damn it, I need you! But I don't need one more 'wounded' to look after. You'll be invalided out when we get back. Until then, you'll have to manage the hospital for the garrison troops. I'll leave you one orderly, and I hope to Hades you can tell him what to do if anyone gets sick. My daughter tells me this knee went out on you a month ago. Why didn't you tell me then?"

"I thought it would go back in, and it did."

"The more fool you. I leave you with one parting thought, surgeon: if my daughter decides to play Psyche to your Cupid, chase her home. It will be much more pleasant for you if I don't have to do it when I get back." He pulled his cloak around him and his voice softened somewhat. "You young fool, I know you didn't wish this on yourself, but you'll have to pay for it all the same."

Justin and Gwytha sat with the baby between them, indulgently watching him wave his fat hands and stare curiously about the lamp-lit atrium.

"He'll have grown out of all knowing by the time you get back," Gwytha said at last, slipping a hand into her husband's.

"Yes, you might even have hair by then, mightn't you?" Justin tickled the soft peach fuzz that covered his head, and the baby gurgled happily. "Son of mine, I think it's time you were in bed." He scooped the baby up and deposited him in the cradle where he could be heard contentedly trying out new noises to himself. Justin came back and put his arm around Gwytha.

"Taking it hard, love?"

"This time I'm really afraid," she said. "I've prayed to every god I can think of to keep you safe. It's that accursed cohort."

"Martius's hard cases? They're no prize certainly, but I think I've made some headway with them. They'll do well enough," he added with a conviction he was far from feeling.

Gwytha too was dubious, but she only said, as she snuggled closer and laid her head on his shoulder, "Then in that case, I think you're being foolish about tonight."

The evening had been complicated by a fierce determination on Gwytha's part that Justin should, if at all possible, leave her pregnant, and an equally strong determination on Justin's that he should not. They had argued about it in whispers throughout most of dinner.

"I don't see what difference you think one more night will make anyway," she whispered now, running a small, coaxing hand up his knee, and Justin began to feel his emotions getting the better of his common sense.

"If it won't make any difference, why are you arguing?" he said a little breathlessly.

"Because I want you to love me," she breathed, almost in his ear, and the hand crept a little higher under his tunic. "It will have to last me a while, I'm thinking."

"And me, you know." He sighed and bent down to blow out the lamp, then stood up with his startled wife in his arms.

"Put me down, you idiot!" She laughed and pounded a small fist on his shoulder.

"Certainly not." He caught her eyes with his in the moonlight and bent his head to kiss her, a long slow kiss that left them both shivering. "Come along then," he whispered, and turned through the dark doorway of the bedroom.

But when he had stripped off her tunic and picked her up again, naked, to lay her on the bed, Justin spent a long time just running his hands over her body, breasts and thighs, her face and even her feet, as if he would memorize every line of her. And she in turn reached out her hands for all the old, familiar places . . . the hard muscles of his forearm, the white scar on his rib cage, the cowlick on his forehead where the brown hair waved wildly in three directions at once.

Only after each had explored and remembered every inch of the other did he pull her into his arms and pin her to the bed beneath him with a grip so strong it startled her. She twisted under him, wrapping her strong slim legs about his back, and together they put a whole summer's lovemaking into one spring night.

And then the morning came, as grey as twilight, with a blanket of fog that blotted out the world. Brave in scarlet and bronze, moving smartly to the sound of trumpets, and pitifully few, the column of the Legion turned its face to the north, and marched into the shifting mist.

XVII

The Road through the Mist

AS THEY SWUNG onto the Corstopitum road, Justin turned and surveyed his cohort, marching behind him in the steady twenty-mile-a-day tramp of the Legions, each man blindly following the one before him into the mist.

Justin could see no more than the first few ranks, and the gleam of the cohort standard to his left. With Hilarion, and now Licinius left behind, he felt himself very much alone with what Owen Lucullus had termed Martius's sharks. To the side of the road he could hear the clip-clop and jingle of the cavalry, and a voice, probably Owen's, raised in song:

Come you bold fellows, and join the Ar-mee—

"Come on then, let's have a little noise to chase the fog away." Justin joined in, and the men behind him picked up the chorus:

To slaughter the Pict and the heathen Parsee—

The sound swelled as the cohorts before and behind them picked up the song and sent it up and down the column. At its head, the Legate smiled as the song reached the First Cohort, and he too joined in, in a surprisingly booming baritone:

And maybe, just maybe (the chances are small)
But maybe you'll rise to be Emperor of all!

A loose stone skittered across the roadway and there was the
clatter of a dropped pilum. "Friggin' fog," a voice said distinctly in
the pause between verses. With a whoop of laughter they caught up
the second verse and roared it out cheerfully. By the time they
reached an ominously deserted Isurium, they had worked their way
through "The Courting of Claudia," "The Three-Day Hunt," and
even an unspeakably rude little ditty about a cavalryman and his
horse.

They pushed past Isurium the first day and set off the next morning at semiquick march. It was a long road north, too long to make
forced march the whole way, but the war band would have to be
checked before it could reach the northern frontier forts. From
the second day, the Legate drove the column hard but he kept them
carefully short of exhaustion.

"Or so he says," Justin said, wearily massaging his calf muscles.
"Me, I feel like I'd hired out for a horse." Feeling lonely with
neither Licinius's company nor Hilarion's, he had sought out Owen
Lucullus, and the two of them were lounging by a fire near the
cavalry pickets.

"Aye, there'll be some sore backsides among my lads for a few
days, I'm thinking," Owen said. "And Number Nine Troop's still so
winter soft you can practically see the boils growing."

"Well, they'll have a long march to toughen up on." Justin heaved
another branch onto the fire.

The mist, which had come down again at nightfall, made each
campfire, each group of lanterns, an entity unto itself. In one of
these to the rear, Flavius was dispensing liniment and much the
same advice to an assortment of leg cramps and saddle sores.

"Ah, what do you know about long marches, young one?" a
grey-haired legionary grumbled, rubbing liniment into his calves.
"Pah! This smells like horse piss! When you've been on as many
marches as I have—"

"When I've been on as many marches as you have, I'll retire to
private practice at Aquae Sulis," Flavius said cheerfully, "and make
my fortune prescribing the baths to fat old ladies. And it's supposed
to smell like horse piss. It keeps old drunks like you from lubricat-

ing their insides with it as well."

There was a shout of laughter and the legionary retired, defeated. "Ha! You'll do fine, young one," a voice called out. "You'll do fine!"

Flavius looked down at his hands in the misty light. "Dear god, I hope so."

In another little sphere cut from the fog by lantern light, Centurion Albinus echoed Flavius in his turn. Kneeling by the lantern, he dug a makeshift altar from the spring turf and pricked his finger over it. "Lord of Armies, grant me what is needful," he murmured. Then he picked up the lantern and went to wrestle once more with the demon whose current habitat was the Fourth Cohort.

Aurelius Rufus, enclosed in his own private world within his tent, wrestled also with the demon of Things As They Are, counting the Legion over in his mind, its strengths (and there were some) and its weaknesses (too many) and the best disposition of both. He thought wistfully of the Victrix detachment and then put them from his mind. If they arrived in time, he would bless the Fates, and if they didn't, there was little use bemoaning their absence. He only hoped young Vortrix was passing the night equally unpleasantly. He sighed and rose to make a final tour of the mist-shrouded camp, not so much for inspection as for the peace of his own mind, soothed by the soft anonymity of the fog.

Helmetless, with his cloak pulled over his forehead against the damp, he made his way through the camp, startling the life out of a very young picket and then discomfiting him further with a short lecture on "What If I Were a Pict?"

Somewhere a pair of voices, their origin muffled by the fog, were raised in song, and the Legate paused to listen. One, a clear true tenor, rang sweetly on the night air, while the second, enthusiastic if occasionally off-key, stumbled along behind. Decurion Lucullus and Centurion Corvus, unless he missed his mark, and he thought he recognized the tune:

> But the General's wife she's happy,
> When he plays his instrument!

The voices finished up triumphantly, and the Legate chuckled. He'd heard the song before, though not since *he'd* become a general . . . an irreverent ballad about a great man's faithful wife who devoted herself to music (and the music master) while her husband was off at war. Aurelius Rufus grinned and made his way toward the cavalry lines. The gods send him more men like those two and he'd make something out of this legion of vipers yet. He approached the camp fire and was about to cough tactfully when the two seated figures leapt to their feet, swords half drawn.

"I am friendly enough," the Legate said drily, and the two swords slid back home in their scabbards.

"Sorry, sir," Justin said. "You're as quiet as a Pict."

"A rare compliment. May I join you?"

"Aye, gladly." Owen dusted off a convenient rock with the tail of his cloak and bowed to the commander. "Pray have a seat on the chair of state."

"Thank you," the Legate said gravely and lowered himself onto the rock. "You make a cheerful noise. I was drawn by it."

The other two regarded each other with horror.

"I used to be quite fond of that song," he continued, "in the days when I used to sing it myself."

"Ah, then you might know a few we haven't heard, sir." Owen looked interested.

"You've a fine voice, Decurion, and I'm told you know more un-repeatable songs than any man in the Legion. I doubt I could outdo you."

"Ah, but there might be one or two I've missed, sir," Owen said. "I'd like fine to learn a new one."

"Hmm." The Legate cleared his throat and hummed softly to himself for a moment. "It may be that I can recall one or two from before your time, Decurion."

The Decurion of Number Nine Troop, limping by with a jar of salve to nurse his saddle sores in the privacy of his tent, was thus treated to the sight of the Legion's commander, huddled in a sodden cloak by the fire, his voice raised in praise of a young lady with the unlikely nickname of the Spotted Mare:

> Oh, Zoë's thighs are snowy white,
> Her breast like the soft sea foam,
> But she can't compare with the Spotted Mare,
> The fastest ride in Rome!

The song ended with a long-drawn whinny, composite of lust and longing, and his two listeners joined in with enthusiasm.

"Now that's a fine song, sir, a fine song." Owen whistled the melody over once to himself to fix it in his mind. "The lads'll like that, they will."

"Mind you don't tell them where you got it," the Legate said. "Tell me, do you always carry on in this fashion? You're the one who began the singing on the march yesterday, I think."

"Ah, the British are always one for a song, sir, or so my mother tells me."

"Perhaps we should send you out like Orpheus, to charm the Picts into submission," the Legate said, pulling his cloak closer around him. "It might work as well as anything else."

"Hades, are we that far gone?"

"Not if the Victrix detachment catches up." He looked old and grey, huddled there in the firelight, and the other two fell silent.

Three mornings later, the Legion marched out of the Corstopitum supply depot, taking with it every available man of the frontier forts, including the sheepish garrison of Castra Exploratorum, which had been unable to prevent the High King's clans from slipping past them in twos and threes to take the war trail north.

There was still no sign of the promised reinforcements, but as they pushed north of Corstopitum, another presence made itself felt, subtly, insidiously, and with nerve-wracking persistence. They never saw the allied war band, but it was obvious that skirmishers had ventured this far south: obvious in the patrols which didn't come back, in the supply wagons cut off from the tail of the column in the mist, in the scattered mules and cut throats of their drivers, in the howling that came down from the nearby hills at night that might be a wolf, and wasn't.

There had been no signal from the north since the first news of the massing war band, and no answers to theirs. What they might find at Trimontium was something no one cared to dwell on.

When they came within first sight of the fort, the Legate called a halt and looked long and hard at the red sandstone walls, ominously silent in the afternoon sun. Finally, he turned back to the Legion, waiting still well out of sight, and the trumpets sang out rest-at-arms. A small knot of scouts detached themselves from the column and melted into the surrounding woods.

They sat as they had marched, in formation, breastplates loosened but not removed, and arms at the ready. The centurions paced along the line, quelling comment and ordering here a breastplate back on and there a pilum brought back within easy reach.

"Are we going to sit here til the little painted devils catch up to us, or are we maybe waiting for reinforcements from fairyland?"

"To hear the Britons tell it, the woods are full of 'em, about a foot high. Maybe they'll throw in on our side!"

"It doesn't pay to mock the people of the otherworld," a young centurion said sternly. "Especially not in their own country. Now put your helmet on and pipe down."

A young messenger from the Legate's staff halted in front of Justin's men, saluted the cohort standard, and murmured something in the commander's ear. Justin nodded, turned the cohort over to his nervous second, and followed the boy.

"Over here, Centurion Corvus," the Legate said. "Follow me, and keep low." He wriggled through the underbrush with a surprising agility (although Justin had long since ceased to underrate the new Legate of the Ninth), with Justin belly-down behind him. Aurelius Rufus held up a hand as he neared the crest of a ridge, and Justin slid into place beside him. Before them was Trimontium, silent and barren. Not even a bird moved in the still air. "You've been in Britain longer than I have, Centurion," the Legate said softly, "and I rate your intelligence rather high. Now what would you say was inside there?"

"I don't know," Justin said after a moment. "It might be full of Britons, of course, lying low and sharpening their spears til we come up and knock on the door. But if the whole war band is this far south, they've made an incredible forced march, and I rather doubt they've done that, for the same reason we haven't."

"Very good, Centurion. Go on."

"Well, it isn't much of a garrison, sir, frankly, and it wouldn't be hard to take, with a lot less than a whole war band."

"So you warned me. Do you think that's what happened? They are in the Selgovae's territory, after all." Aurelius Rufus lay flat along the grass and pulled a straggling branch gently aside for a better view.

"It's possible. Except . . ." Justin's face was grim. "I don't see any signs of smoke . . . or ravens."

"Then what does that leave us? They wouldn't clean up the bodies if they weren't planning to set up housekeeping inside themselves. They'd leave them as a warning, as nastily displayed as possible."

"I don't know why you're asking me, sir," Justin said with more candor than tact. "You know as well as I do what the only other possibility is."

"Let us just say that it is not one I feel like giving voice to at the moment," the Legate said tiredly.

"No more do I, sir." Justin narrowed his eyes and looked long at the silent walls of Trimontium. "Well, at all events, we'll know when the scouts report . . . assuming they make it back."

The Legate gave a grunt that might have passed for laughter in other circumstances. "Very well, Centurion Cassandra, come along back before the whole damn column disappears under our noses." He began inching backward through the heather.

They rejoined the column and Justin took over again from his second, who regarded him apprehensively. The cohort by this time was badly out of formation, and discarded helmets were strewn on the ground. "I . . . they're extremely difficult today, sir," the second said.

"Not nearly so difficult as I'm going to be—" Justin raised his voice, and pitched it to carry "—if this line doesn't dress itself up *now!*" He caught the nearest man to him across the shoulders with his vine staff and stood above him, eyes blazing, as he looked about to retaliate.

"You may have tried that number with Centurion Martius," Justin informed him grimly, "but you'll find it won't work with me. Now get into your armor and get back to your place!" He turned on his heel and strode down the line without waiting to see whether his order was obeyed. The legionary shrugged and settled his helmet on his head.

Midway down the line Justin halted again where three legionaries were gathered about a fourth who was lying flat on the ground. He knelt down and looked at him. "What happened?"

"I dunno, sir. He just keeled over, like."

Justin ran a hand over the man's brow. It was clammy to the touch. "Get him down the line to the surgeon!" The man on the ground twitched and lay still again. "No, never mind. Clear the way!" Justin picked him up, armor and all, and shouldered his way through the gathering throng. His cohort parted before him, and stood gaping after.

As a deadweight, the man was heavy, and Justin was panting by the time he reached the hospital carts, but he laid him down as gently as he could. "I've a patient for you," he said as Flavius came up. "He passed out in line—" He broke off as a stirring began at the head of the column. "Do what you can," he said, and took to his heels.

The scouts *had* come in—all but one, and him they never found—and they stood in an uncomfortable semicircle around the Legate.

"Cease shifting from foot to foot like a centipede and let me have it!" He glowered at them.

There was a pause and finally their decurion spoke up. "Nothing, sir. There is nothing . . . inside. Yon fort is empty as a swallow's nest in the snow."

"What do you mean, empty? There are no dead?"

"Not unless they buried them in the road and paved it over," the scout said. "No living, no dead, not even freshly turned ground. Man, we were *in* it!"

"All right, dismissed. Decurion, you stay." The Legate surveyed the men gathered around him. "Galba, you . . . Corvus, Albinus, Geta, Lepidus, stay here. The rest of you get back to your men and get them ready to march."

And so, after a short and dreadful briefing which came as no surprise to the five who stayed, the Legion marched out, brave in the afternoon sun. They broke the gates of Trimontium, grimly bolted on the inside, and took up their quarters in the barren fort. No salute met them, no sentry challenged, and inside the rats were already growing bold in the granary and the deserted mess hall. The waters in the bathhouse lay still and stagnant, a faint green shimmer of algae beginning to form on the sides of the pools.

There was no hiding what had happened, and an uneasy stirring ran through the lines as soon as the first cohort had turned through the unguarded gates. Trimontium's garrison, wherever they were, had cut themselves finally, irrevocably from Rome. "The gods help them," Justin thought, "if Rome ever finds them."

He settled his men in a barracks that showed traces of their predecessors' hasty exit: broken bits of harness, forgotten cloaks and helmet crests, and a pathetic horseshoe nailed above a doorway for luck . . . a sad mosaic of abandoned loyalties.

Then he turned his back on the grim remains of Empire and

made his stumbling way through the muddy streets to the little temple where a short summer ago he had made prayer with Licinius against today. The Mithraeum also was empty and barren, and the wind had blown drifts of dirt and rubbish into the corners.

"Mithras, Unconquered Sun, Redeemer," Justin began, the litany spilling from his lips unbidden, "Grant us thy aid and intercession—"

A harsh, sobbing breath shook him, and he fell to his knees before the twin altars of the Bull Slayer, the formal invocation abandoned and his plea wrenched straight from the heart.

"Mithras, Lord of Armies—" Justin fought to keep the words in order, and the lost garrison of Trimontium rose up and mocked him as he spoke. "Read us the lesson we need to learn—" he pulled his dagger from its sheath— "but deliver us from the pit of Ahriman." He stabbed savagely with the dagger at his thumb and felt the force that seemed to turned it toward his heart. The point sunk into his hand and bit deep, deeper than he had intended, and he stood before the altar with his blood falling like a fountain on the grey stone.

He staunched it at last with the tail end of his cloak, and rubbed the scarlet pool into the grey stone of the altar.

"Take now the Sacrifice, freely given—" The face of the Bull Slayer seemed to look on him in pity, and Justin fought the visions that rose unbidden before him . . . Vortrix, seeming to look straight at him . . . then Gwytha, warm and welcoming, the curtain of her hair hanging about her face, his heart's companion, who should have been his life's companion . . . and always somehow between her and him, the Legion, scarlet and bronze, shining behind a mist that enveloped everything.

The diffused light of the Mithraeum's one small window gave a hazy, shimmering quality to the face of the god, turned in sadness from the bull beneath him. Somewhere outside a cloud ran past the sun and the light intensified. It seemed to Justin, kneeling before him, that the face of the god wavered and took form again, and two living eyes, burning and terrible in their sorrow, looked back at him. The sanctuary was suffused with a soft glow that he dared not see too well, and he put his head down on his hands on the altar's edge and wept . . . for himself, for his Legion, and for what he had seen in the face of the god.

* * *

That night, when the mist came down again, one full century of the Fourth Cohort went over the wall in a panicked, headlong flight between one sentry's passing and the next. In the morning they were simply gone, and no one knew where, although the choices weren't great.

The next night, a day's half-quick march to the north, double pickets were posted, and young Albinus looked near to a breakdown. Flavius, whose ears were generally pricked like a fox's for news, came round with a cup of something and handed it to Albinus.

"Here, lad, drink this. It is said to be soothing. I quote from the Book of Medicines Licinius is working on," he added. "No, it won't knock you out, but it will give you a somewhat different perspective on life for a few hours. And the gods know we could all use one."

Albinus tossed off the draught and handed the junior surgeon back his cup. "When I was posted here," he said desolately, "I thought it was a promotion—two full cohorts up, and that doesn't happen often—I thought it was for my abilities . . . I had done well . . . but I was wrong. I was sent here to rot because someone thought it was all I was fit for . . . and he was right."

"No, you're wrong there." Flavius laid a comforting hand on his shoulder. "You were sent here because you were needed . . . desperately. Though it's bitter payment for being a good officer, I grant you."

"But my cohort a whole century gone 'unlawful absent.'" On the far hill a wolf that wasn't a wolf bayed at the rising moon, and from the opposite hill another answered. "My fault," Albinus whispered, "my fault . . ." and they both realized that he spoke not of his missing century's desertion, but of its probable fate.

They found them on the next day's march, as they were meant to. From their torn shoe leather and the strands of heather caught in their cloaks and armor, it was obvious that they had been driven hard, probably turned from their flight to the south, and harried northward until they had turned at bay and been cut down like rabbits. Also obvious was the fact that they had not died in the middle of the main north road, but had been flung there as a grisly message for the column that followed them. Eighty men, twisted and stiffened into unnatural shapes, blocking the roadway in a deadly barricade.

On the Legate's order, they halted long enough to dispose of the bodies in proper fashion, the least reliable cohorts being delegated the task of stacking the bodies of the Legion's late deserters. Two hours later, a cloud of black, greasy smoke rising to the sky behind them, the Legion marched out again. Behind them in the late afternoon light, a spine-tingling howl from the hillside followed like a pursuing demon.

The next "unlawful absents" were from Favonius's cohort, and they weren't legionaries but junior centurions, panic-stricken and desperate . . . and they never found them.

After that, all the long, ghastly way to Inchtuthil, they dropped off one by one. Some went "unlawful absent," and their fellows testified as such; some were found a good two miles ahead of where they had vanished, their throats cut and sundry other grisly operations performed upon them; some cried out and fell in the middle of the marching column, a little barbed arrow between their shoulders; and some merely gave up and sat down by the road, to die if they could, or be killed if they couldn't.

The legionary Justin had carried back to Flavius proved to have drunk bad water and was shortly joined by a dozen others. No one died, but it merely heightened the feeling that the whole countryside was poisoned against them.

They reached Inchtuthil at twilight, at the end of two days' full-forced march, while the war band was still massing in the north, the only tangible evidence of its presence the corpses thrown in challenge in the Legion's path and the empty, unexplained numbers on the morning roll. Justin, for whom nothing was clear these days and precious little was simple, wrestled with the horror in his soul and was silent.

Inchtuthil had had a Roman name once—Pinnata Castra—but now the old Agricolan fortress above the Tanaus was deserted and weed-grown, home to the myriad small animals of the forest who had encroached on man's work as man had left . . . bats and mice and weasels, and a half-grown litter of fox kits lairing where the Army's standards had been housed and its altars built. The forest moved back again as the Legate set the Hispana to clearing barracks and rebuilding wall, making of Inchtuthil a human habitation once more. But they felt them there on the outskirts of the newly cleared land, waiting, as if they knew that soon, soon, man would be gone again, leaving the weeds to flourish in the spring rains and the forest to reclaim its own.

But for the time being Inchtuthil was a Roman fort, with clean, orderly streets and the comings and goings of a legionary garrison. Here they would make their base camp for the campaign, set up their hospital and armory, send out their scouts and patrols, and assemble the great war engines that loomed as a testament to Roman engineering over the armies below them. And here, if they were lucky, the Victrix detachment, maybe on the road already, would catch up to them.

And it was here that Justin emerged from the horrors of the march as from a nightmare, and, blinking in the sun of Inchtuthil's orderly reconstruction, pulled himself together and began to sort some sense back into his life. He never knew precisely what had done it—perhaps it was the sight of the Legate ordering his troops to their work with a show of confidence which should only have been engendered by the command of an army twice their size . . . perhaps it was Flavius, dealing calmly and painstakingly with his first surgical command, sitting late over his organization charts in the newly swept hospital, trying to prepare ahead of time for any of a thousand possible crises, and then turning when that was done to read and reread his surgical texts . . . perhaps it was Favonius, who had pulled himself back from the pit after Martius's death and was trying, under the influence of stark necessity, to learn to command . . . or Lepidus, who had been described to Justin respectfully by one of his old cohort as "as big a devil for discipline as you was, sir, and that's sayin' some." Or perhaps, in an increasingly martial world, it was that one note of lightness, in the person of Owen Lucullus, cheerfully putting his troop through its paces, singing old campaign songs in the firelight for the amusement of his general, and sending his clear, true tenor sounding up to the hills in a variety of impromptu ballads on the subject of Vortrix, his ancestry, and private habits.

Or maybe it was the Legion itself, rotten-ripe as it was and stinking with decay, but still a Roman Legion, the Eagles, Justin's beloved Eagles, whose wings overspread half the world, and in whose

service he had found every good thing in life that he had known
. . . loyalty and the companionship of brothers, love, and a sense
of purpose. And oddly enough, it was with the Ninth Hispana, the
rebellious, mutinous, ill-ordered Ninth, that most of these had come
to him. Here he had found Licinius, Hilarion, and now Owen; here
he had known the satisfaction of turning almost five hundred leaderless misfits into a Roman cohort again; here he had found Gwytha,
a lover and companion such as is given to few men, and small Justin,
a child to come after him, the fulfillment of the urge to procreation
that was as old as nature; and here also, he knew, he had met his
dark-side mirror twin in the person of Vortrix, whom this time he
must kill that they might not all go under, Roman and Briton alike.
He didn't know what it was that bound him to the king of the Brigantes, and he doubted that Vortrix did either, but somehow, with
a certainty as strong as life itself, he knew that Vortrix felt it too.
Remembering the battle of two summers before, Justin knew that
this time he would not stay his blade—he could not—and he knew
also that Vortrix would not have stayed his own even then, and that
in that he was the stronger half. It seemed a pity, he thought as he
watched the rebuilding of Inchtuthil around him, that they had
not been born to the same people, he and Vortrix.

And then he shook the mood away as a horse shakes the flies from
its head in summer, and focused in on the activity around him. He
remembered the grim, grey phantoms that had dogged his steps on
the march north, and the horror of the vision that had come to him
in the Mithraeum at Trimontium, but they were faded and far away,
and his own world shone brave and purposeful in the sunlight.

His second came up with a sheaf of duty rosters and he turned
to their inspection. "Hmmm. I wouldn't put Phaedrus next to young
Tertius," Justin said. "And I don't want any of our more excitable
lads within a mile of Cassius's men. Otherwise, they look fine.
Thank you, Centurion."

Justin sighed and wiped a hand across his brow. Cassius was becoming dangerous, a natural rabble-rouser and barracks lawyer of
a type far more common to the legionary ranks than the Centuriate.
His natural instincts for trouble making were aggravated now by a
full-fledged panic in his undisciplined soul, and there was no telling
what he was likely to do. Worse, without the centurion posted with
the Victrix detachment, there was no replacement for him. Justin

knew that the Legate was privately considering breaking Cassius anyway and hoping to Hades that his second, with a good fright in him, would be able to keep his cohort in line. But it would be tricky. Very tricky.

And then the next morning, with the mist waist-deep over the land, the scouts rode in to report the enemy on the march; and there was no chance to make the experiment. Justin saw the Legate's grim, grey face as he listened to the riders' report and knew that the gamble had failed. The Victrix detachment was too late, one way or another.

It was bitter cold in the meadow, and dead still where the Ninth stood formed up in order with the cohort and century standards marking each commander's position. Aurelius Rufus had made a personal inspection of the land and had chosen his ground well. A long valley swept slightly downwards before them, guarded on either flank by rocky hillside and forest. Here they had gathered to meet the war band and try to stop it.

With his bugler and Eagle-bearer beside him, the Legate gave his orders crisply and his staff aides moved from cohort to cohort, conferring with the centurions and auxiliary officers. The mist was beginning to burn off and visibility was growing better, although the far reaches of the valley were still hazy. Now the Legate moved along the lines, dropping a steadying hand on a shoulder or a brief, cheerful word of encouragement, but Justin could see the line quiver like a half-schooled horse, and here and there the flicker of pure terror in a man's eyes. Again the queasy edge-of-the-bog feeling rose in his stomach and he suppressed it, turning to his own men.

"Hold them steady, lads, and we'll turn them back where they came from." He gave them a thumbs-up sign. There were some murmured "ayes" but mostly they stood stock-still and looked at him, and Justin began to feel the hair prickling along the back of his neck. Something was wrong, something more than mere battle nerves.

A moment later he saw it happen. Centurion Cassius and a few of his junior officers were clustered around the Legate, and Aurelius Rufus had a fury in his face that Justin had never seen.

". . . gone mad? . . . a disgrace to . . ." Only bits of words drifted up to him, but as Justin watched in horror, more men pulled out from their places and fell in behind Cassius, including a half dozen of the Sixth. The rest of the Legion turned to watch them, without curiosity but with a kind of suppressed excitement.

"Oh, my god," a voice said softly, and Justin turned to see Lepidus at his shoulder. He made a sudden decision.

"Lepidus, how good a hold have you got on the Eighth?"

"I . . . well enough, I think."

"Then hold them!" Justin said fiercely. "Get back there and hold them! Cajole them, swear at them, baby them, but hold them. And get them around behind and up front to the Legate! Hurry, man!" He turned to his second. "You—don't try to move these, just hold them steady for as long as you can!" He slipped out of the lines and forward, trying not to run, to school the urgency from his face, to look as if nothing had gone wrong.

No man moved to stop him as he pased. They did not seem even to notice him. Every eye was fixed on the Legate among his aides, and the growing circle of men before him. "You are a fool," he was saying in disgust as Justin reached him. "Do you know what the price is?"

"There is no price on honorable surrender!" Cassius spat at him.

"Aye, that's right!"

"We were to have reinforcements—where are they, tell us that!"

"Even our water turns poison—it's an omen!"

"We've no mind to be cut down three to one!"

They chorused around him, and the Legate stood still as granite in their midst. "You will be, if you think the Pict will give you safe conduct," he said softly.

"It's our only chance." Cassius's eyes were glittering and dangerous. "You led us into this devil's land—now you will lead us out!"

"*No!*"

"You can't hold them here. They'll follow me—won't you, lads?"

They jostled forward behind him. "Aye, we follow Cassius!"

"Not all of you." Justin shouldered forward between the Legate's staff. "*My* men don't follow a mutineer!"

"What, your cohort of murderers?"

"No, Cassius, my Eighth Cohort, which were mine long since. I warned you not to fool with my men, Cassius. D'you want to tangle with them now?"

"Corvus, you don't frighten me."

"No?" Lepidus slipped up beside him, and behind him like a wall was a good four-fifths of the Eighth Cohort. "There are stronger loyalties than fear."

"Aye, Centurion, shall I break you in half and prove it?" One of the Eighth stepped forward, towering above his commander. He looked at his hands and then longingly at Cassius's neck.

"No, Clemens," Justin said. "I thank you for the thought, but not yet."

"Roman does not fight Roman," the Legate said, "although I too will remember your offer. Neither does a Roman Army break ranks before the enemy. Now get back to your places!"

"Aye, or we'll put you in them and pound you two feet into the ground to see you stay there," another voice said. Justin and the Legate looked around to see the ranks behind them swelled by a grim-eyed segment of Geta's Seventh Cohort, their commander in the lead.

Cassius hesitated and, for a fraction of a second, the thing was ended. And then a voice cried out, and they swung around to face the end of the valley.

It was hazy, but they could still see clear enough to drop a curtain of silence over the whole Legion. From one side of the valley to the other, and stretching back into the hillside passes, the massed war hosts of three nations loomed ghostly in the fog.

"There! That is what they'd lead you against!" Cassius voice was shrill and hysterical. "Death! Death and destruction, and nothing but their precious loyalties to fight it with!"

"Death!" another man yelled, and the British war horns echoed him. It was enough. The nearest ranks surged and broke like sea foam.

"No!" the Legate yelled. "No, damn you! Back to your lines!"

"Back!" Geta swung his loyal troops around to face them.

"Stand firm, you fools!" Justin shouted above the tumult. "They'll cut you down like rabbits!"

"Not if we don't fight them! Let them have their damn land!"

"No! You will stand and fight like Romans!" The Legate laid about him with his staff. "Look to your Eagle, damn you!"

But it was too late. The Ninth Hispana crumbled like an ill-made wall. They fell away in groups three centuries deep, streaming back away from the valley's mouth, panicked, mindless, trampling their fellows as they went. The scent of fear was in the air and the cavalry horses screamed and plunged. And then their riders caught it also. One troop swung across their path trying desperately to turn them, but they rode through and over them.

The war horns of the British cut through the air, mingling with the sound of chaos. The first wave of deserters stumbled toward the baggage carts and their drivers, seeing a rout, leapt down and fled before them. They ploughed through the rear lines, tipping over carts and snatching what they could from the supply train as they passed. Flavius, standing before the hospital wagons with a sword in one hand and a legionary's abandoned pilum in the other, stabbed one man in the throat as he tried to heave a wagon over, and then they were on him. He dove under a second wagon, and the sound of running feet hammered past him, taking the rear guard with it like flotsam on a river.

Midway down the valley, the Brigantes saw what was happening and surged forward. Their war horns sang out again and one flank peeled off from the rest and streamed down the far side of the valley, howling like wolves on the trail of the deserters.

"Pull back!" the Legate shouted. "Pull back and group!" The handful that was left to him tightened into a circle and fell back over the discarded armor and broken pilums of the Legion. Justin had gathered his old Eighth Cohort, or most of it, about him, and the First Cohort was on his flank, the Eagle of the Legion swaying above them. Of the rest, there was Albinus with two centuries of his men, frightened but grimly determined, several leaderless centuries of Hilarion's cohort, half of Geta's, one century from the Tenth, and Favonius of all people, rallying a pitiful two centuries of the Third about their cohort standard.

They pulled back, somehow in good order, collecting such few of the rear guard and baggage train as were left. Flavius, with young Octavian, was desperately pulling his precious supplies from the hospital wagons.

"Leave them! Come on!" Justin grabbed him by the shoulder and spun him around. "Much good you'll do us dead!"

Flavius caught up his sword and a shield that lay against one of the wagon wheels and fell into line, his slight, unarmored figure sandwiched between Clemens and another burly legionary of the Eighth Cohort.

278

They hugged the valley's edge, and, to their other side, a single troop of cavalry guarded their flank. They fell back in good order, but the war host was closing fast . . . and it was a long way to the dubious safety of Inchtuthil.

"Go! Take them and go!" the cavalry leader shouted. "We'll hold them while we can!" He signaled his troops, positioning them across the narrow mouth of the valley. Thirty stumbling blocks with sharp-pointed spears drew rein and waited. It was the last Justin saw of Owen Lucullus.

XVIII

The Road Home

ALL THE LONG, NIGHTMARE WAY to Inchtuthil they raced, until their breath came in ragged gasps and their hearts were pounding. At the bugle's sound (all the trumpeters were gone) they formed and fought off the screaming blue warriors who had slipped through Owen's wall, then turned and ran again. The Eagle-bearer went down with a spear through his side, but another man caught it up and fought forward. They were in sight of the fortress when the British chariots broke through the last of Owen's Asturians and streamed through the gap, wheels bouncing and rocking over the corpses that lined their way.

But that doomed handful of horsemen had bought them precious time. The sentry on the walls of Inchtuthil saw them coming and, with a scant dozen of his fellows, swung the great catapults around and trained them on the pursuing war host.

"Hold your fire. Steady . . . steady. Wait til our lot are out of range. Zeus defend us!" he added, as he saw the thin ranks streaming toward the fortress gate. Of the Legion that had marched out that morning, only a third remained in the shattered Army flying one step ahead of the war host, for the fortress gates.

"Gone . . . all gone," the catapult man beside him murmured, dazed.

"Steady, lad. Let's bring 'em in . . . what's left of 'em, poor bastards." He raised his arm and the catapult crew wound the great engine back and dipped its sights to the leading edge of the baying war host. The last of the fleeing Legion pulled past the line of fire, and he dropped his arm. "Now!"

A stone as big as three men flew like an arrow from the war engine and fell with all the deadly weight of civilized science on the careening host of chariots. They went down by the score, tangled in their own traces and the flailing legs of downed horses in front of them, and the fleeing army gained another foot. Behind them, the oncoming chariots split with precision around the destruction in their path, and the second catapult swung around to train on the right-hand flank.

"Now, lads! Roll 'em up." The thongs and braces sang and another score went down. Number One catapult, reloaded, bit deep into the left flank. But the war host came on, over and around its dead, the vanguard slipping past catapult range on the tail of its quarry.

"Shorten range!" the garrison commander shouted. "Half the men to the gate. Get ready to let them in and close up fast!"

The Britons were only a spear's throw behind them when the tattered Army turned at bay outside the walls of Inchtuthil, the front line braced against the onslaught as the rear poured through the open gates. Justin, shield to shield with Flavius before the ten-foot wall which guarded the gate, took a chariot pony in the throat with his pilum and it crashed down almost on his feet. The driver leapt snarling along the ridge pole, silhouetted for a moment against the grey sky, until Justin caught him with a shortened thrust and locked his shield with Flavius's again just as a second wave swarmed by the hundreds over the line of downed chariots, with the massed body of the war host swelling behind them.

"Back! Back in close order, we've almost got them in!" the Legate shouted, and the shield wall backed another pace. Every time a man went down, the one behind him stepped up to fill the deadly hole, and still the line held, the Eagle of the Hispana waving above them. But they were dropping fast and if they couldn't make the gate before the Britons broke the shield wall, the war host would sweep in a torrent through the opening. Justin drew a ragged, tearing breath, thrust at a screaming dark-haired warrior clad only in the nightmare paint of the Picts, and backed another pace. He could see little before him over the shield wall; but he knew that Death in the thousands was sweeping with the unleashed fury of a forest fire across what had once been the outer earthworks of Agricolan Inchtuthil, and that soon there would be no stopping them.

And then they were between the wall and the gate: himself, Flavius, and a ragged handful of his old Eighth Cohort. "They're in, sir!" Clemens shouted. "Knock the bastards back for us, damn you!" he added, and as if in answer, the few auxiliary archers of the garrison loosed their precious store of arrows on the pursuers.

"Back and in! Now!" They pulled back and flung themselves to either side of the great gates, as the men behind moved up to slam them shut. Shoulder to shoulder against the onslaught, they jerked the bolts into place and braced them. The weight of the enemy came around the wall and broke against the iron and timber gate.

Aurelius Rufus, his face smeared with blood from a deep gash above one eye, took stock of what was left to him.

"Galba. Still with us, I see."

The Primus Pilus sketched a salute. A deep gouge ran clean across his breastplate and he was blood-spattered from head to toe.

"I want men to reinforce the catapult crews. Strengthen all the gates—they'll be using rams before long. And get some more wall and earthworks thrown up here—" He gestured at the central complex. "I want a three-cohort fort built before they can get through those gates. And I want every man who can use a bow up on the walls now! And get a signal fire going. Maybe Victrix'll spot it."

They came in wave after wave, thundering at the gates, while off to the north the allied chieftains eyed the progress with satisfaction. Justin, on the ramparts with a mixed crew of archers, legionaries, and even the camp cook, a middle-aged Syrian with forearms like an ape, was occupied with picking off the men who were lashing ropes around the gate wall. He hadn't shot a bow since he'd been in Spain and was pleased to discover that he hadn't lost his eye. The string went singing past his ear and another body dropped down at the base of the wall, his fiery hair stained with a spreading pool of red.

"Coming in again! Mark your target." He had discarded his helmet to get a better aim, and his hair hung in tangles about his face. He wiped the sweat and grime from his eyes with the back of his hand and nocked another arrow. But for every man who went down with an arrow in his chest, another came up to take his place, and on the other side of the wall, shielded from the archers, pickmen had set about digging away the mortar. At the nearest catapult emplacement, one of the crews was hurling their winged missiles at any of the main body of the enemy who strayed within range. Favonius, his usually immaculate curls hanging dankly in his eyes, seemed to be commanding them, Justin noticed with mild surprise, and then his attention was claimed again by the sound of falling stone, as the right side of the gate wall slid slowly to the ground.

A thin, pale youth whom Justin recognized as one of the Legate's clerks came up with a bucket of water and a ladle and Justin gulped it gratefully. He motioned the boy down to the rampart floor.

"Get down, lad, you're making a target."

Something hummed past his left ear and the trooper beside him choked and clutched at the little feathered shaft protruding from his throat. The clerk gulped and went white, but he hugged his water bucket to him and inched his way past the dead man to the next archer. Justin, bone-weary and almost beyond fear, stuck his head over the rampart and picked off the Pictish bowman as he ducked out from behind the wall to take aim. And then there was another sliding sound and a cloud of dust and mortar, and there *was* no wall. The path to the gate lay clear.

"Mark the lead men when they bring up the ram," Justin called, "and you can bring down the rest." From the crashing which echoed to his right, he knew that the western gate wall had fallen too.

Flavius in the hospital also heard it. He was probing a spear wound while the orderly held down the man from whose shoulder pieces of shaft still protruded, and he paused only long enough to note that the gate still held. His scavenged shield and weapons lay where he had flung them in the corner of the hospital, and he was back to the work he knew. He felt the forceps close on the last jagged shard. "Hold, brother, it's almost over."

Outside, the inner defensive wall was rising, and all he could see from the window were its builders, grimly setting timber into place. He gave a grateful glance at Octavian, stitching a sword cut at the next table. The lad had guts, he thought. He'd make a good Army surgeon someday. It did not occur to him that until a month ago the same comment might have been made about him. He *was* a senior surgeon now, promoted by the stark hand of Necessity.

"There, he'll do for now." He nodded at the orderly, who had been a supply clerk ages ago that morning. "Bring me whoever looks the worst. And for the gods' sake, find me some more bandages!"

In the corner, those of the wounded who were capable of it were tearing strips from the bed linen, undertunics, and anything else that was handy; and at the western gate, Albinus, caked with dirt and his own dried blood, was shoring up the framework and wishing fervently for some painkiller. To the northward, enough medical supplies for a Legion lay strewn among the wreckage of the hospital wagons. Flavius had managed to salvage only his surgical kit. The few stores left in the Inchtuthil hospital he was hoarding for the most gravely wounded.

The Legate had taken one look at the state of things in the hospital, cleaned his own wound, saw that it was not bleeding much, and tied a strip from his tunic hem around it. Their orderly world had been pulled out from under them, and now they wrestled not only with the enemy but with the unfamiliar. Cooks shot bows, clerks cleaned wounds, and mule drivers took up swords and wondered whether they would know how to use them when the time came. And yet in all of it there was still a certain order, a pattern laid down by the determined hand of Aurelius Rufus. He was everywhere: positioning the catapults, heaving a stone into place on the inner defense wall (they had torn down one of the outer barracks to build it), questioning, ordering, rearranging and encouraging, dealing with each new crisis as it came with the grim expediency of the man who has few options. And as the sun began its last downward course across the sky, the gates still held.

Half an hour later the Britons pulled back. Favonius slumped down beside his catapult. He looked like a sewer rat, his face begrimed and his hands blistered raw, but he chuckled softly.

Justin leaned back against the rampart and laid his own blistered hands in his lap. "They'll be back, you know."

"Oh, I know," Favonius said. "Don't think I don't. But there's a hitherto undiscovered pleasure in spitting in their eye."

The signal beacon was a column of flame against the night sky, but still there was no answering spark from the south, while northward the campfires of the war host were clustered like fireflies.

"What's become of the ones who ran, do you suppose?" Favonius finished the last of the carefully rationed evening meal and dusted his hands on his ragged tunic.

"What do you think?" Justin said shortly, remembering the baying horde that had pursued them to Inchtuthil. "It's best you *don't* think about it," he added more gently. "We've sentry duty in two hours. Get some sleep instead."

Favonius nodded, and they closed their eyes in the weariness of utter exhaustion that banishes even nightmares.

Coming off their sentry shift, they collapsed and slept again, and at dawn they were back on the wall, waiting. The ground below stretched away, alien and secretive in the misty light, and Inchtuthil stood entombed in fog and an unnatural stillness.

"The Pict must be sleeping late this morning," a catapult man said. "Freshening up, like, to have another go at us."

"Wait. Now that's where you're wrong." Favonius squinted into the mist. "Chariots . . . but just three of 'em. And with a green branch, by all the gods!"

The wicker carts rose up out of the mist almost before anyone noticed them, and drew rein within shouting distance of the fort. "Come you up on the wall, Commander of the Eagles!"

"I am here," a quiet voice said, and Justin jumped. Aurelius Rufus looked down at them from the rampart, eagle-crested helmet on his head, his gold-bordered cloak impressive against the sculptured bronze insignia of his breastplate. "What do you want, Vortrix of the Brigantes? You may come nearer," he added drily. "Rome does not fire on green branches."

"Rome would be advised not to." The three chariots moved into clear view, and through the mist the watchers on the wall could now also see the war host, gathered into battle line. Any threat to the three leaders would bring them down like hornets.

Vortrix stood in the lead chariot, stripped for battle and painted according to the custom of all the Britons. The blue stain stood out brightly against his white skin. A cloak of grey wolf skin hung from his shoulders, and his blond hair was braided and tied back from his face with fine leather thongs. His driver, similarly attired, was the lithe blond harper Justin remembered seeing before.

In the right-hand chariot stood a tall, flame-haired warrior in a dark green cloak bordered with scarlet. He also was painted for battle, and his milk-white team danced with impatience, swiveling their small pricked ears at the voices around them. Justin caught the gleam of a golden fillet in the warrior's red hair . . . Brendan, War Lord of the Selgovae. To the left rode the third chieftain, dark-haired and shorter than the lowlanders, and tattooed from head to toe in a complication of spirals and interlocking bands . . . Dergdian, King of the Caledones, the Painted People.

Vortrix nodded to his driver, and the red roan team moved a few paces forward. "Listen, Commander of the Eagles!"

"I am listening," Aurelius Rufus shouted. "Tell me your tale."

"It is this. With the whole of your army, you were outnumbered. Now you have perhaps a third of them left to you—aye, we counted them as they ran, and we know what you began with. You are a brave man, Commander of the Eagles, and we do not like to do murder on brave men, my brothers and I." He gestured at the allied chieftains.

"Then honor the treaty you signed with Rome."

Vortrix ignored him. "I would not order a massacre from choice. Surrender and give over your weapons and live."

"Is that the offer you made Trimontium?"

"There are no dead at Trimontium."

"They are dead to Rome."

"But still they live," Brendan said. "Already they begin to take to them women from my tribe. In the winter there will be babes, and their babes' babes will not even remember that once their forefathers marched with the Eagles."

"The death of a world in two generations," the Legate said. "And this is what you offer us?"

"Trimontium came willingly," Brendan said. "With you there must be a surety that you will not go back to Rome one dark night."

"If I gave over my weapons," the Legate said grimly, "I *could* not go back to Rome. Thank you, no. My world does not die so easily. And I have no great desire to spend the rest of my days with a Pictish slave collar for ornament."

"There are many of mine in the slave houses of the Roman kind," Dergdian said, his voice bitter. "Never again will Rome make a desolation of my land."

"Nor of mine, brother," Vortrix said softly to him. "But a certain one of this Legion gave me my life once. I would like to return the favor if I could."

"Then you are a fool. He will stab you in the back."

"Not in the back, no, although I should go wary all my days." He raised his voice again. "Still, I have no taste for murder."

"Then what of the rest of my Legion?" the Legate said.

"They were dogs for the hunting," Vortrix said shortly. "This is a different matter."

"If the odds upset you, you will no doubt be glad to know that another army of the Eagles is on its way," the Legate said. "Of course, *we* would be willing to take *your* surrender."

Vortrix began to laugh, an honest, pleasant sound at odds with the business of the morning. "Indeed I would not be glad at all to know that. But then I do not believe it either." His voice sobered. "Well, Commander of the Eagles, will you take our peace?"

"I told you, my world does not die so easily."

"I should be sorry to see you die in its stead. It will make no difference in the long run."

"It is my world," the Legate said. He turned down the steps from the rampart.

Below them, Justin saw Vortrix fling up his hand, and their eyes came near to meeting before the three chariots wheeled around to the northward.

"All right, back to your places. No need to stand there gaping." Claudius Galba touched one of the men lightly with his staff. "Tighten up those catapults and we'll give them a nice welcome. And put your helmet on."

Below him, as Justin descended, the Legate stood in the shadow of the Eagle where it had been planted before the inner defenses. Justin approached and saluted, and Aurelius Rufus looked up, as if shaking off some private vision.

"An odd character, young Vortrix. D'you know, I almost believed him when he said he didn't care for murder."

"I think he meant it, sir," Justin answered thoughtfully, remembering the look in the king's face. "But it won't stop him. Any sign of Victrix, sir?"

"Not so far," the Legate said. "Pray for their coming, Centurion."

"I have, sir." A memory of the Mithraeum at Trimontium passed over him like a shadow and he shivered.

As if in answer, a horn rang out on the rampart, and the sound of hooves swelled like thunder to the north. "Here they come! Catapults ready! Take your aim!"

They were up and over the earthworks, their dead scattered by the hundreds before the catapults' deadly aim. But they numbered in the thousands, and still they came, beating like a storm against the gates. The ground was littered with broken chariots and men, and the air hideous with the scream of dying horses, but they clawed and hammered at the gates with a banshee howling that split every nerve. Then, suddenly, above the rising tumult, through the smell of dust and blood in the air, there was another scent, faint at first, then ominously stronger—fire!—burning brushwood stacked against the gates, and the flames slowly eating through them where the ram could not.

There was water in plenty from the Tanaus below the fort, and they soaked the inner gates with it, and poured it from the ramparts; but flight after flight of arrows came over the wall, some of them also burning with pitch at the tips, and the Britons had rigged a shelter above the blaze to run the water away from it. The air was thick with smoke as Justin, among others, worked desperately to reinforce the gates and wet them down.

Arms were issued to the walking wounded, and to every clerk and servant not already pressed into the battle line. Flavius looked at the timber walls of the hospital and shivered. It had never been meant as a defensive position, although it stood now just within the inner wall. But there was no place to move to that would not be in the way of the battle.

"Wet down these walls some more," he told the orderly. "And post some of the wounded at the windows. At least they can sing out if they see fire. I want more water in here too. Fill anything you can get hold of." The baths were outside the inner wall, as was the river intake. When the fighting started, the water on hand would be all they had. The plumbing was old and rotten and there had not been time to repair it all properly. He gave a glance at his borrowed armor stacked ready in the corner, and went back to laying out bandages and his surgical kit. He had wanted the Centuriate originally, but he hadn't come up to the height standard. Ironic, that.

Outside, the smell of burning timber was growing stronger, and they had rigged up a pipe from the river intake to douse the gates.

Albinus, face blackened and coughing from the smoke, stood at the end of a bucket line on the north rampart while the Legate himself directed operations below. Favonius's catapult crew was heaving anything they could get their hands on at the yelling horde outside, while Justin had again taken his place among the archers making the best use possible of their dwindling store of arrows. They were shooting the British arrows back again as well.

The water turned the ground to sticky mud, while the smoke from the burning gates choked them and sent them reeling back to catch their breath. It must be choking the Britons too, Justin realized, as a blue-stained figure staggered back from the gate with his hands to his face. He took aim and the figure dropped, to be lost beneath the trampling feet of the besiegers. In the end, though, it was no use. They had wet the gate from the inside, but the shelter the Britons had rigged over the blaze was sturdy enough to withstand anything they could drop on it. It caught fire itself only when the flames had eaten more than halfway through the gate timbers, and then the rams did the rest. Justin dropped his bow and raced for the rampart stairs. His place now was at the gate, where the sad remnants of his Legion began their last effort to turn the tide.

Today the fog had burned off completely, and the sun lent a brightness and a dazzle to the scarlet and bronze of the Legion and the wild blue war paint of the Britons, as if through the mists of time an ancient struggle had come suddenly into focus. The gates caved in almost simultaneously, with a noise of rending timber, and as the wall defenses were drawn off to reinforce the opening, the Picts began surging over the ramparts as well, silhouetted for a moment against the sky before they dropped down into the fort below. They dropped, most of them, to the end of a pilum, but a few slipped through to take at least one hated Roman with them into the otherworld. Albinus, for instance, never saw the naked, dark-eyed warrior who drove a feathered spear clean through him; never knew that before his body had tumbled from the rampart, Favonius had leapt like a goat from his catapult emplacement and sent the Pict to join him. Or that Clemens, heading down the rampart stairs behind Justin, had paused long enough to grab another tattooed figure by the throat and hurl him downwards on the men scaling the wall behind him.

After that the thin defenses on the rampart held them off as best they could while the bulk of the Legion gathered below them to block the onslaught at the gates. The haunting sound of war horns came down along the wind, and the main body of the war host gathered itself for one last terrible charge. They came like a band of furies, blue as the light that flickered from sword and spear, and they seemed to rise from the ground itself.

Justin, reeling before the wave that surged and broke against the guardians of the north gate, found himself again shield to shield with Clemens, with what was left of his old Eighth Cohort behind and to either side of them. Lepidus was lying badly wounded in the hospital, and Justin, without much thinking about it, had taken command of the Eighth again . . . the troublesome, quarrelsome Eighth that had become under his command a Roman fighting force once more. He was prouder of that than of most things, he realized, as he felt Clemens's solid bulk move up beside him.

The sun was growing warmer now, and Justin looked up at it gratefully in the moment before the howling hosts of the Brigantes broke through the first line of the gate defense and came face to face with the locked shields of the Legion.

They held at first, an armor-plated wedge with its back to the inner wall, braced against the pressure on the northern and western gates. The Selgovae's flame-haired War Lord led his tribe against the left flank, while Vortrix, among his warriors, battled foot by foot to drive the right flank back. The Primus Pilus was dead, and Justin now led the right flank, with the Legate ordering the left. The Eagle of the Legion and the cohort standards of the First, Seventh, and Eighth rode high above their heads. The front line wavered, and soon the main body of the Legion was engaged. Justin drove his pilum deep into a blue-stained body and then lost it as the man fell back and was trampled beneath the battle. He drew his sword and braced himself against the next enemy, a boy so young the spear patterns on his chest were still new and bright. He saw Favonius, trapped between two Britons, go staggering back with a spear wound in his arm, and then he too had vanished in the chaos of the battle.

The small core that was left of the Ninth Hispana was fighting with a unity Justin had never seen it show before, but although they made the British pay for every step, they were being forced steadily back by the sheer weight of numbers. The wall defenses that Geta had commanded were gone, and the whole Pictish wing of the war host was pouring in over the ramparts. A bugle cut through the tumult and the remnants of the Ninth regrouped and fell back, quickly this time, through the openings in the inner wall to take up positions in its fort-within-a-fort, a smaller and more workable defense for their dwindling numbers.

The advancing war host slowed before the closed ranks of the Legion, and for a moment there was room to breathe. Then they surged forward again, a voice that Justin thought he recognized as Vortrix's bellowing for their deaths above the roaring of the battle.

A grey-haired warrior with a twisted torque of bronze about his neck came leaping down at him from the wall, and Justin blinked for a moment as he recognized him—Cathuil, the war paint smeared across the lines in his face, but bellowing like a bull as he leveled his great war spear at the Roman. Justin wrenched himself out of his surprise and threw up his shield just barely in time.

"Too old for this hosting?" Cathuil yelled as he raised his arm to strike again. "Puppies!"

But it was the old warrior's last fight all the same. Justin caught the blow on his shield, and swerved under it to bring his sword up under Cathuil's own shield. He drove it home, and the body crashed down at his feet. After that, the battle was a succession of snarling, blue-stained faces and blood-red blades . . . the smell of blood was everywhere, like a pall over Inchtuthil. Above them, the carrion birds rode lazy on the wind, patient observers of the final struggle.

At last, under the sheer pressure of the advancing war host, a section of new mortar in the inner wall gave way, and they flung themselves against it and poured through. The Legate drew off some of his men to cover the gap, but soon all along the line they were hacking at the stone, tearing it out bit by bit. Finally, a great section gave way and Brendan of the Selgovae leapt howling through it in the midst of his household warriors. He stood high on a pile of broken stone and his flung spear sailed with deadly aim to its goal. Aurelius Rufus, last Legate of the Ninth, staggered and went down.

And the left flank broke with the sudden crumbling of the hopeless as their general's body touched the ground. The right flank wavered too under the added pressure, and in the space of a few moments the Britons were everywhere, and the battle of Inchtuthil was no longer a fight between two opposing armies but a chaos of small wars fought out in corners and down alleyways, wherever a little knot of Romans turned at bay.

The Eagle of the Legion also went down, landing with a crash in the mud, and its staff, thick with the Hispana's gilded honors, lay across the Legate's chest.

"Look to your Eagle, damn you!" Justin shouted, and a burly figure made a dive for the staff. "Hold, you rabble! Hold, and look to your Eagle!" The figure emerged from the heaving throng, and Clemens waved the Eagle triumphantly aloft.

"This way!" he shouted. "If you break, you're done for! This way, lads . . . for the Eagle . . . and for Rufus!"

They rallied then, what was left of them, and backed in good order down the roadway between the storage sheds and the armory. The Britons came after them, blood-smeared and howling like wolves.

They poured over the walls and roofs and down the roadways, in an ever-increasing torrent . . . a torrent that ran red in the sunlight. "Torches here, and we'll light them on their way!" someone yelled, and Flavius dropped his instruments and snatched up his sword. He was standing in the doorway when they reached it, his hands red with blood and his face a fury.

"This is a hospital! Burn it and see who goes with it!"

They halted a moment at the violence in his face, and then with a howl they were on him. The hospital was a beacon flame against the sky by the time they drew back to seek other sport. Flavius lay sprawled in the doorway, his borrowed sword still clenched in his hand and his shield hacked and twisted beneath him. Ringed around him as the flames of his funeral pyre leapt sunward were six still bodies lying in pools of blood. Flavius had come to the Centuriate in the end, after all.

In a narrow alleyway beside the storage block, Justin and a half score of men turned at bay. Their pursuers, men of the Brigantes, advanced on them, and as he prepared to make them pay dearly for the privilege, Justin saw that they were Vortrix's household guard, with the High King himself in their midst. Vortrix recognized him in the same instant.

The High King's face was unreadable, and Justin, behind the shield wall they had stretched across the alleyway, had little time to try. He had snatched up a pilum from the ground, and made good use of it now as the first of Vortrix's men hurled himself at the center of the line. A few feet away, Clemens, with the Eagle in one hand and his pilum in the other, stood wedged between the shields of the men to either side. He was grinning like a fiend, and his pilum was red halfway down its shaft.

"Look! Look to the Eagle!" Justin yelled, and they echoed it as a battle cry down the line.

"Look! Look to the Eagle, and sell dear!"

The man beside him went down, and they were too few to hold the gap. Vortrix was in the forefront now; blood and war paint ran together in a nightmare pattern over his white skin, and he was terrible to look on, not least about the eyes. They were vividly alive, and the light in them burned like a flame, brighter than the blood or the bright, twisted scar that ran the length of his forearm.

Beside him, shoulder to shoulder, was the charioteer, his gentle girl's face transformed by the war paint, and his own eyes catlike and dangerous. He caught the edge of a shield with his own and yanked it toward him while his sword slipped through the gap and another man dropped. Justin shifted to close the gap and, in that instant, Vortrix's blade came down, cleaving through the shoulder of his breastplate, and leaving it hanging loose along his side. Justin stabbed with his pilum, but there was no room to move, and the High King's sword came in again, severing the bronze and leather fastenings over his rib cage. The other shoulder, weakened from a blow early on in the battle, gave way and the whole breastplate slipped down, tangling itself about his knees. Justin kicked at it frantically and it slid to the ground, catching his feet as he tried to step out of it. He stumbled backward through an open doorway into a deserted storeroom; his shield slipped down, and the High King's sword flashed in the sun and bit deep just above his left breast.

Justin's pilum clattered to the floor as he reeled back against the far wall, but somehow he drew his sword from its sheath and stood braced against the stone while the blood gushed from his breast, a brighter red against the red of his tunic. Vortrix followed but halted just past the doorway, his back well to the side of the opening. They looked at each other for a long moment as Justin methodically ripped out the hem of his tunic and bound it around his chest and shoulder.

"I would not have had it end this way," Vortrix said finally.

"Nor I," Justin answered, summoning up from somewhere the ghost of a smile.

Vortrix watched him settle the makeshift bandage, and there was a faint bitter smile about his own mouth as he saw the Roman pick up his sword again and then, with an effort, his shield. "It was for you that I carried that green branch to the Commander of the Eagles. Did you know?"

"I knew."

The High King still stood frozen by the doorway, a hundred miles from the shouting in the street outside. "I remembered that once there was a man who could not slay me while I watched him. You should have done it then," he added fiercely. "I *can*, you see." Over his shoulder, in the alleyway outside, Justin saw the Eagle topple and fall, slowly, as if the motion of the world were grinding to a halt.

"And what price for today's work?" he asked softly.

"That we take our own land again."

"I wonder. You see, the Legate wasn't lying when he said there was another Army on its way. They would have been with us before we marched but for foul weather. The Sixth Legion Victrix," Justin added wryly. "I am told their title is well earned."

"You serve your Eagles well, Justinius. As always."

"No," Justin said sadly. "*I* am not lying either. And oddly, I have still no wish to see your head exhibited on a pilum shaft." He was growing faint, and he braced himself against the wall again as the High King, seeming to shake away his oddly passive mood, came forward suddenly, shield and sword at ready.

Justin somehow managed to block the first blow, although he thought he was going to topple over under its force. Vortrix's eyes were blazing with fury now, whether at him or at the Fate which had trapped them both in this unwanted fight to the death, he couldn't tell. But it was contagious, and it engulfed Justin too with a strength that blotted out the pain of his wound. Neither of them, locked in deadly concentration, saw Galt duck under the door frame, sword still in hand, until, as Vortrix feinted and moved in to strike, Justin brought the wicked little Roman short sword in past his guard with deadly aim, and laid the High King's sword arm open to the bone.

Galt leapt.

"*No!*" Vortrix shouted even as he reeled back from the blow, and Galt halted in midstride. "No, brother. It is my battle."

"You are a fool!" Galt said fiercely. "You are bleeding like a pig! Leave it!"

Vortrix looked for a long time at his arm, where the raw wound cut clean across the old one in an angry slash of severed flesh and muscle. The blood dripped steadily from his fingertips to the floor. "That makes it also my choice, does it not?" he said.

Galt stood stock-still, his face white beneath the dust and paint. "You are the king," he whispered finally. "You have the right."

Slowly Vortrix dropped his shield and took his sword in his left hand. Justin never moved until Vortrix came toward him again. Striving to push back the floating haze before his eyes, he gathered himself to meet him.

Vortrix swung his sword hard, but the blow was awkward and went wide, and the tearing pain in his arm wrenched at him as he moved. Justin, his shield arm growing wearier, struck and struck again, but he was slow and torn with pain from his own wound, and always Vortrix slipped aside or caught the blow on his blade. Neither of them knew how long they fought, each running red with blood and with a growing heaviness in their eyes. But they faced each other, reeling, and fought on.

Then, between one breath and the next it was over. This time it was Vortrix who slipped, in a pool of his own blood, and Justin saw, as if from a distance, his own blade come out and drive deep into the groin, just inside the thigh.

The High King fell. Above him, Justin stood weaving on his feet, and then sword and shield crashed on the stone, and he too went down beside the king, to lie half propped against the wall.

He was still conscious, but his breath was coming in bubbling gasps. The fury was gone now, and there was only a bone-deep weariness . . . for himself, for the lost Ninth, and for the dying man beside him. Vortrix's eyes fluttered open and they looked at each other across the gap that neither could bridge. Galt, knowing that he kept a death watch, was silent. He laid his sword down and turned the High King over gently, pillowing his head on a flour sack.

"Why?" Justin whispered.

"Because I was king."

Justin closed his eyes. "Because I was king. . . ." There was a wealth of loneliness in those words. Because he was king, and it was his right not to live out his days as something less, with a shattered arm. Because no regent could rule effectively with him lingering like a spectre in the background. Because he was king. . . .

"Why could *you* not take the green branch?" Vortrix asked after a moment.

"It was not my choice to make."

"If you had been . . . Commander of the Eagles . . . would you have taken it?"

"No."

"We are much alike, you and I," Vortrix gasped. "There is something . . . twisted in our fates . . . or is it only I who feel this kinship?"

"No . . . there is something."

"And we are Death to one another . . . I have known it would be . . . thus . . . since I spent three nights before the Spear Lord because I . . . slew a kinsman." Vortrix's face was chalky, and Justin, as the world grew slowly more blurry, could hardly hear him. He caught the faint, fierce whisper as if from far away. "There is always a price."

The face of the god of Trimontium wavered before his eyes, and he knew that he too had known what the price would be.

"Your people must make peace," he said urgently. "I was not . . . lying about the Army. There must be something left . . . when the war between us . . . is done."

Vortrix shifted a hand and beckoned Galt closer. But he looked at Justin before he spoke. "Rome has never . . . left anything . . . she rides us down . . . and rides on. . . ."

He turned to Galt and tugged at a ring on his finger. "This only I kept back from the war chest, brother . . . it was my father's and it . . . carries the kingship in the stone . . . take it, and look to my cub for me."

What little fighting still went on had long since passed them by, and the grey walls of the storeroom were silent as the ancient grave mounds where the hill folk once laid their dead. Galt knelt beside him with the green stone in the center of his palm.

"Willingly I will guard your cub, brother. But I am not of the Family."

Vortrix's face twisted. "And which of my . . . family . . . would let the cub or his mother live an hour . . . when I am dead?"

It was unanswerable. The harper turned the ring over in his hand once more and slipped it on his finger. "So. It is done." His eyes looked down on Vortrix as on the quenching of a fire, and the tears that slipped from them unnoticed wet his hand as he clasped it round the king's. "But you must give me truly the right to rule until your cub is grown. Without it, neither he nor I will endure."

Vortrix reached feebly for his sword, and Galt picked it up and held it while the king laid his bloody hands on the blade. ". . . to Galt my brother . . . the kingship of the Tribe, and the . . . right it carries with it . . . until my son shall take his place among the Spears . . . I, Vortrix, son of Arviragus the High King . . . swear it." His eyes fluttered shut, and Galt, knowing that Vortrix did not hear him, still gave the answer.

". . . until that day . . . to rule and to preserve . . . so I swear, Galt, who am the Hound of the Father. . . ."

His eyes met Justin's for a moment, darkly blue as the lakes in storm, over the body of the king. "The time for diplomacy comes to us all, Centurion," he said, and Justin knew that Galt had taken the kingship on his shoulders, and had come close to lying to his brother for the sake of what were now his people.

Justin fought for breath as the stone walls of the storeroom seemed to close around him, and then they dissolved into a grey, swirling mist where the Eagle of the Legion flew in solitary grace, light upon the wind. Somewhere behind the mist was the face of Vortrix, quiet and oddly at rest, as Galt gently wiped away the blood and paint. Justin tried to push away the fog to see it, but it closed in around him, thick and choking. In a single ray of sunlight, the Eagle flicked his wing and was gone, and then there was only grey oblivion.

Galt, alone in the storeroom, looked from one still face to the other. The sun was falling fast in the sky, the shadows lengthening and then fading again as the mist came creeping in around the walls of Inchtuthil. Outside there was silence where the Roman Army of the Eagles lay still in the alleyways and buildings of the fort. To the south, the rest of the Ninth Hispana lay still also, brought down in ones and twos among the trees. Already the carrion birds picked clean their bones, and the wild grasses grew up between them. In the hillside passes of the Painted People and among the broken walls of Inchtuthil, the lost Legion of the Hispana slept.

Galt stood up, fighting off the weariness that seemed to soak into his bones. He pulled the pin from the bronze ring brooch in his cloak and stood looking at it for a moment. Then he pinned it to his kilt and shook out the cloak. He took the dead centurion of the Eagles and slid his body with surprising gentleness to the floor. He put the Roman's sword between his hands and laid his shield, still bright with its jagged thunderbolts and its owner's name and rank, across his chest. And over all he laid his cloak.

He slipped the High King's own cloak from beneath his body and wrapped it around him. And, bearing the shrouded form in his arms, he stepped through the doorway into the light of the setting sun. Before him lay a desolation of broken, twisted shields and broken bodies. The harper and his burden made their way down the alleyway to the inner gate. The sun slipped behind the hills, and as it did, a mouse scuttled out across his path, busy on its own importance. Already the forest was reclaiming its own.

Epilogue: Eburacum

THE COMMANDER OF THE VICTRIX detachment flung himself down on his bed in the officers' quarters at Eburacum and stared grimly at the ceiling. He had just spent a bad morning in the Principia with Governor Falco and the few remaining officers of the Ninth's garrison at Eburacum, and guilt by association had hung heavy in the air.

They had finally made the Channel crossing with the grudging consent and Cassandra-like warnings of the Gesoriacum port commander, and they had had Ahriman's own time of it, too. By the time they reached port, rumors were already flying, and the Victrix commander had collected as many extra troops as he could detach or steal from the southern garrisons and made a forced march north. They knew, even before they reached Eburacum, that they had come too late. But it wasn't until he had been ushered into Centurion Hilarion's quarters that the full horror of what had happened was borne in on him.

The garrison commander looked like a man who had been walking in a nightmare, his thin, freckled face fine-drawn and aged beyond its years. He offered the Victrix officer some wine and told him what the scouts had found.

"I sent them out when the northern forts began to hear stories

299

that seemed bad enough to pass on back to me. I wish now I didn't know." He stared at his wine and then pushed it away from him. "I wish I could get drunk."

The young centurion posted to the Ninth to replace Cassius had also heard the story, and he *had* gotten drunk, which was a mistake, because the Governor arrived the next day, and he was forced to go on parade with an almost terminal hangover. On the other hand, anything was better than wondering whether, if he had held the Fifth Cohort, the Legion too might have held.

The Governor posted the grim details to the Senate and set about pulling the Victrix detachment and the remnants of the Ninth into a force capable of dealing with the Britons who would undoubtedly come howling down about their ears all too soon.

But Galt, who also had his scouts about, saw the well-oiled precision of the Victrix, and used it to force his peace on Brendan and Dergdian.

"The old Caesar left his Eagles to fend for themselves here," he told the allied Council, "but the new one will not." The king's ring winked on his finger in the firelight. "The time for hosting is past. We have destroyed a Legion of the Eagles, yes, but disgraced it also, and that Rome will not forget."

"What do you propose?" Conor asked quietly. ("No, friend, I'll not oppose you," he had told Galt as they stood watching the High King's funeral pyre flame against the sky. "And I am no killer of babes. I begin to think the kingship no great bargain after all. I would not walk in *your* shoes just now, certainly.")

"We must make a peace *now*, while we are strong," Galt went on. "Peace with better terms than we could gain defeated."

"You would simply hand it all on a plate to Rome?" Brendan asked.

Branwen came forward then, from her place at Council as the mother of the young king. "No," she said quietly, and the sorrow in her face stopped the words in their mouths. "We would save it if we could."

And so the thing was done (although Dergdian left the Council early, and they knew that he was an ally no longer), and the one bright spot in Governor Falco's world was the arrival of a delegation to talk peace. He proved both his wisdom and Galt's by setting reasonable terms, and for once diplomacy had its day.

But no amount of diplomacy could ease away the horror of the lost Hispana, and he was not overly surprised when the word came from the Senate. He read the letter grimly, dismissed its bearer, and sent the Optio to summon the Victrix and the remnants of the Ninth.

The Victrix commander found he did not care to dwell on that meeting, and concentrated instead on the problems of the moment. When the rest of the Sixth arrived, the Legate of the Victrix would take over, and he wished him joy of it. In the meantime, he had on his hands an army that was having nightmares, and, the gods help him, Aurelius Rufus's household slaves and his daughter to deal with. So far, the young lady had been as sweetly cooperative as an Army mule.

Licinius, sitting bleakly in his hospital office with his leg propped on a cushion, was of much the same mind.

After the Legion marched out, Felicia had come to the hospital almost every day and made herself useful, fetching and carrying and attending to such cases on morning sick parade as were not of an intimate nature. She worked briskly and cheerfully, a voluminous apron tied over her gown and her hair pulled back out of her way in a knot on her neck, and Licinius found her presence comforting . . . too comforting. He would miss her even more because of these slow, peaceful days, when the Legion marched back and the Legate sent him packing.

And then they learned that the Legion wasn't going to march back, and he and Hilarion had sat up all night together in the hospital, trying to shut out their horror and their loss. In the morning Hilarion had steeled himself and gone to Gwytha and Felicia with the news.

How Gwytha had taken it Licinius didn't know, and Hilarion had not told him. He should have gone to her himself, he knew, but he did not, sitting instead in his empty office alone with his grief, staring at the chair that Justin used to lounge in with his long legs propped on the surgeon's desk. Licinius poured a full measure of wine into one of the green glass cups, and set the second cup rim-down on the edge of the desk in bitter memory of other days.

Felicia found him still sitting there when, escaping from the hysterical weeping of Calpurnia and Theodore, she trudged up the road from the Praetorium. She thought at first that he was engaged in drinking himself into oblivion, then saw that the wine was un-touched.

"I have no comfort to offer," she said softly, "except my own need of it."

He looked up at her slowly, seeming to take in her presence for the first time. "There is none," he said.

"Then we must be each other's." Her eyes were red but she held her voice steady.

"Truly I am sorry." He made a helpless gesture with his hands. "But I have nothing to offer you. I'm being invalided out. I suppose I'll take what little pension I have due me and try to learn farming . . . they say there's good land to be had in the south . . . and I've no mind to spend my life treating rich men's gout. And you will go back to your family and that will be an end of it. It will be better for both of us if we stay away from each other until then."

Then she had dropped her brick. "Licinius, I'm not leaving."

"You're out of your mind!"

"I'd be out of my mind if I let myself be packed off to Rome to live with my aunt! And so I've told that young snirp from the Victrix—he may have my father's fort now, but he doesn't rule me!"

"My dear, no one could rule you," Licinius said tiredly. "Not even your father."

"I'm glad you see it my way," she said sweetly, and he choked. She knelt beside his chair and gripped him hard by the shoulders. "Licinius, listen to me—I grew up with the Army. How do you really think I'd do in Rome? And where have I to go but to you?"

"No!"

"Damn you! I am sick to death of being made unhappy for my own good! I have lost my father, my friends, and my home. All that I have left that I love is you—and now you tell me I'm to kiss *you* good-bye because you are so pigheaded you'd rather be honor-able than happy. Well, I'll wish you joy of your damned honor while I'm reading to my aunt after dinner and fetching her stole and trying not to hear the whispers about 'poor Rufus's daughter—his Legion disgraced itself, you know.' I might even stick it out six months before I killed myself, but you'll have the satisfaction of knowing you did the honorable thing. I hope it keeps you warm at night!" She turned on her heel and stalked out.

That was yesterday, and he hadn't seen her since, although he'd heard on the camp grapevine that she had told the Victrix commander she would go and stay with Centurion Corvus's widow if he was in such a hurry to move into the Praetorium; adding, however, that the only way he would get her on a ship for Rome was bound hand and foot like a slave, and she didn't think her influential aunt would care to receive her in that condition. Whereupon she had slammed the door, smacking it hard into his big toe.

Licinius sighed and reached for his cloak. If she slammed the door on him too, he'd turn the little demon over his knee.

"And so we've all been given our postings," Hilarion said, staring at the floor. "All within Britain too—they don't want any of us running around loose elsewhere."

He had given Gwytha a few days alone with her private grief and then, remembering Justin's parting request, had come hesitantly to see her again. Her face, which, when he had seen her last, had been torn by a pain that seemed almost physical, was tired and without expression now, as if the light had gone out in it before the whirlwind of her grief. But she welcomed him warmly enough and listened as he described that last brutal briefing by the Governor.

"Licinius and Felicia have made terms with each other, I think," he added. "There will be something left for them at least."

"And where do you go?"

"They've shipped me to the Second Augusta at Isca. To the Tenth Cohort," he said with a grimace. "I'm surprised they let me have that."

"And the Legion is broken?"

"Broken and stripped of honors. Even the damned number is being retired. You'll never see another Ninth Legion Anything in this Army."

"Legions have been rebuilt before."

"Don't you see?" he said bitterly. "They don't *want* it back. It's an embarrassment and a disgrace to them, and they don't want to hear of it again ever. May they rot! They're as much to blame as anyone. They could have seen this coming and stopped it!"

"Perhaps that's why they wish to forget it as soon as possible. Rome is like that, I find." Her tone was bitter but there was life in it, and he thought he saw a flash of the old Gwytha. But it tore at his heart to see her come to life only in bitterness.

She put a hand on his. "Don't grieve for me, Hilarion. I will be all right, I promise you."

Her first wild sorrow had almost overwhelmed her, but she had fought it down with the grim determination of necessity, and after two days she had emerged from its grasp with a cold ache in her heart and the ability to see life as it was.

"Will the Eagles go north again?" she asked after a moment.

"As soon as we've troops enough to give the Picts a good fright, we'll take a column to Inchtuthil to bury our dead. Or so they say— myself, I think they'll just bury the Legion and have done with it. They'll be fighting the Picts soon enough anyway."

She thought of Justin, lying cold and alone in that deserted place, and the ache gripped her unendurably for a moment. But Justin was dead, and past caring, and no amount of funeral prayers could bring him back. She picked up small Justin and set him on her knee, finding comfort in his warm baby embrace. "What of the Legion's Eagle?" she asked. They would be trying to get it back, she knew, even though there would be no Legion to carry it.

"The Picts have it, I suppose," Hilarion said. "They walked out of the Council when the Brigantes started talking peace. Rumor has it that they collected the Eagle on their way. The new regent, who appears to have been the king's brother-in-blood or some such, was furious, but he doesn't want a war with the Picts any more than he wants one with us. I don't know what brought him around to this enlightened viewpoint, but I'm grateful for it."

"And how long will this new peace last, do you think?"

"Only until Rome forgets about Britain again and starts to drain off its troops. But we'll have it with us for a while yet, in the south anyway. The Victrix will be busy with the Picts this summer."

Gwytha stared out the window, where a light spring rain was whispering in the apple tree, while the nymphs and dolphins danced in frozen gaiety behind her. "I have written to Justin's mother. Poor woman, it will be hard for her. He was her only child, you know . . . and to hear it from me. But I had to tell her. It would be too cruel to let the Army do it."

"Will you go to her?" Hilarion asked.

"No, I think not. She will ask me, I think, for the babe's sake, and perhaps I will take him to her for a visit . . . she is his grandmother. But no. I expect I will have to go back to my own people after all."

Finn padded into the room and nudged her arm with his muzzle. She scratched his head and hugged the big dog to her. "Poor fellow, you know he's gone, don't you?" He whined and licked her face and then paced away again, making a circuit of the house, his face puzzled and anxious. "He knows," she said. "Poor old boy. And I have no comfort to offer him either."

Hilarion sighed, looking miserably at the floor, and knowing that never in all his life would he measure up to Justin in either of their eyes. "Gwytha?"

"Yes, dear?"

She looked at him kindly and he took a deep breath. "When you married Justin it was because you had to, and I was glad for you both when it turned to love. Do you think the same thing might happen again?"

"What?" She looked abstractedly at him.

"*Need* you go back to your people? I couldn't bear to think of you alone. Couldn't you come with me instead?" That got her attention, and he hurried on while she stared at him. "I won't amount to much, you know. None of us that are left will. But there'll be enough, and I'd take good care of you and small Justin."

"You wouldn't mind another man's babe?" she asked then. "I—it may be there is another on the way."

"Gwytha, Justin was my *friend*. If there is another babe of his, I could only be glad. And all the more reason for you to come to me," he went on, grasping this added argument.

She looked at him suspiciously. "Hilarion, are you being noble?"

"No!" he said, revolted. "I'm trying to tell you I love you. Probably as much as you loved Justin."

"And you'd saddle yourself with a wife who might not ever feel that way about you?"

"It seems to me that maybe that is a kind of love that can be given just once," he said. "How could I be angry that you didn't give it again to me? Many people have married again after such a love and found some kind of contentment. I could give you that at least, I think."

"And *you* would be content with that?"

"If need be. But I am not Justin, and you are fond of me, I think. Perhaps you could learn a different sort of love for me."

"Perhaps I could. But I don't know yet. Hilarion dear, you're taking a risk. Do you really want to?"

"I wouldn't press this on you so soon after . . . so soon . . . but it's now or never. I'll be posted to the south in a few more days, and you'll go back to your people—and—Gwytha, I *want* you and the baby."

"And maybe they don't?" She smiled ruefully and took his hand. "Perhaps you are right. I am of the Roman world now. Best that I stay in it."

The Sixth Legion Victrix marched into Eburacum, standards shining and trumpets singing them on their way, with their own gilded Eagle bright against the sky. And shortly thereafter, the last unwelcome reminders of the Ninth marched out.

To one side, ready to fall in as the ragtag column passed, Licinius and Hilarion waited, with Gwytha and Felicia beside them, while the dogs lay, tongues lolling, at their ponies' feet. In a mule-drawn wagon Januaria sat cuddling small Justin, while in a second wagon Theodore and Calpurnia sat rigidly, their bright, frightened gaze fixed on the road ahead.

Hilarion was in uniform, but Licinius was a dark-haired stranger in a civilian tunic. His instrument case still hung from his belt, and he ran his fingers along it unconsciously until Felicia sidled her pony over to his and took his hand.

Hilarion looked anxiously at Gwytha, but she laid a light, reassuring hand on his arm and smoothed, for his sake, the pain from her face. The remnants of his cohort, bound for postings that would scatter them as widely as a handful of flung pebbles, paused as they passed to salute their former commander, and then they were swallowed up by the column . . . the Ninth Legion Hispana, marching together one last time, so far as the first fork in the road.

As their little cavalcade fell in behind, Gwytha swung about in her saddle, and her eyes locked for the last time on the northern road, sun-baked and empty behind her. Then she dug her heels hard into the pony's flank.

In Rome, the hand of a junior clerk reached out and drew a single line across the legionary rolls.

AMANDA COCKRELL, *the only child of writer parents, has been, at varying times, a newspaper feature writer and a creator of radio and television commercials. She is now chief copywriter and continuity manager for an* AM *rock radio station and its sister* FM *station.*

She holds a degree in Russian Studies from Hollins College and is also an alumna of the Hollins Creative Writing Program. The Legions of the Mist *is her first novel.*

Ms. Cockrell lives in Fresno, California, with her husband, John Crowe, a newspaper reporter, and their seven-year-old son, Jefferson. She is currently working on a second novel.